THE TSCHAAA INFESTATION:
THE PROTOCOL OF SELECTIVE SURVIVAL
VOLUME ONE

THE GATHERING STORM

Marshal Miller

The Gathering Storm:
The Tschaaa Infestation, Vol. 1

First edition, published 2017

By Marshal Miller

Copyright © 2017, Marshal Miller

Cover illustration by Wan Bao 晚豹
Spine image iStock 117150235

ISBN-13: 978-1-942661-54-2

This is a work of fiction. Names, characters, businesses, places, events and incidents are either the products of the author's imagination or used in a fictitious manner. Any resemblance to actual persons, living or dead, or actual events is purely coincidental.

All rights reserved. No part of this book may be reproduced or transmitted in any form or by any means, electronic or mechanical, including photocopying, recording or by any information storage and retrieval system, without written permission from the author, except for the inclusion of brief quotations in a review.

Published by Kitsap Publishing
P.O. Box 572
Poulsbo, WA 98370
www.KitsapPublishing.com

Printed in the United States of America

TD 20170405

100-10 9 8 7 6 5 4 3 2 1

IMPERIAL PALACE

TOKYO, FREE JAPAN

Princess Akiko of the Free Japan Royal Family sat at her desk, looking at the extensive manuscript she had given birth to after many months of labor. As many authors would tell you, producing and writing a book was very similar to giving birth. Some writers had even claimed labor pains in past decades.

She picked up what her publisher had called the final working draft and looked at its cover. It was not a small work, both the subject matter and the number of pages required to record the events had a distinct heft to them. When she was first approached by the publisher from the United States, she had doubts about her ability to complete the project. The first difficulty was that even though a significant time had passed since the events that she would record, the memory of those times was still a bitter one in some ways to her and many others. After all, as a true Samurai Princess, she had played her own active role in the resolution of events. The institutionalization of what was known at the time as the Great Compromise, which had allowed the two dominant species to share dominion of the Earth, was so startling in its advent that she still remembered how almost unbelievable it had been. The fact the Tschaaa were willing to accept the human race as more than just a food source had been a game changer of immense proportions. How this came about was the subject of her book. It was a story that needed to be told while memories were still fresh and yet not so raw that no one would be able to endure the recollection of those events in print.

Without re-reading the entire manuscript, her own impression was that she had truly captured the spirit and reality of the times. Even as a Warrior Princess, she felt within herself the abiding instinctual drive to produce and preserve life on this planet. So she could well understand the historical importance of such a pivotal historical event in the relationship between the two dominant species. After all, it was clear over time the initial invasion it was not to be a passing event but that the Tschaaa, at least some of them, intended to remain. Once they had experienced the environment of the Oceans of the Earth, they could not leave. The life giving reefs, the warm water of the tropics, the sun lit blue waters, and the diverse deep sea life, specifically the Tschaaa alien cousins the Deep Ocean Giant Squid, created a magnetism that imprinted an indelible psychic impression upon them.

Her publisher had been e-mailing her, calling, skyping, and generally yelling at her to "Get It Done". But Princess Akiko refused to be rushed, especially by a pushy American Northwest Publisher who had not been there to see the events contained therein. She must get it right to pay homage to all those who were there. Akiko had tried to say it all in the title page.

"THE GREAT COMPROMISE."

"The History of the Coming of the Tschaaa, the Heroes and Villains the Coming produced, and the Great Compromise, which allowed Two Species of Apex Predators to exist together in relative harmony."

The cover was colorful, with eye catching oranges, reds, blacks and bright whites used to depict all the major participants and events of the some seven years, from the first Rock Strike to the Great Compromise. On the interior page, Akiko had dedicated the work to certain peoples.

"This work of history is dedicated to those who fought, loved, coped, survived and died during the period of the Tschaaa Invasion, as well as to those who created the Great Compromise and made it work. They did not just strive to preserve a certain way of life. They struggled, sacrificed, bled and sometimes expired so that Humanity/Homo sapiens itself as a species was preserved and lived, then could co-exist with their former sworn enemy, the Alien Tschaaa. These members of humanity are truly the Greatest Generation"

She did not care what the publisher wanted. THIS is what she felt in her bones, her heart, and her soul. With just one tweak in this history, Princess Akiko would not be sitting there, the proud mother of twin daughters, both at Military School in order to follow in the footsteps of their Mother. At that thought she still felt a bit of frustration. She had so hoped they would find a different path. However, she had raised them to be just as independent (her Father and others used the term stubborn) as she had always been. Maybe later, after they worked out from under her very shadow, they would strike out in life in a different direction. No matter, Akiko would always be fiercely proud of them. As would their father, the newly elected Prime Minister of Free Japan, as well cousin to Ichiro Yamamoto, a major participant in the history The Great Compromise.

The Princess looked at another stack of papers on the corner of her desk and smiled again. She reached over and pulled the title page of her next work-in-progress.

"BANSHEE"

"The Complete History of the 101st Special Attack Unit and the Sisters of Steel. Madam Presidents Own."

Another work of love from one who was 'there', from the very beginnings. She put the title page next to her final draft copy of her finished first work. The two would tell a companion story of all which had occurred, all that had helped to create and cement the relationship between Humanity, the Tschaaa, as well as related alien species.

She wanted to publish the huge general history as close to the twenty-fifth anniversary of the formal signing of the Great Compromise, which prevented a War of Extinction, as possible. Everyone, especially the younger generations, needed to be reminded just how close of a thing it had been. If not for the actions of small bands and groups of people, the prototypes of the current New Family Paradigm, what Homo sapiens who may have survived Harvesting would either be hiding in caves, mines, deep forests, and jungles, or be service animals, "pets" of the Tschaaa Lords.

"Banshee", much of it about the aftermath of "The Great Compromise", would hopefully be published a year later.

Princess Akiko leaned back in her large padded and form fitting chair and closed her eyes. On and about her desk were pictures of those humans, War Dogs, and even a few Tschaaa who had become part of her story and often her Family. It was hard to believe she had a photograph of her "holding hands" with the Tschaaa Warrior Pilot Dorothy, a then fellow Banshee, just over a year after they had been sworn enemies. Not for the first time did she muse that, had not her fellow Japanese learned with the Americans how to respect and later love formerly sworn enemies, she and her country men and women would still be trying to treat Tschaaa as just so much Calamari, Tako, Squid sushi and sashimi. Now, she counted Dorothy as one of her dearest friends, having faced death together.

Torbin Bender, his wife Aleks Smirnov, Ichiro Yamamoto, his wife Abigail Jorgensen-Yamamoto, Brynhildr Jorgensen, Commissioner Miller, General Reed and of course the Late Madam President, she of the Spine of Steel. Then those of the Other Side; the Director, his Wives Kat and Mary, his best friend the Chief, Andrew the cyborg. Next an image of the Tschaaa Lord called Neptune scrolled through her mind. Memories of times, actions, faces, births and of course deaths.

A large wet tongue made her jerk her eyes open. General, her War Dog from the long line that started with Abigail's K-9 Fuzz, brought her from her reverie.

"What is it, my large and faithful friend," she said as she petted and scratched his ears. Princess Akiko knew that with each generation these War Dogs became smarter and more sentient. Soon…who knew? Maybe someday they would take over, run things better than Tschaaa and Human. For now, he snuffled her, then gazed into her eyes. A true love, as Abigail had with Sergeant Fuzz, a grandfather of General many times removed. Akiko smiled, hugged and kissed his very large muzzle.

"Did I ever tell you the story, My General, how this all was started? How this younger daughter in the Japanese Royal Family became the great and grand Warrior Princess Akiko, heroine of many an anime epic?"

She chuckled as General wagged his tail.

"Well, my good sir, it started well before me, with other heroes and heroines, with perceived and actual villains and monsters. Do you have a while to listen to me? How about if I give you a dog biscuit? Good."

"Now, where was I? I think I'll start with explaining just who was trying to do what to whom, as the Americans say…"

KEY WEST, FLORIDA

The radio woke him up with a Soft Rock hit of the late 1980's or early 90's. Adam Lloyd was awake in an instant, a survival characteristic that had developed over the past 6 years. Although fully awake and aware of his surroundings, he did not leap up. All that would do was lead to an occasional pulled muscle, and upset the other occupant of the huge king-sized bed.

Adam lay quiet, turning his head just enough to see the time on the clock radio. 6:45 AM. The radio station was mandated by him to play Soft Rock music between 6:00 and 7:00 AM., as it was just loud and snappy enough to wake him up without blasting your senses. So far there had been no complaints from other listeners, as if that mattered.

Mary Lou stirred next to him. He looked over and saw that, once again, she had no bed covers on. Her full rounded rear was an inviting sight. She stirred, reaching a hand out to his thigh. Practice told her right where his morning erection would be. He gently pushed her hand back, then reached over and kissed her on her right cheek.

"Later. Don't forget the new arrivals will be at the theater at 9:00 AM. You young ladies need to be there on time also."

"Don't worry. We'll be there, party poop."

Jeanie and Jamey, the two Barbie Doll blondes that looked almost like twins but weren't even related, began to stir in the next room. As usual, they wound up sleeping with their nude bodies pressed up against each other. Adam surmised some time ago that they liked each other's bodies more than his. He smiled. It didn't matter as long as they were there for him when he wanted them. And they always were, all three, for the last three years. They were among the few special women who did not have to explain why they weren't trying to get pregnant as their conquerors demanded.

Adam got out of bed, reset the alarm for the Ladies to 7:30 AM, and then left the bedroom. He went to the connecting door between his office area and the extended living quarters. He locked it behind him to insure privacy. He went out to his living room office, which was built to his personal specifications after he had taken over the Naval Command Headquarters building at the former Key West Naval Air Station. He now had the equivalent of a huge suite, with a large entry way and reception room on the main floor to receive guests and hold staff meetings. His immediate assistant, the Chief, from the days when he was Chief Master Sergeant in the Air Force, had put in a small back- up armory to store his favorite weapons as well as new acquisitions waiting to be tested.

With speed developed through practice he showed, shaved, put on some deodorant and then his undergarments. A high end three piece gray suit with matching tie followed, with his two ornamental as well as functional pistols. He knew what he looked best in. An old fashioned U.S. Flag lapel pin was the finishing touch. Some people thought he was rubbing salt in recent wounds with the pin. The old U.S. of A may not exist as a real entity, but he knew where his roots were. Adam looked at his image in the mirror. He was also proud of his body. He was a shade over 5'10", with broad shoulders, and fairly slim build from lots of gym work outs and martial arts training. Adam thought he cut a fine picture for someone approaching 40. He still had a full head of brown hair and strong blue eyes.

In his mind's eye he thought back to the dream he had last night. It was the same dream he always had before welcoming new arrivals to Key West, one he usually had once a week. For it was not really just a dream. Rather it was the memory of when that first large meteor Rock struck in Atlanta, Georgia, as the Chief and he were meeting in a local diner. One minute B.S.'ing with each other, the next hitting the diner floor as the parking garage with their vehicles was destroyed and the diners front windows were blasted inward. After that, nothing was the same. It became all about survival.

A knock on the outer door broke his reverie and told him that the Chief was here already with his morning coffee. It had become a ritual that the Chief brought him a mug of coffee on such the mornings, usually some high quality blend that he had discovered in his many travels. Chief William Hamilton, of the former U.S. Air Force Security Forces, had done the traveling for both of them during the last six months, as Adam Lloyd had been spending more and more time with the Tschaaa Lord who owned North America, from Panama Canal on up to the Arctic regions. The forenamed area was often referred to as the Reconstructed States of America, although people residing outside the Tschaaa controlled areas often called the area the Occupied States, or the Infested States.

"Come on in, Chief."

A shorter and stockier red headed man with a handlebar moustache entered. Chief William Hamilton, Willie or Chief to Adam, seemed laid back but had eyes that saw everything. He also had a coiled strength that appeared when necessary.

"Here's your coffee, Boss. "

Adam sniffed the mug of hot coffee. Then sipped it.

"This is different. New kind of Columbian? "

"Nope. Bet you can't guess. "

"HMMMM. South of the Border?"

"No Sir. Guess again."

"Someone's home grown stash?"

"No Again. Give Up?"

"Chief, you're just too sharp for me."

"Yep, that's why I stayed a Chief and let you be the Director, with all of the headaches, and I'm the brains behind the throne."

They both chuckled. This private joke had been going on for years. However, both knew the truth behind the jest. They had survived by watching each other's backs, shooting first at times, and running away to fight again on other occasions.

And now Adam was Director Lloyd, of the Reformed States of America. In reality, he ran the Tschaaa owned and controlled real estate, trying to keep as many humans alive and well as possible.

"Actually, I cheated. It's not real coffee from beans. It's a chicory syrup substitute that was popular in Canada. I recovered a small quantity during my trip up to Puget Sound."

"Well, that's why I like you, Chief. You cheat."

Chief Hamilton gave his best imitation of a shit eating grin, then said;

"Oh By the way, she's here."

Adam set down his coffee mug.

"Kathy Monroe? You got her here in time for the orientation?"

"Of Course, Boss. That's what you wanted. I had to do some last minute horse trading, but she's here.'

"By the way,'" the Chief Continued, "She's a lot feistier and more stubborn than you probably realized. She refused my offer of a 'shopping spree' of an abandoned mall or two, something about she can't be "pre-bought" until she hears the offer. I'd watch my balls around her."

"Huh. I guess I will." Who would have thought that a previous Adult Film Star would be picky about her standards in this day and age? The film and television worlds were, thanks to his efforts, just starting up again with regular broadcasts in some areas. A few movies were being made for general consumption. He had not heard of anyone with the wherewithal to start making porn movies again. There were some nudie joints in the old former Navy towns and that was it. Sex was a form of currency in many of the now growing areas of human habitation, but not an official one. Actually, the Tschaaa hoped humans would screw themselves silly, as long as an increase in pregnancies was the result. They liked plenty of food and possible draft animals around. Conversely, those people who said they were Homosexual were long ago sent to the larders, thanks mostly to the efforts of some of the nastier Human minions of the Tschaaa. If you were female, you'd better be willing to at least TRY to get pregnant. Feminist ideas of birth control were extinct.

Adam looked at his watch.

"Let's go and head out now. I want to be at the auditorium early enough to get a good look at the new arrivals before the orientation begins."

"Your wish is my command, oh Great Potentate.

"You know Chief, you can really be corny sometimes."

"Yes, Boss. But it breaks the monotony."

Downstairs at the front of the building, a hard body six foot plus troop in urban camo combat fatigues stood at Parade Rest by a jet black polished Humvee. He came to attention, saluted, then opened the door to the back area. Adam thanked him and clambered into the Humvee, the Chief going around to the other side. Adam noticed the troop had a complete set of Battle Rattle on the passenger front seat, with an assault rifle clipped in a rack on the roof interior. Adam thought he had an additional concealment Kevlar vest under his fatigues. The Chief had tried to get Adam to wear some kind of body armor around the base, but he had refused. If the people believed he was that afraid and did not trust them, all this would quickly fall apart. Trust in him and what he was doing was a primary motivator to the personnel selected for what was now the New Capital of North America. It may not be complete blind trust, but Adam needed it to really function.

Escorting the Humvee in front and back were Harley motorcycles with old fashioned sidecars, two troops per vehicle. Adam chuckled to himself for the at least the hundredth time. Chief Hamilton had a strong predication for "Retro" back to Double U Double U Two whenever he could get away with it and still get the job done. He had even obtained a bunch of BARs, Browning Automatic Rifles, in 30.06 and .308 from where, Adam had no idea. They were carried by the Special Response Teams and were all used and functional.

It was a short five minute drive to the Auditorium. The Humvee pulled up to the back entrance, where an attractive female military member in former U.S. Air force Class As was waiting. Major Jane Grant, a buxom 5'4" 30 something blond saluted Adam. "Good Morning Director."

"Good Morning, Major. And of course, everything is ready to go, as usual."

She smiled. "Of Course, Sir. That's what you pay me for."

"Do I pay you enough? "

"It's not for the pay, Sir, it's for the adventure."

Adam smiled at her, the question and answer a well-used exchange. He noticed that Jane had finally worn a uniform skirt and dark high heeled pumps that definitely increased her already substantial sex appeal. But, Adam did not want to start poking his staff. That was something he learned from his days as a commissioned officer. It always led to trouble. Yes, his Three Ladies were referred to as Staff, but a special Staff outside the normal Chain of Command. Mary Lou acted as his Receptionist and Gate Keeper, with Jeanie and Jamey acting as Social Director's, if this had been a cruise ship. They worked directly for him, outside any organizational chain of command. And all three knew better than to abuse this relationship. Maybe if he ever could resign, he'd grab the Major, make her an Honest Woman, and then screw her brains out.

Who was he kidding?

Major Grant escorted him through the Back, down a hallway, and to the Operations and Surveillance room. The Chief hung back a bit, watching his back as usual. This back room had a bank of television monitors that surveyed the entire Auditorium and the area adjacent, as well as the capability to hack into other surveillance cameras all over him the base. The room was also the Emergency Backup Command Post if the primary one, at the Security Headquarters, was compromised.

After putting the room personnel at ease, Adam quickly took control of one of the monitor stations, using the camera capability of it to pan and scan the crowd of new arrivals in the back of the Auditorium. Six hundred, no, six hundred and one nervous, stressed and possibly scared human beings were drinking hot and cold beverages, eating bagels, croissants and donuts, and milling around, attempting to socialize. This was the largest group of new arrivals he had processed in at one time. It may well be the last one for quite some time. He looked for one person in particular.

There she was. Kathy Monroe. 5' 5" 34D-24-34, 120 pounds, blonde hair primarily from a bottle (who cared?). It looked good. Blue eyes, a smile and perky demeanor that had won over probably millions of men and a few women fans, before the first Rock Strike, completed the package. Adam had admitted it to himself, she was his fetish. Ever since he had first seen her on some talk show years before, defending Adult Entertainment, he had been smitten with her. Bad. Without the Strike by the Tschaaa six years prior, he never would have met her. Now she was going to work for him

Adam also saw his three Ladies arrive and spend a few minutes circulating among the new arrivals, then make their way to the front of auditorium. Dressed to the Nines, high heels and stockings, he saw the other women look at the clothes they wore with a "how do I get those" demeanor while the men tried to imagine what was under the clothes. Adam smiled at the thought.

"Almost time, Boss." Chief Hamilton had slipped up behind him. "By the way, with Miss Monroe, guess how many people are assigned here as of today?"

"I'll bite. How many?"

"Six thousand. Six hundred and sixty six. "

Adam paused. "Let me guess what you are saying. That is 6, 6, 6, 6?"

"Yes Sir."

Adam gave a short laugh. "Well, I guess it's good that I never really studied Revelations."

"Right, Boss"

He turned to Jane. "Major, let's get the show on the road."

"Yes Sir."

Major Grant turned on the Public Address system.

"Good Morning, Ladies and Gentlemen. If you could please find a seat at the rows of tables towards the front, nearer the stage, the Director will be with you shortly. Thank You."

Ten Minutes later, at 9:00 AM, sharp, everyone was seated except for an armed Security Person at each corner of the auditorium. Adam had watched Katy on the monitor take a seat three rows back. Some young stud kept trying to chat her up, maybe recognizing her. If he bothered her too much, Adam would see that he was permanently reassigned to Bumf***ked Egypt.

"It's Show time." Adam said to himself as he took a breath and walked out in front of 601 pairs of questioning eyes.

"The Director, the honorable Adam Lloyd." The Chiefs voice boomed out, not needing help from the PA system. Adam saw some people start to rise, but others who remembered the instruction sheet handed out the day before stopped them. Adam had no need for the trappings of ceremony. People already knew who was in charge; anything else was a waste of time.

Even the hand full of children was quiet. Then again, six years of on again, off again conflict and strife put a premium price on silence.

Adam walked to the center stage, turned and faced the all the new faces.

"Good Morning. Hopefully everyone was able to partake of the beverages and food items provided. I need everyone to have a little energy and caffeine in them so that they can pay attention this morning. The repast, other than those unique breakfast tacos and burritos, were made right here in our kitchens. The tacos and burritos came from the Conch Republic, who will be explained later. Hopefully this helps to allay any fears that you will not be provided for if you all chose to stay here."

A low murmur could be heard in some parts of the auditorium.

"That's right. After hearing today what we do here, what our history and mission are, you may leave voluntarily. If the Chief at times seemed like he was drafting you, well, he has a tendency of being aggressive when he sees something he wants, or something I want." A few nervous laughs were heard.

"Before I share anymore details, my assistants, Jeanie and Jamey, will remove the children to an entertainment room nearby. Don't worry, they have done this many times before and haven't lost anyone yet."

Jeanie and Jamey both had a way with children which was natural and genuine. Adam watched as the two experienced women escorted some dozen children between the ages of five and twelve to the waiting fun room. A couple of the mothers gave them looks that said "If anything happens to my child, you're going to wish you weren't born." This was normal, given recent history concerning children.

After the children were gone Adam continued "Since I do not like to beat around the proverbial bush, let me be clear; you must listen attentively and understand everything I present today. Today is your last chance to have second thoughts, to vacillate, to leave. Tomorrow morning, you will leave, or sign on to be part of a large plan involving all of North America, and possibly more. After that, starting tomorrow, *I* decide if you can leave, when you can leave, how you can leave. "

A person could almost hear a pin drop.

"Now, to fully understand how Key West became the New Capitol and what brought you here, a History Lesson is in order. Trust me, a lot of this will be new to you.""

A power point presentation, run by Jane, began on the large screen in front.

"Almost exactly six years ago today, at 9:13.AM Eastern Time, the First

Rock from Space struck..."

∿

Approximately two hours later, Adam Lloyd plunked down behind his huge desk. Not for the first time did he appreciate the high end padded chair the Chief had found for this desk. On days like this, the added luxury on his weary body was worth it. He still could not really understand why these Orientation Briefings took so much out of him, despite the many times he had done them. Maybe he was just getting old. He'd like to think that it was because he put his complete heart and soul into it, all because of the importance of the assembled humans in understanding where they all stood. And, of course, how they fit into the Mission.

Adam opened a lower desk drawer and pulled out a bottle of Pre- Strike scotch. It was past Noon in some part of the world, he told himself, so he wouldn't be drinking in the morning. He turned his chair around and opened the personal miniature refrigerator, late from some luxury hotel. He took some morning fresh ice cubes from the small bucket and dropped them into a large highball glass. The scotch soon followed. He turned back around, reclined in his chair and closed his eyes, sipping on his drink.

In his mind's eye he replayed the power point briefing Jane Grant had so expertly created years ago. Damn, it had been some four years since he had found the Major and brought her here to be his Executive and Operations Officer. Time flies when you are having fun.

Pictures of the various sized Rocks the Tschaaa Aliens (called Squids by the masses) had shot out of the huge mass drivers aboard Asteroid 18666 always got their attention. Especially when he showed their effects worldwide. Rocks, often with high metal content and unique composite heat shields to keep them from burning up, hit with the size of basket balls to semi-truck trailers. Their speed and mass developed high levels of kinetic energy, causing large bomb like destruction. Just under a thousand the first forty eight hours, another two hundred pinpointed to areas of resistance over the following three weeks.

The people hearing the briefings were always surprised that all the destruction was done without nukes. In fact, just ten nuclear warheads were used during the Invasion following the Rock Strikes. And only four of them were of Tschaaa/Squid origin. The remaining six were human built and detonated. Three of those were Pakistan and India launching on each other, and Iran trying to hit Israel.

Adam shook his head and took another sip of his drink. Stupid goddamned humans. He thought humans were their own worst enemy trying to kill each other even as an enemy was killing and harvesting them as meat prey. The U.S, Russia, and Israel each used a nuke on a main Tschaaa Harvester Ark landing area before it was realized that this strategy would result in a complete Scorched Earth scenario. Besides, it was soon realized that the Tschaaa with their manufactured Greys, Front Men and their client Lizards had developed a very human based Fifth Column movement, using a bunch of sleeper cells of racists, skin heads, bikers, sociopaths, anarchists and self- hating human renegades to attack the rear areas, spreading confusion and fear. One hundred thousand malcontents proved just how destructive Homo sapiens could be against their own species. Some knew they were working for an alien race, others did not. But the fanatic desire to fight against the New World Order, Zionist Occupation Government, Non-Believers, and Mud People was enough for many to not care that a cephalopodan alien race bent on *eating* fellow humans was behind their efforts at destruction. Hate was a powerful thing.

Adam poured a bit more scotch in his glass. Squids. Good name for the Tschaaa. Ten limbed creatures that looked like a graphic novel idea of some Lovecraftean concept of the Ancient Ones. Three to four hundred pounds of a weird amphibian nature, they had some mobility on land. In the Earth Oceans, they demonstrated their Alpha Predator status. The nation's navies were soon decimated. On land, they more than made up for any of the limitations of them being a primary aquatic species with their inventions, mechanical constructions and tactics. Ninety percent of those creations and tactics used in the Invasion were because of the efforts of one Tschaaa Lord. Thus, Falcon destroyer aircraft that looked suspiciously like a star-cruiser from a popular movie series, Delta Fighters that were overgrown versions of U.S. Fighter Interceptors, and Cyborg Warriors called Robocops because they looked like a character in a movie series. Harvester Robots on six wheeled ATV chassis chased people down, took them for slaughter.

The one Lord behind all this was the one to whom Adam reported, worked and paid homage. The Tschaaa Lord who had studied Human culture through their broadcast media to the point his fellow Tschaaa thought him borderline crazy. Adam chuckled. Lord Neptune. Picked that as a human pronounceable name since Tschaaa speak was a series of whale like and dolphin sounds, clicks and rude sounding snorts and whistles. It was also connected to a bit of an odd sense of Alien humor on this Lord's part. The Tschaaa translators made Mr. Spock's machine look very retro. He still remembered when he and the Chief had first almost ran into Lord Neptune and his entourage of young Tschaaa warriors, Harvester Robs, and Robocop Andrew, some five long years ago on Miami Bay.

The now Director was told later by His Lordship that he had been looking for these two crazy humans who ran around trying to keep their fellows from killing, raping and eating each other. It had piqued the Alien's unusual curiosity and sense of humor to locate these humans and try to make use of them. Later, Adam was told by the Lord what the Aliens' great plan was for the human race. At least, Lord Neptune had these plans. A specific type of protocol had been envisioned. Adam came to know it as the Protocol of Selective Survival. They were to be a Client Species, like the Lizards (a reptilian species), the manufactured Grey clones, and the bred from human genome Cyborg Robocop Warriors and Front Men.

Adam opened a folder he used for the briefings and looked at the photos contained therein. The Tschaaa were a spacefaring race who had conquered the bipedal Lizards as well as found the remains of a couple of other alien civilizations. During their travels, they found genetic material from Earth species in some of the remains of one humanoid race. Included were frozen ova, sperm and DNA samples from human ancestors. Lord Neptune told him they were from Gigantopithicus and Homo erectus. He would not say who exactly had these samples just that they were humanoid aliens from an unidentified planet. So someone had visited Earth in ancient times. But along with the human samples and other bits of alien technology, they had unfortunately brought back their undoing.

The Plague. The White Plague that nearly destroyed all the Tschaaa major source of meat and protein.

Adam scanned a series of pictures from the power point slides he used for the orientation briefing. The Tschaaa had moved from sea to land some time in their antiquity, becoming amphibian. Their octopus and squid like structure being modified by Darwinian Evolutionary pressures to incorporate a pliable cartilage rudimentary skeleton. Thus, they could scuttle along for short distances similar to a crab, like a cartoon octopus on tippy toes. At the same time they kept their ability to change the color of their skin to blend in with their surroundings. They became excellent ambush hunters on land.

Adam looked at photos of their primary prey. The meat creatures were a primate looking species, with chocolate colored skin and a face like an Earth tarsier. He looked at the Before and After pictures of what the White Plague did to the primate meat prey. As the Plague progressed, the dark skin became bleached out white. But more importantly, the primate meat became poisonous, especially to the Tschaaa Young. Other mammal species were affected, to a lesser though often still disastrous degree.

Culture collapse, pure and simple, began for the Tschaaa. The closest situation on Earth that Adam could imagine would have been if the African

Maasai tribesman had been told that, after several hundred years of being a culture of cattle herders, meat and beef blood eaters, were told overnight they had to become vegetarians. Or maybe if Muslims were told they had to live on pork products for the rest of their lives. No matter the comparison, the Tschaaa civilization began to collapse. The thought of going completely back to their large oceans for life was not an option, even if they had wanted to return. They had outgrown their original environment.

For the first time in Tschaaa history, inter Crèche general conflict began, with one Crèche that had pushed for a recognition of the sentience of the prey primates and a return to the Old Ways of the Oceans being blamed for the Plague. Before the actual origins of the Plague were discovered, for the very first time in Tschaaa History, a genocide resulted in a blood line all but being wiped out. Then the Human samples were re-found, as was their planet of origin, Earth. Two crash projects were begun by a species that had a history of cooperation many times greater than Earth Humans had ever demonstrated. First, the Tschaaa began to grow human based meat samples in vats, their biological science being much more advanced than the residents of Earth.

The second project was the construction of huge starships to visit the home of the Homo genus. Earth. No longer would the Tschaaa base all their hopes on one idea. Being wedded to their meat creatures on their home world had been their undoing. They would go to Earth, to Harvest fresh Dark Meat and genetic material. The White Plague caused them to think 'White Meat was Bad, Dark Meat was Good', despite the fact that early produced examples of human flesh showed pigmentation of the meat source did not matter. All the Earth hominid samples seemed immune from the effects of the White Plague.

Millions of Tschaaa died due to poisoned meat or malnutrition during the first year of the White Plague. A small breeding population of their home grown primates was kept alive in isolation, and a crash program of vat grown meat products, both from the native primates and Earth based species, was expanded as fast possible. Actual viable individuals were created from the Gigantopithacus and Homo erectus materials. Within twenty years, a viable breeding population for both Earth primate species was created, in addition to the vat grown meat.

The Tschaaa soon found there was a limit as to what could be done with the available genetic material and breeding population. The available sea based food creatures were reduced over the years. The Tschaaa next had problems producing viable Tschaaa offspring with the available resources. These facts spurred the construction of the huge generational Starships as 'the' solution to the crisis. The Tschaaa had the technology of a "warp" or "hyper drive" that cheated the speed of light limitation. However, due to the stupendous energy sources needed to propel craft using these methods, that technology was reserved for smaller scout ships and military raiders. Thirteen huge generational ships were thus produced, each one with the volume and space of an Earth city. Each would carry large numbers of a single breeding Crèche, a bloodline, similar to a huge human extended family. Meat producing growth vats were placed on the ships, as were areas where "families" of Earth primates could be housed as sources of fresh meat.

The final project was the stupendous hollowed out asteroid, known as Base One to the humans. Several Mass Drivers were mounted as oversized projectile weapons in and on Base One, also being used to launch space craft in a pinch.

After some twenty years of construction and preparation, the Harvesting Fleet was launched towards Earth. Acceleration of the star ships was slow, a little over half the speed of light being reached in the first decade. The near Thousand Year Trek began. And make it here they did, unfortunately for humankind. Thus, Adam had to convince the new arrivals that they would not be Cattle, meat for the larders of the Tschaaa. It was roughest when he had to acknowledge the Eight Hundred Pound Gorilla in the room; that the Squids liked human Young, it was their veal cutlets. Always caused some gag reflexes in the audience when that sank in. This system would be successful if the people working for the Reformed States of America and Adam really believed the Director when he said they were a protected class. So far, so good.

The intercom system buzzing brought Adam back to the present.

"Chief is here, Director," Mary Lou announced from the outer office.

"Send him in, Mary Lou." Adam knew the Chief was as much checking up on him as he was coming to discuss any fallout from the Orientation Briefing. It was not uncommon for individuals to ask to leave after Adam had explained the conditions and expectations at Key West. But that could have been communicated over the telephone.

Chief William "Willie" Hamilton opened the office door and closed it behind him.

"Ruminating again, Boss?"

Adam smiled at the oft repeated questioned. "You know me too well, Willie."

"Hell, Boss, we've been together as long as some married couples. Of course I know you."

Adam laughed. It felt good, after the stress of the orientation.

"Here's the bottle. Fix yourself a drink."

"Never turned that offer down." The Chief took the bottle, went to the full wet bar in the corner of the office and expertly poured himself a Scotch on the Rocks. He then pulled up a padded chair and sat near the corner of the desk.

"Kempai, as we used to say to each other on Okinawa."

"That seems like ages ago, Chief."

"Hell, Adam, it was. We are in a completely different age of Homo sapiens development. Thanks to our Squid housemates; and Masters."

Adam took a sip of his drink, then took the bottle and freshened it. He looked directly at the older man.

"Still think about woulda, coulda, happened?"

The Chief snorted. "Hell, Boss, all the time. It would have been a helleva lot simpler if a piece of that rock that broke up over Atlanta as we were meeting up had hit us. Quick, sure, would have been with my wife and kids."

Adam was lucky, in a way. He had been single when things blew up. So he did not have to suffer the pain of a dead wife and kids.

"But," the Chief continued. "We wouldn't be here, saving at least part of the human race. It all worked out with a purpose."

Adam raised his glass. "To the Mission, Willie."

"To the Mission, Adam." They each took a large gulp from their drinks.

"So, Chief, to current business. How many are making noises of leaving after my presentation?"

"Surprisingly, Boss, just the one person who I had already pegged as questionable."

Adam frowned a bit. "Who's that?"

"Professor Joseph Fassbinder's wife, Professor Sarah Broadmore-Fassbinder. You're seeing him this afternoon. She had a burr in her saddle, as they say, the minute I showed up at their survival compound. She let me know she thought you and I were devils incarnate."

"Then why did she come here?"

"I think it was a combination of not willing to let hubby go, out of her control and the chance to tell you exactly what she thinks of you. Maybe throw a drink in your face."

"Well, she'll have a chance at the icebreaker chingadera we have tonight. We'll see if the new vestments I provided her and the other women will soften her. Any children?"

"Nope. I think the Ice Queen's pu**y freezes any potential sperm before it gets to the right place."

Adam began to laugh. There were times when Chief Hamilton had just the right way of putting things.

After he stopped, Adam asked, "Suit and tie, right Chief?"

The older man's face showed his displeasure. "Yes, Boss. I'll put a monkey suit on just for you. But only for you. If you get croaked, my suits are being buried with you."

Adam grinned. "Well. I'll just have to make sure, with your help, me being croaked doesn't happen."

"Still wearing your Glock 26 and SP101 like I asked?"

Adam opened his suit coat. "Look for yourself. Gold plated with a bit of pearl in the handle for the Ruger .357. All showy yet will still blow a hole in someone."

"Well, Boss it's a trade-off. You wear the pistols for me, I wear a monkey suit for you."

"Hey, I thought I was the Director, the head mofo what's in charge."

The Chief showed fake surprise on his face. "You are. You just do this for me because you love me, after all, we've been together as a couple for…"

Adam began to laugh again. "Out. Go harass the troops some more. I have more new people to meet this afternoon."

"One being a sexy blonde with an adult film career…"

"Out. I'll see you tonight, Chief."

"Right, Boss. With bells on."

Adam threw a pencil at him as he left, began to laugh again.

"The character of Adam Lloyd remains one of the most disputed aspects of the history of the Coming of the Tschaaa, often referred to it as the Tschaaa Infestation. Some concluded that Adam Lloyd had acted the part of a traitor in being willing to sacrifice some individuals to save others. For one thing what was to be the criteria of the differentiation between those who would be victims and those who would be survivors? Why should a man who had left the U.S. Air Force as a mere rank of Captain had been given basic complete discretionary power over the life and death of thousands? My research indicated that it was the unique personality characteristics of the Captain that had led to the degree of trust reposed in him by the Tschaaa. What were these points of character in which Adam Lloyd surpassed most of the surviving men of his time? As a Royal Princess, trained in the code of the Samurai, I had been sensitized from a young age to a code of behavior which I found echoed in the particular character of Adam Lloyd. One of the principles of my early training was that 'groundedness' was the first principle of the Samurai. The Samurai must know his Lord. A Samurai who is not a servant has no grounding. But, once knowing the direction in once he is to move, he may proceed with confidence. Adam Lloyd recognized the inevitability of his contact with the Tschaaa or its minions. And thus, he shaped those around him into a proto-organization that would fit the Protocols of the Tschaaa."

"Others have proposed the idea that Adam was a shear opportunist, with possibly a hint of sociopathy, to feather his own nest and insure his own comfort and survival. After all, Adam Lloyd lived rather well during the period in question."

∿

"The third group of ideas was that Adam Lloyd was willing to make the best of a bad situation and take responsibilities for his action because no one else was willing to do so. It should never be forgotten in these times of comparative peace what it was to have every governmental structure lying in ruins. Nor should it be forgotten that complete anarchy reigned supreme in the areas designated Feral. Compared to this reality, the selective harvesting in the areas presided over by Adam Lloyd seemed comparatively civilized. Of course, those conditions were in contradiction to the existence of those in what was eventually called Cattle County."

~ Extract from the Literary Works of Princess Akiko,
Free Japan Royal Family

ATLANTA; CATTLE CONTRY

Martin Luther, Acting Mayor of Occupied Atlanta, wished again for the thousandth time that his Father had not named him after an important historical figure in Black/African American history.

That seemed to make people expect more from him. He rubbed his hand through his graying 40 year old hair. There was a time when someone would have called him 'nappy headed,' which might have started a fight. That time was long gone.

He reached into his top right hand drawer and removed a bottle of Pre-Strike Bourbon and refreshed his glass. Straight up, no ice, this was at a premium to obtain. He replaced the bottle, next to the Luger pistol Joe had found for him. Guns and ammunition were at a premium also. At least for some people. Which was the reason of the meeting with the gentleman who just arrived. The room he was in was a hotel suite in one of the few top end buildings still left standing in down town Atlanta. It was referred to as the Mayor's office now, the original first class hotel chain name quickly forgotten.

A knock at the door, and a huge dark man opened the door. Joe, his aid and protector, entered the room. "He's here Boss."

"Thanks Joe. What name is he using now?"

The former NFL Draft Pick gave a wry smile. "Malcom X. Carter."

Martin grunted. Another young Black Man with delusions of grandeur? God, he hoped not.

"Ask him in, please."

"Right, Boss"

The young African American, six feet tall, muscular, dark glasses, short hair, dressed in a nice dark suit, walked in. Martin quickly noticed he had a Samsonite briefcase hand cuffed and chained to his left wrist. He also noticed that he was the darkest Black man he had seen in years, even darker than Joe. Martin was coffee with cream colored. Hugh, Black Joe had survived through a fluke, Andrew believed. How had "Malcom X. Carter" survived? The Squids had been drawn to darker skinned humans as soon as they noticed the color variations. In a group of African Americans, native Africans, East Indians, Pakistanis, whoever had darker skin were Harvested first. The automated Harvesters Robots would sometimes be overwhelmed with the quantity of Meat available. This would lead to the programed machines to overload and reject those that would at one time be called 'Nigger', but were not the first seized. That' apparently had happened to Joe. The same with this young man?

The Mayor did not offer a hand. "Have a seat, please; Mr.....Malcom Carter is it?"

"My name isn't not important. What I have to offer is."

Malcom, or whatever his name was, set the briefcase on the large desk in front of Martin. He unlocked the handcuff from his wrist and opened the briefcase. As he reached in, Joe as if by magic appeared, his huge hand on a large Bowie knife he kept concealed under his suit coat.

"Careful, Son. Nice and slow. "

Malcom smirked. "Do you think I would have come myself if I wanted to cap someone, Buck?"

Joe started to react, but a look from Andrew stopped him. They had worked together for five years, so Joe knew by a look what Martin wanted.

Inside of the briefcase were three Sig Sauer .40 caliber automatics, in near pristine condition.

"Hmmmm. Seems you definitely have the goods, Mr. Carter."

"Malcom will do for today. How many you want?"

"At least six. Plus ammunition and spare magazines"

Malcom easily answered "That can be done."

The Mayor was surprised. This young man seemed not to have a care in the world. "So...what do you want in return?"

The Gathering Storm

Malcom sat down in the nearby overstuffed chair. He took a cigarette case from an inside suit pocket, removed a cigarette, lit it with a gold lighter, and began to slowly smoke. Martin was an itinerant smoker, could not help but enjoy the smoke. Malcom saw this, and offered him a cigarette, which Martin gladly took. As the Mayor lit the smoke, Malcom began talking

"Let me tell you a story, Mister Mayor. A story of a young man that started one way, and ended in another way. Actually, the word "path" would fit better than "way.""

"His father was a Federal Agent for Homeland Security when the first Rock hit, here in Atlanta. His father had been on the fast track for promotion when all Hell broke loose. Because he worked for the Government, with a Top Secret security clearance, he knew what was happening after the first 24 hours. HE knew who was being eaten and where, and why. He figured that out real quick. He and his partner went to the Field Office, each grabbed a duffle bag full of pistols and ammo, and as many shotguns and M-4s they could carry. They then headed to the suburbs where they lived, and barricaded themselves in their respective homes. They lasted about a week before a Harvester landed nearby, and a sh*tload of those little ATV looking robots started running up and down the street, breaking doors in, looking for humans"

"The Father, defending his wife, two sons and daughter, blew several of those little ATV Robos away before a Robocop showed up. As his two sons and daughter fled out the back, he and his wife took on the Robocop and actually managed to take it out. Five minutes later, a second Robocop showed up and took the front of the house off, leaving the parents for dead. And Harvesting."

"The one son returned, saw his dead parents, grabbed the duffle bag and some of the long guns, and hotfooted it out. Unfortunately, he lost track of his other brother and sister, never to see them again."

Malcom snubbed out his cigarette, and took out another one.

"A month later, the son was back in Atlanta. How he made it there is hard to say. Then, later, a large electronic and physical fence is placed around a three state area by the Squids, and here we are. So, since it near impossible to get out, and if you did, you don't have the firepower to fight the Squids, especially not with some pistols, why do you need my services?"

Martin finished his cigarette after smoking it down to the nub, Tobacco was almost impossible to get.

"It's complicated"

"No, it isn't." Malcom retorted.

"How's that?"

Malcom looked at Martin with an unwavering gaze.

"You are the House Negro of days past; you help keeps Massa happy, and things in the Big House running smoothly. The rest of us are Field Niggers, expendable pieces of meat.

"Now, wait a minute....." Joe started towards Malcom.

"Go ahead, Big Man. gut me. Do you think killing me ends it, fixes it?" Malcom slowly stood up. "First, I, like the rest of us in the 'Death Camp', not the Cattle Ranch that some like to call it, this new Dachau. Everyone is already dead. The only question is the exact time of death."

He pointed towards the briefcase. "Keep those three. But they need firing pins to work. I just came here to see if the Mayor actually existed. And you do. And you need guns to help keep the Field Niggers in line. So you House Negroes can keep Massa from eating you and yours"

Malcom sighed in exasperation. "This has happened before. Some Jews became Kapos in the Death Camps, sold out other Jews to the Nazis. Africans sold Africans into slavery. Revolutionaries sold their own kind to the Secret Police. Hell, people have sold their own children for drugs."

The man called Malcom stared at Big Joe. "So, Big Man, am I free to go?"

Joe looked at Martin, who nodded. Joe stepped back.

"Thank You. Like I said, keep those. As a gift. I have lots of others. If you want more, I need food and specific medical supplies. You see, I plan on keeping us Field Niggers alive past your death. I'll be in touch"

Malcom left. The Mayor sat quietly for quite some time.

"Joe, any idea where his people are?"

Joe Shrugged. "Heard sewers lines, caves, just some place underground. Anyone who claims they have info winds up dead."

"That's just great. A nigger who actually has ideas, not delusions of grandeur."

"Get me lunch, please Joe.'" Joe left him to his thoughts.

Martin Luther stayed alive because the Squids, through Director Lloyd, wanted him alive to run things, to insure breeding, reproduction of the species. He kept order so as to provide certain levels of fresh meat to the Squids. At first, criminals, dope fiends, the "retards" were enough. Now, they are pretty much gone. You cannot keep providing individuals under the guise of malcontents or troublemakers when that applies to 99 % of the population now. Like his Granddad said, it's Nut Cuttin' Time.

Now, who could get some firing pins?

"There were those humans who clearly embraced the idea of a superior Alien Culture represented by the Tschaaa. There were humans who embraced the tasks of controlling other members of humankind designated to be Dark Meat and prime veal for the Tschaaa tables with a zeal not seen since Nazi Death Camp commanders, Cambodian followers of Pol Pot and those Russian Communists who supervised the Gulag system in Siberia. They were soon collectively known as the Krakens.

"Krakens started from a name and symbol for a motorcycle gang formed by one John Talbot, one of the leaders of Renegade Flying Squads that operated as a Fifth Column in the first days of the Invasion/Infestation. Then one Reverend Kray appropriated the name and ancient symbol of the giant Kraken cephalopod sea monster for his Church of Kraken. For Reverend Kray, a religious fanatic of the same ilk as Jim Jones and David Koresh in North America and ISIS leaders in the Middle East, believed with all his heart and soul that he was serving a monstrous ocean dwelling Divine and Ancient God. He soon imbued many of his followers with the same zealotry and fanaticism, often to the point where they ate members of their own species, an act which even the Tschaaa considered as an abomination.

"Even without examining all the mental characteristics and inner motivations of the Krakens, it is easy to identify them as the result of that same old evil and depravity that lurks, waiting to burst out, in the souls of our unfortunate species.

"The Tschaaa in their own evolutionary history had undergone species characterological deformation. My Research from the sources available to me demonstrate that the Tschaaa originated in the seas of their home planet. There original source of protein was of an aquatic nature. The first interface between primate like animals and the Tschaaa on their own planet had been apparently accidental. Over perhaps eons, the original proto Tschaaa evolved into a more highly evolved organism manifesting higher mental capacities and terrestrial mobility. It was then the Tschaaa, led out onto the land by apparent Prophets, began to codify in both writing and deed the culture and belief systems that we now attribute to all Tschaaa."

Extract from the Literary Works of Princess Akiko,
Free Japan Royal Family.

MYRTLE GROOVE, FLORIDA

As Mayor Luther ended his meeting, something was about to happen that would eventually resound up the highways and byways from Myrtle Groove, Florida, to Atlanta. Myrtle Groove could be considered to be on the outskirts of Pensacola Florida and the Former Naval Air Installation that was being rebuilt by Director Lloyd and the Tschaaa. This was why John Talbot, Former Outlaw Biker, now head of his own gang known as Krakens (the Largest Flying Squad left in the Director's arsenal) was there.

The Squids had built a series of fences and electronic barriers that contained what used to be Mississippi, Alabama, and Georgia, give or take a few square miles here and here. Inside were those of sufficiently dark complexion as to be classified as Dark Meat...Cattle. To Talbot, they were all Niggers, Apes and Coons.

As advanced as the Tschaaa were, no system is perfect. And since humans for the most part were now guarding humans, occasionally Cattle got out, contraband got in. That was where Talbot came in. Starting about a year prior, primary responsibility for handling border issues, jail breaks, runaways, whatever you wanted to call them, fell to John Talbot and his ilk. Cyborg Robocops backed them up when it came time to Harvest, so woe to the person who damaged "Meat" without cause. But the heavy lifting fell to John. He was a member of a vanishing special club; one of the some 10.000 humans who had aided the Tschaaa invasion in the United States under the guise of the return of a Great White Master Race.

When some of his fellow supremacists had seen their first Tschaaa, and realized that they were the Superior Race behind the invasion, they had melt downs. Some killed themselves, others headed for the hills, and some joined the Resistance. Added to the ones lost in combat during and after the Strike, less than one in ten remained at the Director's, and the Tschaaa, beck and call. Hell, Talbot didn't care. He had believed in UFO'S and Grey Aliens before the First Rock hit. Now he got paid to catch and sometimes kill niggers and their cousins. He and his people, some 200 men, women and children, were paid in money, drugs, precious metals, booze, and whatever he could salvage. Part of that salvage was strange pussy. Talbot was in Hog Heaven.

Today, someone had whacked two good ole boy sentries for Cattle Country, blown a hole in the fence and now there was hell to pay.

He and his Krakens traveled as a group in a series of fancy SUVS, ex

The Gathering Storm

Greyhound Buses, RVs, Ex- Celebrity Tour Buses, and a couple of converted bank armored cars. They had two old cattle trucks as well, one for a few horses they kept, the other holding a few motorcycles and spare parts. A semi-tractor trailer with ATVs rounded out the transport. Talbot drove a Cadillac SUV. A Jeep Cherokee driven by his Old Lady followed him, pulled his Harley on a trailer. They had twin five year olds, one boy, one girl, who were the next generation. He had a half a dozen younger members who still rode Harleys all the time. The rest of the older members rode in the more comfortable transport. Traditional Bikers were a thing of the past.

Talbot still remembered when he had officially adopted his new colors, the Krakens, some five years ago when Director Lloyd began organizing the remnants of the Supremacists, Renegades and Bikers who had helped support the Invasion. Front Men, Grays and a few Robos had used them to stamp out anyone who questioned the New World Order, but it was too hit and miss. They really did not know how humans thought, instead treated everyone as disposable items. Which was probably the reason why barely 1000 still existed of the Original Flying Squads that had supported the invasion.

When he had adopted his 'new colors', some old school Bikers who hadn't gotten the word that the old way was gone, tried to tell him that he couldn't have new colors unless all the surviving Biker Gangs voted approval, don't disrespect the old colors, there was a way things were done, Yada, Yada, Yada. Talbot, with the help of the Director's personal Robocop, had offed some two dozen of the Old School before they got the hint that the Krakens were the senior club in town. Hells Angels. Bandidos, Outlaws, Pagans, they existed in small isolated compounds. Skinheads and KKK members were still used in some areas to scare the locals, as well as sentries keeping the Dark Meat in Cattle Country. Mostly, since everything was organized around local Committees and overseer Robocops, coordinated through Director Lloyd, the old boogie men had no mission. The Director was also forming military style security forces in San Diego, L.A. San Antonio, Houston, Pensacola, and, of Course, Key West. Since last year, as power, food, shelter and medical began to be provided again in an organized, almost national form, only Talbots People were being used on a regular basis. They were also provided newer weapons and transport.

But the Church of Kraken and the Reverend Kray had risen soon after Talbot had adopted his colors. Reverend Kray had adopted the Kraken, mythical tentacle giant squid creature, as a symbol not long after Talbot had made his presence known. Talbot should have been flattered, but he was actually irritated. He did all the heavy lifting, making the Kraken Symbol to be feared, and then this religious fanatic had stolen his idea. What really pissed off Talbot was when some so-called Krakens, "Churchers" he called them, started eating other humans. What type of sick bastard did THAT?

Now Talbot's people were stopped along the main road, a mile down from the hole in the fence. Hopefully, surviving sentries had kept many people from walking all over the escape route. They had found one piece of discarded clothing, which Talbot had in his gloved hand. He walked over to Dogman. The over six foot tall, 220 pound solid muscle man was built like an Adonis, making women, and any Gay men who may still live, drool with desire. Talbot did not know his original name, the man having always used Dogman for as long as he had known him.

Talbot handed Dogman the child's shirt that had been recovered. The man took it, looked at it, and then walked over to the bus that he had set up especially for him. Dogman had spared no expense or effort to create a state of the art mobile kennel, which resembled a dog spa, as much as a kennel. Inside, he had a dozen dogs of various specialized breeds. He opened the rear door and quickly removed three Black Mask Curs, a now rare breed from the Alabama area. Bred as coon and hunting hound dogs, they had excellent noses to track prey, with jaws and teeth to back them up if the prey decided to fight them before Dogman got there.

The dogs sniffed the offered piece of clothing. Dogman said "Seek." and the three, heads to the wind, took off. The man jumped on a four-wheel ATV he had primed and ready and took off after them.

"Goddamn it. There he goes again." Fumed Talbot," Takes off without a word." Talbot signaled to three young bikers he had wisely standing by to follow Dogman, and they took off in pursuit.

Talbot got back into his SUV to wait for word from the dog handler. That S.O.B. talked more to his dogs than he did to humans, Talbot thought. Dogman had told him once when pressed that he believed dogs were morally superior, not to mention, nicer, than 99% of the people he knew, so why waste his time talking to humans? But Dogman had never let Talbot down. This time was no different. A quarter of an hour later, and one of the bikers radioed back "He's got em." And gave a quick location. Then, shots.

"F**k." Talbot cursed. He yelled over his radio, "Assault Team, Follow me." Talbot took off like the proverbial bat out of hell, with three ATVs and a former Border Patrol Suburban inline. Thanks to the fact that the Director had gotten GPS up and running again last month made the finding of Dogman relatively simple.

An old, large former farmhouse and barn was off the main road by about a half mile. The young Bikers were already involved in a firefight with the occupants when Talbot and the Assault team arrived. With practiced ease, teargas grenades were fired into the structures, as an old M-60 machine gun fired bursts at the firing points. Without warning, a bunch of humans came bursting out of the former farm structures.

"Look at those niggers scatter. Just like a bunch of cockroaches." Somebody yelled.

One fleeing man with a gun fired a shot from his pistol, and then was cut in half by the M-60. Feminine and childlike screams were heard as more shots were fired.

Talbot's men were well schooled in leg shots. It took a little while longer, but some 90% of the adults were down with bullets in a leg, thigh, or knee. The rest, with the children, stopped and went to ground.

"Alright, you black mofos." Talbot yelled over a bull horn. "Hands on heads while you still have a head." A couple of shots rang out as someone still fought back, followed by a burst of assault rifle fire that produced screams. "Cease fire. Cease Fire." Talbot yelled. The shooting stopped. Talbot waited a minute or two for the situation to sink into the Cattle.

"Alright, if you want to survive along with your kids, do as we say, and do not resist." Talbot had already contacted a Falcon craft to respond and Harvest the Dead Dark Meat. Three adults had been killed outright. A fourth was dying from having his testicles ripped off by one of the dogs. A Robocop piloted Falcon could easily handle that small number. This had been arranged and accomplished many times during the last year. One just had to explain ahead of time the threat and don't indiscriminately start killing what the Squids saw as their Cattle, especially the young.

As Talbot supervised the rounding up of the niggers, treating the wounded to keep them alive until they made it back to Cattle Country, one of his Lieutenants, Ray Sparks approached him.

"Bossman, Dogman has a problem. You should come quick."

Sparks was one of Talbot's more level headed men, which was why he made him a Lieutenant. If he said he should come, Talbot knew he had better. Talbot found Dogman cradling one of his dogs. The Black Mask Cur was bleeding, bad, from a gunshot wound. Talbot knew it would die long before they made it back to their convoy vehicles, where there was a vet and a doctor.

"Hey, sorry Dogman. Didn't know one of the niggers got him...."

"Don't" the large man growled.

"What? I just

"Just ...Don't."

Talbot made a lot of allowances for Dogman because of his unique abilities, but this attitude was getting old. Before he could say anything, Dogman turned and walked, carrying his dog to his ATV. On the back cargo rack he had made a padded bed area on which he could strap wounded dogs. With practiced hands he quickly secured his dog. But it was already too late. The dog gave one last sigh, and died. The man stared at his K-9 companion. He bent over, whispered something in the dog's ear, and then gently covered him with a blanket. Dogman turned, and walked towards the Darkies. Before Talbot realized what was happening, the big man approached one of the half dozen children. He grabbed a fifteen year old boy, produced a fillet knife and slit his throat from ear to ear all in the blink of an eye.

Talbot screamed "NO, God Damn It. Stop!" But it had already happened.

The Falcon seemed to appear from nowhere. Dogman calmly walked to the ATV as the boy spasmed and bled out, adults screaming and crying around him. The Robocop in the Falcon quickly took in the tableau, blue light alighting on Dogman as he now stood at the back of his ATV. He looked directly at the Falcon, as he rested his hands on his dead dog. The light went out. The Falcon, using its signature metal tentacles, picked up the dead dark meat, including the boy, and was gone.

"I swear to God, Bossman, those Squids might becoming more human. They understood the dead dog."

Talbot walked over to Dogman, seething. Before he could say anything, Dogman stared at him with those cold eyes he had, and said "They kill my child, I kill theirs." Talbot turned away. What could you say to a crazy mother, who would get fried for a dog? Nothing.

He walked back to his Lieutenant, who had something long in his hands. A spear.

"Look, Bossman. Six guns, a bow and arrow, and a real life Nigger African Spear."

Talbot took the spear, and saw how it had been identified. On the shaft was a brass plate with the words "Waziri, Property of Atlanta Museum of Natural History".

"Boys," Talbot said "we may be taking a trip to Atlanta."

KEY WEST

"To say Director Adam Lloyd was a bit like the mythical creature the Satyr with its legendary sexual appetites was not far from the mark. For he had three full time "Ladies" at his beck and call as well as in his bed when he located one Kathy Monroe, Adult Sex Film Star, an admitted fixation of his. But the larger surprise was, he had another every important role for her to play, that

had little to do with her on screen sexual talents. A role Kathy Monroe would fill quite nicely, to the surprise of many."

"Plus, belying the image of an out of control sexual beast, the Director also was adept at selecting people with more traditional special skills and talent to join him, as well as showing the selected humans the advantages of a Benign Dictator. Adam Lloyd was trying to build a Safe Haven for humanity. It was assuredly not propaganda."

The Great Compromise, Appendix Item #7.
Excerpt from the Sunday Supplement News Article
written by Sally Rand, Great Falls Herald. .

Adam looked at his watch. "It's almost 2:00 PM. Who's next for interview, Chief?"

Chief Hamilton smiled. "Guess, Boss."

"Hmmmmm. Judging by your grin, Kathy Monroe. "

"And that's why you are the Boss, and I am not. Can't hide anything from you."

"Have her come in, please."

"Private interview, Boss?"

"Yes. Please, Chief".

The Chief went out to contact Mary Lou about sending Kathy Monroe in.

Adam felt like a little nervous school boy at his first dance.

"Come on, pull yourself together." He said to himself. Possibly the most powerful Human in the world, and he couldn't handle one attractive woman.

A short knock on the door. "Come in." Mary Lou entered first, announcing the visitor.

"Ms. Monroe to see you, Director."

Adam noticed that Mary Lou was looking daggers at Kathy as she came in, as if she wanted to pull her hair out. Damn, he did not expect that level of animosity. She, Jeanie and Jamey had quickly bonded.

Well, just another problem to deal with. No rest for the wicked.

"Hello, Ms. Monroe. Please, have a seat. Care for something to drink?"

"Hello, Mr. Director. What can you offer.... to drink that is." She flashed him the signature 'perky' smile.

Adam took in all the details of the very attractive woman in front of him. Blonde, blue eyed, with that smile that started in her eyes and then animated her whole face. Nice feminine, but strong looking nose. A firm, strong body, she was wearing fashion designer jeans that were clean, pressed, but had seen better days. A light blue blouse, with the top two buttons strategically unbuttoned, covered, a sheer nylon bra barely containing her gorgeous breasts. He couldn't see her legs because of the jeans, but knew they were great, went all the way up, and made a perfect ass out of themselves. She had a pair of running shoes on, so he couldn't see her feet. He noticed, quizzically, she was carrying an Air Force Flight Jacket on her arm that was too large for her.

"What would you like, Ms. Monroe?"

"Glass of water, with ice if you have it, and a shot of Scotch, neat, please, Mr. Director"

"Coming right up." As he took the ice and glasses out of the refrigerator, Kathy asked.

"'Bartender has the day off, Mr. Director?"

"No, simple tasks I do myself, saves wasted staff positions. And, I will make you a deal.

"If I can call you Kathy, you can call me Adam."

Kathy gave him an impish smile. "You can call me anything you want as long as it isn't nasty. Though I've heard it all in the Adult Film Industry."

"But", she added, "how about 'Boss', for you. I don't think I'm in a position to call you by your first name, even in private. Especially with Mary Lou giving me the 'stink eye'."

Adam stopped for a moment. "It's that obvious?"

"Yes boss, it was. As soon as I walked up to her desk, I got the feeling she was ready for a good old fashioned Bitch Fight. Don't want one, but won't back down if she tries."

Adam shook his head. "No, that won't happen. She knows that would definitely displease me."

Kathy shrugged, then took the two offered drinks from Adam. "Kempai" she said and tossed the scotch back, then began to sip the iced water.

"I really missed ice cubes. And I need that Scotch to settle my nerves." She set the two glasses down on the small nearby end table and looked at him with serious eyes.

"Like you said, Boss, I like to get to the point also." She took a breath, then asked;'

"Why Me? Other than the obvious. You have a huge collection of my porn movies you want me to autograph."

Adam reappraised her. He should have realized that to survive the last six years and still be in one piece took someone with special qualities. Especially someone who, because of her reputation, could be in someone's private stable of F**k Dolls. Adam and the Chief had broken up several slave rings the

The Gathering Storm

past few years. Why humans, under the threat of extinction, couldn't stop from enslaving other humans he could not understand. The Tschaaa did it to humans because we were draft and food animals, a different species. Forced slavery of their own species was alien to the Squids. Traditions and protocols let every being know their place in Tschaaa society.

"I would be lying if I said it had nothing to do with your career DVDs," Adam admitted.

"But, though I have the equivalent of a schoolboy crush on you, your physical talents are not the main reason I had the Chief look you up. I could have found enough of a lookalike to satisfy my baser side."

"Well then, Boss, if it isn't just my good looks, or my sexual talents, what is it?"

Adam paused for a moment.

"Remember an eternity ago when a porn producer said in an interview your perkiness went a long way at five in the morning?"

Kathy smiled. "I thought I was the only human being that still remembered that."

"Well, there are two of us. You seem to have the unique ability to project a positive, upbeat.....aura I guess I would call it, even over electronic media, radio, television, internet, you name it. Some people would say you are just a good actress. I say that you have the genuine ability to project your positive thinking, demeanor, that inner you that really exists. You see the potential best in Humanity, don't you? Despite the seedier side of life you saw in porn, and definitely all the crap you have been through in the past six years, you refuse to accept that things will always be bad."

Kathy gave a little snort. "Never give up, never surrender. That phrase was in a comedy. But I take it to heart. Also Illegitimi Non Carborundum. Don't let the bastards get you down, in very bad Latin"

Adam smiled. "I like a variation of a movie quote, turned on its head. "Positive Vibes, Moriarty, always with the positive vibes."

They both laughed, and again Adam saw that special spark she had shine through.

"I need your ability, what one man called 'perkiness at 5:00 AM'".

Adam stood up and walked over to the large window overlooking the bay side of the Base.

"We are at a crossroads as a species. As nasty as things are, it could be worse. We could all be lined up tomorrow and shipped off to the Harvesters. Every part of the world could be turned into a Dachau and an Auschwitz, a Pol Pot Killing Field, the ultimate Siberia. "

He turned around and faced Kathy. "Our Lordship and a few others see potential in our Species beyond being a piece of veal. The Tschaaa have the technology in a pinch to grow us in vats, similar to the Grays." Adam gave a wry smile. "Lord Neptune said the result is the equivalent of Vienna sausage in a can, but it would still be edible with the Tschaaa equivalent of catsup."

Kathy licked her lips, then spoke. " So, you think I have the ability to help you keep things on an even keel, to help people keep on going on, day to day, working towards a positive outcome. Specifically, we are kept alive until we are seen as a needed, productive junior partner, so to speak, to the Tschaaa."

"And, my unique...'perkiness' as you call it, is that unique?"

"Yes, "Adam replied, "Yes, it is. I have made damn few mistakes in reading people's ability, how they can help us survive. And that is all it is about. Survival."

Kathy sighed. "Well, I have had stranger proposals. I guess, Boss, I could smile at you, bat my baby blues, and say... (Kathy put on a little girls voice) "Sure Daddy Warbucks. Whatever you say." She went back to her normal tone of voice. "BUT, we would both know I would be feeding you a load of horsesh*t."

"So, Boss, let me lay it out to you. You see this flight jacket, the one that is too big for me?"

"Sure," Adam Replied. "I was going to ask you about it. The Chief and I are former Air Force."

"Well, I may have handled a lot of... joysticks in my former career, as it was, but I was never a Pilot. My Fiancé was."

Adam sat down on a padded chair facing Kathy, and waited. He knew she would tell him the story in her own good time.

"He was a Fighter Pilot the day the first Rock hit, the first Strikes. He'd given me a ring the week before. Me, a Porn Star, barely beginning in mainstream films. Usually playing horny young things, and I wasn't so young anymore. He knew the Air Force brass wouldn't look too kindly at a Wife whose claim to fame was f**king and sucking, to be crass. The Officers Wives Club would have imploded. So he planned on getting out, and, using a few connections I had, to fly In Hollywood. Computer graphics can do wonders, but actual hotshot flying sequences are hard to beat. Not to mention ferrying execs around. The Rocks hit, the Squids showed up, he started fighting."

She gently patted the jacket. "This was his old Flight Jacket. He had just been issued a new one of some great, fantastic new material. There is, or was, I guess, some News Footage made by a very gutsy photographer of an Air Force Fighter with a wingman attacking a Harvester Ark coming in for a landing near L.A., on Day Three. The Harvester was hit by a missile and went in. A Delta went after the wingman and, somehow, was out maneuvered and shot down also by the same pilot that had hit the Ark. A couple of minutes later a Falcon appeared. It hit the fighter with one of those so called tractor beams they have. Apparently, the Tschaaa wanted to see who could take out a Harvester ans a Delta with inferior technology." Kathy blinked back tears.

"The Fighter turned into the Falcon and rammed it before it was immobilized. The Falcon bellied in, pieces of the Fighter imbedded in the body of the space craft.

Adam and Kathy were both silent.

"How do you know...it was him?"

Kathy swallowed hard. "The wonders of digital film technology. A close up showed his tail number and, his handle and nickname painted in fairly small letters near the cockpit. "Chubby" was his handle. And yes, he definitely had a large "Chubby", at least large enough for this adult film actress. I should know, I'm an expert." A single tear rolled down her left cheek.

Adam looked at the jacket. "His name tag, it's missing"

Anger flashed across her face. "Yeah. A c**t at the ranch house I and some others were holed up at didn't like the goo-goo eyes her so called boyfriend was making at me. She stole the nametag, burning it to get back at me." Adam saw a feral grin on Kathy's face appear that he wouldn't believe was possible. "She won't try that again with anyone anytime soon. I tore into her, tried to rip her tits off, which were defiantly not as nice as mine. I ripped all her clothes off, beat the crap out of her, tried to scalp her head and her p**sy. Here, look at this."

Kathy, as if she had known Adam for years, opened her blouse and slid her nice right breast out of her bra cup. "See this? That little scar is from her trying to bite my nipple off. I returned the favor. She still had two when I left her, but I bet you she has scars."

Kathy slipped her breast back into her bra.

"Well, so much for perkiness." She buttoned her blouse as she stood up.

"What do you think you're doing, Kathy?'

"Leaving, of course. Damaged goods, Boss. Who you think I am was me six years ago, that's not me now. Thanks for the hot showers, the trip, the Scotch, but I think...."

"Kathy, Sit Down."

"No, I....."

"Sit. Down."

Kathy saw a hard look in Adam's eyes. She saw and felt a cold rage behind the apparent calmness that scared her speechless. In some other life, Adam may have become a hired killer, an assassin, a serial killer. This iciness was instead, here and now, allegedly in charge of saving humanity as a species.

She sat.

"This is not going to turn this into a pity party." Adam walked over to his bar, poured two glasses of Scotch, put some ice in a third glass, and walked back to Kathy.

"Here,"

"'Thanks"

There was a pause.

"Boss?"

"Yes, Kathy?"

"Can we move over to that nice overstuffed sofa of yours? I could stand some more comfort. It's been a long time."

"Sure"

They settled into their new seats and Adam began.

"Everyone has lost someone. The Chief and I were having breakfast together in Atlanta one minute, all hell broke loose the next. But we survived. The Chief's wife and kids did not."

Kathy had a chance for a conversation with the Chief on the rather long trip back to Key West. He had felt her out, she him. She knew of the destruction that had happened around Atlanta, which had set into motion the chain of events that led them to Key West and Lord Neptune. The Chief had matter of fact talked about the complete strangers they had killed when certain people tried to hi jack their vehicles, their equipment. No Regrets, no emotions. And now the Director. The same, if not more, icy strength. Kathy shivered internally.

"What I said during the briefing was all truth, no bullsh*t. Everyone has to make the same decision. Can they survive here, or does this set up offend them."

Adam took a drink. Then fixed her with his piercing blue eyes.

"So, Miss Monroe. You tell me. I told you what I expect, what I want. What you need to do for me and the Tschaaa Lord. No more, no less. Your decision." Cold, almost a feral demeanor. Adam Lloyd was the Alpha Male, no question. Kathy kissed him. He kissed back. A quick fumbling and shedding of clothes and he was sucking and kissing her fantastic breasts. She expertly stroked his erection, as he reached into her panties and the soft furry flesh they concealed.

"Wait, Kathy." He pulled his pants up enough to make it to his desk and retrieve a package of lubricated condoms. "You do not have to try to get pregnant."

She giggled "That's nice. Now hurry up and screw me. It's been a long, dry spell."

Adam quickly discovered that Kathy's expertise was not just movie hype. She expertly rode him, knowing just how to prolong his erection without climax. Finally, as she neared climax, she began using muscles he didn't know existed, and he literally exploded to climax.

Adam lay back, exhausted. "Excuse me, Boss" and Kathy went to his private bathroom. She returned quickly, and pulled his head towards her pubis. "If you don't mind?"

"Of course not."

Twenty minute later, the two Humans laid back on the sofa.

"I told you it has been a long time."

"I'll be honest with you, Kathy. This was not planned this way."

She wrinkled her nose at him.

"Doesn't matter, Boss. It happened. I liked it, you liked it. Both of us a lot. " She looked at Adam.

"The question now is....what's next?"

Adam frowned. "Normally I have everything planned out to a T. As much as I may have fantasized about you, I wasn't going to try and make you a concubine. The large part of what I told you about your abilities in communicating a special message IS the reason why you are here. Seeing you on that local broadcast from San Diego was pure luck. It was just a test on connecting the West coast directly, real time, to here."

"And the rest of the reason was you had the hots for me."

"Alright, yes, mea culpa, I had the hots for you for years. But, remember what I said about the mission being 'The Mission'?"

"Yes Boss."

"That's true, no bullsh*t. I believe I can save what is left of the human race."

Whether he was mad, delusional, or both did not matter. Kathy saw in his steely eyes that he believed what he just said.

"So, Boss, what's next?"

"I set you up in a private apartment here. You are going to be a Special Assistant dealing with Message and Media Communications. I came up with the title, so don't laugh."

"I learned never to laugh at the one who signs the check, Laugh with them, not at them."

"And, since we are dealing in truth right this minute, if things work out like they just did, you move in to my suite with me"

"Uh, Boss, don't get mad, but a fourth wheel is great on a car; a fourth for Bridge is okay. A fourth woman in your bed, even a powerful stud like you, is a recipe for disaster."

Adam looked at her. "Three have worked for almost a year. Why not one more?"

"Boss, Sir, I know you are the ultimate decision maker here. But please, trust me; even you can't change human nature. Mary Lou will not accept more competition."

Adam began to realize that this conversation had more to do with his small head than the head on his shoulders.

"We'll discuss the future details later. I did have a suite planned here for you. Here is the key. The Chief can show you where it is. There are some work clothes and some appropriate clothes for tonight there.....No Protests. I provided all 600 new arrivals with the right attire for tonight, no favoritism."

"'Yes Boss." Kathy kissed him on the cheek. "I start work tomorrow? Where? "

"See Major Grant at Communications, There is a map in your room of the Base. 8:00 AM and don't be late. You may work directly for me, but Jane will not allow anyone to slough on assignments I gave. She also helped me developed the program I have in mind."

"'Then, see you tonight, Boss?"

"Of course. It's my party. I also reserve one dance with all the Ladies I can handle, so be warned."

As Kathy finished putting her clothes back together in preparation to leaving, she turned towards Adam. "One last thing, Boss."

"Shoot"

"I am nobody's Bitch, unless I want to be. Threaten me, beat me, screw me over, and I still will not be yours, or anyone else's, including Mary Lou, the Chiefs, even the Lord Squid's, Bitch. I'll die first, after I cut someone's testicles or tits off."

Adam looked at her, saw iron in her. "If you think I'm trying to make everybody into someone's Bitch, guess again. My survival plan involves humanity's lot improving, not being a permanent whipping boy. Or meatsicle."

In a flash, Kathy's famous perky smile returned. "Sorry, Boss, didn't mean to be such a downer."

Adam waved her comment away. 'Don't worry. I want honesty. And, you are not going to be anybody's Bitch. A nice squeeze maybe, not a bitch."

Kathy giggled. "Aye Aye sir. See you tonight."

After she left, Adam sat down behind his desk. Life had just thrown him an unexpected curve ball. Kathy was just supposed to be a pinup with some excellent communication skills that would help The Mission. He had fooled around with many a woman in the last few years. The closest he had ever come to the idea of having a long term relationship with was Major Grant, or Mary Lou. Even then, the spark wasn't there that could distract him from his ultimate goal.

In one face to face meeting, Kathy, a former porn star, had him thinking more serious thoughts about his personal future than anyone had in five years. At least any Human.

He shook his head. He had to be careful. He needed an honrst to God love affair like a submarine needed a screen door. He called Chief on his radio phone. "Chief, so far so good. Check with Mary Lou, see if she needs any help rounding up the last few newbies I planned to meet with."

"Will do, Boss." Kathy's "Boss" had a definite ring to it the Chiefs did not.

∽∽

Professor Joseph Fassbinder sat in a comfortable padded chair in the waiting room. Ten feet in front was Mary Lou's desk. Although he was in a nice chair that definitely made his tired rear end feel rejuvenated, Professor Fassbinder was far from comfortable. He was as nervous as a High School Senior meeting his date's hard ass Old Man for the first time. The only thing that helped take the mind off his tension was Mary Lou. He kept thinking that she reminded him of some old time celebrity beauty that he had seen in some books or magazines his Father had. Joseph had looked in those books and magazines and realized he looked an awful lot like Charles Lindbergh, the formerly famous pilot, lanky tallness and all.

His Father. was long dead Luckily he died just before the Invasion. His Mother wasn't so lucky.

He mentally shook himself. Don't go there. That memory would just screw him up right now.

Then it dawned on him. Bettie Page. That's who Mary Lou was a spitting image of. Long deceased Bettie Page, the Pinup and Bondage queen.

Mary Lou caught him staring at her, and gave him a quizzical look.

"Sorry." He mumbled and looked away.

"Just say it." It took Joseph a moment to realize that Mary Lou had spoken to him.

"UH, excuse me?"

"I said, just say it. I look just like Bettie Page."

Joseph Blushed, and stammered.

"Oh come on now, Professor. Do you think you're the first man who noticed that? Or who told me that? I take it as a compliment."

Joseph was saved by the telephone ringing.

"Right, Director" Mary Lou said, then hung up the phone. "You're up, Professor."

As he unfolded his lanky frame from the chair, Mary Lou gave him a wry smile. "We'll discuss Pin Up Queens at a later date."

That didn't help his blush at all.

He went into the Director's office, and Adam Lloyd met him with his hand extended before he was halfway towards his desk.

"Professor Fassbinder. It is an honor. Glad you came."

He shook the Director's hand, stunned that he was being greeted like some long lost relative or celebrity. The Director acted as if he knew everything about Joseph that was important.

"Please, have a seat in this nice overstuffed chair. Believe it or not, it is of local manufacture."

Joseph sat, liking the effect the chair had on him. It was so comfortable that it seemed to suck all of his fears and insecurities from him. Alien technology involved? Who cared. He had been living on edge since the first Rock came down. Somehow he and his wife, Professor Sarah Broadmore-Fassbinder had survived in a small enclave in a state college town in California. A small community of intelligentsia, writers, professors, talking heads from the media, a couple of former government officials had bonded together and scraped enough food and supplies together to survive. Then, a week ago, Chief Hamilton had showed up on their doorstep. At first, there looked as if there was going to be a fight, as some believed they were about to be Harvested. Although off the beaten track, everyone knew that the Eyes in the Sky could find most anyone if they wanted to. And, the group had just started using the reconstructed Internet the month before.

Chief Hamilton soon disabused them of the fear of being Cattle after all these years, though he had enough firepower, people, and a Robocop that would have made any fight definitely one sided. Then the Chief had asked for him and his wife. Sarah did not want to leave. She spit venom in her words when she told the Chief what she thought of Quislings and anyone who talked to Squids. A poly-sci professor, well published before the first Rock Strike, she had been a central figure in many a controversial protest or movement to include television appearances.

She had influence, people listened. Now, she had little, just enough to survive. But, she refused to give in on 'principle'.

Joseph knew you cannot eat principle. Principle did not provide medical supplies for the few children in the group. When he realized that The Chief wanted him to come, bad, in the name of the Director, but was unwilling to force him, Joseph surprised himself with some hardnosed wheeling and dealing. Before they left, a large amount of food, medical supplies, and fuel for their generators had been provided. Some toys and clothes appeared for the children. They were looked on as Saints by those who stayed behind, principles or no. He somehow convinced Sarah that this was the chance to tell the Director to his face her opinion of him. Then, if still alive, they could leave. After living with death so long, the concept of it no longer scared him. After you are dead, being eaten or buried or cremated, macht nichts.

Now, he was face to face with the Director.

"Can I get you a drink, Professor?"

"Why, yes. I would die for a cold beer."

"Well, that's easy. But I didn't ask you to come here to die for a beer. One cold beer, coming up."

Joseph was surprised when the Director walked over to the bar near the large picture window

in the office and drew a pint of ice cold beer from a hidden keg. He thought for sure the Director would have servants, underlings to do this. But, other than Mary Lou controlling entry, there was no one near his office. The cold beer was divine. He closed his eyes and almost cried.

"That, Professor, is locally brewed Conch Republic beer. Don't ask me how they make such good beer in such a humid climate, but they do. And, while you enjoy your beer, let me show you something."

The Director went to his large desk and retrieved something. He then walked over to Joseph with something that seemed oddly familiar.

"Here, Professor. Remember this?"

It was a bound copy of his self-published dissertation, "Star Trek, Star Wars, and Babylon Five: How Do We REALLY Get From Here to There at Greater than Light Speed."

Joseph was astounded. He turned the dissertation over, and then opened it to find numerous notes written in the margins.

"Where did you get this? I didn't print that many, and every one of them should have been burned up by know. They make good kindling."

Adam chuckled. "Where, it was found at the University of Miami Library, and it was probably on the road to a fireplace when I found it. It was said at the time of publishing this showed signs that you were the next Einstein, Michiro Kaku, et al."

Joseph smiled sheepishly. "Well, it did get me a government grant and a security clearance."

"Even with wife and all?"

Joseph knew then that the Director knew almost everything. His wife's political leanings had been a problem. A bigger problem was that she basically let him know he was selling part of his soul if he took the money and position. But, positions in theoretical physics and space engineering did not come every day. He soon found out he could apply for Astronaut Training as a civilian.

So, even though his wife never really forgave him, he took the money and position.

Then the Rocks hit. He and his wife hid out in a cabin in the Santa Fe Mountains in California. The cabin belonged to a close friend who had come up with the plan that if there were ever a large scale disaster that affected the social framework, they would meet at the cabin. His friend and family never showed.

The Nuclear or Long Winter caused by all the crap thrown up into the atmosphere caused one of the coldest winters on record. They barely survived in the cabin, although his friend had it well stocked. When a half assed summer that felt more like winter rolled around, he and Sarah dug their way out and headed down out of the mountains. They managed to make it to some friends of his wife near a State College she frequented in her travels for various causes. Hunkered down, they survived. His wife and her friends spent an awful lot of time 'Navel Gazing', having grandiose discussions about political systems that no longer existed. They seemed to think that everything was temporary, that this was just a societal cycle like all the others. They failed to grasp the permanency of the Squids, as if they would suddenly disappear and humankind would argue politics again. Fat chance. He used his engineering background and some practical stuff he learned during summer jobs in school to keep things running and food on the table for the some 100 adults and children. Then the Chief showed up. And now he was here. Joseph sipped his beer, then set it down.

"Director, I know you know all about me. And my wife. The chances of us ever agreeing on the path of humankind vis a vis the Tschaaa are slim to none."

"Sooo...why did you come here then? Curiosity?"

Joseph paused, sipped his beer again, then answered.

"I wanted to see just how organized you were. And, yes, I wanted to see why you were interested in me. I was able to dicker for some supplies for the people I just left, so, if I never see another day, at least I have done something for some fellow humans. Not a bad epitaph, considering I could have been hamburger six years ago."

Adam surveyed him. It had not been a good six years. The Professors tall slender build was now in desperate need of fattening up to keep him from looking like a poster child for anorexia research. He also had the beginnings of the proverbial Thousand Yard Stare.

Adam tossed him a thin folder. "Here, this is part of the answer to the "Why Me" question everyone asks. "

Joseph opened the folder and examined two photos and a page of single spaced typing.

"A flying saucer. So, the Squids have flying saucers. They also probably have unicorns for all I know. What does an alien flight system have to do with me?"

"Easy, they can't get them to work. There are two of them. They are not Tschaaa technology. They are apparently some kind of interstellar or interdimensional craft that uses a propulsion system that is alien to them. Sounds like an attempt at a joke, doesn't it? Alien to the Aliens."

"Oh come now Director. How can I help a species that is light years ahead of us in technology? Why do they need some out of work Professor?"

"Here, look at this folder," Adam tossed another one at Joseph.

"Now this, I understand. Looks like a variation of one of those commercial space planes, pre- Strike and Invasion that is."

"Well, Professor, you may not believe it, but The Tschaaa need help with both. And before you start pontificating on how much farther advanced the Tschaaa are than us; let me tell you a story."

"But first, another beer, and some popcorn." Adam called Mary Lou on the intercom and requested some popcorn. The then he drew another beer for Joseph. By the time he handed the beer to Joseph, Mary Lou was walking in with a huge bowl of warm, fresh theater style popcorn, fatty butter and all.

"Ah, the meal of champions. Beer and popcorn. Thank You, Mary Lou."

Joseph couldn't help but ogle Mary Lou a bit as she bent over with the popcorn. Damn, she must be Bettie Page's alien clone.

"Sir, how do you get fresh popcorn?" Joseph asked.

"Liberated a brand new machine from a brand new movie theater that was opening the day the first Rock hit. Plus, a ton of makings. The theater opened and closed the same day. Hell of a spate of bad business luck."

He sat down as Mary Lou left, closing the door.

Adam sipped at his own beer as he fed a handful of popcorn into his mouth.

"One of my guilty pleasures. Now, where was I? Oh, that's right. Imagine, if you will, you were on the Mayflower in route to the New World. But this Mayflower is the size of a large ocean liner. But, the voyage takes a thousand years." He took another sip of beer.

"Now during this voyage, you have plenty of food, but it is rather boring. You have books, films, computers, libraries, theaters, sports."

"Not bad, so far. But the intellectual stimulation of the books, libraries, etc, is good for the first hundred years or so, as you eventually read, watch and enjoy what is available. Your fellow shipmates do create some new material, but there are thousands of people to share it with."

"Your scientific and educational studies are fine for the first hundred years, but, with limited resources, things become stagnant. And, in a closed society, no outside stimulation."

He sipped his beer. "We humans, about this time, would start trying to kill each other in competitive sports, limited war, etc. This may provide some artificial stimulus for at least part of the population, so some would strive to come up with new ideas, equipment, and the such, to dominate the others, usually to obtain the best mate, sexual partner. After all, we are just nasty monkeys."

Adam continued. "As long as we limit our violence, at least some of us will survive, and we would not be brain dead with boredom. Well, the Squids aren't human. They do not war on each other. Their competition is limited so offspring have less of a chance of being injured. The breeding and birthing areas are large complexes along reefs and outcroppings in the ocean, so it would be simple to wipe out thousands if two Crèches went to war. That is an anathema to their culture. Duels between individuals are few and limited in scope. They only become gravid every sixty days, and do not even think of having sex with a female that is not in the mood. They are as large as the male and just as nasty if they want to be. Breeding females have been selected through thousands of years of selection in each of the Crèches. Inferior females are sometimes sterilized. Young bucks compete in demonstrating accomplishments, in fighting other species, traditional predators for a chance to mate with one of the Breeders. Occasionally, a non-selected female is allowed to reproduce, just to keep a little biological diversity. But nowhere in their culture was a form of competitive warfare ever practiced."

Adam grabbed some more popcorn, as did Joseph. The Professor had forgotten how good simple pleasures were. "I claim popcorn is as habit forming as crack cocaine is, but it can't kill you. Well, unless your cholesterol gets to the level that your heart explodes."

Joseph laughed at the image, and then stuffed more popcorn in his mouth.

"Anyways, about one hundred years from Earth, the Squids began to become extremely stagnant. Intellectual development came to a near standstill. Young bucks took on very stylized form of competition, the equivalent of dance competitions or poetry readings. Some made a name by re-examining the work of some ancient brain, then memorizing it and reproducing by rote. They developed a stagnant bureaucracy along the lines of Ancient China, before the British came in and helped force opium on them. They managed to keep the Breeders breeding, but only fifty percent of the offspring survived past the first year. Lord Neptune, who told me this, said it was as if the young never developed the will to live. Even though the Breeders normally give birth from two to very occasionally eight to a litter, some during this period were lucky to produce one viable offspring that lived past the first year."

"Want another beer?"

"I'm fine, Director. I have to watch it or I'll be loopy. We didn't get a lot of beer in California,"

"Point well taken. Well, not only did the Squids have problems, but they had trouble with reproduction of their Grays, the clones, and the Robocops. The clones in the vat became only about 15% viable; the Robocops were producing only 50% viable offspring. The genetic material of these species seemed to be wearing out. Whether cosmic or background radiation was leaking through to the occupants of the ships, no one knew, or seemed to care." Adam sipped his beer again.

"Then, our Lord reached majority. And, though some think he is just this side of insane, a rare condition amongst Squids, he soon got a reputation for 'getting things done'." Adam looked at the clock. He still had time for the rest of the story.

"He monitored our TV and radio transmissions incessantly. This may be what helped keep an intellectual spark alive in him that was stagnant in others. He was the one who designed the Falcons, the Harvest Robs. Hell, he basically developed the whole Harvest Ship system. Otherwise, the Squids would have just hit us, the young bucks slaughtering us the best they could in the first five years, then start getting ready to move on. At the best, we would all be living in caves right now. Although Lords more Senior than him got the so called plums, like Africa, everyone knew who was behind Cattle Country, creating great breeding stock, helping to organize large ocean breeding areas here on Earth. Most of the older Lords were afraid to let their Breeders leave the Ships."

Joseph looked at Adam in a quizzical manner.

"You have a question that you are hesitant to ask. Spit it out. You're not going to the Gulags; I've heard it all before."

Joseph took a drink of his beer, a deep breath. "So, Lord ....Neptune helped make our slaughter efficient. Just like Himmler and company did with the Jews. So why cooperate with a butcher?"

"Because, Professor, the alternative, extinction as a species, is worse. If the invasion had gone worse, if the Squids had attacked as they originally planned, a disorganized mass, they would have been quickly frustrated. Then, instead of a thousand rocks, try two, three time as many, plus a few dozen nukes. They would grab some breeding stock, and leave us with a world freezing from the lack of sunlight thanks to a decade of Nuclear Winter. And, instead of one segment of the human species, the darker skinned races, being the major source of Meat, we would all be. We would have no worth, other than as chickens in a factory farm."

Joseph looked hard at Adam. "That is an awful cold and mean decision. And selfish. We sold everyone else for the Great White Race. "

"No, the human race. Actually, human species, as race is an artificial construct to explain local population variations due to environmental effects. We keep the so called genetic basis for our "races" in the DNA of the survivors. But, at least we survive as an organized species, rather than maybe, at best, small isolated bands. And, we rebuild our Pre-Strike civilization."

"Our Lordship has worked to convince the others in the idea of our long term worth, not only as Meat Cattle, but as worker bees, like the Grays, Lizards and Robo's. It *is* the lesser of two evils. And remember, unlike the Jews in Europe, there are no Allied Countries to come to our rescue. Ever."

Silence. Joseph stared ahead. Adam knew his mind was trying to come to grips with this. As was his heart. Adam continued with his explanation.

"Our Lordship realizes that the Tschaaa needs us, a young species with lots of potential, which is not stagnant. And, he has convinced the majority of the Other Lords of our worth, at least in the short term. He has so far convinced them to give his Protocol of Selective Survival a chance."

And because of that, in about two months, a revamped Space Plane will be launched to Platform One. I want you on it. You will look at those 'Flying Saucers' onboard a Tschaaa Generation Ship."

Joseph mouth dropped open. "Humans? Going into Space, and not as a slab of beef? I don't believe it." He gulped his beer. "I changed my mind. I need another."

Adam laughed. He stood up and went to get another beer. Joseph sat stunned. And his mind was fighting a battle in which only he could decide the outcome. Now was his chance to go to Space, to explore the Universe from outside Earth's atmosphere. But he would be the equivalent of a trained service dog, of use only as long as his Master, the Tschaaa, had a purpose for him.

Adam came back and handed him his beer. Joseph sipped on it, staring into blank air. Adam waited calmly. He knew that Joseph had to get his mind around this. And decide. Finally, Joseph spoke

"Director, this is no bullsh*t, right? This isn't some cosmic joke? I know we are well past the Twilight Zone "To Serve Man, "episode, but is there a hidden agenda?"

"No, Professor, there is no grand conspiracy. No hidden human experiments. The Tschaaa are really not that complicated. They are a species that developed due to evolutionary pressures and the occasional chance variation in their DNA, similar to humans. They just happened to develop earlier than we did, being an older species. And now, a stagnant species in this part of the Galaxy."

"Director, can the Tschaaa.... keep their word? Is that a concept they have?"

"You mean Honor? Yes, they do. But, we are still an inferior species, so it is complicated. They may use some of us as a food source, but they do not torture other creatures, like some humans have done. You are either a threat or competitor, a food source, or, in the last thousand years or so, a client worker species that can perform a function that will help the Tschaaa survive and reproduce. We can be all three on Earth, but in Space, all us live ones will be client workers. The Tschaaa, as much as they like fresh kill, have limited space for live food animals on their star craft. Fresh frozen and an amount of vat grown flesh will for the most part suffice until they reach another planet with a meat species. Except, of course, the huge ships taking the meatcicles, human sperm, ova and breeding stock back to their Home World. That is for the survival of the Tschaaa left behind."

Adam sipped his beer. "The one caveat to that is if you die in space and they have your body, you will be eaten as fresh kill. Nothing personal"

"What if we ate one of them?"

"They know we ate squid, calamari, octopus, all literal cousins to them. No problems as they expect one species to prey on another, a la Darwinism, if necessary."

Adam took some more popcorn. "What they do not understand is the idea of cannibalism. The fact that we can eat our own species is the ultimate perversion. They do not have Jeffery Dahlmers. A Tschaaa who realizes he ate his own would go catatonic, then die."

Adam chewed on some more popcorn. And before you ask, how do I know? Well, our Lord showed me a recording of a catatonic Squid. Killing your offspring, even by accident, or eating Tschaaa flesh causes them to go catatonic, then, stop breathing. A disaster that wiped out a breeding area on their home world led to the surviving adults, who were the caretakers and mothers, to go catatonic. Out of 29 adult survivors, all but one died within a week."

"How about the one exception?"

"A Breeder, she became one of the few "insane" Tschaaa around. They treated her like a Shaman, or Oracle of Delphi. Happens once every hundred years or so."

"Professor, we as a species have a wide range of behavior, called cultural variations. Maybe that keeps us vibrant, adaptable. The Tschaaa do not have variations. The Tschaaa have developed a very narrow range of cultural behavior, and definitely no equivalent to our idea of race. The homogenous nature of their culture probably resembles that of historical Japan, pre-World War Two."

"Then what, how do Crèches fit into things?" Joseph asked.

"Strictly as extended families, all within a specific cultural norm. They form a hierarchy much like the traditional Mafia Families did. They insure no one gets out of line, and reward success amongst the young males. Females are Breeders and Caretakers, only limited numbers are anything else"

Joseph sat silently again. An old expression was that you could see someone's gears working in their head when they were deep in thought. Adam believed the expression fit Joseph to a "T"

Finally, Joseph spoke. "It's a big chance that all this is a fantasy. But, I can't turn down the chance of humankind in Space again, even in a service capacity. We deserve the stars."

Adam smiled. "Good. You'll be given more details tomorrow, after this has all really sunk in. You can change your mind by tomorrow morning. After that, you are literally under my control. Understood?"

"Understood."

"One for the road?"

Yes, Director. I will need to be well lubricated to explain this to Sarah."

Adam looked at him intently. "Professor, if she wishes to leave, she may. If she stays, I will find her something to do to use her teaching experience. But, she follows the rules, like everyone else. '

"Yes Director... May I ask one more question?"

"Shoot. "

"Do you ever think of telling the Tschaaa ... to Go to Hell? To make one last stand at resistance?"

Adam smiled "All the time. So does the Chief."

He finished his beer. "And you will not believe me, but I have told Lord Neptune on a regular basis that I still have those thoughts. He laughed. Yes, Squids have a form of laughter, and humor. Someday, I'll have to write a book on that subject. And, after he laughed, he told me that, like the Borg, "Resistance is Futile" unless I really wanted another thousand Rocks to rain down on us. He knows that if the roles were reversed, the Tschaaa would have to accept or die. Once again, total acceptance of the rule of Darwinian Selection based on some ancient religious belief, some Protocol. Someone is always at the top of the food chain, and dictates to others who eats whom. As long as they can breed, the Tschaaa will do what is necessary to survive as a species."

"Director, how many humans have died during the institution of these... Protocols?"

"From what we can glean about the casualty rate for humans, from the Panama Canal to the frozen North, today there are about 100 million humans.

The Gathering Storm

That includes us in the occupied areas, the Resistance, some four million Cattle, and an indeterminate number of ferals still in hiding."

He let that sink in for a moment before he spoke.

"Now if you will excuse me, I still have a few things to take care of before our Social tonight. Mary Lou here will show you out." She magically appeared at just the right moment.

"Thank You, Director". Joseph said, and shook his hand.

"Thank You, Professor."

∿∿

Sometime later, the Chief knocked on Adam's door, then entered.

"Boss, it's almost six o'clock. The Social starts at Seven."

The Chief already had a suit and tie on, the Social the only event that forced him to wear them.

"My suit takes just five minutes to put on, Chief. Have a seat and you can brief me on what else you found out there."

"Oh another poodle gun... Sorry, M-16, with a complete military sight package. A small amount of ammo with it, including twenty rounds of match grade hollow point. No other military stuff. Most places have been picked clean in six years."

Out of a small kitbag he seemed to always have with him, the Chief pulled a smaller sized replica of a Col Peacemaker. He handed it to Adam.

"This is for you. Six shots of twenty- two Magnum. It works; I tested it and loaded it."

Adam frowned "And this is for...?"

"Remember, Lord High Executioner?"

Then Adam remembered. He wanted something smaller, but effective, in case he ran into any more Baby Rapers in his midst. The Nine Millimeter he had used then had created a Hell of a mess with a short range shot to the head. He still remembered earlier today when he had told all the new arrivals that he was the Executive, Legislative, and Judicial Branch all rolled into one. Then he had told them he was the Lord High Executioner also, and about him handling in person mistakes he let in. Like a certain serial pedophile. Judging by the silence and the looks on their faces, they believed him.

"Thanks, Chief. Here's hoping I don't have to ever use it."

"I'll drink to that idea, tonight."

Adam slipped it into a locking drawer in his desk

"What about the air defense system I have you working on?"

"Four former ship mounted Phalanx systems ring us, plus a five inch and a three inch gun. We have over a hundred Stingers on various mounts, and one old Chaparral system with Side Winders. We are short ammo for the Phalanx, but I think I found some more in San Diego,"

"And, the Gunship's about to fly. Plus, two GAU 30 ex A-10 weapons are in route, with over a thousand rounds of ammo. Also one 20 millimeter Gatling is being recovered off of an F-15."

"Well, short of a general war, I think we have enough firepower."

"Yes, Boss. We have enough for a small war. And for land forces. Eglin will have four M-1 tanks up and running this week, added to a dozen Bradleys."

The chief slapped his forehead. "I forgot. We have a hundred AT-4s, a dozen SWAWs and six Dragons anti- tank weapons coming, so we won't have to rely on those RPGs I 'liberated' from Cuba."

The Chief had done some wheeling and dealing with the small groups of survivors in Cuba. For food and other supplies, he had gotten a scrapload of Cuban Cigars, plus RPG launchers and a hundred grenades of various manufactures. Wheeling and dealing like this had also obtained a thousand hand grenades, Claymore Mines, and even a few anti-tank mines, from various sources in Central and South America.

"Find anything else interesting, Chief?"

"No new evidence of any cannibalism. I think we have pretty much nipped that in the bud. The Church of Kraken has helped, since His Lordship sent that recording to the titular head, the Most Reverend James Kray, explaining what being a Tschaaa really means."

Some humans had a unique ability to develop new belief systems at the drop of a hat, coming up with some new revelation to explain the Meaning of Everything. Creating a new religion based around the Tschaaa and some traditional Pagan beliefs was what the Church of Kraken was. The problem was that early adherents felt that to be Kraken meant you ate human flesh like the Tschaaa did. Lord Neptune, at Adam's prodding, developed a filmed recording explaining that the eating of one's own species was an Abomination that would result in a quick trip to a Harvester, after Adam and Company were allowed to "tenderize" the blasphemers. When your new Gods local rep tells you directly that you are screwing the pooch, one usually listens. At least in public.

On the Base, there were some one hundred members of the new church. Amongst the Conch Republicans, close to a fouth of the some 5,000 humans were Converts. They bent over backwards if Adam mentioned that the Tschaaa Lord wanted something done.

"Well, Chief, let me put my party clothes on and we will get going. By the way, this will probably the last one of these we will be doing for a while. I think I need to get everyone settled before we bring anymore newbies in"

"What about the Cubans?" The Chief had cultivated six surviving Cuban Military members and their families who had helped him obtain some of the left over hardware, not to mention Cuban Cigars and, for the Tschaaa, sugar cane. Apparently, raw sugarcane was something that did not exist on the Tschaaa Home world, though something similar but not as flavorful did. The Tschaaa here had suddenly developed one hell of a sweet tooth. When some 90 percent of the Cubans had been Harvested, thanks to their relatively dark skin of the populace in the early days of the Invasion, the survivors hid in the hills. Cuba had been split between the Tschaaa Lord that controlled South America and Lord Neptune in a resource sharing agreement. The South American Lord was not that interested in the Islands so he had let Neptune take over the Cuban area after a week of hectic Harvesting. A small Crèche breeding area was set up in the warm waters. When Adam and he Chief had come on the scene and made a foray looking for salvageable goods on a depopulated island, they had made contacts with the survivors and had brought back a bunch of raw cane, not only for everyone's sweet tooth but also for possible ethanol production. By pure chance the Tschaaa had tried eating some of the cane as it resembled a bamboo like plant from their Homeworld they used for medicinal purposes and "teeth" cleaning (The Tschaaa had their version of dental structures).

One taste and it was a match made in Heaven. Now a small group of humans tried to keep some of the fields producing, as well as harvesting wild plants. Adam had brought some plants back, and was growing some in their green houses. He was also trying to get some fields growing near Miami. The Tschaaa young would eat all they could find, and the Breeders claimed it helped during their pregnancy. Now there was another reason to look kindly at humans other than as a snack. The six surviving Cuban Military members and their extended families, some fifty men, women and children, wanted to relocate to the Base. They were entirely beholden to the Chief for providing supplies that kept them alive, and would do anything for him.

"Well, let's bring the families over in a few of months, with the caveat that they help us keep the sugar cane available. It gives us a nice bargaining chip with Lord Neptune and the Lord in South America."

"Yea." the Chief said, "Lord Neptune acts like a kid in the candy store when you mention sugar cane."

"Okay, it's settled. Now, let me get ready for the Social."

At two minutes before 7:00 PM, Adam entered the large auditorium, now a large party room. Round dining tables had been set up with colorful table clothes and decorations. Along one side of the auditorium was a long buffet, with fresh fruit, vegetables from the large greenhouses and hydroponics area, as well as a lot of Asian dishes. The Conch Republic had a section of fresh seafood, including shark steaks, and at the end was the supposed children's section, hotdogs, hamburgers, shredded beef and grilled cheese sandwiches. But, as normal, the adults could not stay away. Decent meat of any kind had been a rarity until very recently in North America, other than for those who were good deer and wild cattle hunters. Urban populaces were meat and dairy starved.

But it wasn't the good food only that put everyone in a good mood, nor the free beer, and pay as you go bar(with all new arrivals discovering a small cache of U.S of A Bills, still legal tender in civilized areas , in their rooms). No, it was the women folk. Every woman had been provided with a formal dress that was tailored for them. Adam had found some dozen former dressmakers, designers, and tailors and convinced them to come to Key West. As they had been starving, it was an easy decision. Also, he now had several young apprentices gleaned from the children brought in the last four years learning the ropes. Not to mention some hairdressers and makeup artists, survivors of Hollywood. The results at these Socials were always surprising, and astounding.

Women, who a few days before had the beginnings of the Thousand Yard Stare, were now alive, attractive, and sometimes downright ravishing creatures. As Adam began to make the rounds with the Chief, mingling, no ceremony, a woman would suddenly come up to him, grab his hand, or hug him, or kiss him, usually speechless. The husbands of those married would be there, usually in the background, letting Adam and the Chief know with a look "Thanks for making the Love of my Life live again." A more than occasional tear would threaten to ruin make up, and Mary Lou, Jeanie and Jamie would hustle the woman off for a quick repair job. Maybe it was a crass fantasy that he was perpetuating on some very vulnerable people, Adam did not care. He could not save all humans, but he could make a difference in a small number, one day at a time. If some of them felt beholden over an act of kindness, so be it.

As he was extricating himself from a bear hug that a very small but powerful woman had put on him, his Spider Sense told him there was someone behind him. Before he could turn around, he heard "Hello, Boss." There was Kathy. The dark blue long dress looked like it had been spray painted on her, hugging every part of her body just right. A slit up the left side showed an expanse of nylon leg that took his breath away. Her blonde hair was up, showing off her exquisite neck, with a few long curls teasing her ears and shoulders. For the first time in a very long time he was speechless.

"Well come on, Boss. How do I look? This is first new party dress I've had on in about six years. A woman needs to know she still fills a dress in all the right places. Well....?

He finally found his voice. "Kathy Monroe, you look absolutely stunning."

Kathy wrinkled her nose at him, smiling. "Ah, you probably tell all the girls that." Then she looked past him, her mouth still smiling but her eyes now wary. "Battle stations, Boss," she said, and Adam turned to where she was looking.

Professor Sarah Broadmore-Fassbinder, all dressed up, was coming at him like an enemy battle cruiser, full steam ahead. He believed for a moment she actually planned on ramming him.

Sarah had always been attractive, with a slim, athletic looking body. She used to run pre Squid and still had shapely runner's legs. She was a 5'6"brunette, with nice breasts that were definitely still perky. But now, her face reflected her past.

Years prior there was a female Representative from Colorado that was also attractive. But, she had a look on her face most of the time that looked like a combination of constipation and Stick Up Ass syndrome, especially when someone disagreed with her strong feministic views. Men physically stronger than women? Even when presented with scientific evidence to the contrary, women and men were the same, except men had the evil penis that must be controlled. And if they were not the same, Dammit, she would MAKE them the same by the power of Law.

Sarah had the same constipated, frustrated look, reflecting the belief she could change reality by sheer force of will.

"Good Evening, Professor. And if I may say so, the dress is quite becoming on you."

Sarah Broadmore-Fassbinder stopped short of slamming into him, smirking at him.

"Well, Director. Glad that you recognized me. Though I expected to meet you earlier when you had that meeting with my Husband."

"Sorry, but the meeting had to do with your husbands abilities, not yours."

Adam saw her jaw tighten. "So, your plans do not include strong, professional women. I should have realized you have a stereotypical view of the female gender when you provided all the women with these frilly clothes. Do you think you can disarm all women with a bit of frill, a piece of ribbon, so that we will be the traditional 1950's housewife from ' Leave It To Beaver'?"

"No, Ma'am. I thought everyone would enjoy a chance for a little 'dress up' men included, which is why every man received a suit tailored for him. That's why everyone was measured before arriving. Not for a coffin, that some rumors have stated. A little bit of good old time Western Civilization does wonders on morale, in my experience."

"Do you wonder that we would have some apprehension, given the last six years?"

"No Ma'am, I don't. Contrary to popular belief, I lived through the last six years also. I am not some clone grown in a tank like some have claimed. And, to counter your statement about the role of women here, in this group of humans you see here tonight, you will find six medical doctors, ten nurses, five biologists, two agriculturists, ten security personnel, seven mechanics of various types, four computer geeks, a mathematician, two engineers and a theoretical physicist, all blessed with female genitalia. I look at what you can do, not what gender you are. Trust me, with Tschaaa medical technology, if it were important, gender modification is a lot simpler than Pre-Strike. But it isn't important. What you can do for the human species is."

"But you still limited your one on one meetings to a few men."

"'And one woman. Let me introduced you to Ms. Monroe....'"

The professor cut him off, purposefully not acknowledging Kathy. "You can't be serious. You compare a video whore to women with real accomplishments?"

Adam began to burn internally, though he did not show it. Dealing with Aliens, you learn how to control your outward emotions. But before he could reply, Kathy did.

"Hey, Lady. I'm right here. And yes I read, write, and understand English quite well. So, if you think, I don't understand being insulted, guess again."

Sarah still refused to look at her. "As I said, some whore who showed her ass on film is hardly an example of professional accomplishment."

"Well, your husband seems to like it." Kathy shot in." But, as uptight and dried up as you are, I can see why he would notice another woman."

Sarah's mouth dropped open, then snapped shut, and she took a step towards Kathy with murder in her eyes.

The Chief seemed to appear out of nowhere and stepped in between.

"Now Ladies. This is a fun time, not a fight time."

"Of course you would come to the defense of some white blonde bimbo" Sarah snapped.

"You probably never met a woman of color that you didn't want to own. How many slave owners are in your family tree?"

"That's enough, Ma'am." Adam broke in. "In the street vernacular, don't let your mouth write a check your ass can't cash."

"Oh, of course. The savior of the human race. So where are all the dark

The Gathering Storm

faces, the brown faces? How many did you help slaughter?"

People were beginning to notice there was a conflict nearby, and were beginning to stare.

Others moved to other side of the auditorium, glancing back nervously.

"Ma'am..." Adam Began.

"It's Professor! Quit trying to pigeon hole and demean me with chauvinistic titles. I earned my Professorship through hard work. Not by f**king someone."

"Ma'am," Adams voice was ice quiet. "Shut Up."

Sarah, hearing something in his tone that sent a chill up the human spine, stopped and sputtered a bit.

"Chief, you have that picture of your family?"

"Always, Boss."

"May I have it please?"

The chief produced a laminated photo that had been well worn. Adam took it carefully, and stepped in close to Sarah.

"First, Ma'am and Sir are honorific words that show good manners and respect. They were good enough for my Mother and Father, they are good enough for me. Second, who do you see in this picture?"

Sarah looked at it, and began to get a bit pale in the face. "A... dark skinned woman of Middle Eastern descent and two children that look ... mixed race."

"You see, the Chiefs wife was a darker skinned Afghani who he saved from being killed due to some honor killing bullsh*t for being nice to Infidels. They got to know each other, fell in love, got married."

Sarah tried to look at the Chief. "Ah, Chief, I'm..."

"Shut up." That ice voice again. "Guess what happened to them that first day?"

"I...."

"Shut up. The question was rhetorical. A well-educated Professor knows what "rhetorical" means yes? Don't speak. Just nod your head if you understand."

Sarah nodded her head.

"Good. They were probably Dark Meat in some Squids larder. And I know of former Black friends from the Air Force who were probably some Tschaaa Breeders snack the first year."

"Yes, I made a choice to save who I can. Sorry that most of them have lighter skin. And oh, by the way, I was the Godfather to those kids when his wife converted to Christianity, which would have gotten her killed doubly by her own people. She survived all that, until an Alien Invasion. Bit of a Cosmic Joke, don't you think?"

Adam got nose to nose with Sarah.

"So do not *ever* accuse the Chief of being some racist assh**e feeding dark skinned kids to the Tschaaa. And, Ms. Monroe is here because she has a flair for communication and seems to brighten people's lives up a bit with her perkiness. Some characteristics I think you lost well before the first Rock Strike."

Adam stood up straight. "Oh, Mary Lou. Glad you joined us. Please join the Chief, Kathy and I for a drink at the bar." Adam took both Kathy and Mary Lou's arms and escorted them to bar.

The Chief paused for a moment, putting the picture of his family away. Looking over the top of Sarah's head, he seemed to speak to no one in particular. "Too bad that some people walking and talking today are just as dead inside their heads as my family is dead for real." He went to join his friends.

"I'm sorry, Director" Mary Lou began, "I tried to head her off, but some young stud tried to pick me up and got in the way."

"No harm, no foul. She had her sights on me. Some time tonight she would have got me.

"By the way, Ms. Monroe, please accept my apologies for those boorish comments."

Kathy wrinkled her nose at him "Boss, she was right. I did show my naked ass for a living. But, I think I am a bit too well educated and smart to be a bimbo."

"Then why did you show your ass?" Mary Lou asked with a cocked eyebrow. She was wearing a dress that fit her body as nicely as Kathy's, slit up the side showing shapely leg.

"Needed the money, and found out I could make a goodly sum. Then began to go Mainstream Hollywood. The Squids showed up as I was on the way to an audition, the rest is history."

"Oh" Mary Lou said.

Mary Lou gave Kathy a look that meant she was sizing up possible competition. Why she seemed so protective when she was already sharing her bed with two other women Kathy could not figure out, especially since Kathy had made it a point to stay in a separate apartment.

"Excuse us Ladies, the Chief and I need a moment with the Major Grant."

For once the buxom blond had saw fit to wear a nice evening dress that showed off her well-endowed figure, slit up the side and all. Kathy looked at her appraisingly.

"If you are checking out Jane for a possible roll in the hay, she is straighter than straight."

"Now, Mary Lou, why would you assume I like women that much?"

Mary Lou mirked. "I checked out you films. You seemed to really like having women sit on your face, and vis a versa."

The Gathering Storm

"Well, you have heard of acting, haven't you? And if you think trying to have an on screen orgasm with a guy you don't like is hard, try to do it with a gal." Kathy gave Mary Lou a bit of a sideways glance. "But, you share your bed with the Barbie Twins. So, female attraction isn't new to you, is it?"

Mary Lou looked her in the eyes. "What I do with Adam is private. I know that he has already, 'tasted your wares'. But let me assure you that you're not the first, nor the last. The Director's randiness is legendary. It is a form of stress relief from having to watch people die, and knowing that each day you have helped condemn thousands of what were once called People of Color to being pieces of meat, literally.

"And," Mary Lou continued, "I will be blunt and say that I don't trust you. My gut says there is a hidden agenda hanging around you. So, if you hurt Adam, I will mess you up."

Kathy stared back at Mary Lou. "I always wondered what it would be like to get up close and personal with the late Bettie Page. You could be her twin. So, let me tell you, I am nobody's Bitch. If you want a fight, you've got one. I am willing to be friendly, but I won't be walked on."

The two women, inches from each other, stared into each other's eyes. Mary Lou broke the stare down. "Alright, now that we are both on notice, may I suggest we make the best of a bad situation for the Director's sake."

"Agreed." Kathy replied. "Shake on it." She extended her right hand, and Mary Lou took it in a firm handshake. Both women held the handshake for a few extra seconds gauging each other's strength. Both quickly realized that neither one was a push over. They released each other's hands.

"Nice handshake, Mary Lou. You're used to dealing in a Man's World, aren't you?"

"Yes, Kathy, and the same to you."

Adam returned at that moment. "My apologies again, Ladies. Getting acquainted, are we?"

"Yes" Both women answered in unison, each giving the other a small smile.

"Good. Because we will all be working together over the next weeks and months. Now, those drinks."

∿∿

Sarah was seething when her husband walked up. She was angrier with herself than the Director, angry for allowing the Director to so dominate her. She should have said more, she should have.....

"Well, that was special."

"Shut Up, Joseph." She snapped. She was so God Damn MAD.....

"Ouch! You're hurting me." And she was staring into her husband's eyes, noses nearly touching as she realized his right hand was digging painfully into her left bicep. He had never laid hands on her before.

"You just don't get it?" he hissed. "This is not some intellectual exercise. This is F**king Real."

He continued." The Tschaaa are real, human cattle are real, and the Director's power and mission are real. And he made me an offer I cannot refuse, to quote the Godfather."

His hot breath was in her face. "Do you think I will die for you, now? Maybe six years ago, sure as Hell not now. I have watched you and your pointy headed friends' complete intellectual masturbation while I and a few others found the food and supplies needed to survive. I have put up with your artful disdain that I 'dare' work with the U.S government, because I wanted Space."

Joseph was shaking with anger. Six years of stress and frustration, of listening to her sarcastic statements of intellectual superiority, of his physical love for her that was rejected, of barely surviving. And now, in this place, she dared to dictate what was right?

"You can stay, you can leave, you can go f**k yourself. I don't care. You have burnt me out. I'm staying. I'm doing what is right for me."

He stepped back, letting go of her arm. He let out a long sigh.

"You used to be a beautiful, vivacious woman. I wanted children with you. Now all I want is to be quit of you. Have a nice trip back to California. I need a drink." He turned and walked off.

For the first time in a long time, Sarah's private thoughts were not enough company.

Adam and his small party had obtained their drinks by know. There was a no host bar that was pay as you go. However, Adam had insured that in the pocket of ever man's suit paints was a twenty dollar bill to provide funds for a few drinks. Not to be sexist, females also received like funding, safety pined to the evening gown provided. Beer and wine were free, though 75% of it was Conch Republic locally brewed and vinted. The beer, more of ale, was quite good. The wine varied from bottle to bottle. The bartenders provided kept an eye on the patrons. They knew that many had only passing contact with alcohol in the past six years, so it was easy to drink too much.

However, most of the attendees made a bee line to the food offered free of charge. Several tables set up buffet style provided various Asian cuisine as well as types of pasta. Fresh fruit and vegetables from the extensive greenhouse and hydroponics area were often the first fresh food the new arrivals had seen in months, other than the occasional apple. Once again, tears of gratitude

The Gathering Storm

were evident, especially those mothers with their children. Malnutrition was a thing of the past here in the Keys. It was odd but the most popular section was one that Adam had originally set up for arriving children. That was the hamburgers and hotdog grill. After the first run on this simple food, Adam had ensured that in all future Socials, there was plenty of good old beef and pork hotdogs and hamburgers. He had even added a large roast for French Dip sandwiches. As usual, there was a bit of a line.

"Boss, where do you get the meat?" Kathy asked.

"We now have a herd of beef cattle and some pig pens here on Base. In addition, we obtained some cattle, especially some good old nasty Texan Long Horns, and introduced them wild on vacant areas near Homestead and Miami. They are enough like African Water Buffalo that they quickly adapt to the Everglades and other rural areas. So, anyone can have some beef on the hoof if they hunt it. And, Long Horns are big and tough enough to give anyone fits, including the 'gators. Oh and we do use alligator meat, which tastes a bit like chicken."

He pointed to two long tables set off a bit by themselves, with a large flag above them.

"And, Conch Republic Sea Food. Here, let me introduce you to someone."

"Then can I eat? I'm starving."

Adam chuckled. "Yes, this will only take a minute. And he will be slighted if I do not introduce you to him."

They walked up to the sea food tables, and saw a tall, slender man with a large but well-trimmed grey beard, He was dressed in a caricature of a Military Class A Uniform coat, with oversized shoulder boards containing five stars on each.

"Kathy Monroe, May I Introduce the Admiral, leader of the Conch Republic."

The Admiral broke into a large grin at the sound of his name and the sight of Kathy. Two gorgeous near six foot tall high heeled Amazons, one blonde, one brunette, flanked the Admiral, dressed in evening gowns that fit as well as Kathy's. They were more than just eye candy, as they scanned everyone and everything around the Admiral. They flashed smiles at Adam that said "High, Old Friend".

The Admiral took Kathy's right hand, clicked his heels in good German Kaiser Imitation and kissed her hand.

"Madam, it is indeed an honor. I probably have the largest remaining existing collection of your work, including your cable and mainstream work. Will you marry me?"

Kathy's mouth dropped open a bit, quickly recovered, and she replied" Why, we have just met, Admiral.......?"

"Just Admiral. I don't need another name. I know who I am, and so does every else in the Keys."

Kathy wondered if the elevator in his head went all the way to the top, and if it ever had.

"Now Admiral, "Adam interjected "She just got here as my guest. Decorum requires sometime for courtship before one pops the question, don't you think?"

"You are quite right, Director. How crass and crude of me. But, please Kathy, remember me before you become betrothed to another."

Kathy flashed him her signature smile. "Of course I will, Admiral. I do have a weakness for men in uniform."

The Amazons rolled their eyes at this, which the Admiral either did not notice, or preferred to ignore.

"Now, Admiral, could you please show Kathy your excellent repast?"

"Of Course. COOKIE." The Admiral bellowed, and a short man in a chef's hat appeared. He had a steaming plate of fish, crab, lobster, cornbread and silverware all ready to go.

"Compliments of the Conch Republic."

Kathy's eyes went wide, and she glanced imploring at Adam with an "I need food, now" look.

"Thank You, Admiral. Now, if you will excuse us, Ms. Monroe needs sustenance."

"Only if you promise to bring her back."

"Of Course, Admiral."

Adam escorted Kathy over to a nearby round table, and watched as she sat down and began to eat. A pang of conscience hit him as he realized that Kathy's diet had probably been hit and miss over the last few years, and here he was playing politician. She ate in a concentrated manner, not sloppily but like one who did not know when her next meal would come. It took her about five minutes to realize he was watching her, blushed, swallowed and sat her fork down.

"Hell of a date I am. You buy me dinner; I ignore you and stuff my face."

Adam looked at her intently. "Sorry. I forgot that this spread I take for granted is the first you have seen in years. I will admit I have a selfish streak in me that what I think is important is important to everyone. I'm fat, dumb and happy, and forget sometimes most people in the last six years are not."

Kathy took his right hand in hers. "Adam, you saved me and this whole auditorium of people from a continuous hand to mouth existence at best. And now I know you are working hard to provide this, "spread" you call it to as many people as you can. You need to apologize to no one. The Squids need to apologize. But I know that is impossible. It would be like me apologizing to a beef cow for eating meat."

She sighed, let go his hand, and took up her fork again. "I am not going to let guilt about how I survived and others did not spoil my appetite. But, please, I hate to eat alone. Please get a plate and join me. I have not had decent sea food in years."

Adam chuckled. "Your wish is my command. I'll be back in a minute. "

He went and obtained a matching plate of seafood, much to the enjoyment of the Admiral and his cook. He went back, sat down and began eating.

Maybe it was the effect of the company at the table, but the food seemed much more flavorful than ever before. He ate in silence for a few minutes, stuffing his face. Then he realized Kathy was now watching him intently.

"A penny for your thoughts, Ms. Morgan."

"You need to enjoy life more, Boss. I can tell that usually eating and drinking to you is just fuel for the engine, to keep you going. You need to enjoy the proverbial fruits of your labor."

Adam looked at her. This so called porn star had a wisdom and insight that was hard to ignore. And, he had a warm feeling in his lower body regions that wasn't just from the good food.

"Point taken, Kathy. But, I have to keep the eye on the prize."

He took another bite, chewed, swallowed, used his napkin to pat his lips and wipe his hands. He then stood up.

"Please excuse me, but I must mingle. Everyone must have access to the Director tonight. A dance later, if you please?"

Kathy flashed her smile and wrinkled her nose. "Of Course. But Mary Lou may fight me for it.

Adam chuckled again. " No need for that. Everyone who wants a dance gets one, even if I have to stay here all night. Although I try to get around the Base, some people won't see me again for weeks. Now, finish your meal, and relax. I will talk to you later."

He walked towards the other side of the Auditorium, Kathy watching him the whole way. She took a deep breath, and slowly let it out. A lot of people believed Adam was just this side of Hitler or Pol Pot.

But he wasn't.

This was hard.

"Even as Director Adam Lloyd set up sanctuaries for his Chosen, as well as began providing some of the lost amenities and trappings of 21st Century civilization, Pre-Infestation, others in the non-occupied or controlled areas of the world were getting by on their own. The inhabitants of the Feral areas, some near Tschaaa controlled areas, tried to leach and scavenge what they could without drawing the attention of the Cyborg Robocops and other Tschaaa minions.

"However, there still existed free minded people who firmly remembered what the world had been before the coming of the Tschaaa. Some of these people set up Free States or Countries.

"In the center of the former United States of America existed the Unoccupied States of America. Those who had fled there, away from Tschaaa control, had not just traveled to hide. For as in days of the Swamp Fox Colonel Francis Marion during the American Revolution, they ran away to fight again another day."

Excerpts from the Literary Works of Royal Princess Akiko,
Free Japan Royal Family.

MONTANA, UNOCCUPIED STATES OF AMERICA MALMSTROM ARMED FORCES BASE

Torbin Bender sat waiting for the Commander to finish speaking, literally twiddling his thumbs. The former Marine Sergeant, Navy SEAL and Delta Force Team Member, now field promotion Captain, was up next. He had a power point presentation that should knock the socks off all the occupants of the briefing room.

This was a Big Deal. In the room were representatives of Free Japan, as well as a few ragged representatives from former Russian controlled areas known as Free Russia, primarily from Siberia. This was a first attempt to organize a world coordinated Resistance to the now firmly entrenched Alien Tschaaa. He had to provide information they all needed and hopefully wanted to hear. The situation was still unstable, but Torbin felt his data was as reliable as possible. Six years of the Alien Occupation had still left pockets of Ferals and Free Agents who provided information on the activities of the aliens. Torbin enjoyed the field craft, the nitty-gritty operations in the unsecured or Tshaaa controlled areas. Sneaking around worrying about being discovered by the minions of Tschaaa brought back memories of his days in Delta Force and the SEALS.

However, this Intelligence Officer role was giving him fits. He was a Field Ops man, not a prog, not a REMF. He had recently managed short field ops, permitted after he told the Commander he was getting cobwebs in his combat reflexes. He had been in on the first capture of a Quisling renegade biker, one of three who tried to sneak into Montana by the back roads. This had been the first probe or enemy recon in months. Torbin was ordered to interrogate him after he had been softened up a bit, which had helped provide further information for this briefing.

As he waited for General John Reed, his Commander and former U.S. Air Force pilot to finish speaking, he looked at his Captains bars, still found them alien looking. He was 'enlisted material', never wanting to become an Officer and a Gentleman despite his four year degree. But a well over sixty percent casualty rate in the Lower 48 States, amongst surviving military of all branches after the first 48 hours of the Invasion, had led to some drastic promotions. Total casualties counts in this war usually meant 90% Dead, and then eaten.

Torbin was built like an Olympic Athlete, just under six feet tall, brown hair, blue eyes, with a profile befitting a TV Soap Opera Star. He had become a certified Physical Trainer in civilian life, after eight years of Active Duty, five of those in the SEALs and Delta. His four year degree was in Education, as he enjoyed teaching, so being a trainer combined his desire to instruct with his desire to remain physically active. He had stayed in the Marine Reserves, which led to his recall in the first 48 hours. Due to his SEAL training, he helped lead a hasty attack as the senior NCO in a 30 man Assault Platoon in the first 72 hours. The target, a Harvester Ark outside of what was left of Marine Corp Air Station Yuma, Arizona, would mark the last time the Squids tried to Harvest in the desert. The brass saw it as a chance to obtain some good Intel, maybe some prisoners, as the alien Squids seemed to have landed in Yuma by mistake. They were proving to be fallible. The problem was, humans were much more fallible, and the Squids had the 'high ground'... Space.

His mind scanned his memory, quickly jumping from scene to scene. He had survived, but others, including a young Army Lieutenant, had not. A C-130 Special Ops Bird pilot, an Air Force female Captain, flew tree top level and dropped them off and picked them up in the middle of the night just outside Yuma, Arizona. He had spent a night of passion with the pilot after the mission. Both had needed the affirmation that they had survived by having a nice, warm human body to hold, and love. She had dropped off the face of the Earth after that, never to be seen again. As had millions of other humans.

The information, photos and video he and the others provided, especially his up close and personal contact with a Front Man (which the creature did not survive) provided much needed intelligence on the Tschaaa and their minions. But it was too little too late. And just afterwards, he found out his younger brother William, an Air Force pilot, had been killed. He had died a hero, but he was dead nonetheless. Torbin would trade ten heroes for the chance of having a beer with his brother again any day in the week.

What was now referred to as the Battle of Yuma Overpass had gotten him "noticed". So when he and numerous other military types had fled to the now Malmstrom Armed Forces Base, a certain newly minted General John Reed had found Torbin and latched on to him. Which eventually got him a Battlefield Commission and then stuck him doing briefings when he would much rather be kicking ass and Taking Names. No rest for the wicked.

"Captain?" General Reed's voice cut into his reverie. "You're up."

It took a moment for Torbin to reorient from his memory to the here and now. He stood up quickly.

"Huh, sorry Sir. Wool gathering again."

"Well, like they say, times a wasting."

"Yes, Sir."

Torbin scanned his audience. There were eight male representatives from Free Japan. Free Japan had embraced a return to a form of traditional pre-Commodore Perry Code of Bushido infrastructure. This return to traditional Bushido culture was an attempt to deal with the horror of the demon like creatures trying to kill and sometimes eat them, although the Japanese had been successful in keeping their 21st century technology.

From former Russian areas, primarily Siberia, the Russian Military personnel were six, three of them were women. The women were all age 30 or younger, the Russian men in their 40's. Torbin thought of mistresses or former Russian intelligence officials attempting to insert operatives using sexual attraction. Probably the latter, as all three women were attractive but had the air of military training. Any mistress that existed would not make the dangerous trip to the U.S just because Poppy promised an exotic vacation that did not exist anymore. Plus, Russian and Soviet spy habits die hard.

Three young U.S.A. Butterbars were in attendance, one male, and two females, apparently ordered to get this updated briefing before going operational. Either he was getting older or they were getting younger, as the three young officers looked barely out of High School. The two females had dark complexions, one African looking, the other East Indian. Then Torbin remembered that a year ago a dozen Humans had escaped from Cattle Country and made it here. They must be from that group, definitely motivated to get some payback. That had been the last group to make it out, at least this far North.

Torbin began; "Good Evening, Ladies and Gentlemen. I know it is getting late in the evening, and we have all had a rather long day, so I will be as concentrated in my briefing s possible."

Torbin clicked the power point on, the first screen displayed showing North America, divided by shaded colorings into Squid controlled areas, feral areas, and then the Unoccupied States of America, once Montana, Wyoming, Colorado, the Dakotas, Nebraska, Kansas, Parts of Minnesota and Idaho, and off by itself, the State of Alaska. The Interior of Canada was listed as feral or unorganized, even though Torbin knew of some former Canadian Military Units that had fled to the Northern Provinces, the extreme cold keeping the Tschaaa out.

Both Coasts, the Great Lakes, all of the Mississippi River area, and the southern part of the Missouri River were colored as under Tschaaa Control, as was the Gulf of Mexico, Florida, Baja California, and the Panama Canal Zone. The Columbia River area between Washington and Oregon was shaded as in flux, the Tschaaa and their minions trying to reclaim the river from the horrible effects of the Hanford Nuclear Storage Area detonation, not to mention the volcanic activity of Mounts Rainier and Saint Helens. The Oceans, other large bodies of water, and the areas of land extending about twenty miles from these sources of water were firmly in Alien Control. Human naval vessels had almost ceased to exist.

The Japanese representatives had used low and slow aircraft to fly to Alaska. The Russians had crossed the Bering Strait in a Soviet era hover landing craft, the Tschaaa disliking the cold winter seas and ignoring the movement of smaller craft anyways. If you stayed away from their breeding areas, humans could get away with limited sea travel. The Russians had linked up with the Japanese and made the arduous overland trip in two weeks to get to this briefing. Torbin hoped they found the briefing worth the effort

Using the cursor, Torbin pointed out the areas of interest. "Us, Them, No Man's Land, since about six years ago." He pointed to the former states of Mississippi, Alabama, and Georgia.

"Cattle Country. As far as we know, the largest, organized, human meat stock breeding and containment area the Squids have on Earth. Three to four million souls reside there. And it is made up entirely of people with darker pigmented skin, due to a psychological fixation by the Squids that Dark Meat is 'best', is cleaner, safer. "

The dark skin of the two female Lieutenants made it difficult to see if they were blushing with anger, but the tightness of their mouths told him that they wanted to invade the area, tonight, and free their former friends and relatives. Which Torbin knew was not going to happen anytime soon. He pointed to Key West, Florida.

"The Capitol and Control Center of Squid Occupied North America. And home to what we believe is the most important Tschaaa Lord on Earth. Why so important, you ask? Because, though not being the most senior, they were his plans that were used for the Invasion. His specifically developed the technology, the tactics, and the decision for a long term stay. This has its good and bad sides. The worst scenario, which almost happened, would have been a much longer bombardment from space, more nukes, after which when the Tschaaa had sufficient meat in their larders and DNA material for meat reproduction, not to mention viable breeding pairs, they would leave. However, we could be nearing extinction now, instead of just beaten."

"We know this because we managed to slip a couple of agents down there. Plus, Director Lloyd, the Tschaaa puppet leader, tells everyone within earshot what the original plan was, and how things could be worst. The Tschaaa, at least the Lord in charge of North America, thinks hiding anything from humans is a waste of time and effort. OPSEC and COMSEC are apparently foreign concepts. At least once they take control, the idea someone would try and revolt or resist is an 'alien' concept." That got a few chuckles from the fatigued participants. Torbin continued.

"This Lord, who apparently has a sense of humor as well as knowledge of western mythology, calls himself Neptune, after the mythological Ruler of the Sea. He was the one who convinced the other Lords to allow Breeders into our oceans. Before that, they were going to remain on the Generational Ships that are in orbit. But Lord...'Neptune', convinced them that our oceans were very viable places to raise their young. Now, they have large, permanent breeding areas along all the coastlines in the more temperate areas of Earth."

"This is a good lead into 'know your enemy'."

Torbin went to the next slide. It showed a very dead young buck Tschaaa, all spread out on a large platform. The quality of the photo caused all the personnel to lean forward intently, with some whispering in Russian between two of the male senior officers. Torbin knew what was on their minds. How did the Americans obtain such a prime specimen of Alien Squid? The Japanese and Russians had only been able to obtain incomplete bodies due to combat damage.

"This not so little guy came into our possession much undamaged at the beginning of the second year of the Occupation. His Delta Fighter crashed in a corn field in North Dakota. Actually, it was what was left of a corn field, thanks to the Nuclear Winter that was going on. A very nasty snirt blizzard, that's snow mixed with dirt blown about by high winds, seemed to have knocked him down, and interfered with the Eye in the Sky locating him. At least no one came looking for him until what passed as spring occurred a year later. A patrol of ours scavenging for food and anything else of use found the Delta, saw the body inside, now frozen, and started screaming for attention." Next slide showed a different angled view of the same Squid.

"We now know Tschaaa are very closely related to our cephalopods here on earth in form and function. They combine characteristics of our Giant Pacific Octopus and larger Squid species. They have a thick body that resembles a rounder, more domed octopus, but ten appendages, eight arms and two specialized tentacles. They have a limited what we would call a skeleton made out of a type of cartilage. This prevents them from squeezing through small openings like a true octopus, but gives them extra body and frame strength that enables them to motivate on land more like a crab, for short distances, by rising up on their appendages supported by this frame. They have a combination gill and lung system that makes them a true amphibian, though they exist best in an ocean environment."

"Average weight is around 160 kilos, about 300 to 350 US pounds, so you can image their appendages are strong in order to be able to motivate on land. There is very limited dimorphism in the Tschaaa, the Male and Females being about the same in size." Torbin clicked to the next slide, which showed a detailed illustration of Male, Female, and Young. "Average appendage span is about six meters, their arms a bit stubbier than our octopi or squids as related to body size. The Males have two longer tentacles, similar to Giant Squids hunting tentacles, with specialized grasping fingers, five per end. The Females two tentacles are shorter, with grasping appendages which are slighter, smaller and, almost dainty is a good concept."

Torbin used the laser pointer to illuminate the tentacles.

"Why the difference? Because the larger male tentacles, besides used to manipulate tools as well if not better than our hands, are also used in mating. Though the Males have a fairly big shaft like penis, for some reason the penis is used as the backup means to deliver their sperm. The Tschaaa seem to prefer implanting their sperm into the Tschaaa version of a vagina with their strong, long and sensitive fingers. The smaller, dainty tentacle hands of the Female, though capable of intricate tool use, are designed to caress, stroke, basically excite the Male during the mating activity, to include the erect penis."

The three Russian Female Officers whispered something amongst themselves, then began to giggle until the senior Russian male gave them the Stink Eye.

"Now, after the two Squids do the 'nasty', that is have sex, what happens next?"

A fuzzy photo of a female Tschaaa with what first looked like four large buds or bumps emanating from her body.

"At First, scientists believed that they actually 'budded', that the young grew inside out into buds, like a plants, then broke off to swim free. Now, we know that, like marsupials (almost), the very tiny, young are expelled from the birth canal, then attach themselves to some very small nipple like structures in pouches near the base of the females' arms. There they grow in size, looking like large bumps, taking sustenance from their mother. Next, at a total time of one year, they have the 'Second Birth', where they break free from their mother. At this time they have the capability of swimming, both by arm locomotion and the siphon jet routine our native squid use. However, they stay near the birthing area for the next five years, tended by non-gravid females as the Breeder Mothers get pregnant again."

Torbin displayed a picture of several representative female Squids.

"Females have limited options in Tschaaa society. Some ten percent are chosen, based on their genetics, to be full time Breeders. Each Breeder gives birth about every twelve to thirteen months, depending how fast a male can get his tentacles and sperm into the Breeders naughty bits after the 'Second Birth'. They normally have from two to four young at a time, sometimes six, very rarely eight, and, once every one hundred years or so, a Breeder has a litter of ten. This is a 'Big Deal', taking on basically religious and supernatural like connotations. The easiest way to explain it would be if one human woman had a virgin birth in Christian belief every hundred years, producing several Jesus of Nazareth. Eighty five percent of the females spend their lives caring for the young of their Crèche. Before everyone thinks this a form of misogynistic slavery, in Tschaaa Society, know that the young are *everything* to the Tschaaa."

Torbin let that sink in. "All females involved in the production, care and maintenance of the young, both male and female, are treated with the utmost respect. They, after the Young, get the bulk of the fresh cuts of meat. A lot of that would be classified as "veal".

The Russian women, though professional military, became a bit pale when they realized what human veal was to the Squids. One of the Butterbars looked like she was having trouble keeping her last meal down.

"The last five percent are allowed to be Warriors, Technicians, Scientists, whatever the males Squids do, and are treated exactly like them when it comes down to resource allocation. You see, males compete to climb up the social ladder so that they can do the Nasty with a Breeder. Like Alpha Males in the animal kingdom, if you are not Numero Uno in a pack, the chances of having sex with a female is slim. Once in a great while, a regular female outside of the selected breeding lineages is randomly selected to be impregnated. This is to provide a little random genetic variance to prevent a line of Royal Idiots from taking over. There is no English Royal Family in the Squids." This elicited a few laughs.

"Now, why is all this is important in relation to the so-called Lord Neptune, you may ask? Well, his birth mother was one of the randomly selected females to add genetic diversity. She then proceeded to give birth to ten Tschaaa." Torbin let this sink in. "That's right. He and his brothers and sisters, littermates, were the closest thing to royalty, or supernatural leaders that the Squids have. He was told he was special, which may have made him think in a special way, to our determent. While the Tschaaa were getting stagnant in the thousand year long journey, Lord Neptune was just the opposite. Although the Senior Lords tried to limit his effect on the way things were done, he used his 'specialness' to push for new things. And, he found sufficient supporters so that ninety percent of the weapons and equipment used against us were either his new idea, or his modification of existing designs, including that equipment taken from the alien races the Squids ran into during their travel into Space. He spent years studying our transmissions, and knows us possibly better than we know ourselves in some ways He seems to be step ahead of us on any given day. So, if any one Tschaaa is responsible for kicking our ass, it looks like him."

"But," Torbin continued" he also is the one pushing the idea that we are potentially of more use than just being a nice cut of meat. He seems to want to make us the equivalent of 'working dogs,' as well as maybe draft horses. He and the Director talk about the Protocols of Selective Survival. These concepts have probably kept us from being Nuked and Rocked back to the Stone Age as the Tschaaa leave our Solar System. That, and the fact that their Young seem to love our Oceans."

"Their home world seems to be almost eighty percent Ocean, with ninety percent of dry land being around their Equator. Although Squids can take cold water thanks to their copper based blood, like our squids, they do not like it. And, their Young need warm seas the first few years to develop well. "So, we get the Arctic and Antarctic Oceans, parts of Alaskan and Canadian northern waters. They get the rest of the Oceans."

Torbin changed slides.

"Now, what and who else did the Squids bring with them? Let's look." Pictures of Grays and Lizards appeared. "Since the Second Week of the Invasion, we have seen few of them. Possibly because they make better targets than they do soldiers."

The senior Russian Officer, a Colonel Antonov, cleared his throat loudly.

"Yes sir, you have a question?"

"My young Captain, you talk with a tone of knowledge and experience in combat. But, I see large complexes in these northern states, and fair numbers of Americans. We Russians fought tooth and nail for the Motherland. Now, three quarters of us are dead. How do we know that you are not just spinning tales to assuage your well know American conceit and pride?"

Torbin looked at his Commander. General John Reed, though a former Air Force Puke, and not a Marine, knew his stuff. Now, once again, they had to deal with someone playing "Quien es Mas Macho" when they should be thinking of killing Squids.

"Colonel," General Reed began "You have seen our photos from Yuma, Arizona, correct?"

"The Battle of Yuma? Yes, we have watched the DVD. It is like many combats we had in the early days of the Invasion."

"Well, Colonel, Captain Torbin was an enlisted Marine then, and was the highest ranking person to survive. He got his people home after getting all that film evidence and destroying the Harvester. I think he knows how to deal with aliens."

A young Japanese Lieutenant choose that moment to spring to rigid attention, began rambling in Japanese, then bowed to Torbin, as his Colonel Tanaka started to tell him the equivalent of 'Sit Down, Boy.' in Japanese. He sat down at rigid attention. Colonel Tanaka stood, bowed slightly to General Reed.

"My apologies, General. Lt. Yamamoto was overtaken by the emotion of the moment. Please, Captain, continue."

Torbin looked at his boss. The General, knowing by now what Torbin was thinking, having been through a special Hell with him the last few years, gave a little nod.

"Colonel," Torbin asked, "may I ask what the good Lieutenant was talking about?"

The Colonel paused, and then said in perfect English, "Captain, Lt. Yamamoto lost his family to one of the few Harvesters that landed on Japan. They seemed more content to hit us with a few 'Stones', and then strafe us from their aircraft. He has seen your film many times, and wishes that is what he could have done in Japan."

Torbin knew his family was gone, but was sure they died in an early large Rock Strike near San Diego, California, other than his Brother, William, who died fighting. He did not know what he would do if he knew that his Father and Mother had been butchered on a Harvester. Torbin came to attention, and bowed to the Lt. "Please, accept my condolences. My parents died quick, my brother in combat. But I, too, wish I could have done more."

Colonel Tanaka looked at Torbin. "You come from a military family?"

"Yes Sir. My Father was a Ranger, my Brother was an Air Force pu... I mean, pilot. Past generations have also served in the military, including World War Two, in the Pacific."

The Colonel drew himself up a bit, then, in a formal tone, "General, Captain, may I present Lt. Yamamoto, a descendent of Admiral Isoroku Yamamoto, who died fighting America in World War Two. The Lieutenant hopes to carry on the Yamamoto name with honor. Which he has so far, in direct combat with the Tschaaa."

The Lieutenant snapped to his feet again, bowing deeply to Colonel Tanaka and began to rattle off in Japanese again.

"Yamamoto-San. English, Please." Colonel Tanaka snapped.

Yamamoto took a deep breath, and then said in perfect English. "You do me and my family great honor, my Colonel."

"No Lieutenant, it is you who do us honor."

Colonel Tanaka continued speaking. "That family Samurai sword the Lieutenant carries with him always has accounted for eight Tschaaa Warriors."

Colonel Antonov snorted. "I am sorry, but, how do you expect us to believe he has killed eight 'Squid" with a sword, when we only see them in aircraft. We fight robots and those Giant Warriors they have."

"Because, Colonel, the Islands of Japan have been selected for what we call Special Attention."

"How so?" Asked General Reed.

"Because of the Fukushima nuclear plant meltdown and contamination we suffered before the Invasion, after the tsunami. The Tschaaa seemed to be hesitant to eat us after the first few days, due to residual radiation that can still be detected in some areas with sensitive instruments."

One of the good-looking female Russians, a black haired brunette, took that moment to chime in.

"That is like Chernobyl. We had no reports of Aliens any nearer than two hundred miles from Ground Zero. They are afraid of radiation contamination." For this comment, she received another Stink Eye from Colonel Antonov.

"Yes, Ma'am." Torbin interjected "The Squids are hyper sensitive about a contaminated food supply for their Young." He turned to Colonel Tanaka. "So, what have the Squids been doing in Japan?"

"Their Young Warriors sneak ashore in ones and twos, sometimes up to four. They hunt and kill, and leave the bodies behind, the only occasions in which we have heard of this happening. They seem to be testing themselves, bringing only hand cutting weapons with them."

Colonel Tanaka looked at his Lieutenant with the look of pride a father would have for his son.

"Yamamoto-San has proven the superiority of traditional Nippon Bushido swordplay on land eight different times. Tell them, Lieutenant."

"They seem to underestimate what a katana can do. You slash a couple of appendages off, they freeze for a moment, thus giving you the chance to slash and then impale their brain by going through their eye."

Torbin mused about being 'Billy Badass' with a rifle. But a fricking sword?

"You must be fast, Lieutenant."

"He is, Captain, he is." Once again Colonel Tanaka took the role of the proud father.

"Gentlemen. Please." Colonel Antonov interjected. "Can we now continue with the briefing? I can assure you that everyone in this room has seen their share of conflict and deprivation. My staff and I are tired from a very long and arduous journey." Now that the Colonel had lost his chance to one up everyone, he wanted to change the subject.

General Reed looked at Torbin. "Think you can finish expeditiously, Captain?"

"Yes Sir. Now, let's look at the other players and their toys in what has become a nasty dance of death……."

∿∿

Two hours later, Captain Torbin crashed on his rack. He had a private room, befitting his rank and accomplishments. But he would trade it all in for a combat post.

There was a knock on his door. Now what?

He went and opened the door, to find Lieutenant Yamamoto standing there, a bottle of Scotch in one hand, and a bottle of Sake in the other.

"Captain, please. I would like to share a toast with you."

Torbin smiled. "Ah, Lieutenant, you know my weakness. Any self-respecting Marine cannot turn down a drink offer, especially Scotch. Do come in. Find a seat. I'll get the ice for the Scotch. Do you want the Sake warmed?"

"You have drank with Japanese before?"

"I have had a drink with just about every cultural group on Earth. I hope one day to have a drink with the Tschaaa just before I blow their brains out."

They were soon sitting down, enjoying the quality libations Yamamoto had provided.

Torbin noticed for the first time that Yamamoto seemed taller than the normal Japanese, 5' 10" at least. Torbin had accessed the limited Internet they had set up using the military based servers in the Unoccupied States and found a photo of Admiral Yamamoto. There was a family facial resemblance, but the Lieutenant was definitely leaner and taller than his ancestor. Probably inherited from the non-Yamamoto side of the family.

"So, what is your first name again, Lieutenant?"

"Ichiro. And yours, Captain?"

"Torbin. A family name. Tor for short, which is sometimes mistaken for Thor, but I am definitely not the Marvel God of Thunder."

"Ah. You read comic books."

"Ichiro, if I may call you that, 99% of kids of my generation read comic books, of one kind or another. But your Japanese Animae gave a kick start to all future animated forms of entertainment....until the Squids showed up."

They were silent for a few moments, musing about childhood joys probably gone forever.

"Are you a pilot, Tor-San?"

He snorted. "Not even close. My brother was, he went to it naturally. Why do you ask?"

"You had an accurate grasp of the Tschaaa Deltas, the Falcons in the briefing. We know of the thirty two millimeter electromagnetic cannon, the three inch guided missiles used in actual combat. Although we now have limited fuel, we still intercept the odd Delta that attempts to penetrate our airspace. Like the raids by Tschaaa Warriors from the sea, they act as if it is a test, a game, a real life video game."

"But" Ichiro continued, "you Americans do not seem to have an operational Air Force of any capability. Is that so?"

Torbin chuckled. "Yes, that's true. We're trying to piece together aircraft as we speak, but have maybe a dozen of all types available. The Squids targeted our airfields and airports, as well as sabotage by the Quisling Renegades, all which knocked our aerial 'dick' into the dirt. We have substantial ground to air defenses available, but that is good for point defense only.'" Torbin did not mention the somewhat operational ICBMs that were still scattered around the former Northern Tier bases. But, even if they all still worked, they would only either cause another Nuclear Winter, or contaminate the living areas still under human control. Human kind may not recover from either one.

"But, we do have a good deal of Intelligence Assets. Because Lord so called Neptune left so many pockets and centers of non-Dark Meat humans alone, to survive on their own with just some Robocops keeping an eye on them, we have a lot of sources of information that keep track of Tschaaa. Squid Watching, Ichiro, is the only 'hobby' some humans have left."

Torbin looked at Ichiro. "You are a pilot."

"Hai. Yes, I was finishing Pilot Training when the Tschaaa attacked. It took me a few months longer to become fully certified due to combat losses in aircraft and fuel. But, I saw my first aerial combat a year to the day after the first Stone Strike."

"What was it like?"

Ichiro gave a beaming smile. "Exhilarating. I knew I was born to be a Warrior. The Deltas, there were two, instead of the normal one. We found out through some recovered Tschaaa electronic records we were able to translate that 'littermates' from small two Young litters, like our human twins, often had a bond that few others have. They live and fight together until they either succeed in their efforts to pass their genetic seed on or...... they die trying."

Like innumerable fighter jocks before him, Ichiro began demonstrating the aerial combat with his hands.

"They came in at close to Mach three, though we know they can go faster on their scramjets. But, they wanted us to intercept them, to fight. I and my three flight mates accommodated them." Torbin had never seen a more animated soldier or pilot. He also seemed to have a photographic memory, the way he demonstrated the entire combat, relating what each aircraft did and when.

"They fired their electromagnetic cannon, one round from each cannon, the finned shells traveling some 2000 meters a second. And, as you know, they have an organic limited Artificial Intelligence in the warhead that key on moving objects, using their fins and tiny maneuver jets to twist and turn after us."

Ichiro jumped to his feet, almost knocking his drink over. "But my Squadron Commander, Major Chiba, had planned for this. He had installed rear facing target marking rockets on our jets. When we fired them, at the shells, their quick movement caused the fined shells to turn towards them. Chaff and flares traveled too slowly to attract the AI. But these rockets were quick.

"The Tschaaa Delta Pilots seemed surprised by this tactic. They turned their now well-known 15 plus gravity turns, boring towards the rockets also."

"I threw my fighter around in the air, and was on the tail of one of the Deltas for a moment. Before he could use his Gravity Pulse Engine to accelerate out of the area, I fired every weapon I had. The tough skin and frame of the Delta, though very strong, collapsed under my weapons. My first kill."

Ichiro paused, and then sat down, his demeanor suddenly becoming more subdued.

"But the surviving Delta did a 15 'G' turn and latched on to me, and shot me from the sky. I ejected, and my parachute opened. As I swung to Earth, the Delta looked as if it would make gunnery run on me, dangling in my chute, apparently seeking revenge for the loss of his Twin. Then, it happened."

Ichiro paused, and took a large gulp from his glass of Sake.

"Major Chiba cut in front of the Delta, and turned directly into the Delta, ramming him, as pilots in World War Two had sacrificed themselves for others, for Japan."

Ichiro was silent. Then he spoke. "'On that day, I swore I would kill ten Squid for Captain Chiba. I have two more to kill."

The two warriors sat quietly. Torbin then stirred.

"A toast, Ichiro." Torbin interjected. "To all our comrades in arms, who have died, fighting the good fight. May their memory never disappear."

"Hai. Kempai." They emptied their glasses, and Torbin refilled them.

"Before we are completely shitfaced, Ichiro, I must have you show me how you kill a Squid with your katana."

Ichiro laughed. "I am willing, but we are short a Tschaaa to use as a victim."

Torbin slyly smiled. "Watch my magic, Ichiro."

He walked across the room, and pulled a large frame from the shadows into the room's center. Up at the top was a rather thick roll of unknown material.

Torbin stood off to one side. Ichiro, sensing something was up, stood up, right hand on his Katana hilt that he carried in his left hand.

"Ichiro, please meet a special guest." Torbin pulled a restraining tie and a very exact 3-D representation of the recovered Tschaaa from the crashed Delta, unraveled to the floor.

Torbin took a breath to speak, and it was all over. There was a blur of motion, the sounds of slashing. The 3-D representation was sliced in three pieces, along the axis of the Squids tentacles. Ichiro was standing stock still, his two hand gripped Katana impaling the Squids right eye perfectly.

Torbin gulped. "Well, so much for that training aid."

Ichiro smoothly sheathed his Katana. "I am sorry if I destroyed something you need. It was an automatic reaction."

Torbin walked over to his desk and retrieved his K-BAR fighting knife.

"So, if the Tschaaa had a blade......"

The katana blade was already at his throat.

"Uh, remind me never to make you mad."

Ichiro sheathed his katana, and bowed. "I apologize, Torbin-San. I have drank too much.

"Oh no you haven't. I wanted an example, and you gave me one. Have you always been this fast?"

"Yes, Torbin-San. Some medical specialists once said I have the fastest reflexes in the Japanese Defense Forces. Why, I do not know."

Well, Hell, I do. It's Karma. You are supposed to slice up Squids. Here,

The Tschaaa Infestation, Vol. 1

another drink, if you please."

At that moment, there was a light knock at the door. "Who the Hell....?" Torbin strode over, and flung open the door, K-BAR still in his hands.

The three Russian female officers were standing there, a bottle of Vodka and glasses in their hands. The senior one, the Captain, cocked an eyebrow, and looked at Torbin and his knife.

"Well, I see you are playing with your Man toys. May we join?"

Torbin paused, then answered. "I have never turned down three pretty women with a bottle of vodka in my life." He stood aside, bowed, and swept his arm towards the center of the room, beckoning entrance.

"Come into my parlor, said the Spider to the Flies."

The three women laughed, and then entered. They all wore matching fleece work out gear, as if part of an Olympic sports team. One Brunette, one Blonde, one bronze colored Redhead all about 5'5" and around 130 pounds of fit woman hood. The sweats were baggy enough to conceal some of the curves, but not all.

Aleksandra, the senior ranking woman with dark black hair, saw Ichiro. "Good. More company"

Ichiro stammered, and tried to move towards the door. "My... apologies, Tor-san, but I must go..."

"Whoa, old hoss. You cannot leave me outnumbered three to one. Even a Marine has his limitations."

"I ... I... "Ichiro stammered again.

"Excuse us for one minute Ladies." Torbin grabbed Ichiro by the arm and escorted him to his back bedroom.

"Ichi", he began, "Are you married?"

"Well, no, I..."

"Good. Then think of these Ladies as three wandering Geishas come to entertain the conquering Japanese Samurai."

"But..."

"Lieutenant. You owe me for the training aid. And it is also in the name of good international relations."

Ichiro sighed. "I owe you for the training aid. And for you, Tor-san, I will sacrifice myself. "

Torbin wondered if Ichiro was bullsh**ting him with the last statement. But it did not matter. Three specimens of outstanding womanhood were in his room, and must be provided service becoming of their ranks and positions.

"Good. Follow me."

"Ladies, in the name of full disclosure, there is absolutely nothing of any intelligence value in my room, so if you have any ideas...."

The Gathering Storm

Three gorgeous women were standing in his living room, with just panties on.

Aleksandra caught his eye "I think, Mister Spider, that the Flies already have ideas of their own."

It was going to be a long, rough night.

∾∾

Torbin awoke with Afanasii, the Blonde, gently kissing his back. He glanced at the

Clock. Five A.M. Due to the late night briefing, and trip fatigue on the part of the visiting military members, the General had told everyone that he did not want to see anyone before Noon. This could not have come at a better time. He started to turn towards Afanasii when another set of lips began to kiss his chest. Aleksandra, the Captain, was demanding attention. He tried to position himself equally between the two women, then they became cognizant of what the other was trying to do. Rapid fire whispered Russian began between the two. Torbin did not speak Russian, but he could imagine, by the tone of voice, what was being said;

"It is my turn. No, it is not. Yes, it is, quit trying to pull rank, we are in bed. Let go, Slut. Do you want your ass kicked, fat cow? Try it, Bitch."

Suddenly the two women slid down to the end of the bed, stood up and began to wrestle. Despite being trained military members, passions caused the conflict to quickly dissolve into a hair pulling, biting, scratching catfight. They fell to the floor, cursing in hushed tones as if no one would notice. Torbin watched as they grabbed each other's breasts, cruelly twisted and scratched their mounds of beautiful flesh, tried biting each other, Torbin decided it was time to stop them.

"Ladies. I have hot water in my shower. And high quality shampoo."

They froze in place, untangled hands from hair and breasts, stood up as if nothing had happened. They made a beeline to the shower. Inna, the bronze redhead, apparently watching the conflict, had untangled herself from Ichiro on the couch. The mention of a hot shower and American soap products apparently had magical powers, after a long and dirty trip. Torbin chuckled at the vive la difference of womanhood and stretched. Ichiro was beginning to snore, so Torbin got up and went to the couch. He bent over and whispered in a high falsetto voice into Ichiro's ear, "Oh, my big Samurai, wake up. I must have more."

Ichiro smiled with closed eyes, reached a hand up, muttering some pillow talk, felt Torbin's beard stubble. His eyes popped open, and he began to curse in Japanese, as he tried to untangle himself from the blanket. Torbin jumped back, laughing. "Rise and shine sweet cakes, if you want some hot water in the shower."

Ichiro recovered, stood up with an embarrassed grin on his face. "You Americans are always such jokesters."

"Oh come on, Ichi-san. I saw those Japanese game shows your people used to produce. You loved practical jokes. We even started copying them."

Ichiro looked at him. "You did say a hot shower?"

"Yes sir. You just have to share it with three Russians."

Ichiro's face broke into a broad grin, and he marched towards the bathroom in his boxers, showing off an extremely cut muscular torso, whistling some Japanese military tune. He definitely was adaptable.

∽∽

"My examinations of the workings of the Director's organizational skills revealed he had an excellent knack for finding people with the expertise he needed for certain specific projects and functions. Often, these people came with emotional and personal baggage that must be dealt with in order for them to fulfill the desired task. But of course, all surviving members of the human species at that time had psychological, social and emotional scars from years of the threat they or their children would be eaten by the Tschaaa, myself included."

"One such married couple who the Director had located, Professors Joseph and Sarah Fassbinder, would have much to work out before they played important parts in the history of the New Capital of Tschaaa Controlled North America, Key West."

Excerpts from the Literary Works of Princess Akiko,
Free Japan Royal Family

NEW CAPITAL, KEY WEST

While Tobin was waking up Ichiro, Joseph Fassbinder was also being woken up. But he was not in bed. Instead, he was propped up against a small tree about two blocks from the Auditorium.

After his blow up with his so-called wife, he had made a concerted effort to get sh*tfaced. He needed a good drunk; he deserved a good drunk, so he worked at and obtained a good drunk. He had used all his liquid assets at the bar, just before being cut off by the bartender. When the barkeep was distracted by a very attractive, and apparently single young woman in a revealing cocktail dress, Joseph had swiped a bottle of whiskey from behind the bar, and disappeared towards the exit, bottle expertly concealed under his suit coat, which was a tad loose due to his undernourished lanky frame.

The security troop let him leave, as they had been told some of the new personnel had assignments in the morning. And besides, this was basically a free 24 hour installation, with the perceived threats coming from the outside, not the inside

He had wandered for a while, making a concerted effort to finish the near full bottle in the shortest amount of time possible, before being forced to use the tree as a support. He then passed out.

Joseph heard a male voice "Sir, Sir. Time to wake up. The party's over."

Joseph found himself looking into the face of one of the biggest men he had seen, in full battle rattle. He saw stripes on his arm that Joseph recognized as a Sergeant.

"Sorry, Sergeant. I guess I dozed off and lost track of time." He tried to stand up, and fell forward, being caught by the Sergeant.

"Whoa, Sir. Just sit there down for a moment until you get your balance. We do not need a busted face the second day here..... Oh, Good Morning Ma'am."

The Sergeant tried to prop him up against the tree to free his right hand for a salute. Joseph proceeded to fall backwards. Another, smaller set of hands helped catch him, and he heard a woman's voice. "Good Morning yourself, Sergeant. It looks like my morning run is going to be interrupted."

She looked at Joseph. "Good morning, Professor. I take it you did not make it back to your quarters last night."

Joseph managed to finally focus his eyes enough to recognize Major Jane Grant in a set of running shirt and shorts that did very little to conceal her voluptuous body.

"'Good Morning.... Major. Umm, where am I?"

"Whew, you smell like a distillery. And you are a few blocks from my quarters, a shower and some coffee. Sergeant, if you could help me with transportation, I will take this problem off of your hand. I need to try and get him to work today."

"Yes Ma'am. Thank you Major. This saves me a lot of paperwork."

Ten minutes later, with the help of the two additional sets of hands, he was sitting on the Majors couch.

"Thanks for the ride, Sergeant."

"Oh, thank YOU, Major. Good luck." Joseph heard the front door shut.

He started to nod off again, but was woken up by two feminine hands unbuttoning his shirt. He started to protest, and then decided he liked the feel of the hands and the nice smell of the owner.

"MMMM, I like your perfume, Major."

Jane laughed. "That's called O' De' Sweat, Professor. It's easy to come by around here. And, if you help me, this will be a lot easier and quicker. You desperately need a shower."

Between the two of them, he was nude in the shower in ten minutes.

Joseph leaned against the stall wall, cool but not cold water from the shower head beating on the top of his head, then running down his face and chest. He just might live.

Suddenly, the shower stall door opened, and another body entered.

"Gangway, Professor. I need to clean up too. No touching without permission or you will be singing soprano. Looking within reason is okay. "

Jane turned the shower head so that the water was now on her athletic body. Joseph turned his head sideways enough to look at her. He had not seen such a nice body in a long time. Her large, firm breasts must be close to 36D, and, she was a natural blonde. He leaned against the stall wall and drank in her loveliness. Jane quickly washed her body and hair. She rinsed the shampoo from her hair, then turned towards Joseph and began washing him.

"Uh whoa, Major. We haven't been properly introduced." Joseph protested as Jane's hands began washing his whole body with a washcloth.

"Oh, be quiet. You don't have anything I haven't touched or seen before. And I and the Director do not like to work around men with drunken sweat on their bodies."

She paused for moment. "Well, that part still works. I guess you're not as drunk as I thought."

Joseph blushed and started to turn away, but could not. He was standing at attention when Jane said, 'Okay, you're clean enough. Out of the pool."

In five minutes he was sitting on a clean towel in the kitchen, trying to conceal a still fairly prominent erection. Jane came up and tossed him a set of boxer shorts and a man's shirt.

"Here, I wear these around my place when I'm relaxing. They should fit you, you're pretty skinny right now. Professor, you need some meat on your bones if you are going to ride a rocket in a couple of months. "

He looked at Jane, and she smiled.

"To properly introduce myself, I am Major Jane Grant, the Director's Operations Officer. You are Professor Joseph Fassbinder, soon to be helping us obtain regular space travel again, with some help from the Squids, of course."

Joseph sighed, and said "Major, I wish to humbly apologize for this trouble. I owe you."

Jane handed him a cup of hot coffee, and two large donuts.

"Here, this will help soak up the alcohol. And, no, you do not owe me anything. First, because we all work together here to survive in a crazy world inhabited by BEMs ...Bug Eyed Monsters."

Jane took a sip of her coffee. "And , two, do you remember a Marcia Brand when you started Mission Specialists Training for the Space Program, just before the Rocks hit?"

Joseph got his wheels turning in his head, remembering a different time in a different place.

"Yes, I do. She was one of the sharpest young ladies I have ever met. She was training as a Spaceplane Co-Pilot, the youngest ever accepted."

"She was a Cousin of mine, who was like a sister. She had the utmost respect for you. And, a bit of a crush, also. She told me you were one of the nicest people she had ever met, as well as the most brilliant. But in my book, nice beats out brilliant."

Jane took another drink of coffee. "She's dead now. Unfortunately, probably some Squid fed her remains to their young. I also help you in her memory, as she would have wanted it."

A tear appeared in Jane's eye. "Excuse me." She walked out to her bedroom.

Times like this reminded Joseph that just about everyone had been screwed over in one way or the other. They were all just making the best of it. The Tschaaa had changed human dynamics drastically, most likely forever. Now, they tried to keep a resemblance of humanity while trying to survive. Damn. Joseph put the boxers and shirt on, and they did fit. He had lost a lot of weight, and not in a good way. He wolfed down the donuts, suddenly starving.

Jane came back with his suit pants that she was brushing out, and a windbreaker.

"These will do today. We do not stand on formality, unless you're in uniform. Those standards are tougher. Although Ms. Monroe, because she will be on camera and in the public eye as a representative of the Director, will realize it will be like she is in the military."

At the mention of Kathy's name, the memory of what Sarah had done flooded back.

"Major, I need to apologize to Ms Monroe for....."

"Never mind. Ms. Monroe is the proverbial tough cookie. It was water off a ducks back."

"Now, if you will excuse me, I need to finish getting ready." Jane walked back to her bedroom.

Only then did he realize she had been standing there in panties and bra. He had not been this relaxed with a woman in years.

∿∿

Adam was moving a little slow, thanks to a late night entertaining the new arrivals. He had literally danced with all those who wanted. More than one wife had danced with him just long enough to whisper a thank you in his ear, especially those who were mothers. And, of course, Mary Lou, Jeanie and Jamey had each tripped the light fantastic. Then, Kathy had tapped his shoulder.

"My turn, Boss, if you please."

She had a smooth rhythm, and, as he held her, he noticed strong back and shoulder muscles he had not noticed during their earlier passion. She held him quite firmly, with strong fingers and arms that befit someone who worked at keeping fit. As the song ended, Kathy kissed him on the cheek.

"Time to turn into a pumpkin. I need to get a good night's sleep as I think Major Grant will try and work my ass off tomorrow. "

Adam smiled. "You're posterior is much too nice to be worked off. You'll do just fine. I'll be in contact when I can."

Kate wrinkled her nose and flashed her signature smile. "Just remember I wouldn't mind some quality one on one time also. Especially if is horizontal."

Adam laughed. "Don't worry, how could I forget."

Kate squeezed his arm. "Night, Boss." She literally slinked off, her smooth sexy walk drawing many an appreciative stare from the males in attendance. And a few bruised arms as wives let husbands know that they were keeping an eye on their men folk.

Now, 7:00 AM the next morning, Adam once again wished that he had a clone, so he could be in two places at once. But the hard truth was that Duty Called today. He had to meet the Lord.

His radio phone pinged.

"Yeah, Chief."

"Boss, I have a Professor Sarah Broadmore who says she 'really' needs to see you. Her husband is missing."

Sh*t. He needed this like he needed a hole in the head. "Send her up, Chief. Mary Lou has the morning off."

Adam quickly dressed in his Tactical pants and Shirt, which he wore when travelling to visit the Lord Neptune. He waited out by Mary Lou's desk in the front office.

Sarah came through the doors, dressed in slacks and shirt. She had her hair tied back in a pony tail that should have made her look younger. But her face was pale, and she looked like she had aged ten years.

"Morning. So Joseph is missing."

Her chin quivered, and then she regained some composure. "He never came back to the room last night. He started drinking, and then disappeared. He has never done this before. Ever."

Adam looked at her. Hard. "Do you blame him? You basically acted like you'd just as soon castrate him, me as well, than spend any time with him as his wife."

Sarah's chin quivered, a tear appeared, running down her left cheek.

"Ah Sh**! Turn off the waterworks, Sarah, I'll help find him. I need him a lot more than apparently you do. Here, a box of Kleenex. Sit here by Mary Lou's desk."

He punched in Jane's phone, and pinged her.

"Morning, Sir! If you are looking for a certain Professor Fassbinder, he is all cleaned up and headed towards the Science and Engineering Building."

Adam stared at his phone. "Major, have you been hiding that fact you are clairvoyant all these months?"

"No, Sir. Just trying to...anticipate your orders. Sir."

Adam chuckled. "Could you please stop by my office for a moment?"

"Yes, Sir."

Adam turned back to Sarah. She began sobbing. He stood there. He had never been married, never lived with a woman, prior to bringing his three Ladies here and moving them in. He knew that Joseph had loved her dearly once. And she may have killed it.

Sarah finally stopped, blew her nose.

"Director, what will become of me?"

Adam paused. "That is up to you."

She laughed harshly. "Really? I am only here because of Joseph. Why didn't you just kill me and dump my body in the mangroves?"

"Because, Sarah, contrary to what everyone thinks, I actually do care about my 'fellow man'....and woman. I did not lie at the briefing. You can stay or go this morning. We will provide transportation back to where you lived."

Sarah sniffed, blew her nose again. "What can I do here?"

"Well, Professor, you could teach. I was told you were quite the interesting lecturer in your early years. As long as you did not try to ferment revolution, stir crap up, you could help teach the younger folks. Most had their formal education interrupted. And, I do believe they are the future."

Sarah looked at him. "Don't really have a choice, do I?

"As I said before, yes, you do. I want actual volunteers. I'm working to turn North America back into a livable place again, not just a place where people survive in a hand- to- mouth existence. And, we have made great strides in the last year in the Tschaaa controlled area. Food is now being distributed. We are setting up hospitals again. Televisions, radio, the Internet are making a comeback. It takes time after an all-out war. Look at World War two and the Marshall Plan."

"Well, Director, what about the rest of the country? What about the Cattle Country, the Unoccupied States?"

Adam shook his head. "I can only help those whom I have the power to help. And, the Tschaaa would just as soon let the interior states go to Hell, as they have nothing the Tschaaa want. The Tschaaa leave them alone, hopefully they leave the Tschaaa alone."

Adam continued. "And I know that you are going to say things are unfair. Well, the Universe does not have a 'fairness doctrine'. Creatures are born, live and die every day on various worlds, all based on variations of Darwinian Evolution. The strongest, fittest, do survive to procreate, and work their way to the top of the food chain. Unfortunately, what we would at one time have referred to as People of Color are at the bottom of the food chain. And if we, if I am not careful, we could be right there with them."

Sarah was silent. Adam knew she was trying to deal with her inner conflict of her survival verses fighting the unfairness situation. She did not want to admit she had no power right now to make a difference. Rights and fairness are concepts that work when all sides come from a framework of the same basic moral concepts. If the side with the power decides that your opinions do not matter, and they have no recognizable moral conscience, then the world turns to Hell real quickly. The Squids were the Nazis, and Humans were the Jews, humans existing due to the sufferance of the Squids. Sarah took a deep breath, and then let it out slowly.

I guess for once in my life I will have to admit I am pretty powerless. That is a concept completely foreign to me."

"Believe me, Sarah, you are not alone. I had to come to the same conclusion five years ago."

She stood up and looked him in the eye. "I will do as you ask as long as I can for my own, and Joseph's, survival. When I can no longer, I will tell you."

Adam smiled. "Fair enough."

Major Grant arrived at that moment, slowly approaching the two.

"Director, you called."

"Good Morning, Major. Would you be so kind as take the Professor back to her Quarters so that she can freshen up a bit, and then see that someone gets her to the Training and Education Section?"

Jane smiled. "My pleasure, Sir". She turned towards the Professor. "Ma'am, if you would come with me, please." She escorted Sarah to the winding staircase that led up to the Director's Complex.

As the left, Adam sighed. "I'm getting too old for this sh*t." He went back to his office and retrieved his satchel and briefcase he needed for the meeting with Lord Neptune. This had all the makings of a very long day.

Jane had a Security Troop drive her and Sarah to her quarters. She walked Sarah up to the door, where Sarah finally spoke to her. "Major, if I may ask, how is Joseph?"

"As well as can be expected" Jane paused. "Professor, I know little about you and cannot live your life. But, please take this as true friendly advice. Your husband is a fine man, well respected by some survivors here who knew him before the Rocks. If you want to continue being his wife, please, cut him some slack. There are those here that would willingly swap places with you, and be his partner. I think you have one more chance as he's a man of honor who loves you."

Sarah looked at Jane, blinked back some tears, and finally said. "Thank You, Major. I will strive to remember that."

"Please give me a call when you have a chance, Professor. I mean that."

"Thank You. I will."

Jane left Sarah and walked back to the vehicle. As she was driven to the Communications and Broadcasting Center, to meet Kathy Monroe, she thought, what a f*cking Idiot that woman was. She wished she would have met Joseph ten years ago.

∿

The aforementioned Joseph was in front of the Science and Engineering Building, trying to figure if it was too early to check in for work. Then, the most colorful former Fed Ex delivery truck he had ever seen pulled up. Written on the side in large red, white and blue letters was "CONCH REPUBLIC EATS. DRINKS. SUNDRY ITEMS. YOU WANTS IT, WE GETS IT."

Joseph noticed that the driver's side had been modified by cutting a large access window with a small counter as the bottom sill. The window was open, though it looked like there were large fold down flaps inside to secure the opening. Emanating from the mobile kitchen inside were the most delicious odors and smells. His mouth watering, Joseph began checking his pockets for money. All he found were some coins left over from his bout of drinking.

He then checked and found his wallet. In a wallet pocket he found something he had almost forgot he had, His Lucky Two Dollar Bill. The Director said they still used good old 'green backs 'as tender, as there were so many left in relation to the numbers of survivors. But, he had this bill for so long. His stomach growled.

Then his Lucky Two Dollar Bill generated luck once again.

"Professor Fassbinder! Is that you?" A female voice called out.

He turned towards the voice as saw an attractive young lady with red hair and freckles approaching him. Right behind her was a young man, red hair and freckles also. Instantly he noticed a strong family resemblance.

"It IS you. My God, I thought someone was making it up. You did survive." The young lady started to throw her arms around him, but stopped when she saw the confused look on his face.

"I'm Sorry. Of course you don't recognize us. Remember Sandy and Samuel Olson, the "Olson Twins"? We were first year aeronautical engineering students in you class. We bugged the crap out of you until you let us help you with your research project."

Then recognition flooded in. The Olson Twins. They were young geniuses who had started college at age 16, and had managed to get assigned to his department. He eyes teared up as he recognized another human being from his past that had survived. They were few and far between.

He threw his arms around her as he yelled "My God! You made it." Soon she and he were both crying. Other people coming of the building gave them space. Scenes like these repeated themselves all over the former U.S.A., as survivors found family, friends, co-workers, and former neighbors found a familiar face. It was the new reality. Next Samuel was hugging him also. They remained clasping each other for about another half minute, before they stepped back from each other. Joseph looked for something to wipe his eyes with, and a voice from the food truck called "Here. Just give it back." And hit him with a rolled up towel.

He and his found friends used different corners to wipe eyes, blow noses. The Olson Twins gave him a quick update (without going into gruesome details). They had somehow survived in the basement of a school dormitory that had been an old Civil Defense shelter in days gone by. It even had some old rations and survival hard candy that kept them alive for a couple of months. They emerged, bumped into a couple of other survivors, and headed for the hills. After the first couple of months, the fact they were 'red headed white people' seemed to result in them being ignored by Harvesters. Pale skin and freckles seemed to put them off. Living hand to mouth, three years later they bumped into one of the Director's Foraging Expeditions, saw what side of the bread the butter was on, and joined in. The young fresh faced youngsters were gone, replaced by seasoned survivors.

"Are you hungry?" Samuel finally asked.

"Yes, but I am short of funds. Maybe the Department will give me an advance..."

"Forget it. My treat and I'll order for us. The Mystery Meat Burritos are to die for."

Joseph frowned. "Mystery Meat…?"

Samuel and Sandy laughed. "Don't worry. It is good quality meat. They just won't tell us all the different types that are in it."

Joseph soon had two large burritos, and a bottle of Near Beer. To insure adequate and potable water, pasteurization of drinks in one way or the other was called for. Thus, the Conch Brewery made Near Beer, probably one percent alcohol on a good day was a staple. They sat down at a nearby table, apparently provided to service the meal truck.

"Oh. Wait a minute, please." He took the towel that had been thrown at him and walked to the truck.

"Excuse me. Here is you towel back, rather used. Thank you so very much."

A gorgeous woman with jet black hair looked at him, locking eyes, and smiled. "Don't mention it. Just remember the Conch Republic was there when needed. And also, we're here every morning, rain or shine. Come and spend money, eat, get Gas!" As she turned away, he saw her hair covered a large scar on the left side of her face. Even then, she exuded attractiveness second to none. Sandy giggled as Joseph walked back to his friends.

"And Jolene, one of the Admirals many Daughters, captures another heart. Will the spell last? Or is the Professor able to break the magic that enslaves so many, including my brother."

Samuel blushed a bright red. "You'd better be glad you're my twin sister or, female or not……"

Sandy laughed. "If I were not your twin sister, then I would be on the verge of having a good old fashioned cat fight with the local women for your attention! You see, my brother is seen as a very desirable catch by the local Conchettes. A couple have already come to face scratching and hair pulling over him." She snickered. "But not Jolene, much to his frustration."

Samuel kept blushing. "Just because I'm more attractive to the girls than you are to the guys isn't my fault."

Joseph broke in before he stuffed his mouth with burrito "So there is a lot of interaction with the locals?"

Sandy answered, "In a word, Hell Yes. They provide a lot of the local amenities, including not only this meal truck but a couple of cleaners, some stores, restaurants and, my brother can attest to this personally, a bunch of bars and entertainment spots. Including at least two brothels."

Samuel couldn't stop blushing. He mumbled. "Just you wait."

Sandy continued. "After you get settled, we will take you for the grand tour." Joseph felt her hand on his thigh beneath their table. He suddenly realized that the 16 year old student was now an auburn haired beauty, who was giving him smoldering looks. Did Key West make everyone a bit randy?

Samuel looked at his watch. "Eat up! Then we will take you in and introduce you to our Section Chief."

Still chewing on the best burrito he had ever tasted, Joseph managed to mumble, "Ours?"

Sandy smiled. "Yea, you're going to be stuck with us again. We're assigned to the same project. And, we may be going up in the Spaceplane with you."

The day was getting curiouser and curiouser.

∿∿

"Even in War, or in some ways, especially in War, close friendships are developed even as relationships with others on the proverbial same side become extremely acrimonious."
Excerpts from the Literary Works of Princess Akiko,
Free Japan Royal Family.

MALMSTROM ARMED FORCES BASE, GREAT FALLS, MONTANA

Torbin was headed over to the Main Hanger on what was once Malmstrom Air Force Base, now Malmstrom Armed Forces Base. It was just before Noon, and he had already been up for hours. At 8:30 AM, he had been the first customer at the Base Exchange, flying through the relatively well stocked women's undergarment section. Creative scavenging of abandoned towns in the surrounding former States, as well as into Canada, had produced a large supply of various a sundry items. And, with the population of the Unoccupied States a great deal less than pre-Invasion numbers, there was room for surpluses. In addition, various cottage industries producing consumables had sprung up among the locals.

Other than hits on the Northern Tier Military Bases, there had been only cursory attempts at Harvesting. The Tschaaa wanted to stay near the abundant Oceans, the Great Lakes, as well as those areas with the majority of Dark Meat, once that was figured out. The ability and experience of the Northern Plains States population to weather very bad and cold weather had led to a fairly high survival rate during the 'Nuclear Winter' that hit most of the United States. Thus, now there was a basic population and resources to build an organized Resistance. In addition, the new U.S. A offered a safe haven for survivors to flee to, especially people of color.

Torbin knew the clerk figured he was some pervert when he bought a quantity of women's unmentionables, all of very similar sizes. A little prompting of Aleksandra had helped confirm his suspicions based on his, shall we say, sizing experience, and he had sought to buy everything he could. He then grabbed some feminine hygiene products, perfumes, deodorant, makeup and frilly, female doodads.

His last stop was at the silk screening and embroidery shop ran by his friend Mike, a disabled Gulf War Vet. Torbin had provided him with lot of ideas for his products, including "I kissed a Marine and all I got was this lousy T-Shirt." He bought three.

Mike looked at Torbin with the "You have got to be kidding" look he often gave him.

"Ask me no questions, and I will tell you no Lies." Torbin told him.

"Tell me later, over a beer. You're buying." Mike responded. Torbin grinned, and then left.

He put together three identical packages, then tracked the Russian Female officers down at the chow hall, away from their male counter parts. He did a hit and run mission, not giving them enough time to open the packages. Now, all of the Military Missions personnel were meeting at the Main Hanger for the next part of the briefings.

Torbin saw the three Russians, and made his way towards them. As he approached he noticed something was wrong. The three women were tense and stiff. Then he saw Aleksandra's black eye, which almost seemed to be getting darker as he looked.

"There you are, Captain." It was Colonel Antonov, walking up to him. His face was flushed, and looked a bit unsteady. As he neared, Torbin smelled cheap booze on his breath and exuding from the pores of his body. He came up and poked Torbin in the chest with his left index finger "I will decide what my officers receive. You ask permission before you attempt to buy their attentions and favors. Now, you will take the items back, or I will sell them when we return to Russia."

Torbin grabbed the Colonels finger and bent it painfully back, sideways and down, all at once, nearly breaking it. He then shoved the Colonel back.

"Where I come from, IVAN, you don't beat on womenfolk or junior officers just because you're drunk and pissed."

Antonov's face went white. He swore, and grabbed for a small pistol concealed under his fatigue blouse. Torbin saw red, reached for his concealed K-Bar he always carried.

Ichiro seemed to appear from nowhere, and expertly tapped the Colonel's wrist with his sheathed katana. The pistol fell to the tarmac, and Ichiro then struck it like a hockey puck, sending it skittering away. He began to bow and apologize profusely. "Oh, many pardons, Colonel! I am so clumsy sometimes. Here, let me retrieve your pistol."

"YOU SLANTY EYED LITTLE APE!" Colonel Antonov yelled it before he realized what he had said. A stone faced Ichiro Yamamoto stopped bowing and stood up, his back straight as an arrow. In what was probably just a second but seemed like minutes as time perception slowed, Tobin saw Ichiro shift his feet and body. At the same time, his right hand grasped the katana's hilt, tensing for a draw.

"CAPTAIN! What is going on?" General John Reed's Command Voice cut through the tableau, freezing everyone and everything. The General was not a big man, being a fit 5'9", medium build, with graying dark hair. But some people have that ability to immediately take charge and demand obedience by their voice, presence, and demeanor. Luckily for everyone involved, General Reed had this Command Presence ability.

Tobin turned towards the General and saluted smartly. "Sir. Just a little misunderstanding, Sir."

He then noticed that Colonel Tanaka was at General Reed's side. Ichiro saw his Colonel also and, before anyone else could speak, spat a couple of rapid sentences in Japanese to Colonel Tanaka. Immediately, Tanaka, stone faced, stood ramrod straight and impaled Colonel Antonov with his stare.

"At Ease. Everyone!" General Reed commanded. 'I do not know what happened, but this is MY base. We do things my way."

He turned towards Antonov and sized him up immediately. "Colonel, you are drunk. That may fly in Russia, but not here. Go sleep it off."

Antonov glared at the Russian Females, and spat something at them in their native tongue.

"NO, Colonel. You will *not* 'take care of them later'." General Reed commanded. "Do you think you are the only one who speaks Russian? Like I said, this is my Base. Now, go to your quarters before you mouth writes a check your ass can't cash."

With this, Colonel Antonov stomped off.

The Gathering Storm

"Captain."

"Sir!"

"Escort these personnel to the Hangar. We need to get this show on the road."

"Yes, Sir." Ichiro and the Russian Females, came to attention, saluted the General, about faced and fell in behind Torbin. With near practiced precision, the five officers marched in step to the Main Hangar. Colonel Tanaka gave a short crisp bow to General Reed. "General, I do not wish to intrude, but there is a matter of honor..."

"Colonel, with all due respect, after the Squids leave, you can have all the duels over honor you want. Hell, I'll probably volunteer to be a Second. But right now, I've been tasked to form an Alliance out of very limited resources. And, since we here in the U.S.A. have a civilian government in control, War or no War, I do what I'm told. So, sorry, everything else is on hold."

Tanaka took a deep breath then let it out slowly. "I understand, General. Please accept my apologies if Lt. Yamamoto has caused you any difficulties."

"Colonel, Lt. Yamamoto reacted the way any young man with a sense of decency would react. Yes, I saw the black eye. But, since I'm the 'old fart in charge', I have to keep the men from fighting each other so that they may fight the real enemy. Agreed?"

"Yes, General. I will explain this to Lt. Yamamoto."

"Thank you kindly, Colonel. Now, I think you will find what is in that hangar very interesting...."

When Torbin and his little formation reached the Hangar, they found that the rest of the personnel from the previous briefings the day before were already in attendance, their attention focused on what was in the Main Hangar. No one else had seen the outside action, and Torbin was not about to share the situation with them, to include the three Butterbars.

Towards the back half of the large Hangar was the center of everyone's attention. A tall man was hosing down a Tschaaa Delta that was propped up and supported by a series of large jack stands. A large drainage tank set up around the aircraft was catching the run off. This was a different craft than the Delta in the photos from the briefing the day before. Torbin told the Russians and Ichiro to find some seats in the small set of bleachers that had been set up, and he approached the tall man with the hose.

"Afternoon, Pappy. "

Without taking his eyes from the task at hand, Pappy responded. "Hello, Captain. I see we have a fairly large audience today. I hope they are sufficiently rested."

"As well as can be expected, Pappy. You about ready to begin the Dog and

Pony Show?"

"Just as soon as I wash this thing off one more time. Despite all of our decontamination, I still keep getting fluctuating readings of high radiation. I can only surmise that the organically grown skin has pieces of radioactive dust and crap imbedded in the odd spot here and there. I hope one more wash down will free up the crap causing the readings. As it is, I would limit direct contact with this bird to about five minutes. I have exposure strips for everyone to attach to their pockets so we can keep track of their exposure. "

"Thanks, Pappy. Well, let me get them handed out, then I'll introduce you."

Five minutes later, exposure strips handed out, Torbin began.

"Ladies and Gentlemen, if I may have your attention. The tall man with the hose and salt and pepper hair is Peter "Pappy" Gunn. He is a former Army Chief Warrant Officer, who told our elected officials that he would not be re-drafted into the Military when they tried to about five years ago. But, he said he would work as a Civilian Consultant as long as we kept him supplied with cigars to chew on and cold beer." There was some light laughter.

"So, Madam President agreed, and here he is, all six foot six of him. He is related to another famous 'Pappy' Gunn of World War Two Fame. That Pappy became famous for cobbling together various weapon systems to use on our aircraft in the Southwest Pacific, back when Japan and the U.S. were at war. I bet you that if we had known the Squids were nearing our neighborhood, the war would have ended real quick."

Torbin continued. "Be that as it may, our Pappy Gunn is carrying on a proud tradition of figuring out all things weapon related. Thus, he will go into much more detail concerning the threats and weapons I mentioned yesterday. Please pay attention, as Pappy has a wealth of information to pass on in a limited amount of time. Pappy."

Pappy Gunn walked to the front of the bleachers, all six feet, six inches of him. Tall and lanky, he had a reputation of somehow twisting and wrapping his frame into and around the piece of equipment he was examining. And, somehow, he always managed to figure out to some degree or another how something worked.

"Afternoon. I know the good Captain gave you some information on whom and what we are facing in this conflict. Here, in this Hangar, I hope to pass on some more details on weapons and threats of the Squids. And, hopefully you will share some information with me. Every little bit helps, and even after six years of fighting with an enemy that has little concept of information security, there is still a lot to learn."

He turned and walked back towards the Delta. He had learned years ago about projecting ones voice, so he did not need the provided microphone to be heard.

"We obtained this little gem just two weeks ago. A survivalist from Idaho walked all the way from near the Washington-Idaho border to tell us about it. He is in the hospital being treated for radiation exposure, as he was in and around this Delta prior to us de-contaminating it. Not to mention how much he was exposed to thanks to the Hanford Mega Explosion. "

Pappy pointed to the starboard side. "This Delta was apparently in the air when Hanford blew, and all this area here took some blast, heat, and various types of energy that fried the right ramjet and singed that area forward."

"The Squid pilot must have been a hotshot as he found a long stretch of highway in Southwest Idaho and landed this bird. "

He pointed to the three large wheels, one in the nose, and one projecting from each wing.

"This landing gear, and I use that term loosely, are wheels that were added as an apparent after thought. They only have large coil springs to absorb landing shock, and the brakes are equivalent to a 1955 Chevrolet sedan. So, the Squid must have been good to keep from bouncing off the road into the ditch. This craft was clearly designed to operate from space and return to a low orbit station."

Pappy continued. "The Squid was nowhere to be found, so we assume a Falcon picked him up. How much radiation he absorbed is hard to say, but since the Geiger Counters were having fits when we found the Delta, there is a good chance he is buried in a lead box somewhere, if the Squids ever bury their dead."

"The radioactivity is the reason, we believe, no one tried to salvage it. We know the Squids are sensitive about all types of contamination and poisoning, as they are afraid their Young will be affected. The original plague that killed off much of their meat supply, their primary food, must have been devastating."

"The Squids left everything behind. So, we found in the craft the following."

Pappy motioned to an Airman in a decontamination suit the wheel a cart close enough to the bleachers for the personnel to see. Pappy used a laser pointer to help in the examination of the equipment mounted on display boards.

"This medieval looking thing is their equivalent of a crescent shaped sword or ax. See the thin wire or cable strung between the ends of the crescent? That is a monofilament, a monomolecular strand of condensed material that has the capability of slicing through all known metals when enough force is applied to it. We have one good report of a Robocop using one to slice off the barrel of an Abrams main tank gun. The curved blade on the other end of the four foot shaft has a point on it made from a tungsten alloy. Makes a dandy can opener on soft skinned vehicles."

Ichiro raised his hand and said "Mr. Gunn. We have seen a cruder version of that, where there is sharp blade suspended in place of the cutting strand. "

Pappy looked at him quizzically. "Oh really? What was the situation?"

"Young Tschaaa Warriors are raiding our shore areas, coming from the sea, looking for individual combat."

"That's very interesting. I would like some more details when you get a chance."

"Hai! Of course, Sir."

Pappy continued. "And of course, a large multi charge pulse rifle. We usually see these in the hands of Robocops, but, at least in the early days of the Invasion, the Squids seemed to have carried them also. They can penetrate the side armor of a tank at close range."

He then pointed out a long projectile looking object, just under two meters long.

"The three inch missile, launched from the Delta, although some multiple ground mounts were seen at the end of organized resistance. The missile is guided by an organic based Artificial Intelligence seeker, which bore sights on anything moving. Once it gets locked on, the Rube Goldberg looking mass of little holes, that are actually maneuver rockets openings, somehow twists and turns that thing around like it was fluid. The warhead is equivalent to our old three inch explosive shell, overkill on a jet fighter, somewhat effective on ground targets. Usually only one or two mounted per Delta."

Pappy then moved a bit closer to the aircraft itself. He used the Laser pointer to outline the salient features of the craft.

"That long thin cone looking nose contains a high energy plasma pulse weapon, the science of which we are just now figuring out. It can blast through a tanks armor at a thousand meters, no sweat. At longer ranges, even though the pulse or beam dissipates in atmosphere, it still contains enough umpff to fry electronic guidance and radio systems. Humans in the open are dead. The only good thing about this for us is that the amount of energy or charge for this weapon seems to be limited. We have reports of Deltas using it at full power twice in one mission, no more. "

He continued. "These two barrel looking protrusions near each side of the cockpit are just that, barrels. These are the downsized version of electromagnetic rail guns, which fire 32MM long dart like projectiles at two thousand meters a second. The kinetic energy is sufficient to blast most of what it hits. They also have an organic based AI system that tracks motion, and small retractable maneuver fins that allow them to twist and turn after the target. When the velocity drops at very long ranges, there is still a small explosive charge in the warhead that goes off a second after impact. It's rather anemic, but can blow the head off an unprotected human, hole a thin vehicle body, and shatter cockpit glass."

"They are fired in pairs, with only ten in a drum for each gun. No spray and pray for Squids, everything is based on guidance."

Pappy then pointed to openings near the cockpit.

"As was mentioned before, two scramjet type engines that can propel the Delta to at least Mach 3.5 by our radar track, but examination of the engines show a potential of Mach 5 or more. The rear nozzles can be tilted five degrees in any direction, aiding in maneuvering. The center large engine is a type of gravity or magnetic pulse engine, which is used to kick the Delta into Outer Space, or accelerate from zero to five hundred knots in a second from a standing start. We are still trying to figure it out. The cockpit is a self- contained unit that is filled with heated water when a Squid flies, so the cushioning effect plus Squid body design means high G, instantaneous maneuvers have little effect on them. The cockpit IS the G suit. A small crude oxygen tank is used to keep the water oxygenated for the Squids. Their gills work well enough that they do not need a separate pressurized air system."

Pappy Gunn faced his audience.

"The Delta, like most Squid machines, is some 90 percent organic in nature. This means, the outer shell is grown like a crustacean's mantle. This system makes for a very tough piece of equipment, like metal armor in its capabilities. We shape metal and ceramics to make our equipment, the Squid's can grow theirs, then have metal and ceramic add-ons as needed. Thus, small low orbit maneuver rockets are embedded in the organic body after the Delta is grown.

All these characteristics results in an air and limited spacecraft built for hit and run strikes from low orbit. They land on Earth only rarely, or in this case, because the Squid flew too close to a nuclear blast."

"We have yet to recover a Falcon. We do have some Jim dandy news film of one being rammed by one of our fighters and going in."

'Not Again'. Torbin thought. He tried to steel himself for watching the news footage once again. He should be used to it by now. But when a large television monitor was wheeled in front of the assembled personnel, and the footage began to play, Torbin stood up abruptly and walked to the latrine. He washed his face with cold water, and then stood by the sink. He had seen a lot of people die. But he would not watch his brother William die, over and over again on film. Not for anything or anybody. He waited while Pappy finished covering what was shown on the news footage, knowing it was over when one of the Japanese Officers entered the latrine. He exited and almost ran over Ichiro.

"Torbin-San. Are you well?"

"As well as can be expected, given the circumstances."

He continued walking outside the Hangar. He closed his eyes and let the sun warm his face, taking slow, deep breaths. He felt a familiar touch on his arm, and opened his eyes to see Aleksandra Smirnov, blackened eye and all, standing near him.

"You knew the pilot in that news footage, the one that rammed the Falcon."

Torbin took another breath and let it out slowly.

"Yes, Captain, I knew him. Hell, Ma'am, I grew up with him! That was my brother, William."

Aleksandra stood near him, silent.

"He went the Officers Route, joined the Air Force, I guess to show his Jarhead older brother by one year that he was better at something. And after all the sh*t I went through, the action I saw before he even got his wings, he goes and gets himself killed being a hero."

He noticed Ichiro was still standing nearby.

"Torbin-san, all Japanese pilots have heard about the American who took down the three Alien craft from stories told by surviving American Servicemen in Japan. But, we have never seen the recording before. Some believed maybe it was an exaggeration. Now, we know it was not."

"No, Ichiro, it happened. But a day doesn't go by that I wish it was a myth, an exaggeration, and -William will magically appear so that I can buy him a drink. But that's not going to happen."

Torbin took one more breath, and then turned to walk back into the Hangar to complete the briefings.

"Well, like my Grandpa used to say, daylights awastin'. Shall we finish this?"

As they re-entered the Hangar, Ichiro said a little prayer to himself, and thought what an honor it was to have met Torbin Bender. He prayed that his Ancestors would help keep his new friend safe. He tightly gripped his family sword, its hard reality giving him a measure of comfort in an uncertain world.

It had been another long day for the General. One in a long line of long days. He sat at his desk, wondering if he would ever have a "normal" day again. Then he realized he was having trouble remembering what a normal day was like. Master Sergeant Johansson, late of the Minnesota National Guard, knocked on his door jam, stuck his head in and announced "Captain Bender here as requested, Sir."

"Good, Send him in, please."

Torbin marched in, saluted at attention, "Reporting as Ordered, SIR."

"Thank You. Please, have a seat, Captain."

"Sergeant Johansson", the General called out, "Go ahead and take off. Please shut the door when you leave."

"Sir, I could stay, I have ……."

"Sergeant, did I stutter?"

"No Sir. Have a nice night, Sir." After he heard the outer door shut, General Reed looked at Torbin.

"Relax, Dammit. That's an order." He reached into his desk, and pulled out an unopened bottle of 12 year old Scotch. He then stood up, glared at Torbin when he started to stand, and walked over to his small refrigerator.

"Well, I guess that jerry rigging the Sergeant did was good. It's making ice again."

General Reed put ice cubes into two glasses, and went back to his desk, setting one glass in front of Torbin. With practiced ease, he opened the bottle of Scotch, and poured a good two ounces in each glass.

"This is single malt Scotch. I never thought I would be pouring it for and sharing it with a Mustang Jarhead Captain, but here we are."

Torbin looked at the General. "Well, sir, I never thought I'd be sharing 12 year old Scotch with an Air Force Puke General, Sir. No offense meant, General."

General Reed chuckled. "None taken, Torbin."

They sat in silence for few moments, sipping and enjoying the Scotch.

General Reed reached into the left hand drawer of his desk and pulled out a double picture frame. He set it on the desk so Torbin could see it.

"Torbin, how long have we known each other?"

"Almost five years, General."

"Ever seen these photos before?"

"No, Sir, I haven't.'

"That was my wife, Ivana. Those were my two boys, Matt and Mark. She is the reason I speak Russian."

Torbin looked at the photo. The woman was a knock out with dark hair, a models body and smoldering eyes. "You wife is beautiful and you sons good looking. "

"Yes, they are….were. I assume they are dead, as she was visiting relatives in Russia, outside Moscow, when the Squids hit us. "

He took a large slug of Scotch, then refilled both glasses.

"I met her when I was an Air Force Attaché' at the Embassy in Moscow. I was a young Light Colonel, never married, fast burner. I had been an A-10 Driver, then a Special Ops pilot when I wrangled the Moscow assignment as part of an intelligence gathering effort. I wanted some career broadening as I wanted General's Stars."

General Reed took another drink. "I met Ivana at some Embassy function and fell madly in love. She was an interpreter, spoke better English than I did, and taught me Russian. I was told that marrying a Russian National, thanks to Putin and company, was probably not a good career move. But she was, literally, no bullsh*t, my first, and only, great love."

"So, I set my horizons lower, married her, and got her to the U.S. She became a citizen while pregnant. We had our sons, one after the other, and were talking about a daughter. I was going to retire and work for some think tank, as I had made some good contacts over the years. I managed to make Full Bird, was looking for a Reserve assignment so I could bow out gracefully."

He drank again. "Then, the f*cking Squids showed up. Now, I have Three Stars, going on Four, no family, and a near impossible mission."

He looked at Torbin. "This is it. I got this assignment because I speak Russian, can get things done, follow orders, and, if I do say so myself, I am one motivated individual. Torbin, if this fails, we putter along for a few decades, maybe a century. We revert back to a pre-industrial society, and all, 'this'... becomes the stuff of legends. That is, if the Squids just don't decide to hunt us all down. If we succeed, and can really hurt the Squids, find some way to start wiping them out, the survivors will probably leave. Or, if we believe our friend the Director, they accept us as equals or the Top of the Food Chain again." He paused for a moment, in thought.

"Or, we die trying. Which isn't the worst thing that can happen. Existing as an intelligent side of beef, waiting for slaughter, *is* Hell."

Torbin sat silently. Then he asked. "General, why aren't you a Marine?"

General Reed laughed. "Funny you should ask that. My father told me he would be proud of me if I chose the military as a career. But, that he would kick my ass around the block if I joined the Marines."

Torbin stared. "Why, Sir?"

General Reed took another drink. "My Grandfather had been at Iwo Jima. He told my Dad stories that had a lasting impression on him about charging up the beach. My Dad said he did not raise a son to be cannon fodder." They sat and drank for a while longer. Then the General said. "Thank you, Captain, for the excellent company. Now, it is time to turn in."

"Thank You, Sir, for the excellent Scotch." Torbin rose, saluted. "General, I don't consider myself cannon fodder. But I will charge up a beach for you, for all the humans left. Just say the word, Sir. "

General Reed looked at him. "I know you would, Son. That is why you're here."

"Now, hit the rack, Captain. We have another busy day tomorrow."

"Aye Aye, Sir." Torbin turned and left. General Reed sat still for a moment.

The Gathering Storm

He then put his wife and children's picture away, finished his drink, and stashed the bottle.

He wondered again what a normal day would be like.

∿

El Segundo: "He is here, my Sire and Lord."
Lord Neptune: "Good. Insure the Director is brought here most haste. I have much to discuss with my most favored Human."
Excerpts from the Literary Works of Royal Princess Akiko,
Free Japan Royal Family.

Transcription of translated Intercepted communications between Tschaaa Lord Neptune, Lord over North America, and his Tschaaa Second in Command, known as El Segundo.

KEY WEST

As General Reed was preparing to leave his office, Adam Lloyd was just returning to his. He walked in plunked down on the overstuffed sofa. Damn, he felt tired. Maybe he was getting too old, though late Thirties had not been old at all six years ago. The threat of winding up as a cut of meat may cause premature aging.

"Director, are you back?" It was Mary Lou. She had the morning off, but, the trooper that she was, she came in and stayed around until he returned. She still had on her office attire of blouse, skirt and high heels.

"Yes, Mary Lou, I am. Finally. Today, Murphy's Law was in full force."

He looked at her. "You can take off. I need to unwind and make some notes from my meeting with Our Lordship. But first, please come here." He stood up as she approached, gently grabbed her shoulders, and kissed her softly. He let her go. "Thanks for caring and checking on me."

Mary Lou smiled. "Any time, Adam."

Just then he heard a knock from the Mary Lou's office and heard "Hey Boss, are you back?" It was Kathy.

Mary Lou started to say something but Adam responded first. "Yes Kathy, come in for a moment."

Mary Lou tensed up, and stepped back. Adam thought that she was almost getting into a self-defense stance. He would have to keep an eye on this "relationship" between her and Kathy.

Kathy entered and gave Mary Lou a challenging look before flashing her signature smile at Adam.

"Just want you to know, Boss, Major Grant tried to work my butt off, but I survived, and loved every minute of it."

Adam smiled." I told you that you would do just fine."

"Well, thanks for the chance, Boss. And as I can tell you have had a long day, I will see you later. Good night Boss, Good night, Mary Lou."

"Good night, Kathy." Mary Lou said with a little too much syrup to it.

"Sleep tight, Kathy." Adam said, as she winked at him, turned, and slinked away.

Adam saw Mary Lou staring at Kathy's ass as she walked away.

"A penny for your thoughts, Mary Lou. "

"She tries too hard. She wiggles her ass every chance she gets for effect. I don't trust her."

Adam gently put his left hand on her thigh. "Hey, who's in charge here?"

"You are, Director."

"Have I done pretty well so far?"

"Adam, this is not about you, it's ….."

"It's about you being worried that I'm thinking with my little head rather than my big head. Mary Lou, you're a knock out, Jeanie and Jamie are knock outs, and now Kathy is a knock out. As much as I care about you, I am still focused on what needs to be done. And no new sexual object, as you see her as, is going to influence the end game, my end game "

Mary Lou blushed a little. "I'm sorry, Director."

"Adam, not the Director, will be in bed later on. I expect you to be there also."

Mary Lou gave him a bit of an impish smile. "Just me or you want all three of your Ladies?"

"I'll leave that decision in your capable hands. Now, the sooner I can finish here, the sooner I will be to bed. So please excuse me."

Mary Lou kissed his cheek. "See you later." She turned and went to the attached suite.

Adam sighed. Things seemed more complicated. Maybe it was because today was such a pain in the ass day. Starting with the Professors wife, continuing to his trip to meet their Lord, today had been one pain after the other. Adam sat down again and replayed the day in his head…..

The Chief had given him a ride to the small boat dock at the most southwestern point of Key West. Adam rode in the ex-U.S. Postal Service small four cylinder Jeep in the left seat, steering wheel on the right. The Chief had the 50 Caliber Sharps rifle he had recovered during his last scavenger trip, rounding up the most recent new human arrivals. After dropping off Adam he was headed to the Firing Range to test out some Sharps reloads and plink a few practice rounds out of his .45 automatic. They pulled up to the dock, and Adam got out, taking his briefcase and satchel from behind his seat.

For the umpteenth time, the Chief asked," Need me to go along, Boss?"

"No, Chief. Our Lordship still only wants one human at a time talking to him. If I get whacked someday, you'll then get the chance to tell him the news. And then you get to do that until you get whacked."

"Well, Boss, I guess I keep you from being whacked. I have no desire to take the trip by myself."

Adam chuckled. "I guess I'm stuck for the time being, then. "

The Chief put the Jeep in gear. "Well, be careful Boss. I'm not there to hold your hand."

"Loud and clear Chief. I'll ping you on the radiophone when I head back. Have fun shootin'."

"Always, Boss, always." He drove off.

Adam carried his satchel and briefcase to the Open Fisherman tied up at the dock. The boat was supposed to be maintained by the Conch Republic as a symbol of their connection with the Base. But one look at the boat and Adam knew that someone was either getting lazy or purposefully ignoring maintenance. Adam checked his satchel, that had two bologna sandwiches, a greenhouse apple, two Conch Republic Near Bears, and a bag of stale pretzels (for seasickness nausea), just in case he became stranded. He'd eaten a left over cookie and a couple of soda crackers, and drank a full glass of purified water before leaving, just enough salt and water to ward off dehydration or other heat related problems.

Also in the satchel was a sawed off twelve gauge with two black powder rock salt loads. In a small shoulder holster he also a five shot replica of a .31 caliber Colts Baby Dragoon pistol, also loaded by the Chief with five black powder loads. The black powder was to create enough fire and brimstone to scare off any wandering Squid Juvenile or Early Teen who felt a need to prove themselves with a human in a boat. The Tschaaa did not like sulphur and flame coming in their general direction, despite their transition to land, so it was used to scare off the young. Their early development in the Ocean of their world was sans fire, other than underwater volcanic activity and thus, like most wet skinned species, did not like sources of heat too close. Despite their evolutionary development they, similar to human's fear of snakes, kept some old intrinsic fear from their days as a more primitive species. The shot and rock salt were for people who might want to engage in some low level piracy.

Adam started up the Open Fisherman and soon realized just how rough the twin engines were running. He swore, and pinged up the Chief on his radiophone.

"Yeah Boss"

"Chief, this so-called boat may make it there and but not back. I don't have the time to screw around, so if you don't hear from me is about five hours, send somebody out towards the Marquesas Keys looking for me. Otherwise, you're stuck with my job."

"Will do, Boss. And I'll light a fire under the Admirals ass also. They get enough stuff from us that keeping the agreement about the boat should be a given."

"Roger that. See you later, Chief"

Adam, the boat untied, headed out with all the due speed he could muster. Marquesas Keys was at one time a series of tiny islands and reefs in a circle in a National Wildlife Refuge almost due west of Key West. Just a tad under 20 statute miles away, it was now a huge circular domed shaped complex of several stories, mostly underwater. It was nicknamed Squidville, as humans had seen few Tschaaa structures up until its building. Around it and the Dry Tortugas were a series of large Tschaaa Breeding Areas, Crèches or Beds in and near the many local reef structures. The domed complex itself housed Tschaaa versions of workshops, construction factories, laboratories, development centers as well as landing berths for both air and sea craft.

Here resided their Lordship, named by himself in homage to Human mythology as Lord Neptune, King and Ruler of the Great Seas.

He had a great sense of humor, especially the absurd. Adam wished he could pronounce his Tschaaa Name, but Lordship "Neptune" had told him "Do not waste your time. Our Translators work fine translating our voices to human speech. You trying to speak our language would just make us laugh so hard we would get nothing done."

Adam believed him. The one thing the Lordship had been from Day One in their relationship was honest. To the fault, no matter how cruel the truth can be sometimes.

Adam managed to make the trip in just under an hour, with the twin outboards badly overheating the last mile. He nursed the Open Fisherman up to the entrance dock he always used, and managed to get it shut down and tied off before the engines seized. Waiting for him was a young Adult Squid Adam had named El Segundo, after a character in a Western he had seen years ago. Adam was probably one of the few humans who had learned to tell Squids apart fairly accurately. And El Segundo had been meeting him for almost a year now, had taken the name as his own. The Tschaaa wore no translator, just giving him the "Welcome Sign" with his two 'social tentacles' that Tschaaa used in greeting. Since these two appendages were also the ones used for sexual intercourse/primary impregnation, not to mention intricate equipment use due to the sensitive fingers on the ends, Adam often mused what humankind would have been like if Men waved their cocks at each other as a form of "welcome". But then again, humans were perpetually horny, so there would have been constant erections, with the resulting attempts to screw everything that moved, so communication would have been even more limited.

Humankinds attempts to deal through social mores with their 365 day a year sexual "season" was a constant source of wonderment and mirth to their Lord Neptune. The Lordship believed the limited time that male and female Tschaaa were 'in the mood' for sexual relations gave them more time to deal with more intellectual pursuits. After all, they did achieve interstellar flight before Mankind.

Adam stashed the sawed off 12 gauge under the boat seat, along with his small pistol. He kept a cheap but sharp 'Made in Pakistan' knife on his hip, and brought the satchel and briefcase.

He walked along the walkway constructed for items the Squids preferred to keep fairly dry, while El Segundo swam alongside. The Tschaaa could motivate on land, but were so much more efficient in the Ocean that there was where many preferred to remain. The fact that Earth's gravitational pull was about 5% more than their home world gave them another reason to prefer water locomotion over using land.

He walked through the entrance way into what at one time would have been through the Keys series of small land masses, but now was directly into a huge dome, 90 % of it under water. The dome, "Squidville" to the humans, now covered almost all the above water reefs, mangroves and spits of the Marquesas Keys Refuge. How many stories were below sea level, Adam was unsure but it was at least several. It was a good fifteen minute walk to the doorway into the Lordship's combination throne room and work area. Then, it was a few moments more until a person saw him. Once he reached the doorway, he was on his own.

Adam walked slowly up to the Tschaaa Lord's receiving area. In a sudden flash of light, a large image was projected on the nearby curved wall. He heard a loud booming human voice.

"I AM THE GREAT AND POWERFUL OZ."

"DO NOT AROUSE THE WRATH OF THE GREAT AND POWERFUL OZ."

And there were Dorothy and Company projected on the wall. Sh*t. He'd been watching Old Movies again. Self-named Lord Neptune loved to view, study, and just enjoy all forms of human Pre-Invasion Mass Media. Tschaaa films, books, other information media usually resembled National Geographic Travelogues and Science Tapes, with large historical musical dramas, similar to human operas, relating some of the great incidents in Tschaaa history. Fiction, other than the Young's versions of Grimm's Fairy Tales and Aesop Fables (intended to instruct also) did not exist. Making up 'stories for fun' was seen as a waste of time or mental aberration.

Which was why, if he was not so above the other Tschaaa in his abilities to handle Earth and it's humans, he probably would have been sent to the Tschaaa form of a mental hospital.

Tschaaa did enjoy jokes and humor, but most of it was along the line of Three Stooges slapstick, Farts, Practical Jokes and the occasional Your Mama is So Fat street insults, usually by Adolescents and to other Adolescents. Adam just knew that if the Tschaaa had such a thing, His Lordship would have been a combination standup comedian and writer for situation comedies, and be very successful.

His Lordship was reclining in a large, modified hot tub. Though amphibious, the Tschaaa still preferred their original liquid environment. He was waving his social tentacles in signs of complete mirth and laughter. Adam knew he was also blowing bubbles from his gill slits, a sign of pure belly laughter. Adam approached him, smiling; palms open towards him in a sign of mirth also.

"Ah, Director! My favorite Human. I see you noticed my new entrance images. I found that film of yours just the other day. Such a prime example of human Fantasy."

The Translator produced a human voice that reminded Adam of a combination of Shakespearean trained movie actors coming from the London Stage. Adam knew that Lord Neptune never did anything by chance, probably spent many hours before coming up with the right Lord Voice. Tschaaa speech to human ears sounded like a combination of porpoise clicks, Sperm Whale tones and lisping hissing. Although reproducible with computer enhanced technology, human vocal chords were not designed for that type of communication, and there were a few sounds above and below the frequencies that human ears could not distinguish. As had been proven in the study of whales, certain of these frequencies and tones in ocean water could be heard for miles, resulting in excellent long range communication. Thus, the Tschaaa Adolescents and Young(those older than five years), when they left their Crèche birth areas to roam the Oceans as part of growing up, were never really out of ear shot of

Adults.

Adam chuckled. "Yes, your Lordship, the Wizard of Oz is a movie classic. Tell me, are you thinking of changing your "human name' to the Wizard?"

The Tschaaa Lord laughed again. "No, my Director. Although I am great and powerful, I definitely have no need to hide behind a curtain. Now, Sir Human, come closer and have a seat in the chair provided. I have much information to impart to you, and I imagine you have some updates for me. "

"Yes, Sir. And, By the way, I have something you will like." Adam reached into the satchel and produced a couple of large stalks of sugar cane.

Tschaaa eyes were large, sensitive, and accurate, literally having eagle eye capabilities. So, Lord Neptune knew what Adam was removing from his satchel before it was completely in view.

"Ah. Some more of that delicious sweet cane. Please, hand it to me, kind sir."

His Lordship reached out a social tentacle to Adam and gently took the sugar cane from Adams proffered hand. He placed one stalk up, out of the hot tub, and then gently fed the other into his mouth, hidden from view by facial tentacles.

"If for no other reason, thanks to the cane, I think I have convinced the greater majority of my fellow Lords that humans can be of greater service than just sources of meat."

"You could not grow sugar cane yourself?"

"Outside of the natural environment, it would probably not be the same. We can grow many things in our organic tanks and vats, but the results are never as good as those things produced naturally. Which is why we never grew any Tschaaa Young in the tanks, not to mention it would seem.... perverted I think is a good word. The Grays, some Bipedal Warriors, those who you call Front Men, are the only higher life forms we have attempted. We eventually found or produced enough breeding pairs to result in natural growth of the Cyborg Warriors, Robocops you call them, and other human relations, as natural growth produces a much better product."

"So, Sir, the same with your original 'meat' creatures?"

"Yes, Director. When the Plague hit, in order for growth in the tanks and vats, we eventually produced sufficient non affected sperm and eggs of our Meat Creatures to start producing fresh Meat. The results, though edible in the strictest sense, were very... disappointing. This led to the Great Voyage here."

"Now, Director, on to other matters. How did your recent arrivals turn out?"

"Fine, Lordship. We now have over 6600 humans on Base. And, I located Professor Fassbinder, that scientist I told you about."

"Excellent! I expect him on the Platform when your new Spaceplane flies. Hopefully, he can discover the secrets of those two Saucers." Lord Neptune slowly chewed on the sugar cane.

"And, you obtained that blonde female you were looking for?"

Once again, he had no secrets from His Lordship.

"Yes Sir, I did. She will be one of our prime 'faces' representing our human government in our mass media. I hope she will assist us in convincing the majority of humans that we, and by exportation you, as the face of the Tschaaa, are not Bogeymen. The days of widespread Harvesting is over and that we have a chance to become junior partners in your interstellar civilization."

"Again excellent. And of course, being sexually desirable to you helps also, yes?"

Adam Smiled. "You know me too well, Your Lordship."

Lord Neptune laughed. "Your species constant sexuality is a source of mirth and wonderment to us. It is a mystery to the Tschaaa that you obtained the level advancement that you did, with you having constant sexual relations, or at least desires of such."

"Well, some of our human scientists believe that competition among us for mates actually spurred us to do great things."

"Like war on your own kind, Director?"

Adam sighed. "Unfortunately, some of our best advancements were sped along by warfare."

Lord Neptune's two social tentacles went high up in the air, denoting surprise or incredulous belief.

"But you killed many of your own young."

"Yes sir, that too".

His Lordship was still and silent. Then he spoke.

"Hopefully, our patronage will affect your behavior for the better."

"We can only hope, Sir."

"Well, enough of that. Come, Director. Look at what I have been doing."

Lord Neptune slid out of the hot tub, and began to slither along the walkway like the oversize cephalopod that he was. He did not waste energy by rising up on his eight arms, to walk almost crablike, that Tschaaa could do if they were in a hurry. As always, he reminded Adam of a large, many legged bearlike creature, due to his size and weight.

Even slithering, the Tschaaa could move quite fast, and Adam had to walk quickly to keep up.

The Human and the Alien were soon looking at a large bay where a Falcon was being worked on by Tschaaa Grays.

"I obtained this from Europe. The Tschaaa Lord there is too lazy to repair it. I took it off his hands, as you humans would put it. Unfortunately, many of my fellow Lords have little foresight, have lost much of their drive to plan, to

The Gathering Storm

create. Too many Elder Tschaaa are content to stuff their stomachs with the very available Meat, with little concern of how it was harvested, who provided it."

This was a complaint that Adam had heard on many occasions. Adam knew that if not for His Lordship, things would have been very different. The Tschaaa had no history of long term organized warfare among their species. They fought with other species on their Home World for survival during their evolutionary climb up the development ladder. No other species had the level of intellectual development, so none developed advanced tools, weapons. The Tschaaa, at some time lost in myth and history according to his Lordship, had evolved into an amphibious species, and expanded onto land. That had led to a great evolutionary change in diet, when the Tschaaa had discovered the species of Meat Primates.

Something about the difference in this protein, different than the fish and sea creatures the Tschaaa had eaten for millennia, had led to a change in eating habits, and thus in culture. Soon, the Dark Meat Primates were the main source of protein rich sustenance of the Tschaaa Breeders and Young. For some reason, despite their high development in all things organic and its uses, in all forms of biology and genetics, DNA genomes, etc, no Tschaaa scientist had ever bothered to see if the chemistry and the hormones in the primate meat may have had an effect on Tschaaa morphology and biology. Did the type of meat protein help give a boost to Tschaaa intellectual development? Adam thought it was fascinating that, just at the time the Dark Meat became available, the Tschaaa, according again to his Lordship, took a huge leap in evolutionary development. They became more organized, the size of Crèches increased, and they began to cooperate on a global scale. Adam believed it was a definite cause and effect scenario. The fact that Tschaaa intellect suffered during the time the primate meat protein was very limited in quantity and quality was another strong indication.

"Come, my Director, I have some other developments to show you."

Adam followed him over to a table where a three foot object was covered by a tarp.

"Please, have a look." His Lordship said.

Adam removed the tarp. Underneath was a slab-sided object that was clearly a shoulder fired weapon. Adam looked at an 8x10 piece of paper covered in plastic that was attached by a large rubber band to the weapon. He took the paper and read the clearly human printing. The author had excellent calligraphy. The document stated that the shoulder weapon was a downsized version of the electromagnetic rail guns mounted on the Delta's. With a loaded magazine of forty 50 grain long nail shaped hardened steel projectiles with tiny pop out fins for stabilization, total weapon weight was just less than twenty pounds. The projectiles were fired at a velocity of 1600 meters per second, give or take a few, which caused devastating effects to soft targets down ranged. Recharging of the electromagnetic battery could be accomplished with a recessed hand crank (if you had a lot of extra time on your hands), a photoelectric cell (much more efficient than human photoelectric cells), or by plugging a pull-out charging cord into a standard 110 outlet.

"Please, Director, try it out on the piece of metal taken from one of your garbage dumpsters."

The target was some fifty meters away and already had been used for target practice, judging by the holes in it. The weapon had a pistol grip at the rear part, containing the magazine of .17 caliber ammunition. There was a large vertical handgrip set some six inches back from the apparent muzzle. Despite its bulk and weight, the basic super rifle was well balance and easy to manipulate. After following the directions to insure it was loaded and chambered, (simplicity in itself) he mounted it to his cheek. A holographic sight was automatically projected in his line of sight. All he had to do was put the red dot on the center of the target and squeeze the trigger. No felt recoil, a supersonic crack from the high velocity round following a buzzing sound from the action. Even from fifty meters, Adam could see the near instantaneous impact flash. The hole produced was larger than the .17 caliber projectile. Adam looked down at the weapon.

"A human designed this."

His Lordship signed amusement. "Once again, My Director, you demonstrate your superior intellect."

"Now, watch what was designed to use it."

Adam felt rather than heard the Tschaaa verbal command given in a frequency beyond his hearing range. From the shadows came a six and a half foot figure. The biped looked like a human Soldier, combat uniform and all, wearing a gas mask. As it walked up and stopped some six feet from the Tschaaa Lord, Adam saw that the figure was not wearing a uniform. Rather, the organic skin/mantel was molded into the shape of human attire, gas masked face and all.

Lord Neptune's octopus camouflage abilities demonstrated themselves when his flesh began to automatically try to match the coloration of the approaching biped due to his excitement. "This Soldier, as I call him, was developed at my behest by a human mated pair on Platform One. Another mated pair developed your shoulder weapon. The humans in space have produced great dividends for me. I am looking for more when others are sent up in two months in your Space Plane."

His Lordship signed for the Soldier to leave. "They have the mental capacity of about a five year old human. They are designed for basic problem solving, but specialized for following orders. In addition to combat, they can also perform more mundane everyday functions. They will supplement the limited supply of Grays and Cyborgs. So far, one hundred have been produced in the growth vats. Now, if I can just convince my unimaginative fellow Lords to use them, my satisfaction will be complete.""

He motioned Adam to follow him to the Tschaaa equivalent of a Lounge. As they moved, His Lordship Continued.

"I have also repaired five Deltas, something no one else is doing. In addition, they are set up for ground launch using what humans call JATO rockets. Three are at Cape Canaveral, one here, one in the large Baja California Complex."

The Gulf of California/Sea of Cortez had been literally closed off and connected from shore to shore in one huge complex, including a large Breeding area and manufacturing section. Every other major port city up and down both former United States Coasts and the Gulf of Mexico had some form of a Tschaaa complex. However, since the Marqueses Keys were his Lordships base of operations, it had the most developed equipment and facilities, despite the average two mile diameter.

They arrived at the lounge, and His Lordship deftly obtained a drink for each of them from a refrigeration unit. His had a long tube, so that he could drink it with his mouth concealed by his face tentacles. Adam knew there were some teeth structures under there that made humans nervous. The Director's drink was a bottle of Conch Brew. The Tschaaa Lord clinked his container against Adam's bottle. "A toast to much more useful collaboration between Tschaaa and humans."

"I'll drink to that," was Adam's reply.

They each drank, the Tschaaa Lord reclining in the Tschaaa version of a lounge seat, Adam in a human chair.

"Director, I have often wished, despite what we have accomplished, that I had the power to travel back in time, to before the Plague, where things were simpler."

"Well your Lordship, there is an ancient human Chinese Curse; 'may you live in interesting times'."

The Tschaaa Lord laughed., blowing bubbles thru his gill slits.

"That fits the situation perfectly. In addition to dealing with stagnant Elders, reduced ability of our vats and tanks to produce viable Grays and Biped Cyborg Warriors due to worn out DNA, now I must deal with my own Young Tschaaa demanding to go help the Asian Tschaaa Lord in his Japan 'operations'."

Adam looked at him quizzically. "You mean, Harvesting Operations?"

"No. Apparently the Young Tschaaa Warriors are conducting what you humans term as 'raids' on the coasts of Japan, fighting with traditional blade weapons, as well as incursions by Deltas, looking for aerial conflict. It provides thrilling experiences they claim they cannot have anywhere else." Lord Neptune gave the Tschaaa equivalent of a sigh.

"I guess it could be worse. Too many Tschaaa had been satisfied with sitting around, getting fat on the over-abundance of food. At least they wish to do something."

He took another sip from his drink." And I have been given only limited resources for the production of replacement equipment. The new weapon I showed you, I can produce only one a day. I am repairing Deltas in Baja California, after having produced only sixty new ones in the last six years. Using modified humans, we have created 250 successful new what you call Robocops, Cyborgs, since the Invasion. Though superior in nature, these do not replace losses. The new Soldiers, I can produce one a week after the initial production order. All because the Elder, stagnant Tschaaa have no foresight."

The Tschaaa had no history or concept of long term wars or combat operations. Thus, the idea of a war production plan was alien. It had taken Lord Neptune 60 years of wheedling, nagging, politicking, even actions nearing deception (alien to Tschaaa) to produce the equipment for the initial Invasion. And this was with the reports from Scouts and over 60 years of radio/television transmissions providing specific information on the threat humans could provide to any invader. The idea of real-time 'replacement equipment' was not a concept they had ever had to deal with. Things were used up, and then maybe a replacement was grown or produced, at a slow pace. Before the Plague, Slow and Steady Won The Race.

After it, it was still like pulling teeth to convince the older Tschaaa to adopt new ways of doing things. Even competition for position in society had been stratified one way for so long that there was only so much upward mobility. Despite all this inertia, His Lordship had created a revolution, a firestorm based on his will and motivation alone. He had designed and implemented the organized, long term Invasion and Harvesting Plan, replacing the disorganized Raiding Plan originally agreed upon. Everything now flowed from His Lordships concepts and ideas, no matter how slowly.

"Now, my Director, I must inform you of two very important matters."

He sipped his drink again.

"Your amateur astronomers must have mentioned that our large Crèche ships are moving."

"Yes Sir. Last week." Adam also had some professional people, with security, working at the McDonald Observatory in West Texas, but he did not advertise that fact. It was an island in a sea of a so called Feral area.

"Well, the mile long Crèche Ships are moving to set up a dive into the gravity well of the Sun to obtain a sling shot launch outside the solar system. This is to occur by the Ten Year Mark in Earth years."

Adam sat silent. Then spoke.

"So it is true. You plan to leave.'"

The Tschaaa Lord paused. Then spoke. "Only 30 percent of the Tschaaa, 50 percent of the Grays and the so-called Robocops, and one percent of the Lizards are leaving. And, the Ship of my Crèche will stay on the Dark Side of Earth's Moon."

Adam looked at him. "So the Tschaaa will be here for the long haul."

"Yes, Director, Adam, Earth's Ocean have become our New Home."

Adam sat silent for a full minute. He knew he must choose his words wisely.

"This situation is going to cause a lot of fear, hate and discontent when it gets out. Humankind always kept a hope in the back of each person's mind that the Earth would be under human control again, at least during the next lifetime. It was a light at the end of a tunnel."

Lord Neptune signed regret and compassion with his tentacles.

"I hope that you can help convince the rest of humanity that it is in their interest to work with the Tschaaa, to be client species as our Lizards, second only to the Tschaaa Lords in power and control."

He continued. "I have worked hard to put you in a position that, each day, Tschaaa become more beholden to what services and items that humans can provide, not just as Cattle And it has worked. In the next year, I will have either influence over or control of the Tschaaa dominated areas worldwide. All unrestrained Harvesting that still exists in some areas will be gone very soon. Next week, I will begin providing you with the most advanced medical nanotechnology and organic medicine that will eventually increase human life spans by decades. I will turn over the rest of the Near Space communication grid, resulting in human life near to where it was six years ago. And more of you will have access to Outer Space."

Adam asked "What about the Feral and Rebel areas?'

"If I have learned anything from the study of humankind is that you can adjust your belief systems and morality when the proverbial grass is greener on the other side. Though the concept of 'lawns' is very strange to me. "Just look at Nazi Germany, the Soviet Union, and Communist China. People adjust when it is beneficial for them, especially if the alternative is much worse"

"But the Jews, the dissidents, go to the Camps and the Gulags." Adam stated.

"Yes Director, as you have said yourself, the Universe is not fair. We will need Cattle, Dark Meat. Your so called People of Color will continue to be sacrificed."

Adam drained his beer. He had always feared that it would come to this. That he would keep millions alive with hope, to have the situation slapped in their faces. For those that made excuses in their mind that if you waited long enough, things would change better for the Cattle, that dream just disappeared. There would now be a permanent class of Humans, and one of Cattle, same species, different life. The Protocol of Selective Survival in its ultimate form.

"Well. Your Lordship, I guess I have my work set out for me. Hopefully you can support me in my attempts to control the situation. There will be some strong resistance from a certain percentage of humans, and there may be an attempt at organized armed conflict from the Rebels. I may need some help from your Crèche."

"Of course, Director. We will make this work, as we have with all our endeavors." The Tschaaa Lord signed positive feelings and happiness with his social tentacles.

"I have one lesser item of possible conflict. Please look at this picture." He handed a photo to Adam. The creature on it looked like someone's idea of a Sci-Fi nightmare. Six limbs, four of them long thin legs that branched several inches from the bottom into two long toe like structures each. The front two limbs were arms with large five clawed hands. Long hair like structures run up and down the arms. The face was basically two huge eyes above a large teeth filled mouth, with an extremely long tongue. The body was circular and resembled an Earthly crab's domed shape.

"What, Sir, is this?" Adam asked.

"It is a beast from our Home World. We used to hunt it for sport. It is about five of your feet tall when its legs are extended, and is about 120 to 140 pounds. The hair like structures on the arms are very similar to your porcupine quills, and just as sharp. The closest name we could translate it to in Earth English would be 'Eater', as that what it does for most of its existence. Its stomach can stretch and extend some two feet below its body when full, at which time the Eater prefers to fall into a deep sleep like state so that it can digest totally the prey. It eats almost anything, and its' very strong gastric acids can break down anything short of depleted uranium. Oh, and it reproduces asexually. After it has stuffed itself several times in a row, it buds out two young from its back, which 'hatch' about a week later. The young remain around the adult just long enough to see it feed. Then they understand the concept, and go out looking for their own food. They will not eat their own kind."

Adam kept examining the picture. "Why are you showing me this picture, Your Lordship?"

The Tschaaa Lord wiggled its arms in a sign of consternation and embarrassment.

The Gathering Storm

"Some Lords had brought examples along with them, trying to hunt them in specially designed areas on our large ships. The limited area greatly reduced the sport to a quick one on one fight, so that the activity soon fell out of favor onboard. "

"Then, what you would refer to as a Mr. Bright-eyes decided that releasing them on Earth would result in two things. One, there would now be room for the traditional hunts. Two, the Tschaaa Lord saw it as a means to harass the Chinese Populace, whom he did not think had dark enough flesh to make them very tasty. I believe he thinks the Eaters will displace some of the human populace, which displeased him in the first year after the Rock Strike by refusing to cooperate and harassed his coastal breeding areas."

Adam knew that harassing Breeders and Young was a death sentence. Now it looked like an entire culture maybe sentenced to death not for Meat but for Revenge.

Lord Neptune sighed. "Unfortunately, Eaters breed like your rabbits, and are constantly on the move. It has been an Earth month since the introduction of a dozen or so. There are reports of sightings in Eastern Russia, and they seem to be moving towards Europe and former area of Korea."

Adam knew the Korean peninsula was almost barren of life, thanks to North Korean resistance. The Eaters would soon move on.

"Can they swim, Lordship?"

"Yes, they can, although they are land creatures. They seemed to have originated in our Ocean."

"Well, I now have an interesting and unique subject for Kathy Monroe to discuss during a broadcast." said Adam

"Excellent." His Lordship exclaimed. "And the primary subject will be the Crèche Ship movement?"

Now it was Adam's turn to sigh. 'I will start with a story that the Tschaaa are exploring the Solar System and asteroids for usable resources. I will hold off on mentioning the Sun Dive for as long as I can. I need time to get set up for panic and violence."

His Lordship gave a sign of compassion.

"Director, Adam, I have one more question. It is rather...theoretical in nature."

"Like we humans say, Sir, Shoot."

The Lord paused for a moment. Then he asked, "Could you be my Friend?"

Adam was caught off guard. What brought this on? He had to be careful in his answer or he may suddenly disappear.

"Well, we refer to our dogs as Man's Best Friend. But most humans stopped eating dog meat decades ago. And we bred them to be our 'Friend'. Dog and

Man both greatly enjoy physical contact with the other. But that took at many thousands of years of development, of change from wolf to dog and primitive man to Homo sapiens."

He could tell that Lord Neptune was in deep contemplation. Then, his Lordship spoke.

"I hope you and I can find a way to speed up the process. Thousands of years is much too long a time. Once your species can accept the division between Client and Cattle, Man and Meat, Dog and Wolf, I think the next step will result in humans being the Tschaaa's Best Friend."

The rest of the conversation was small talk. Adam did say that Talbot and his Krakens had asked to go to Atlanta in Cattle Country to see who was behind the organized breakout that had just happened.

"I leave those day to day details to you, My Director. Just insure they have communications with a Falcon or two in case some… 'Harvesting' takes place. I dislike wasted Meat."

"Yes your Lordship."

The Tschaaa Lord looked at Adam intently.

"Just for your information, I at one time contemplated making Talbot a Director."

"Oh?" Adam said.

"Yes, I had that idea for about one second. He lacks what you humans refer to as finesse, what we Tschaaa refer to as 'gill cleaning' the ability to clean another's gills quickly and efficiently, with pleasure, not discomfort. "

"Yes, Your Lordship. It goes without saying that I am glad you chose me instead."

"As I am glad, Director, as I am glad."

Adam left soon thereafter, with assurances that Andrew, the Robocop assigned to Key West, would soon be by with new nanotechnology, and to assist in beginning preparation for the dissemination of information about the Sun Dive and its aftermath. As Adam left, he thought of Andrew. He was one of 250 successful modifications of more recent Earthborn Humans to what was almost a total Cyborg interface, a Robocop. There were 254 volunteers selected, and 250 were successful, an extremely high success rate. As far as Adam was concerned, the end results were superior to the original Bipedal Cyborg Warrior, developed from Gigantipithicus and Homo Erectus DNA. Not only did Andrew and his Brothers have more natural cognitive ability, independent of computer interface, but as he grew first as a human child, he had the natural understanding of the human experience on Earth.

Did Andrew see Adam as a 'friend'? Now that was an idea to ponder. Andrew was still basically human, though the computer brain interface produced a very fast and varied mental process, the abilities to handle various tasks and different lines of thinking all the same time. Adam wondered if he still really 'thought' like a human. It was surprising that only four of the human/information system interface attempts failed. His Lordship said all four went insane and had to be 'dismantled'. Adam believed it was due to a tight selection process from thousands of applicants, and that volunteering to become something both less and more than human led to an initial good mindset for success. But, all the applicants also had to accept the fact they would be completely subservient to the Tschaaa, 24 hours a day, no private life. They were literally 'wired in' to the massive Tschaaa information, communication and data processing system, with instant contact. This meant they could have no secrets. And, they had to accept Harvesting Dark Meat personally. Thus, a large percentage of applicants must come with a preconceived notion of racial superiority. Due to the size requirements, close to a seven foot minimum upon complete modification, most were of Nordic Stock from Northern Europe and the former U.S., with a few tall Irish, Scottish and light skinned Spaniards and Italians. Adam had gotten word that a call for more Volunteers had just been released in Europe. Knowing the rather limited amenities and creature comforts, especially decent food, Adam was pessimistic they would find a dozen applicants who could meet the size and health requirements.

Maybe they would extend the call to North America.

Adam was escorted by El Segundo back to the dock. The Tschaaa offspring of His Lordship gave him a respectful wave of his tentacles and disappeared beneath the waters. Adam sat in the boat for a few minutes, eating one of his sandwiches and drinking a bottle of Near Bear. Out here was one of the few places where he could be truly 'alone'. He still needed private time, wrapped in his own musings, hard to find at the Key West Base, the New Capitol of North America. Adam stretched, looked at the abused boat engines and shook his head. Well, here goes. He turned the blowers on, which sounded as if the fan bearings were shot, then waited. After a couple of minutes, he cranked the engines. They started up, and then the port one literally burst into flames. Luckily the fire extinguisher still worked. He shut everything down, then sat on the bow. He looked at his watch. Well, he was already pass due for contacting the Chief, so he reached for his radio phone.

Then he heard an engine. It sounded like a Skidoo Wave runner. He shielded his eyes from the sun and caught sight of the sea craft approaching from about ten o'clock to his reference. It was a large two seater, with one figure on board. He stepped to the stern of the Open Fisherman and waved to the Skidoo. At that, the driver accelerated towards him, cutting the engine back to idle at just the right moment so that the craft coasted to a near stop next to Adam's Boat.

Adam used his boat hook to hold the craft near.

"Ahoy, Captain. I guess you must be the Director." A slightly sultry and strong sounding female voice emanated from the driver/pilot and told Adam the operator was a woman.

"Yes, Sailor, I am the Director. You must be my ride." Adam looked at the young lady. She was a well-shaped, about 5' 6" in height, rather buxom woman, dark brown hair tied back in a bun. The woman had definitely strong looking well defined arms and shoulders, strong looking but still feminine, not steroided out. She definitely worked at staying fit.

She flashed him a small smile. "Begging the Director's pardon, but I'm a Coastie, so I prefer Guardsman. We are bit sensitive about being lumped in with Swabbies."

Not only fit, capable, but a bit feisty. Adam smiled back. He did not readily recognize her, but he knew he would soon come to like her.

"Sorry, Ma'am. I'm a former propeller head, Air Force. We get confused on the water."

Her smile disappeared as she looked past Adam. 'We've got visitors." It was then that Adam noticed the Coastie had a Beretta M-9 in a shoulder holster, with a magazine pouch and large fighting knife balancing the opposite side of the rig. She reached for the pistol as Adam turned and saw two adolescent Squids pop out of the ocean, each having a large edged weapon pointed to the humans. Adam knew the two Squids were doing the equivalent of demonstrating their 'maleness' by challenging a couple of humans near a Tschaaa breeding area, authorized or not. And sometimes, like human Teenagers, they acted out with violent results.

"Stop Right There, Fishheads." The Female Coastie bellowed, quite authoritatively. The Squids stopped, moving their arms to stay afloat and in place. Their eyes focused on the Coastie, ignoring Adam. He had the boathook in his hands, still hoping the situation did not come to blows. Once before it had been necessary for Adam to let fly with a black powder load in order to scare an agitated Squid away. He knew injuring one could lead to problems. But he was not about to be slapped around, or watch one of his people get skewered. Adam thought he heard some Squid clicks, a couple of low tones. The two Youngsters then blew their gills in the Squid version of a belly laugh, and flipped a sign with their social tentacles that Adam had come to understand. Adam snickered as the two Squid disappeared beneath the waves.

The female Coastie looked at him quizzically "What was that about, Sir? Was something funny?"

How not to offend a professional woman? "First, what is your name, please."

"Heidi Faust, Petty Officer First Class, Sir." She smartly saluted him, her hand no longer on her pistol.

"Petty Officer Faust, please do not be offended, but the Tschaaa think that all....large breasted human females are Breeders. They do not understand our sexuality. To them we are a bunch of randy monkeys. The sign they gave meant something similar to apologies for interrupting mating."

Heidi Faust flushed a bit. "I should have shot the assh*les. I was born with big breasted genes. What's their excuse, assh*le genes?"

Adam began to laugh, and after a couple of seconds, so did Heidi. Adam finally stopped. He did not get a reason to laugh like this very often. It felt good.

"I take it, Petty Officer, that you are my ride."

"That be me, Sir."

"Well, let me stow my briefcase and ditty bag, and we can get moving." Adam, while Heidi held onto the side of the boat for stability, secured his items in a hatch beneath the rear seat. "Here, Ma'am, have a Near beer. Not enough alcohol to worry about."

Heidi flashed Adam a smile that lit up her eyes. "Thank you, Director. It is getting warm out here."

Adam clambered on behind her like riding a large motorcycle. Heidi began drinking the Near Beer.

"So tell me, how did a former U.S. Coastguardsman get here?"

"The Chief, Sir. Found me up the Coast by Miami, trying to survive fishing where the Squids would let me. I and a couple of Swabbies , plus some civilians, hooked up after everything feel apart, stayed where it was warmer when the Nuclear Winter kicked in. I had my Coast Guard Cutter blown out from beneath me by an underwater mine the Squids were so nice to provide. I was the one and only survivor."

Adam looked at her profile as she finished off the Near Beer. "So why work with the creatures that killed you shipmates?'

Heidi tossed the empty bottle purposefully at where the Squids had been, a definite sign of protest.

"They stopped eating us, I got tired of living hand to mouth, and the Chief made me an offer I couldn't refuse."

Adam Grinned. "The Chief had a way of doing that. Can you use that knife?"

She gave him a bit of an impish grin. "My folks ran a Gym and Dojo outside Palm Beach. I was doing Judo and later Gracie Jiu Jitsu from the time I was five. I met my boyfriend there later.

"He taught me Filipino Eskrima knife fighting. We joined the Coast guard together." Suddenly her face and eyes clouded. Adam had seen that look a thousand times before. Everyone she was talking about was dead.

"Sorry. Did not mean to pry."

Heidi gave him a wry smile. "Not your fault, Sir. Every survivor I've met has lost someone. After a while, you are glad to be alive."

Heidi had a nice sensual face, full lips, and with a strong German nose that looked good on her. She had hazel eyes that flashed when she laughed. How had he not noticed this lady before? The Base wasn't that crowded.

"I do not remember meeting you, Petty Officer. Why not?"

"You were supposed to, right after the Chief recruited me. That was a bit over a year from me losing my Cutter. You were really busy then, so..."

Adam grinned at her. "Well, it was my loss. Which is one of the reasons I instituted the initial briefings and socials, so I could meet everyone. You slipped through the cracks."

Heidi grinned back. "So, Director, I think we need to head back before the Chief thinks we are goofing off."

"Hell, the Chief 'knows' I goof off every chance I get. Let's go, then, Petty Officer.

"Aye Aye, Sir."

Adam wrapped his arms around Heidi's waist to hold on. He felt the strong, supple strength in her stomach muscles. She accelerated and they were soon hauling ass back to the Key West Base.

The close proximity of a sensual, attractive woman, the vibration of the Skidoo, his body rubbing against the Petty Officer soon produced an embarrassing erection that Adam tried to hold away from Heidi's body. However, he had to hold tight as Heidi Faust was hauling ass with a competency born of experience. Adam kept hoping that the attractive Petty Officer would not notice. He was wrong. Just Under an hour later, as they were about a mile from shore, Heidi cut their speed to an idle. She turned her head towards Adam. "Director, if I may be so bold, is that a gun in your pocket, or are you just happy to see me?"

Adam did something he did not do often. He blushed.

"Please, don't take it the wrong way, Petty Officer. I don't take advantage of my position....."

Heidi let loose with a, strong throaty laugh. "All due respect, then you are the first person I have ever met that hasn't, at one time or another, including me."

Adam sat with his pelvis still thrust up against Heidi. Despite his embarrassment, he still had an erection.

Heidi winked at Adam." I'm not offended, Director. In this day and age, with a lot of people already a slab of meat someplace, worrying about normal human body reactions is a waste of time. Actually, I'm a bit jealous of your

The Gathering Storm

well known Ladies. A Good Man can be hard to find. Or is it a Hard Man is good to find?" She laughed again.

Adam laughed also. Damn, but she had a good sense of humor.

"Seriously, Ms. Faust, if you are as good as you say with that knife, I could use the lessons. Chaperoned, of course."

"Any time, Director. But just remember, I'll be one of the most dangerous things to a man with an erection; a woman with a sharp knife"

With that last comment, Heidi accelerated like a Bat out of Hell, Adam having to grab on tight to keep from falling off. Smart Ass Coastie.

∽∽

Now, back in his office, he was grinning like an idiot alone in the office. He definitely would take her up on her offer, if for no other reason than she made him laugh a lot. He looked at the time. He started to go to his quarters. Then he stopped. He had on just a pair of shorts now, and noticed he was getting an erection from the memories of the day. Damn, but the situation seemed to make him horny a lot. He wondered if the Tschaaa had a hidden means of creating randiness. He turned and quietly walked out the door, down towards the suite where Kathy resided. He lightly knocked on the door, and the blonde opened the door, wearing just a short, shear robe.

"Adam, I thought you would never get here." she whispered. She pulled him in, and quietly closed the door behind him. Placing her arms around his neck, she leapt up and wrapped her strong legs around his waist, her naked pubis rubbing his erection.

"Come here, you." She ordered.

An hour later, he extricated himself from Kathy's arms, kissed her cheek, and quietly padded to the apartment door. He put his trunks back on, and returned to his office. As quietly as possible, he went to his private bathroom and took a shower. He made sure he washed all of Kathy's scent off him, then got out and dried off. He then walked nude back to his master bedroom.

Mary Lou was sleeping in the oversized bed alone, slightly snoring. He slid into bed next to her, and spooned up next to her luscious behind. He kissed her shoulder, and then went to sleep.

"Whether they resided in the Feral Areas, Tschaaa Controlled Areas, or the Free States and Countries, humans still discovered or rediscovered Love and Family. This is a constant of the Human Condition, sometimes resulting in often strange and stressful situations."

Excerpts from the Literary Works of Royal Princess Akiko,
Free Japan Royal Family

MALMSTROM ALLIED ARMED FORCES BASE, MONTANA

Torbin was tired. These long days added to some of the emotional upheaval around was finally getting to him. Despite his excellent physical shape, everyone had their limits. He was beginning to suddenly feel old. When he walked up to the door to his quarters and found it unlocked, a jolt of adrenalin woke him up. He unscrewed the nearest hallway light. Then, his K-Bar in his hand, he pushed the door open, low rolled into his darkened front room.

"It is I, Captain. And I am unarmed." It was Aleksandra.

He stood up, and saw the Russian sitting in the dark on his sofa.

"And how, may I ask, did you gain access to my quarters?"

She sighed. "I am a trained intelligence operative, a spy. Of course I was trained in how to get into locked rooms."

Bingo. Torbin re-sheathed his K-Bar. "So, now that is out of the way, what's next?"

"Come here, my Torbin, and find out."

An hour and a half later, he was holding her close in his bed. She was gently caressing and scratching his chest with her fingernails.

"Thank you for defending my honor, my Captain. It has been ages since a concept like honor has been part of my life."

Torbin stoked her lush hair. "You deserve better, Aleks. Life since the first Rock Strike has made things hard enough, without us humans treating each other like bovine excrement."

"You mean bullsh*t?" Aleksandra replied.

Torbin chuckled. "Here I am, trying to be all gentlemanly and correct, and you go all earthy on me."

Aleksandra raised herself up from Torbin's shoulder and looked into his

The Gathering Storm

eyes. She kissed him on the lips, slow and sensual. "You deserve better also, Torbin. And, give me a chance, and I will show you 'better'."

"Promises, promises." Torbin mumbled as he put his arms around Aleksandra and pulled her close.

There was a loud banging on the front door, and someone called his name.

"What the Hell?" Torbin exclaimed as he rolled out of his bed. He grabbed his K-Bar, and padded naked to the door. "This had better be good," he yelled as he yanked open his door.

Two large Military Police Officers were at the door. They took one look at Torbin's state of undress, and the Senior Sergeant asked "Are you alone, Captain?"

"No, he is not." Aleksandra called from the bedroom door, sheet wrapped around her.

"Sorry, Ma'am, But I must ask how long you have been here with the Captain."

"An hour and a half at least. Why, Sergeant?"

The second Military Policeman was relaying the information on his radio. He then told the Senior Sergeant. "It happened within the last half hour. Even Captain Bender can't be in two places at once."

What Happened, Sergeant?" Torbin demanded

"Ma'am, Sir. The Russian Colonel was found dead with a broken neck. It looked like it just happened."

Torbin was stunned. Aleksandra broke the silence first.

"The General is at his office?"

"Yes, Ma'am.

"Come, Captain, we must go there. Thank You, Sergeant."

"Yes, Ma'am." The two Military Police left. Five minutes later, after some rapid dressing, the two Captains were in route to the Commanders Office.

All the other Russian Officers were there when Torbin and Aleksandra arrived, as was Colonel Tanaka. Torbin entered, and saluted. "Sir."

General Reed saluted back. "I understand you have an iron clad alibi, so there is no reason to ask you what you've been doing." He gave Aleksandra a knowing look, which she returned with typical Russian stoicism.

"So, now we need to start a full investigation ....."

The Russian Second in Command, Major Romanov interrupted. "With all due respect, General, that is not necessary. Especially since we have more important fish to fry."

General Reed looked at the Major like he had suddenly grown an extra head.

"Major, how in the Hell can I explain to your government what happened without an investigation. My own Madam President will have my ass if I don't cross the T's and dot the I's, so I can imagine what your government will want to do to me."

Major Romanov sighed. "General, they will say nothing. My Cousin was a Pig, always was a pig. Yes, he was my cousin. But he was a pig who survived because he knew where the skeletons were hidden, and he abused his underlings. No one in my family liked him. He was sent here hoping he would screw something up so bad that he could be shot before he could use his information to blackmail his way out. So trust me, General, you will be doing everyone a favor by agreeing that the drunken ass fell and broke his neck."

The Major paused. "Or, you can start an international incident by accusing foul play and setting back plans for a counterattack on the Tschaaa back months, if not years."

Silence. Torbin realized that for once in his life, he could have heard a pin drop. General Reed then let out the air had been holding in his tight chest.

"Major, I do not usually agree to not searching for the truth. 'The Truth Shall Set You Free.' I believe that. But, the Mission takes precedent over my belief. So, I agree with you. I ask that you communicate directly with your government. "

He turned to Colonel Tanaka. "Any problem with the Major's ideas, Colonel?"

"No, General. You both have more say in this matter than I. I bend before your decision."

Major Romanov then spoke again. " I do have one favor, General."

"And what is that, Major?"

"The three young female Officers will need to stay here on detached duty indefinitely. I know my pig cousin has already communicated via our secured radio relay some remarks questioning their loyalty. They will be, shall we say, pressured, about his death, whether they know anything or not. I do not want them harmed unnecessarily."

General Reed rolled his eyes to the ceiling "What in the Hell have I gotten myself into? All right, that's it. No more deals. Now, shall we all go back to bed? I'll have my mortuary officer prepare an Accidental Death finding and prepare the body for shipment back."

As everyone began to leave, the General called Torbin back.

"Captain, since you have such a way with women, especially Russian women, your additional duty is to get the three young officers integrated into our command structure and mission. They will also need to be quartered near other women, if possible. But bottom line is this...everyone works. Hard. Kapesh? Clear?"

"Crystal clear, SIR."

"Now, get some sleep. That's an order."

Torbin saluted smartly and left. General Reed sat in quiet contemplation for a few moments, then removed the picture of his wife and son from the desk drawer. "Darling, days like this, I wish I was with you instead of here. I miss you, and the presence of all these Russians makes me miss you more. But I know you would want me to fight the good fight. So, I stay." The General kissed the photo, and put it back in his drawer.

Time for bed. Tomorrow was going to be a long day.

KEY WEST

Joseph Fassbinder woke up and saw that it was still dark out. Surprises of all surprises, he was sleeping next to Sarah in their shared quarters. His thoughts drifted back to the end of the previous day, his first day on the job. Joseph had stayed at his new office until almost six o'clock. His supposed new boss, Mike Jones, had been so dispensational to him, letting him basically know that what Joseph wanted he would get, no questioned asked. Mike had given him the impression that if Joseph wanted to take over as supervisor of the Aeronautical Physics, Engineering, and Space Travel Section (what a mouthful) he would be on cloud nine. Like Joseph, he was a scientist first, and administrator second. Joseph did not rise to the bait.

Then, he had to walk back to his quarters. He had no idea what Sarah had decided, or if he would see her again. No matter what happened, he had not been looking forward to the potential that his relationship with his wife would probably not be better. As mad as he had gotten, he still loved Sarah.

Joseph saw the large food van, known as the Roach Coach in local slang. He remembered some signage that beer and alcohol was available starting at 4:00 PM, Happy Hour. He decided he would need some liquid courage.

He walked up to the serving counter and saw the comely Jolene sitting on a chair towards the back of the large interior. She was holding a large bag of ice on her scar. Joseph started to back off, when she saw him.

"Afternoon, Professor Fassbinder. Can I get you something?" Jolene stood up, still holding the bag of ice to her face. Joseph tried to avert his eyes, feeling that he was staring at her injury. He began to stutter.

"'Let me guess. You need a stiff drink. And, you are wondering about my scar but are too polite to ask."

"Huh," Joseph stuttered. Jolene gave a nice, pleasant and genuine laugh. "First, a shot of home brew whiskey on me. Then, the story you want to hear."

Joseph blushed. "How did you know my name?'

"The three of the Roach Coaches, as we are called, have free access to the base. We Conchies hear and see everything. We know who is here before they know. But, we are friendly and respectful, so no dirty laundry will be aired. Here, take your drink."

Joseph took the highball glass containing poured brown liquid over ice. He sniffed, and then sipped. It was surprisingly smooth for home brew, but with still with a kick.

"Why...Jolene is it? This is quite good for home brew."

Jolene smiled. "Distilling secrets of the Admiral, my adopted Father. Actually, he calls all us young 'Conchettes' his Daughters, and treats us like we were his own. Woe to the person who disrespects one of us."

Joseph sipped his drink. "Do not worry. I am not in the habit of disrespecting young ladies."

Jolene flashed a wide smile at him. "I like being called a Lady. I think I'll like you, Professor."

Joseph started to blush again, and Jolene gave a bit of a belly laugh at his discomfort.

"Relax, Professor. You'll get used to normal human interaction. You don't have to look over your shoulder here, contrary to rumors."

Jolene put the ice bag on her face again. Joseph sipped his whiskey, enjoying the simple pleasure of a Pre-Squid normal activity.

Jolene then put the ice bag down. "The ice is to stop phantom pain I get sometimes. Doctors tell me there is no reason why my pain still occurs, other than nerve memory of some type from my original injury. But I'm lucky as I should be dead."

Joseph raised an eyebrow. "Dead?"

"Yes, dead. About a year after the first Rock, a member of the so called new Church of Kraken decided that he wanted a piece of me, both sexually and literally. The early members decided that they needed to eat human flesh like their new demi Gods, the Tschaaa. They wanted to 'be' a Squid."

Jolene poured herself a shot and freshened up Josephs drink.

"I owe the Director my life, literally." She threw the shot back. "That is smooth, isn't it? Well, just as the asshole was beginning to cut on me, hence this scar on my left jaw line, the Director showed up out of nowhere. He had apparently just been contacted by His Lordship Neptune a week or so prior, here in the Keys."

Jolene's eyes had a bit of a faraway look to them. "I have never seen anyone so angry before. But it was a good anger, the kind from seeing the weak and innocent being hurt and you stepping in to stop it."

"Anyways, Director Lloyd wound up hacking the asshole to bits with a machete. He literally took him apart piece by piece. Then he and the Chief

The Gathering Storm

bandaged me up. The Admiral showed up, saw what had happened, and has respected the Director ever since, Tschaaa or no Tschaaa."

Jolene stared into Josephs eyes. "The Director has saved everyone he can. He saved me, he saved many others in similar situations. So, all that sh*t about him being a Monster is just that... sh*t. He saves who he can. And I am living proof."

"And," she continued, "He offered to fix my scar once the Tschaaa started providing their superior medical supplies. I said no, as I think it serves as a reminder of what could have been."

"Besides, I think it gives me character." Jolene laughed.

"Now, Professor, one for the road, take a couple of beers with you, and go make up with your wife."

Joseph's mouth dropped open. "How…"

"I told you we hear everything. I'll see you here tomorrow."

Sarah had been waiting when he got to the quarters. There were some more tears, he found out she had a job, was staying, and almost begged him to stay with her. He again realized that he still loved the woman he had married. And, there had been a sea change in her.

"I'VE been a … c*nt. There, I said it. You saved me and all I could do was rag on you. I'm sorry, please forgive me."

Ten minutes later, after such a long dry spell, he couldn't remember the last time they had made love, Sarah literally screwed him stupid.

He looked at the sleeping woman next to him. They were quite good together in bed, always had been. Things had just got in the way. Now, it was changing.

After everything that had happened today, he was beginning to wonder if there was something in the water.

"While some groups of humanity attempted to retain or re-discover basic cultural norms and morals, others sank into a morass of depravity and bizarre behavior that is hard to comprehend by many. Possibly a Citizen of Ancient Rome from the reign of Emperor Caligula could more readily accept and understand what occurred on parts of 21st Century Earth."

Excerpts from the Literary Works of Princess Akiko,
Free Japan Royal Family.

CATTLE COUNTRY, ATLANTA

A couple of days had passed since his meeting with Malcom whatever the hell his real name was. The Mayor did not care, for tonight was Fight Night.

In an old sports auditorium, Mayor Luther's version of Bread and Circuses was about to begin. He had soon realized after he took over as Acting Mayor that base entertainment helped take peoples mind off of reality. And Fights, violence, seemed to attract the populace more than most things. Add his alcohol supplied by the monthly supply drops and he put on quite the party

The last three Fights had shown a pattern of success. Mayor Young had found that Female Nude Catfights floated everyone's boat. And the prize for winning was the almost irreplaceable. The woman who won obtained complete protection for her children. No chance of any Veal being seized from her family. Thus, there were no shortages of volunteers. Tonight, two five foot two, 110 pound large breasted East Indian women were fighting. Their only protection was eye goggles to protect them from gouging each other's eyes out. Blind women did no one any good. And, the referees would keep them from killing each other. But, Mayor Luther knew that the fight, like the previous ones, would be a bloody biting, scratching, hair pulling, kicking, punching and screaming Bitchfight. And it was the first of a three fight scorecard.

The second was a couple of Black Americans. The third was two dark skinned Filipinas. He tried to keep the fights within the ethnic groups as there was enough animosity already without adding to it. His technicians had gotten the Jumbotrons to work, so everyone could have a good view of the tits and ass when the women went after each other. And, he was burning DVDs for sale to the highest bidder. The winner got the freedom from having family members eaten, as well as a few bucks and other incidentals. The loser got to come up to the Mayors box suite to service whoever the Mayor wanted serviced. Last time, he had two losers fight in front of him, while the third loser performed fellatio on him while he watched the scratching and biting. He came so hard he almost choked the Bitch

The roar of the crowd told him that the two East Indians had entered the arena. The two women were so evenly matched they could have been twins. They both had Bollywood good looks, so he hoped his medical staff could keep them from suffering any permanent scarring.

The two attractive women entered the arena from opposite ends. Other than the goggles, the only other adornment was a red or blue thick ribbon tied on their left arm. This was to help in identification, primarily for betting purposes. No one really cared about their names.

The Announcer ran through the standard litany of their respective sizes, weights, etc, as well as general rules, which were almost non-existent. Then, in the time honored tradition, he yelled over the PA system. "Let's Get Ready to Rumble!"

Both women, their shoulder blade length long hair thick and loose, charged each other like two linebackers. They slammed into each other in the center of the arena, breast to breast, clawing their sharpened fingernails into each other's faces and necks. They screamed and cursed in their native language as they tried to knee each other in their pubis, and fell to the soft grass as their legs became intertwined. Clumps of hair from were ripped form each other's heads as they rolled around on the ground. The crowd roared with approval as the fight intensified. Blue managed to use her legs and feet to flip Red up and over her, resulting in a short break in the grappling. Both women sprang to their feet, then began to circle each other with clawed hands.

Red lunged and dug her nails into Blues substantial breasts. Blue screamed and began kneeing Red to make her let go. Red slapped Blue hard across the face with her right hand, and tried to follow up with her left. Blue tucked her chin to her chest and began throwing hard punches into Reds tanned breasts, smashing them back against the woman's rib cage. Red backed up, covering her breasts with her arms, and then lashed out with her feet, aiming at Blues lower body. Blue wrapped her arms around Red's right leg as she kicked, digging her fingernails into the soft skin of the shapely thighs. She pulled the leg up, throwing Red off balance. They tumbled to the grass, Red clawing at Blues soft skin as they fell.

They began to roll on the ground again, arms wrapped around each other in bear hugs, clawed hands gouging and scratching each other's back as well as buttocks. Suddenly, Red let loose with a high pitched scream. It was soon evident that Blue had clamped her teeth onto Reds left breast, and began to worry it like Terrier with a rat. Red screamed again and dug her fingernails into the neck and throat of her rival, tried to force her to release her bite. A trickle of blood was evident from Red's breast, as she clawed at Blue's face. A fishhook by Red into Blue's left cheek finally resulted in release of the bite. Otherwise, Blue would have had her mouth ripped open.

Blue managed to dislodge the fish hooked finger, and then bit the offending hand. Red cried out and began beating Blue on her head with her free hand, the hammer-strikes eventually resulting in the hand to be freed.

Red pushed herself back from Blue with her legs and feet, and tried to stand up. Blue threw herself at the other woman, her hands again clawed. She raked

Red's breasts, now smeared with blood. But Red was still in the fight. Now it was Blues turn to scream with pain as Red clawed at her pubis. Blue went into a Virgin Clutch, trying to remove the cutting fingernails from the most sensitive of areas. Red tried to force Blue onto her back as she dug into the pubic mound. Then, Reds right breast swung too close to Blue's mouth, and Blue bit her nipple, hard. Red screamed "Nooo." as she believed she was about to lose her nipple. She let go of Blue's pubis and clawed at the woman's mouth, again going for a fishhook.

Once again Blue stopped biting, and then began kneeing Red in her stomach and crotch. Red scrambled back, shoving Blue away from her. The two damaged and bloodied combatants managed to regain their feet, but were clearly winded. The red bloody scratches and gouges on their bodies were mute testimony of the sharpness of their fingernails and the savagery of their attacks.

They circled, cursing each other. In a sudden move, Red made a dive for Blues legs. She managed to dig her nails into the others thighs for a moment. Then Blue smashed her elbow down on the back of Reds head. The stunned woman went to her knees. Blue trapped Reds head between her strong, shapely thighs, and then rolled to her side. She bent, reached down and began to claw at the undefended butt cheeks and thighs of Red. Red, still partially stunned, tried to pry herself loose from the trapping thighs. She regained enough of her senses to use her own teeth. Blue yelped as Red sunk teeth into the inner thigh area. Blue responded by hammer fist blows to Reds back, until the pain and damage to her thigh forced her to release the other woman's head. They rolled apart, both clearly the worse for wear. The crowd began going completely nuts.

The Mayor grinned, and then guffawed. Damn, what a fight! This would be talked about for months to come.

The two combatants got to wobbly feet. Both had tear stained faces from the effects of the vicious pain they had inflicted on each other. They circled again, trying to regain their breath.

Red sprang a kick to Blue's pubis, but she caught it on her outer thigh. Then Blue lunged forward and drove a combination of fists to her rivals stomach and crotch. Red tried to cover up with her arms and hands. This let her face unprotected. Blue closed on Red and sunk her teeth into the woman's jaw line on the left side of her face. Red screamed and again tried to claw herself loose from the damaging bite. Blue shifted her bite to the neck, drawing blood. Then a knee smashed into Red's pubis. Once, twice, Blue slammed her knees into Reds hairy femaleness. Red staggered, and appeared about to collapse. Blue grabbed her rival's large breasts and, tugging and yanking, used them to keep the woman on her feet. She then slammed her knee into Red's pubis again.

Red sagged. This time, Blue let her fall to the ground. Blue then straddled and sat on the stunned Red in a classic School Yard Pin, her knees pinning Red's shoulders to the ground. Blue reached back with her right hand and clawed the rival's pubis, paying her back for the attack on her own genitalia. Red cried and moaned, then began to sob. Blue cursed something at Red, then, to the howling appreciation of the crowd, spit in her face. Twice. Blue used her hands to smear the spittle all over Reds face, as the defeated woman's heels beat a powerless drum beat on the ground. Blue rolled off Red, and somehow had the energy to stand up. She placed her bare right foot on Red's face and pressed it into the grass. Blue raised her right fist in the sign of victory.

The crowd went wild. Coins began to be thrown at the victor, as cash would not reach the arena floor.

"Where did you find these two, Joe?"

The big former pro football player gave the Mayor his signature grin. "Oh, you know Boss, words gets around to me. Seems that Red tried to fuck Blue's husband. They were going to fight in the street when their people told them to fight for something real, not just sex. So, here we are."

"Goddamn. I *knew* there was something to why they seemed to hate each other. Well, get Blue and Red cleaned up. I want to talk to them, and then Red gets to have some more fun and games."

Mayor Young's erection was straining to get out when Red and Blue showed up in his box suite just before the next match. They had both cleaned up rather nice, though they had swelling and bruising. Red would not look at Blue, instead looked at the ground. The Mayor tossed Blue a large envelope. "Your reward. Certificate stating you and your family are exempt from Harvesting, unless you or someone commits a felony crime. Also some money and chits you can use. You are one tough woman. Care for a drink?"

Blue looked at him and a bit through him. *'Damn'*, the Mayor thought. He had heard these East Indians were prideful, but she acted like he had dog-sh*t on his shoes.

"No, thank you, Mayor. May I leave?"

Mayor Luther sighed. "Yes. Good Job. You are going to be a legend." She said nothing, just bowed and turned to leave. She glanced at Red. "Leave my Husband alone, or I will gouge out your eyes." Blue hissed at Red. Red kept looking at the floor as Blue left.

The Mayor looked at Red. "Well, you lost. But the fight was so good, I decided to find something for you." He tossed her an envelope. "You have dispensation for One Year. Then your family can be Harvested."

She looked at him for the first time, surprise in her eyes. "Thank You. Oh Thank You."

"There is a little cash there too. You are going to be a legend also. Later, you can fight someone else for permanent status if you like." He looked at her. She was beautiful, damage and all. "Now, please come here. You do have to be introduced to Mister Trouser Snake before you leave...."

∽∬∽

It was early the next morning when Mayor Luther awoke in his suite, Red cuddled up to him. He did not know her real name and did not care. She had quickly decided what side of the bread the butter was on, and, for that matter, who supplied the bread. Red had shown such an intimate knowledge of the Kama Sutra that the losers of the last two bouts received only cursory attention from him. Red let him know that she had nothing to return to, she had no children yet. So, she was now the Mayors Main Squeeze.

She had tried to screw his brains out all night, knowing that for a man like the Mayor, that attitude cemented the deal. If she performed like this on a regular basis, Hell, she could stay forever.

The mayor kissed her nice rounded ass and extricated himself from her grasp.

He took care of his toilet and was getting dressed when he heard a small knocking on the outside door to his suite. He went to the door and peered through the peep hole. It was Joe.

"What's up, Joe? "

"Mayor, we have a problem headed this way, fast. It's that Cracker Talbot and his Kraken Flying Squad. They're on the outskirts of Atlanta."

"WHAT? Coming here? What the F*ck, is he nuts? There are a half a million Niggas just waiting to kill his Cracker ass. Nobody has that many bullets."

"Well, Boss, he already kneecapped two young bucks that got in his way, and a Falcon traveling near them harvested a third. After that, everyone scattered."

Most of the survivors the Squids classified as Dark Meat had begun to centralize around the major Pre-Rock Strike population centers in the former tri-state area, mostly because that was where the food and other supplies were delivered to by the Squids at first, Director Lloyd and his people. Attempts to organize some type of subsistence farming on earlier fertile lands were mostly failures. During the past year, instead of Falcons dropping supplies, large balloons and dirigibles were being used for the supply drops. Definitely not as accurate, they made up in tonnage. As long as he and the other "Mayors", representatives of the major population centers, supplied a monthly quota of "Meat" to the gigantic Harvesting Center in the former port of Savannah,

Georgia, the food and other supplies kept coming. When in the beginning, organized resistance to the 'Quotas' was attempted, two things happened;

1. The food and supplies stopped, and people began starving, fighting, even eating each other.

2. The Robos and their Falcons began random Harvesting in the middle of the night, usually starting with buildings being blown up around people.

3. As they fled the fire and destruction, People of Color were unceremoniously snatched up and slaughtered, sometimes while suspended overhead. There was nothing like blood raining on someone's head to create a quick attitude adjustment.

The survivors chose the "Mayors" to talk to the Tschaaa. In a flash, agreements were made, and once again the age old process of basically buying and selling people so that others could survive began. Now, an average of 5,000 Cattle were required delivered to Savannah for "processing" each month, including a substantial number of Veal Units. Most of the fresh Dark Meat went for feed for the Squid's Young. The Mayors and their helpers had to insure delivery, or else the Falcons came looking, with the help of the Cracker Krakens. The sad part was that some individuals were willing to sell their own young. But, since abortions were common place in some communities Pre- Strike, it wasn't that difficult a leap. However, Talbot and Company never came this far in to Cattle Country. Not ever. Talbot must have suicidal thoughts, Robocops or no Robocops.

"How close is he?"

"Within the hour, he should be here, barring a major firefight."

"F#$K!" the Mayor exploded. "Just when I start enjoying myself, this sh*t happens. Get the office ready, Joe, for their arrival. I'll be there shortly."

"Sure, Boss." Joe left. He knew the drill.

Martin Luther went back to Red and woke her up.

"Honey, something's come up. Stay here in the suite. There is some food and drink in the refrigerator, some DVD's near the TV, some women's clothes in the closet. But, just do not leave. In fact, lock the door when I leave. Understand?"

Red could tell he was worried. And she had no desire to screw up a good thing. She had found a protector and sugar-daddy and did not plan on blowing it.

"Anything you say, Mayor."

Mayor Luther stroked her cheek. "When we are alone, call me Marty. As you can tell, I like you. So, like me back and we will get along just fine."

Red smiled. "Yes, Marty." She reached up and kissed him. Maybe he wasn't so bad after all.

Mayor Luther quickly dressed and recovered his Lugar from beside the bed.

He had decided a long time ago that if Talbot and Company came for him, he would fight. So, tonight may be the night. Or maybe not. He met Joe at the office. He had a couple of the Mayor's security people standing at the door to the office, each with sawed off double barreled 12 gauges, obtained by Joe from God Knows Where. The Mayor poured himself a shot of bourbon and threw it back. He needed it to help settle his nerves. Then, he sat back to wait in silence. About a half hour later they heard a large number of engines in the streets nearby, followed by some shouts and a single gunshot. The Mayor sat frozen, staring at the door to his office. Next, a commotion like a herd of elephants was heard coming up the stairs and then down the hallway.

"'HEY, NEGRO. Watch where you point that shotgun unless you want it up your ass."

Mayor Luther and heard that voice before on the telephone and recognized it as Talbot, Cracker One.

Talbot and company burst through the door buy using the two security men as battering rams, sending them sprawling at the foot of the Mayor's desk. Joe stood with his hand on his great Bowie, standing still but ready to explode into action if necessary. Talbot looked at the Mayors' aid. "Joe. Long time no see. I still say you would have been one of the best players in the NFL if not for the Squids. But then again, we wouldn't be having all this 'fun' now would we."

Talbot looked at the Mayor. "Hey, Marty. Sorry, but we had to gut shoot some nigger outside that got too close. The Falcon has already Harvested him, so there's no mess to clean up. But I digress. Lieutenant Sparks." Ray Sparks stepped up with a long pole like object. Talbot took it and tossed in unceremoniously on the desk with a resounding clatter.

"Look familiar, Mayor?"

Martin Luther saw it was a spear. He picked it up and examined it. It took him only a few moments to notice the information plate on the shaft. Property of the Atlanta Museum of Natural History' it read.

"I never was one to hang around museums, Mr. Talbot. "

Talbot grinned. "I never thought I would see the day when homegrown niggers carried African spears in America. I mean, we used to call you 'Spearchuckers' but I never saw one of you actually have one, a spear that is. Until the other day, when we tracked down those niggers and coons that broke through the fence in the Florida Panhandle. And now, the question is how an African Spear from a museum in Atlanta, Georgia, wound up in Florida."

He glared at the Mayor. "Do you have an idea?"

The Mayor paused, and then answered. "Someone stole it from the Museum. The place has been closed since just after the first Rock Strike, six years ago. "

Talbot kept staring at Mayor Luther in silence. Sweat began to knead up on

The Gathering Storm

the Mayor's forehead. He had no idea what else to say.

Talbot broke the silence. "I know you don't know. Hell, you're too busy porking the losers of your Catfight Extravaganzas." Talbot chuckled. "Yes, we have heard all about your little circuses. Wished I could have gotten here sooner to watch the last one. I heard you record them, Right?"

"Yes, we do."

Talbot slapped his hands together. "Good. I want a copy sent to me. As well as a dozen good looking Ho's. Well, at least as good looking as a Darkie can be. "

Talbot walked over and sat on edge of the Mayors desk. "We won't stay long, as the 'natives' are getting restless. Sounds like an old Tarzan movie, doesn't it?"

"But, after we leave, you have seven days to come up with the Ho's, the recording of the fight, and seven dark bucks who get to accept responsibility for the breakout. Send them to Savannah with notes pinned to their asses stating they are the seven who planned it, and we will call it even. Kapeesh?"

Martin Luther hesitated. The populace would know what was happening when seven men were suddenly grabbed, above the quota, which they had just filled.

"I said, KAPEESH. Understand?" Talbot roared.

The Mayor jumped in his seat. "Yes, I understand."

"Good. Now, as much as I enjoy your company, time to go. Oh, make sure you get us the Ho's. Otherwise, we have the Robos start Harvesting at random."

Talbot got off the desk and strode to the door. "Goodbye, Joe. See You Next time. Hell, you might be Mayor then." He began laughing at his joke, joined by the other Kraken Squad Members as they all barged out the door. The two now empty shotguns were tossed into the office by the Tail End Charlie.

"Don't forget the DVD of the fight." the Major heard from the hallway. The Mayor was shaking with anger and fear.

"You okay, Boss?" Joe asked.

"Fu*k. As good as I can be. At least I'm still alive." He used his shaking hand to pour himself another drink.

Talbot and his Krakens clambered down the stairwells to the street below, bellowing and laughing. They just loved to f*ck with Niggers. As they joined the security team guarding their transportation, Talbot noticed a tall, muscular very dark skinned man leaning against the wall of the building across the street. He seemed to be watching them without a care in the world, ignoring even the Falcon circling the city overhead.

"Hey, Dark Meat. What are you looking at?" Talbot Yelled.

"Just some White Meat done f*cking with Hiz Honor, the Mayor."

Talbot laughed, and walked towards the uppity coon.

"My, my, we have a set of balls, don't we? What's your name, Meat?"

"I go by Malcom these days. And you, Sir, what name do you go by?"

"Talbot, of the Krakens, and no, not that Church. In the old days we would be a Biker Gang.

Now we're the biggest Son Of A Bitch in the Valley." His men laughed.

"Don't you know you could wind up dead if you piss us or that Robocop flying around off?"

Malcom gave one short "Ha." Then spoke. "We are already dead. We were dead the day the Squids showed up. It's just a matter now of when we stop being the walking dead and become truly dead meat. "

Talbot looked at him. This Nigger, with his very dark skin, was one of the smartest humans Talbot had met in the last few years. How had he stayed alive?

"Pardon me for asking, but how did a 'Negro' with skin as dark as yours, not been Harvested by now? The Squids, you know, love Dark Meat, the darker the better."

Malcom shrugged. "Just lucky, I guess. Mind if I ask you a question?"

"Go ahead. This is one of the most interesting conversations I've had in a long time."

"Did you have fun with Hiz Honor, the House Nigger?"

Talbot stared at Malcom. Then he started laughing, as did all his men. He laughed so hard that he almost fell over. As he wiped tears from his eyes, he said to Malcom. "You know my man; I sure hope you're around the next time I have to visit the Mayor. You're a hell of a lot more fun than he is."

"Who knows, Talbot of the Krakens, I may be the Mayor when you return."

Talbot laughed again. "Well, Malcom of the Walking Dead, your luck is still holding. Most darkies standing around eyeballing us would be dead by now. So, yea, you could be Mayor soon. If you are and I have to look you up, you can buy me a drink." Everyone laughed, including Malcom.

"Sounds like a deal to me, Talbot of the Krakens."

Talbot laughed, signaled it was time leave. "Time to leave, Malcom. See you next time, I hope." He climbed into his SUV, and accelerated down the street, his units soon falling in behind.

As the sound of the vehicle engines began to fade, Malcom straightened up from his position on the wall. He looked up to a fifth story window in a building two blocks away. He gave a high sign to the Sniper manning the homemade Fifty Caliber bolt action sniper rifle. Malcom knew that if he had taken Talbot out, all Hell would have broken loose. The Fifty probably would not have taken out the Falcon. But man, it would have been a fun few minutes.

The Gathering Storm   III 131

And when you're already "Dead", it's the little fun things in life that get you through the day.

∿∿

"The Director Adam Lloyd became quite adept in his special form of propaganda. With the assistance of Kathy Monroe, the perfect on screen image and messenger for the Protocols of Selective Survival, the Director began spreading the word about the New Age the Tschaaa were bringing to humanity, at least part of it."

"But not everyone who received the message accepted it. This was especially true of those humans residing in Unoccupied States of America."

Excerpts from the Literary Works of Princess Akiko,
Free Japan Royal Family.

KEY WEST, FLORIDA

The last few weeks had been very busy for Adam, Kathy, Mary Lou and the Chief.

And, as it was very busy for them, thus the whole base became a literal beehive of activity. Adam lit a fire under all departments and sections, knew that the information he had just received from his Lordship had put a premium on getting things done as fast as possible before pushback from the populace occurred. Only he and the Chief knew the full story of the Tschaaa Ship movement, though he knew the scientists and astronomers still alive could easily figure by the developing angles of trajectory the possible final destinations of the ships. It would be a while before the true final results of the Tschaaa movements and plans sank in to those with the knowledge to figure things out. Then, it would spread amongst the general populace like wildfire.

Before that happened, Adam needed to have a buffer, a cushion in place to soften the blow that the Squids were here to stay in large numbers indefinitely. No small centralized colonies, the Tschaaa breeding areas would be huge and worldwide. So, Kathy began broadcasting all the benefits the Tschaaa were suddenly providing. Cell phones, the full Internet, a national power grid, superior nanotechnology and organic based medicine for everyone in the Tschaaa controlled areas, as well as fresh food and produce finally being produced on restructured farms. Of course, the greatly reduced population helped by reducing the overall need.

And Kathy was the perfect spokesman, just as Adam had believed she would be. Her hot looks attracted those men, and a few women, who wanted to watch eye candy on the reconstituted nationwide broadcasting system. Her proverbial and legendary, at least among the old adult movie industry, 'perky' demeanor woke many a person up in the morning with a smile. Even with hard news, some not good, Kathy managed to soften the blow with her delivery. People soon found out when she interviewed people she was not some air headed bimbo. Instead, they saw she really cared about her fellow humans. The initial prime example was when the first "Eaters", reproducing and traveling at an exponential rate which no one foresaw, hit the West Coast.

Despite directions from Adam, Kathy had finagled a security team (Adam heard there were almost fist fights over who could go with her) and air transportation to the Oregon Coast, near where the Columbia River met the Pacific, all behinds Adam's back. This really pissed off Adam when he found she was near the radioactive contaminated Columbia River, but she was already there when he got the word. Kathy had an ability to convince those around her that yes, what she wanted had been cleared with the powers that be, and it was such a "good" idea that, Hell, why not, anyways, permission be damned. Near a small active port created by the Tschaaa, Kathy had interviewed some of the first humans who had contact with the Eaters and lived. They were with Tschaaa and Robocop overseers to salvage metals and electronics from the abandoned buildings, houses, vehicles and boats left up and down the Oregon and Washington Coast. Somehow, some Eaters made it to Mainland America, possibly on an abandoned former Chinese barge that seemed to belong to some smugglers. China, now run by Warlords, knew that the Occupied States were creating disposable goods and wealth once again, as well as providing surplus food. The surplus was both fresh and left over canned and dry goods salvaged from abandoned malls, shopping centers and warehouses in Harvested Areas. So, smuggling started again. The Tschaaa Eye in the Sky surveillance system did not care about some slow moving surface vessels at this late date, as long as they stayed away from Breeding areas and Cattle Country.

Adam had watched the taped interviews with a mixture of pride and seething anger after the fact. One minute, a young couple of humans, with two young children, were talking about these weird creatures they had seen. Then a couple of Eaters had attacked seemingly from nowhere. Kathy kept broadcasting, as she back peddled, pushed the husband and wife to safety, putting herself between the Eaters and the kids. The Eaters were hauling ass down an expanse of sandy beach, saw a bipedal lunch within reach. The attack had happened so fast, and the threat was so new, that the security team was flatfooted for a few seconds. Kathy screamed at the creatures, waved her arms to attract the Eaters from the young couple and their children. It worked. She was seconds from death, but the kids were escaping. Assault rifles and shotguns, finally on target, blasted the two creatures to bloody bits six feet from Kathy, on camera.

As the security team approached, Kathy was heard to say off camera, "Well, that was kind of scary, wasn't it, Boys and Girls?"

Then, Kathy was hugged by the mother of the two children, thanking her between sobs for distracting the Eaters and helping save her kids. Great film that showed, Squids or no Squids, humans still cared and sacrificed for other humans. Basic humanity could still exist.

Kathy then, perky smile back, talked with the security team as they did a quick examination of the remains, before everyone realized that where there were two, there could be more. Then, they bum-rushed her off the beach, along with the young couple and their children. "Hey, Guys, it's hard to run and broadcast at the same time, you know." She quipped, and then giggled.

Adam personally reamed the security team a new asshole for; 1. Letting Kathy convince them that a several day trip to the West Coast was somehow authorized, and; 2. Almost getting her killed. Then, he gave them medals and bonuses for courage in face of a new and very dangerous enemy. Kathy became the symbol of What Was Right with the government. After all, if she worked for the Director, and she put herself in harm's way to save others, especially children, then it was logical that the Director and his people must still have a strong spirit of humanity. They care. This broadcast also reached the Feral and Unoccupied States of America.

So called Feral Areas began to have access to power and the grid, as they tapped and hacked in, with Adam's people purposefully looking the other way. If the so called Enemy is actually helping make your life better, easier, it is hard to convince people to risk their lives attacking it.

Adam knew the Unoccupied States of America were leeching power and Internet capabilities from the Controlled Areas, but he did not care. Once again, they may think twice of knocking out the new found grids and benefits if it hurt their populace. And everyone began to know Kathy.

(What no one else knew was that Adam had Kathy picked up by Andrew in his Falcon, and rushed back to Key West. He then had him carry her, cursing, to his office. Behind closed doors, he had screamed at her, pulled her pants down and spanked her like a five year old on her bare ass. All the spanking seemed to achieve was some screams of protest, a randy Kathy, and a quick session of hot sex.)

Now Adam was packing his ditty bag and briefcase again. The Chief, Kathy, Mary Lou and a security detail accompanying them were to fly to

Cape Canaveral for a truly nationwide special broadcast about the Pending Spaceplane Launch. This was one subject that seemed to generate a lot of positive feedback from the surviving populace. It pointed to the fact that, at least for the people outside Cattle Country, the Tschaaa were trying to better their lot in literally astronomical proportions. Why would they do that if they planned to eat them?

Mary Lou came into his office. "Ready, Boss?"

"Finishing touches, Mary Lou. Is Kathy here?"

"Yes". Still with the icy demeanor concerning Kathy. They were like oil and water, did not want to mix. The fact that Kathy was now becoming a household name did not help the relationship. It had gotten to the point that both women did their best to show off their best assets when they were around Adam in his office, or in the broadcast studio. Slightly lifted skirts, a little more cleavage, leg shaping high heels and nylons, all came into play. This was bizarre because he was having sex with both of them when time permitted behind closed doors, so he had intimate knowledge of their bodies. And both knew he desired them. It seemed like they were showing off to each other, saying "Look at this. My boobs and ass look better than yours."

Today, they were wearing almost identical blue pants suits, tailored to accentuate every feminine curve and body part. And they kept glancing in each other's direction, occasionally locking eyes.

Adam knew people were randy and sexually competitive, but this was beginning to get ridiculous. He was thinking of having a three way talk with them after work someday. That was, when he had the time. Right now, he needed to get the show on the road

He rounded up Kathy and Mary Lou and they headed down to the main building entrance. The Chief met him curbside in front of the building, a look of frustration on his face.

"Boss, two of our three security troops are down for the count with some nasty food poisoning. I can find two more, but it will just take a few."

"Are the pilots armed?"

"Yes, Boss."

"Well, grab a couple of you Special Briefcases for us, and let's hit the road. The trip in the Gooney Bird is going to take a while as it is, and we have a busy schedule. I don't need more delays. The Pilots and Flight Engineer will just have to do double duty, if necessary. Besides, Cape Canaveral has Tschaaa security out the ass, several Robocops and even some Lizards floating around."

"Okay, Boss. Let's head to the airport."

The lone remaining Security was a Sergeant Jackson, a tall blonde haired man who had come in the last group of New Arrivals. Chief Hamilton had told Adam that he had an extreme Gung Ho attitude, having been the child of a White Supremacist that hated Darkies before the Tschaaa appeared. He thought the Squids had been a Godsend. Adam never really trusted fanatics. It had been his experience that people of extreme views were hard to control, and it was not unknown for one to suddenly become just as fanatical about a view once held as opposite. People such as these seemed to just enjoy being fanatics, the basis of their fanaticism being secondary.

But, he seemed to be completely beholden to the Chief, who he appeared to treat like his long lost savior. And because the Chief was loyal to Adam, Sergeant Jackson must be loyal to Adam by default.

They arrived at the Key West Airport, where the re-engined DC-3 Gooney Bird was being prepped for takeoff. Part of a small fleet that had operated out of the Florida Keys pre-Strike and Infestation, this plane had the original Pratt and Whitney engines replaced by a more modern Turbo Prop, which upped the top speed and load carrying capability. It was set up to carry some 20 passengers quite comfortably, some of the seats modified to face each other over small fold down tables.

Mary Lou and Kathy had purposefully sat opposite of each other, which piqued Adam's curiosity. So, after a smooth take off, he began doing some surreptitious people watching as the Chief played Old Sol with a well-worn deck of cards. Sure enough, periodically, the two women were giving each other the Stink Eye Stare. Adam was pretty he saw a couple of single finger salutes flashed at each other when they assumed no one else was watching. He clenched his teeth. This had to stop. Without warning, the plane lurched. At the same instance, Adam heard a loud "Bang" from the port side engine, which belched smoke, then stopped.

"Ladies and Gentlemen, this is the Captain. As you can see, the port engine just sh*it the proverbial bed. I will be looking for a field to set down on. Please fasten your seat belts. Thank You."

The Pilot and Co-pilot were both former Air Force and Airline Pilots that had survived the last few years by being very good at what they did. After thousands of hours of flying, this was the first serious in-flight emergency that Adam could remember.

An old civil aviation field, only just cleared off by the locals at Adam's behest and payment, was found north of Miami.

"Director, do you have anyone following us?" The pilot asked over the intercom.

Adam unbuckled his belt and went to the cockpit. "What do you have?"

"We have an old Cessna 172 shadowing us all of a sudden, ever since the engine blew This makes me very nervous."

"You and I both, Captain." Adam quickly went back to his seat with the others. He noticed Sergeant Jackson was staring at Kathy, like he expected her to say something to him. Infatuation in times of crisis? No time for that.

"Alright people. You know the drill. Rig for possible crash landing, seatbacks up, tables stowed, put you head down on your knees, hands on the back of your neck just before landing. Kathy, Mary Lou, quit screwing with each other."

There were two surprised looks. "'Don't say anything. We have a Cessna 172 behind us, which may have up to four people jammed in it. Chief, Sergeant Jackson, prepare to repel borders when we roll to a stop."

"Yes Boss." The Chief checked the special briefcases he had stored under the seats.

The approach the Captain made was flawless, and he greased the DC-3 onto the runway with one engine. Adam planned on giving him a bonus. As the plane was braked to a stop, Adam and the Chief were already out of their seats. Sergeant Jackson was still staring at Kathy with his bright blue eyes, who now seemed to notice the stare. "Care to join us, Sergeant?" Adam asked, and then was staring down the barrel of Jackson's M-9 Beretta. To say he was surprised was an understatement. Jackson then spoke the first two words Adam had heard the whole flight. "Good Bye."

Adam sensed the Chief start to throw himself at Jackson. Then the Sergeants head exploded as Adam lost his hearing to a loud gunshot. Mary Lou screamed as everyone was spattered by Jackson's blood and brains. It took a few moments to realize that Kathy had a large caliber two shot derringer in her hand. No time to ponder. The Flight Engineer hauled ass back to Adam, who waved him off.

"Problem taken care of. Get ready to help us with the Cessna."

Adam and The Chief each popped open a briefcase. Adam pulled out an MP-5K sub compact submachine gun with a twenty round magazine. The Chief pulled out a sawed off double barreled twelve gauge from his case, then grabbed up the M-9 Beretta the dead assassin had dropped. The Flight Engineer had a well-used M-2 Carbine with a thirty round banana clip he had kept stashed somewhere.

"Stay here Ladies, and get down." Adam, Chief and the Flight Engineer made their way to the rear hatch door.

Mary Lou stared at Kathy. "Where in the Hell did you get that?"

"Around", answered Kathy. "A girl has to keep her secrets."

Mary Lou grabbed Kathy's left bicep, digging her sharp fingernails in. "I told you not to f*ck around when it concerns Adam."

Kathy dropped her Derringer and sank her fingers of her right hand into Mary Lou's pants covered crotch.

"Let go of my arm, Bitch." Mary Lou shoved Kathy back, and Kathy released the other woman's pubic area. "This isn't over, C*nt." She hissed. "I know." Kathy hissed back

Adam, Chief Hamilton, and the Flight Engineer scrambled out of the Gooney Bird and used the tail plane as cover. The Cessna was taxing towards the DC-3 and began to slow some fifty yards back.

"Shoot first, ask questions later." Adam said, and he began to empty his weapon's magazine into the Cessna. The Flight Engineer opened up also with good accuracy. Some forty rounds later, the Cessna, its gas tanks unprotected, its body unarmored, began to come apart and burst into flames. A figure bailed out of the passenger side door, went into a roll, then popped back up, firing some kind of assault rifle. Adam pulled his Glock 26 and began firing as the Flight Engineer fired the last rounds in his Carbine magazine. Someone hit the individual and he went down,

"Damn it. You didn't let him get close enough for my twelve gauge." The Chief protested.

"Well then, go ahead up and check for survivors, Chief, if you want something to do."

"Okay, Boss, will do." Chief Hamilton swung wide and came at the Cessna from a ninety degree angle.

"What's your name again, Sergeant?" Adam asked the Flight Engineer.

"Forrest, Director. "

"Well, Sergeant Forrest, your shooting just got you a healthy bonus. Thanks."

"Thank You, Director. I haven't had this much excitement in ages."

Chief Hamilton called back "Everyone in the Cessna is toast and dead. The guy on the runway bought it also. Shot to the head."

"Damn. No one to question. Chief, come on back."

Adam quickly turned around and went back into the plane. He found Mary Lou and Kathy glaring at each other., seething. The pilots had un-assed the plane and were making sure the fire was out on the port engine.

"All right, Ladies. All is secure. Kathy, where in the Hell did you get that gun?"

"I brought it with me. No one asked, so no one knew."

Adam looked at Kathy hard. "I don't know what was going on between you and Sergeant Jackson, but for someone that didn't seem to have a lot of contact with anyone before, other than the Chief, he seemed very intent on you. Any Ideas?"

"Christ, I don't know. Look, I just blew someone's brains out. You may be used to that, but I sure as Hell am not. I get stares all the time."

"Maybe if you didn't flash your pussy around so much like a street whore, you wouldn't get stares." Mary Lou yelled. Kathy and Mary Lou lunged at each other, going for the others face.

Something seemed to click in Adams brain, a threshold had been reached, and then passed. Kathy felt steel trap fingers around her throat, with a duplicate grip making Mary Lou's eyes bug out. Both women had their heads shoved hard against the Gooney Birds bulk head. Fear almost made the women pee their pants.

"That's it." Hissed Adam. "This sh*t stops now. I have more important matters than to referee a catfight. Understand?" He was squeezing their throats so hard all they could do was croak. Adam released his grip and the two women almost fell over.

"I said, Understand?" Both women managed to say "Yes. " Rubbing their throats.

Then Kathy, for the first time in years, began bawling in pure rage.

"This is just f*cking great!" She screamed. "I save your ass, my ass, the C*nt's here ass, and I get *choked*. I almost get eaten by some six legged freaks on a beach and I get SH*T." She sucked in another breath.

"Fine. Well, F*CK YOU ALL! I quit! So go ahead and shoot me. Otherwise, I'm f*cking gone!" Kathy stormed off the plane, almost bowling the Chief over who was just about to re-plane. Mary Lou started to say something, but a cold, icy stare from Adam shut her up. Adam took a deep breath, and then followed Kathy.

The Flight Engineer Forrest was standing outside looking at the assault rifle the Chief had recovered from the body on the tarmac when Kathy stormed up, grabbed it from him, and began marching down the field. Where she was at, where she was going, she did not care. She just had to get away. She had never felt so betrayed, so rejected. She cried more than she had done in years, pent up emotions now cascaded out of her. An image of her dead fiancé, the pilot William, flashed through her mind, and she cried some more. She began to wish she had died with him.

Then, strong arms wrapped around her and lifted her up off her feet. She started to kick, to struggle. Then Adam said in her left ear. "Kathy, stop. I'm sorry. I owe you my life."

Kathy froze. Then she went limp, dropping the rifle in her hands. Adam put her back on her feet, now having to hold her up as the shock of what had happened began to finally penetrate her anger. He turned her around, she buried her face in Adams chest and she sobbed.

"Kathy, please listen. First, I don't make it a habit of laying hands on women, abusing them. Second, whether you want to hear it or not, I love you. I love Mary Lou. Hell, I love the Barbie Twins in my own way. But I love the Mission, my Mission, to save as many members of the humanity I can, first and foremost."

He sighed. "This is not the first time somebody has gotten close to me and tried to off me. It just has not happened in quite a while."

Adam gently tilted her face up and looked into her tear filled eyes. "And, it is not the first time someone got close to me, to try and kill me, then changed their mind."

Kathy started to speak and Adam put his fingers on her lips. "Hush. Jackson believed he had a connection of some sort with you. I think you may have been contacted by someone after the Chief contacted you. You still love and miss your hero fiancé and hate Squids, who I am working for as much as I'm working for my fellow humans. So, you have entertained some ideas of revenge on the nearest, biggest target. Me." Adam paused, then continued.

"Then, for whatever reason, that idea changed. I'd like to believe it is because I am such a sterling example of excellent humanity. But I know it isn't. And I do not need a reason. Things have just changed. As things change in this screwed up world, I have learned to accept things and move on. I have to."

He looked deep into her eyes. "I need you. The people need you. Whether you like it or not, you are becoming a symbol of Hope. Hope for a better tomorrow for at least part of mankind. But if you want to leave, I understand. You just saved my life, so I owe you yours."

Kathy looked at him. Her mind was trying to go in several directions all at once. Somehow, she refocused her thoughts, got past the awful hurt, feeling of lost. She took a deep breath, and then spoke.

"Adam, my Fiancé's name was William. I miss him so much it still feels like an ice pick in my gut. Even six years later. Maybe it's because I have an idealized memory of him, frozen in time. Hell, I don't know, I'm no psychiatrist. It just is." She swallowed the lump in her throat.

"I also love the Hell out of you. You remind me of William, and yet you're different. I was ready to hate you, to play you. Now, I can't."

She was shaking, some from the post shooting effects, some from fear of what she was going to say.

"I knew 'of' a Jackson type individual. I did not know it was him. I have not had contact with anyone since just before I arrived. I was supposed to contact someone by passing a note through a mailbox in the Conch area of Key West. I never did. That is the truth, Adam. If you wish to kill me, I think you would be doing me a favor. It would end the pain."

Adam looked at Kathy. Maybe someone made of stone would have shot her, in the head, leaving her body for the bugs and scavengers. Contrary to what the Rebels, the Darkies, the general populace believed, he was not made of stone.

As he often had to do before, he made a decision, no turning back.

"Kathy, this stays between us. It ends here. If you want to kill me later, I will probably help you. I suddenly feel very old, very tired. I will not give up on the Mission. But, I may not be able to see the end."

Kathy kissed him. "Don't you give up! You aren't perfect, but you're here for a purpose, otherwise you wouldn't have been able to save so many people, and delay the end of us all."

"Yes" she continued. "You have done that, somehow. Don't forget that, whatever your failures."

She wiped her eyes, smearing makeup. Then, she flashed her signature perky smile. "It's ShowTime again, Boss. I'll swallow the pain if you will."

Adam thought for the thousandth time what cruel God had thrust this role on him. Why had he not been killed six years ago in Atlanta?

"Okay, back to the plane"

He walked Kathy back, and then went straight to Mary Lou sitting on the plane. He knelt before her seat.

"Mary Lou, please forgive my physical abuse. I lost my temper and should not have. You have every right to kick me in the testicles the first chance you get. I am sorry. Please forgive me."

Mary Lou took his face in his hands and kissed him. "Boss, you did what you figured was right. I owe you too much to hold a grudge."

Then she took a deep breath. "May I speak to Kathy, alone?"

"No fighting, yes."

"No fighting, Boss"

Mary Lou found Kathy outside the plane, staring at the burning Cessna.

She walked and stood beside her. "Kathy, I owe you for saving Adam. I was completely helpless. You were not." She took a deep breath. "I still don't trust you, and I don't know if I can like you. But, like we said that first night we talked, we need to call a truce for Adam's sake. Okay?"

Kathy turned and looked at Mary Lou. "Truce. But we are going to have to accept the 600 hundred pound gorilla in the room. We both love Adam, and he f*cks both of us. You're as sexy as Hell, and so am I. It's too bad we couldn't come to a ménage de trois type situation, but, like you said, we don't really like each other right now. However Adam loves us both. And don't argue, he told me. I'll let you call him a liar if you don't want to believe me."

Mary Lou looked into Kathy's eyes and knew she told the truth.

"Okay. Truce. But my original warning stands. Don't f*ck Adam over, or I will f*uck you over."

The two beautiful women looked at each other. There was still a part of them that wanted to scratch and claw each other's bodies, faces, beat the crap out of each other. But, that would cause pain to Adam. So, truce.

They went and sat on the plane, as the two Pilots tried to obtain alternate air transport. The Port engine was scrap.

"Someone placed a small explosive charge on the engine, small so that it wouldn't be noticed." The Captain told Adam. "'I don't know if the dead Sergeant planted it, or someone else did. It was done. It was enough to really trash the engine, though."

Adam grunted. "Well, I guess my Security Chief has a sabotage investigation on his hands. Thanks, Captain. By the way, the way you and your Co-Pilot greased this Gooney Bird onto this field with only one engine did not go unnoticed. Look for a bonus."

The Captain shrugged. "Part of the job, Director. Besides, you don't know it, but I owe you big time since that last group of newbies came in."

Adam looked at him quizzically. "How so?"

"You and the Chief found my Daughter and Son in Law. And now, I'm going to be a Grandfather. Now, Sir, excuse me while I get you another plane to ride." He turned and went to radio Key West.

Not for the first time, Adam allowed himself a small feeling of self-satisfaction. Three more lives in the plus column. Now if he could just reduce the minus column.

MALMSTOM AIR BASE, UNOCCUPIED STATES OF AMERICA

Aleksandra was helping Torbin put his Dress Uniform together, something he had not worn since being commissioned. He and Aleksandra looked at him in the full length mirror.

"Torbin, your Marine Corps Dress Uniform has to be the most colorful uniform I have ever seen. I am jealous." The Russian Captain said as she brushed lint off him.

"Yes, but don't you think I fill it out nice? Especially the front of my pants?"

She playfully slapped him. Then she kissed him. "You are a typical crazy American Yankee. Why did I have to fall in love with you?"

"Fate, kismet, whatever. Besides, you are a hard ass Russian. Why did I fall in love with you?"

Aleksandra grabbed his right hand and pushed it to her left butt cheek.

"Squeeze it. It is not hard. It is firm, but soft and sexy. You are wrong again, Americanski."   They kissed. War time romance was rough and dangerous, especially when both people involved went into Harm's Way. But, when you found someone who fit you, who completes you, danger be damned.

Aleksandra gently pushed him away. "Let me finish helping you, Torbin. You must look perfect for your Madam President. Tomorrow, the rest of us meet her. Today, it is your time."

Torbin felt embarrassed. The General had told him the President, who had somehow managed to sneak onto the Base without any fanfare, had specifically asked the General for his presence ASAP. She apparently had an award or medal to give him, and then wanted some one on one time with him, about what, no one knew.

A few finishing touches and he was a handsome Marine in traditional Dress Blues. Aleksandra squeezed his arm, and sent him on his way. Torbin marched smartly to the Generals Office a few blocks away, the light exercise helping to quiet the butterflies in his stomach. He was field troop, a combat Marine, not a REMF. Getting awards and attention from big wigs, especially Madam President, was not his cup of tea. Rubbing shoulders with a combat team In Harm's Way was his idea of fun, not rubbing shoulders with the upper Chain of Command.

He quickly covered the distance to the Generals Office. His NCOIC waved him towards the door. Torbin Bender sharply knocked on the door, and entered the Generals Office upon hearing "Enter." He stopped in front of the Generals Desk, smartly saluting." Reporting as Ordered, Sir."

Out of the Corner of his eye he saw Madam President sitting in a comfortable padded chair. No staff, no Security. Probably the most famous woman in North America, she was a legend.

A very fit 5'6"attractive woman, firm chin, straight yet feminine nose, nice lips; she was noted for her attractiveness. She had a nice 36 inch chest that she had not allowed to get in her way when she played sports, including Judo. Her full head of shoulder length brown hair now had small streaks of gray, yet she still had a young, vibrant demeanor. Is she wasn't Madam President; Sandra Paul would have been classified as a very desirable Cougar.

Her Pre Squid political Critics had written her off as a Conservative Bimbo because of her good looks, Midwest demeanor and her uncompromising politics when it came to a Strong, Moral America.

She had weathered many a political caricature of her, her family, her background, her residence in Alaska. Now she had the Last Laugh. 99% of her critics were dead, many eaten.

The Gathering Storm

The joke she made was "They were right. I was too tough. Yes, too tough to eat."

She stood up and walked towards Torbin. He turned towards her, still at ramrod attention, and snapped a parade field perfect salute. To his surprise, Madam President returned it with the same parade field precision. "Madam President. Reporting as ordered, Ma'am."

"At Ease, Captain. And I do mean At Ease, Relax. You Marines seem to be unable to relax past a stiff Parade Rest. Now, RELAX. That's an Order."

Torbin tried to let the ramrod in his spine relax. He managed to obtain a 5% decrease in his stiffness.

Madam President chuckled. "Well, I guess that is all I am going to get. General, let's all have a sit down around your coffee table. And break out that bottle you have hidden in your desk. I and the good Captain could use one."

Torbin found a chair, was given a drink, and finally began to relax a bit. Madam President suddenly produced a very normal large female purse that matched her dark blue women's skirted business suit. Torbin couldn't help but notice before they sat down that she had great legs, filling the shear nylons perfectly.

"After reading your file, Captain Bender, I know you hate pomp and circumstance. So here. A Distinguished Service Cross, a Special Medal and Citation from the Japanese Government, a Hero of Free Russia Cross. Congratulations. And I do mean congratulations. Your country recognizes your unique abilities. And you have managed to keep a cobbled together alliance between three remote countries in its early stages going and expanding.

"Begging your pardon Ma'am, but it has been the General...."

"OH Stow It Marine." General Reed ordered. "Accept the fact that, despite you wanting to do everything combat related, and are excellent at it; you now have a new skill set. You are an excellent diplomat also. "

Torbin blushed. The last thing ANYONE had ever said about him was that he was diplomatic. His idea of diplomacy was a two by four to the head to get the attention of the other parties involved.

Madam President continued. "The Japanese Government left Lt. Yamamoto, soon to be Captain, here in your tutelage in order to assist Pappy Gunn in adapting Tschaaa technology to our uses. Now, we have a nearly operational Delta. The three Russian female Officers have been a Godsend in developing trusted relations with the Russians. You were instrumental in keeping them productive and happy. And every time something improves, your name is involved somehow."

Madam President took a large sip from her drink. "Good Scotch, General. My husband was a Scotch drinker, and he got me to like it. "

"Anyways, where was I? Oh yes. I don't know if somehow you just exude good fortune or what from your pores. All I know is that, every project you touch becomes golden. So, don't argue with Your President."

"Yes Ma'am."

Torbin took a drink from his Scotch to help settle his nerves. He had trouble taking compliments.

"Now, Captain, the Bad News. An attempt we orchestrated to whack Director Lloyd recently failed. Our Agents are all dead. All except one that WAS an Agent for a short period, but was apparently was turned by the Director. Again."

General Reed snorted in disgust and frustration. "Lloyd must be a combination of Svengali and Rasputin. No one seems to be able to keep a level of hate against him once he starts talking to them."

"Especially women, General. Captain, the woman who we inserted into Lloyds inner circle was Kathy Monroe. I believe she was you late Brother William Benders girlfriend."

Torbin Froze. Then, he spoke. "Actually, Madam President, they were engaged to be married."

"An Air Force Captain was going to marry a Porn Star? I can't imagine his commanders would have liked that."

"Ma'am, he was going to resign his commission."

"For a Porn Star, who made her living servicing strangers in front of a camera? Why in all that is Holy would he entertain that thought?"

Torbin slowly stood. "Madam President, General, with all due respect, they were madly in love. I know. I met her. And War or no War, that's my younger brother we are talking about. If dueling were legal, you would be challenged for questioning his honor. Ma'am. Sir."

Torbin felt a white hot anger. He knew he was probably looking at the end of his career, but F*ck Them. Family was Family, dead or alive. You do not disrespect them.

Madam President looked intently at Torbin. Then she spoke. "You're right, General. Captain Torbin has the requisite toughness and intensity. I apologize for the crass test, but I needed to know just how much of a spine you have."

She stood up and extended her hand. "Please accept an Old Tough Broad's heartfelt apology. I know what it is like to have your family besmirched. And, then lose them."

Torbin knew she had one daughter still living. Her husband, son, another daughter were dead. He took her hand and had to control himself from crushing it. His brother was one subject that was still very raw to him, even six years later.

"Captain, we have a very tough and classified mission for you. This is why only the three of us are here right now. Director Lloyd and his Tschaaa Lordship seemed to have the unique ability to figure what we are going to do before even WE know what we are doing. The three of us will plan it. You will pick the Team that you will use. Everyone will only know what they need to know to do their job. Only We Three will have the full mission plan. Understand?"

"Yes Ma'am." He stared into the Presidents Eyes. "What do I have to do, Madam President?"

"You, Captain Torbin, are going to help me Nuke the Tschaaa Lord and capture or kill Director Lloyd".

∽∽

"Even at this much later date, some twenty five years after the events, there are still those who find it difficult to understand why very highly educated and scientific minded individuals bought into the Protocol of Selective Survival based promises made by Director Lloyd. Some say that, much like those who aided the Nazi's Final Solution or the racism based Greater East Asia Co-prosperity Sphere of Imperial Japan, anyone who aggressively helped Adam Lloyd in his projects must have been evil or deranged.

"However, I do believe there is one extremely salient difference when you compare the events of World War Two and those of the Tschaaa Invasion and Infestation. The Tschaaa threatened to kill and eat everyone, if humans were not found worthy of Client Status. So, despite the Tschaaa preference for those of darker skin, many members of the Alien Species would just as soon feed we humans to their Young as to wait for us to prove our worth for something other than being a menu item. Thus, a select few humans as well as Tschaaa believed they had to prove humanity's worth as being more than just tasty protein.

"At one time, horses were treated as wild game. Then, the Mongols and others found they could be ridden and pull war chariots. Suddenly, they had a much more important role than being just another source of meat.

"But of course, in a pinch, horses could still be eaten."

Excerpts from the Literary Works of Princess Akiko,
Free Japan Royal Family.

CAPE CANAVERAL SPACE CENTER, FLORIDA

It had been a tense day for Professor Joseph Fassbinder. When word had come that the Director would be delayed due to the failed attack, Joseph's initial fear was that everything would be delayed. He had busted his butt to get himself and the Spaceplane ready for launch and he did not want the launch date to be set back, for fear that it would be cancelled. So when he heard that Adam Lloyd and Company were again in route, he breathed a sigh of relief. His wife Sarah had remained at Key West, as she was involved in setting up a truly adequate education system for the increasing youthful population. Now that she had a function that actually helped people, she was much happier. She still had her basic beliefs concerning the unfairness of it all, but she was making the best of it.

Joseph had been in a crash course of physical fitness and nutrition to get him ready for space. So, lots of food, lots of exercise, and long hours as he prepared everything technical for the launch. He had filled out some so he did not have the look of a walking cadaver, but he would never be fat. He still had the slim build and resemblance to a World War II era Charles Lindbergh. The meeting scheduled with the Director and Kathy Monroe was for a Broadcast showing everyone in North America just how close they were to launching back into space. Because of this, security was tight. How many Robocops there were, he had no idea, only that there were lots. Also Lizards. And, a few of a new Soldier Class of artificial beings, grown in the tanks like the Grays. Human security was rather slim, but there were a couple of people who had worked at the Cape Pre-Rock Strike, so they had intimate knowledge of the set up. The Cape had been spared destruction, one small rock had hit the main administration building and that was it. But strikes at Homestead Field, Miami, and other parts of Florida had led to the area eventually being pretty depopulated. Only in the past year had Director Lloyd located enough scientists, engineers, and support personnel to start full operations again. Because of the Tschaaa breeding areas located up and down the Florida coast, the Director always had access to a substantial amount of Alien support. Many younger Squids were seen both in and out of the water, working around the Cape in numbers seen only around San Diego and the Gulf of Baja. And of course, they provided all the sea based security. Needless to say, any human wanting a swim had better find an inland pool.

Joseph was meeting the Director's party at the base of the main launch gantry. The huge size of the structure made the humans and Tschaaa in the area appear like ants in comparison. Next to Joseph was Andrew, the Robo assigned directly to the Director.

"The Director should have let me escort him here, Professor," Andrew said in his signature baritone. "Then no one would have considered attacking him."

"Well, Andrew, you know the Director wants to appear as independent as possible. But you could have forced him to accept your security presence, couldn't you?"

"I have been directed by his Lordship to follow the Director's directions as long as he isn't trying to commit the equivalent of suicide. Otherwise, he can make as many mistakes as he wishes, as long as the ultimate desired results are eventually reached."

Joseph mulled that over in his mind for a minute. "And the ultimate desired result?" Joseph asked.

"Full integration of humans into Tschaaa operations, especially in near Earth orbit." Andrew replied. A thrill coursed up Joseph's spine. So, the Director hadn't been exaggerating. He looked at Andrew. He knew that the Robocops were completely integrated into the Tschaaa computer and communication system, knew everything the Tschaaa knew, and were incapable of lying. The Tschaaa had infused them with the same inability to deceive in communications that the sea creatures had. This, in Joseph's opinion, was weird. The Tschaaa, like their Earth bound cousins, had the ability to change their skin into camouflaged colors in order to blend into their surroundings. Yet somehow, the idea of deception, of using lies and equivocation to hide ideas had never developed in their society. hysical hiding was one thing, maybe even physical ambush of prey. Intellectual hiding was another matter.

The Sun was low in the sky when the Director and his party arrived. Joseph and Andrew met them as they exited the Humvees that had picked them up at the nearby airfield.

"Professor. Good to see you."

"I am much more pleased to see that you got here in one piece, Director. This type of excitement is not the type an astrophysicist wants."

Adam chuckled. "But being launched on the end of a roman candle, in a new, untested aircraft, is the type of excitement YOU like, right, Professor?"

Joseph knew Adam had him there. What he was about to do was not exactly safe. "Well, Director, I guess one man's refreshment is another man's poison."

The Director looked at large Andrew. "Nothing to say, Andrew? No lecture, no I told you so?" Andrew turned his head ever so slightly towards the Director.

"Would it do any good? I have given you numerous reasons why you should be more careful. I have offered you time and again my services as transport.

Yet, you refuse."

"Well, Andrew, you know I must be approachable, must seem very human to those around me. Flying around in an Alien Aircraft with a huge Cyborg makes me appear to be less than human, and definitely not approachable."

Andrew replied "I believe you are just stubborn, Director. So, why should I waste my breath on a Man who is as stubborn as a mule? I believe I shall ask the new information database that will have the new form of Wikipedia to have a picture of you next to the term 'stubborn ass'."

Nobody said anything. Then Adam began to laugh. "I forget that under all that hardware is still a Man, born of woman, with a sense of humor, if now somewhat limited. Someday, you might want to try a Standup Comedy Circuit."

"Why, Director, when I have a readymade audience already?" Joseph would later swear he saw a twinkle work its way from Andrews Eyes, and past the Robocop's protective Visor. They laughed, which helped release some of the tension from he failed attack.

"Come, Professor, let us head towards the Admin Building. A little bit of planning, then everyone needs to rest. You and Miss Monroe will be broadcasting live tomorrow from here in front of the Gantry. At that time, everyone will see for themselves that yes, we are really about to launch back into Space."

KEY WEST, FLORIDA

Professor Sarah Fassbinder, now Primary Teacher for some two dozen children, ages six to sixteen, had all of her students on the main athletic and parade field at 8:00 AM. She had decided that a few calisthenics and a walk around the track every morning helped get the children's blood flowing, as well as use up excess energy and relieve stress. Six years of living under constant fear of being eaten, of living hand to mouth, with no structured education, made it difficult for the young humans to sit still in a regular structured classroom. Plus, the older children were given the responsibility of helping and keeping track of the younger, both in and out of the classroom. Sarah was trying to reintroduce basic human interaction among non-related youngsters, many who had no contact with other children while in hiding, as well as the habit of structured education.

"All right, young ladies and gentlemen. In the immutable words of our Military Members, you know the drill. Robert, lead the others in a few calisthenics. Then we take our walk around the track. I want you older ladies and gentlemen to review with the younger what the assignments are today. Alright, let's get started."

Sarah had forgotten how much fun it was to teach, to help educate young minds, make them think. Now, she was doing what she had originally trained to do in University. Somehow, she had been sidetracked into philosophical navel gazing and fighting the Establishment rather than teaching. Then the first Rock hit, and everything was frozen in time. Now, thanks to the Director, she had a chance to live, to teach again. She may hate what he was doing, picking who lives and who dies at the behest of the Tschaaa. But, she could not hate him anymore. She could tell he did care about his fellow humans, and did what he could to help as many as possible to survive. She often wondered if he bled inside every time he thought about the Human Cattle he helped condemn to the slaughterhouse.

A blurred form entered her peripheral vision, at first her mind said "dog". Then she saw the six legged horror. It must have been hiding in the drainage ditch on the edge of the field. It did not really matter where it came from, as it reached an eight year old girl and literally clamped its wide mouth over the complete upper torso. Sarah screamed and charged the creature. No weapons to fight a clawed and toothed predator, she did not even think. She was a mother cat protecting her young.

The screams from across the fielded grabbed Major Grants attention. She was cutting across the fields in route to a meeting in a nearby office. She was trying to get caught up on a few small projects while the Boss was away, as the Director could be a major distraction. Now, everything was forgotten, except for the word "Eater". The creature was a duplicate of the two that had been filmed trying to eat Kathy. Six limbs, two ending in clawed hands, with a huge, oversized mouth full of teeth; they got their name because they lived to eat. And now one was eating a young girl.

Jane automatically ran towards Harm's Way. She was Military, which was her job. Part of her said "You dumb Bitch, you have no weapons. You're dressed in blue uniform slacks, blouse and low quarters. What are you going to do?" The other part said "find a weapon."

In between her and the children was a five foot metal fence stake, the type used to secure temporary wire fencing. It was still stuck in the ground, apparently used to mark some pre-measured distance on the field. She grabbed it and tore it from the ground. By rights, that was physically impossible. Even a fit 135 pound zaftig female should have had difficulty pulling a metal rod out that had been pounded over a foot into the ground. But, call it Divine help, the fight or flight response that causes overproduction of adrenalin, or whatever gives humans the ability to lift 2000 pound cars off of their kids, Jane had it. Jane grabbed and yanked the fence stake out in one motion, just as Sarah threw herself at the eater. The Professor screamed, scratched and clawed at the body of the horror, until a blow from one of the limbs caught her on the edge of her jaw, cold cocked her. Two of the older boys rushed the Eater as this happened. A flick of one of the forelimbs flipped quill like hairs off its forearms, impaled the skin of the approaching boys just as porcupine quills impale an attacking dog. They screamed in pain, temporarily halted in their assault.

One of Jane's old boy friends, dead some six years, had competed in the javelin throw in College. He had taken her to the sports field when he practiced, and she had tried it a few times. While not good enough to compete, she had not been bad. Now, everything he had showed her came back. The Eater, the eight year old girl stuffed into its expandable stomach, was looking for a place to depart so that it could digest its meal. Just as it began to move, the fence stake/javelin slammed into the corner of its large right eye. It let out a howling scream no one at the scene would ever forget. Then Jane was on top of it. She threw her whole weight onto the stake, driving it through the eye into what passed as a brain in the creature. It shuddered, regurgitated its last meal, and died. Jane started to grab the regurgitated girl, and then screamed in pain as her hands were singed by stomach juices from the Eater. One of the older boys ripped off his sweatshirt and tried to wipe off the girls face. The flesh began to slough off the skull. The boy turned around and vomited. Jane grabbed her radio phone from her pocket and began screaming into it. "EATERS. At the Sports Field. Everyone get here NOW!"

She heard Sarah behind her scream "Susie!" Somehow she tackled Sarah and held her down, keeping her from the digestive acid covered body.

∿∿

The Hazmat team carefully washed and cleaned the area around the dead bodies of the Eater and the girl, making sure the very corrosive stomach acids were all neutralized. Jane had her hands treated; luckily she suffered the equivalent of first degree chemical burns, nothing deeper. Sarah was sitting in the back of the ambulance, sobbing. Jane went to her. "Sarah..."

"It's all my fault. They were under my care. I'm no f##king good!"

Jane grabbed and shook her, with painful hands and all. "Sarah. LOOK at me!" Sarah's eyes finally focused on Jane. "There was nothing you could do. Eaters are like a force of nature. Like a pissed off bear in the woods. Hell, I saw you jump on that damned thing. You're lucky it didn't rips out your throat."

Sarah managed to catch her breath. "I should have..."

"You should have nothing. You were doing your job. Which does not include taking on Alien life forms. That's my job." Jane stopped, and began to tear up. "Ah Christ! It's mine and the other Soldiers and Police's job. And, we let it through."

Suddenly, Sarah was calm. Steeliness appeared in her voice "Now look here, Major. You're a damned hero. That thing could have killed, hurt others. You killed it with the equivalent of a spear. A Spear! And you beat yourself up? What are you, Nuts?"

The two women stared silently at each other.

Then Jane spoke. "I guess I am a little nuts. But, I'm sane enough to know you have a class full of students that really need their teacher now. The teacher that almost sacrificed her life for them."

Sarah took a deep breath, and then let it out. "You are right, the living need me. And, Major, they need you also. No recriminations, no guilt. Just help us prevent this from ever happening again. Deal?"

Jane managed to smile. "Deal." She yelped when she tried to shake hands "Damn, this is going to hurt for a while."

"Yes, Jane, it will. It will hurt. But, I think we can get through it, with a little help from our friends" Sarah stood up and hugged her. Then, she stepped back, and wiped her face with the edge of the blanket the paramedics had wrapped her in.

"Well, I guess I need to go to the Kids. Thanks again, Major Grant... Jane. Oh. Can someone get a hold of my husband and let him know I'm alright?"

"Done and done, Professor. See you later." They both turned to leave when suddenly Jane turned back.

"Sarah."

"What is it, Jane?"

"Joseph is one hell of a lucky man."

Sarah smiled. "Thank you." She went to her class. Their parents would need a lot of help getting through this.

CAPE CANAVERAL, FLORIDA

Adam stood by the launch Gantry, giving Kathy and Joseph some last moment direction for the upcoming broadcast.

"Joseph, just relax and follow Kathy's lead. Not only is she a natural, but she has a lot of experience in this type of broadcast. We went over the basic questions, but I want this to be real and genuine, not some canned crap. Joseph, I need people to see your true feelings, beliefs about this space mission. Just relax and act like you're having a conversation with me. Or better yet, imagine that you are in bed with your wife, having a nice talk about the business of the day."

Kathy giggled. "I think the Professor would have something on his mind other than what is going on here if he was in bed with his wife. At least I hope so." Joseph blushed.

Adam gave Kathy a small glare. "Now see what you've done. I can't have him blushing during this broadcast. He is going to be one of the new Space Heroes of humanity." Joseph blushed more. Kathy began to laugh.

"Stop that. You're makeup is going to be ruined."

"Boss, I know you run everything, and know a lot. But trust me. I'll make sure this runs smoothly. The Professor will do just fine once we start talking."

Adam sighed. "I sound like an old woman, don't I? Don't answer that. I will leave this in your capable hands, Kathy. "

Large Andrew appeared from nowhere. How a being so large could move in so a quiet and unobtrusive manner was a mystery. He said. "Director, an Eater attack just happened on Key West. I have Security Control on the line." He pulled a handset from a hidden recess in his chest plate and handed it to Adam.

Adam paused for a microsecond, and then went into high gear. "This is the Director. Report." He stood silently, listening to the Controller/Dispatcher on the other end. They all knew with practiced ease what the Director needed and wanted when he said "Report".

Kathy was frozen with memories of her close shave with the Eaters in Oregon, all caught on camera. Joseph stood still. This was out of his expertise and experience.

"Thank You. Keep me posted." Adam looked at Joseph. "An Eater attacked you wife's class. She's okay. One of her students is dead. You are going to fly back with me on Andrews Falcon. Okay. Andrew?"

"Of Course, Director. I am at your service."

He looked at Kathy. "I really need all your ability to communicate over that big eye we call broadcast television. This is going to be breaking news, no copy. Quick transition from the original subject to the Eater threat. Use film from your attack. You have more experience dealing with them than anyone else around. I need you to prevent panic, and prevent anything from derailing this Space Mission. I may have complete basic control, but panic can screw up the best planned activity. People must know that things are getting better, that we are in control, that they are safe under Tschaaa oversight. Understand, Kathy?"

The Gathering Storm

She took a deep breath and let it out. "I'll handle it, Boss. I'll make you proud." Kathy looked at Joseph. "Take care, Professor. Get your wife safe and sound and I will take a rain check on this interview." She kissed Joseph's cheek. "See you later."

Kathy made a bee line to the production and broadcast technicians and began to brief everyone on what was going on.

"She is definitely not a dumb blonde, is she, Director?"

"No Joseph, she is not. Come on, you get your wish. A ride in a Falcon."

Joseph had always wanted to get on board a Falcon, but not this way. The loss of anyone at Key West Operations Base was painful as the population was still small enough that most people had at least a passing knowledge of everyone else. However, the child and teen aged population was still so limited that everyone recognized all of the young humans. Now one was dead, killed in a horrible fashion. While getting settled on board the Falcon, Adam Lloyd gave him a quick rundown on what had happened. An Eater, hidden probably in a drainage ditch, had caught Sarah's class completely flat footed. Sarah had almost been killed trying to defend her charges. By shear chance, Major Grant had been nearby.

"Let me get this straight, Director. Jane Grant killed this creature with an improvised spear??"

"Yes, Joseph, she did. Only our Security Police and Soldiers normally go armed. I think that policy changes as of now. Having a feral population of very dangerous creatures on your door step requires drastic measures. I'm going to have as many people armed as possible. Everyone is going to be required to help provide for their own defense."

"I think you have a bonafide hero on your hands, Director. Killing a nasty Alien with a spear is not something people, even the military, train for."

Adam smiled." Yes, I know. I knew that from the first, when the Chief and I recruited her, she was special, and was capable of great things. She definitely just proved it in spades."

"Time to strap in, Gentlemen." Andrew's voice boomed over the speaker system. The Falcon was not set up for comfortable passenger travel. Andrew had the pilot's chair, with another similar chair just behind it. Behind those were four very basic 1950's style airline passenger seats. The cargo hold was just for that, cargo, to include collected meat. Adam and Joseph strapped themselves in. Then, the Falcon levitated and shot straight up, reminded Joseph of a high speed elevator suddenly rising. Then they accelerated straight ahead in the proverbial blink of an eye. Joseph felt a slight acceleration, but not to the extent he believed he would. Before he could comment, the Director spoke.

"Acceleration dampening system, Professor. This craft can create a small field that counteracts gravity and acceleration, at least in the passenger area."

Joseph had a bemused look on his face. "And they need me to give them advice on spacecraft? I think they have sold themselves a bill of goods."

"I disagree, Professor. If for no other reason than the Tschaaa have become rather stagnant. Even before the long trip here, they were of the 'slow but steady wins the race' species', lacking true flights of genius that often fuels great discoveries. Humans still have that spark. And, we are here."

"My God." Exclaimed Joseph, "How fast were we going? And I felt virtually nothing."

"Over Mach 3, Professor. Give or take a couple of decimal points" Andrew answered over the intercom.

"And it was smoother than riding in a luxury car. I sure would like to have one of these. This Falcon makes our Spaceplane look like a Model T. I understand you could fly to the Moon and back in this."

"You are correct, Professor." Andrew Replied. "Falcons can fly between planets. Maybe someday, Professor, you will have that chance. But right now, one step at a time. Prepare for disembarkation."

Andrew had landed them in the middle of the sports field where the attack had taken place. Two vehicles were there to meet them. No sooner had they cleared the Falcon than Andrew accelerated straight up, out of sight, with little or no noise. A Delta, superior to human fighter aircraft, still looked like an also ran when compared to the Falcons. Joseph wondered what other marvels he would discover when he took the Spaceplane up to Platform One.

"Professor, you wife is at her classroom. She has an overly developed sense of duty. Please take her home and help her rest. That is an order." Adam said it calmly but with a bit of steel in his voice."

"Yes Sir." Joseph answered.

"And, tell Sarah we know how she tried to defend her wards like a she bear defending her cubs. That will not be forgotten by me or the parents of the children."

"Yes, Director. I will be sure to tell her that, in spades. I don't expect my wife to almost get her killed on a normal day in school."

"Please tell her I would like to see her after she has rested and depressurized. Now, I must track down Major Grant." The two men took the separate vehicles and went their separate ways.

Joseph found Sarah in her main classroom, reviewing the class roster when

The Gathering Storm

he walked in.

"Joseph! What are you doing here? How did you get here so fast?"

"A quick ride in a Falcon, thanks to your heroics. And I have orders from the Director to take you home and rest."

"I, I can't do that Joseph. I still need to talk to all the parents, to explain what happened. They need to hear it from me. The children were in my care. I am responsible." As she talked, her tone began to take on a shrillness that told Joseph one thing. Traumatic shock was beginning to set in. He went to her as she stood up to argue with him. He threw his arms around her, kissed her on her forehead, and then hugged her tight.

"Goddammit, I thought I lost you."

Sarah sputtered, then grabbed him tight and began to sob into his chest. They stood that way for what seemed like an eternity, but was actually a few minutes as Sarah cried out her fear and frustration. When she was finally finished, she looked up at his tall, still gangly self.

"You have always been too damn tall to kiss right. You should have married a tall Amazon, not a normal woman like me."

"You, my dear, are far from normal. I know that, the Director knows that, and now the rest of Key West knows that."

"All I did was get myself knocked silly, Joseph. Jane Grant is the real hero. She killed the f*cker... pardon my French."

Joseph took her face in his hands and kissed her long and deep. "Dearest, you put yourself in danger with little or no hope for success. With no training of any kind to fall back on. That takes true courage."

Joseph kissed her again. "I have been ordered to take you home. Right now, the Director is in no mood for disagreement. So, wipe your eyes. Then we go. There is a car waiting for us outside."

Sarah took a deep breath, and then she sighed. "All right, Joseph. No argument from me today... I 'm too tired."

Then she looked into his eyes. "I love you, Professor."

Joseph smiled at her "I love you, Professor. Let's go home."

ᨆ

Adam found Jane Grant at her desk, trying to compose an After Action Report, typing in on her computer with her injured hands. Adam growled at her staff when they tried to snap to attention when he entered the office.

"At Ease, dammit. I'm not a four star General." He barged into Major Grant's office, shutting the door behind him just short of slamming it.

"Director, I'm just trying to get this done while it is fresh in my mind...." Jane said as she jumped up.

"Go home and rest, Major. THAT is an order."

Jane froze for a moment, and then her shoulders slumped a bit. "Yes Sir. I'm leaving". Then Adam was hugging her. "If you ever get yourself killed pulling a stunt like that, I will be royally pissed. Trying to break in a new Ops Officer and Jill of All Trades and Master of Most is too damn hard."

Adam let her go and stepped back. "By the way, I already heard someone refer to you as Wonder Woman. Being a hero is going to be a pain in the ass for you."

Jane began to tear up. "I was a few moments too late, Director. I had to watch a young girl being eaten."

Adam produced a silken handkerchief and handed it to her. "Here, Major, wipe your eyes, blow your nose. Then, go to your quarters and let your hands heal. The fault for the girl's death stops at my desk. I have gotten way too complacent. An assassination attempt, then a young girl is eaten in front of her classmates. Time for me to buckle down and do my job."

"I started a formal inquiry into the assassination, Director. The Investigators are working on it as we speak...."

"That is enough, Major. Go home and rest. Let the rest of us earn our pay. Okay?"

Jane smiled. "Yes Sir. Heard and done" She winced when she picked up her cover.

"Hurts?" Adam asked.

"Yes Sir. My hands and my gut. I keep wondering if I had been walking just a bit faster, been a few minutes earlier, I could have been between that bastard Eater and that little girl."

"Then you would have been out of position to do what you did, and you and Sarah Fassbinder would be dead along with that little girl. Plus maybe that thing would have killed other children, who knows. I don't know its mental processes. What I do know is that you used a metal fence post to make a throw which would have made an old Olympic Javelin Thrower envious. Everything happens for a reason. Don't second guess yourself. You did what you could, and killed that horror. That means a lot. To the people here and to me."

Jane suddenly kissed Adam's cheek. "Sorry to violate protocol, but thanks, Boss. You opinion means the world to me."

Adam smiled. "Thank you, Major. Now, please, Rest."

"Yes Sir."

The Gathering Storm

∿

After viewing the remains of the Eater at a special room setup at the Biology and Animal Husbandry Section (Part of his Department of Resources), Adam called Chief Hamilton on a secure line.

"Chief, thanks to Major Grant, we have one dead Eater here. The question is, how did it get here so fast? The last report was from a sighting near San Francisco a week ago. So, a couple may have moved down the coast from Kathy's contact in Oregon. But, all the way across the continental U.S.? Give me a break."

"Well, Boss, we did just have that first convoy of trucks from the West Coast to the East Coast, bringing all that surplus and salvaged stuff. Maybe one stowed away."

"No, Chief, that trip took eight days. And, after spending that many days cooped up, an Eater, at least from what His Lordship told me, would have come busting out of the truck trailer like a bat out of Hell. Someone would have either been eaten, or at least seen it."

"Boss, go to the Source. Ask the Tschaaa how this could have happened. "

"That is a good idea. I'll get Andrew to get me a secure video hookup with Our Lordship. Talk to you later."

"By the way Boss, when you get a chance, watch our broadcasts. Kathy is creating newscast history for a new generation to follow. Fox and CNN would be eating their hearts out if they still existed. "

Adam had always thought she would work out. Now, he knew for sure. "Gotta go Chief, I'll call you later."

∿

He contacted Andrew, who met him at the Director's Office. From his many bag of tricks which were part of his Cyborg body, Andrew pulled a small monitor screen connected to a video phone. He silently made direct contact to the Tschaaa Lordship thru his complete interface with all things communicative and computerized. The image of the Tschaaa Lordship known as Neptune flashed onto the com screen.

"Director. Andrew told me what happened. You lost a Young One to an Eater."

While the Tschaaa Lord's translator broadcast his language into English, he manipulated his social tentacles to communicate Extreme Sorrow and Distress. Adam had been given a video dictionary of Tschaaa sign speech, as important to Tschaaa as facial expressions and voice inflections were to humans. Adam had never actually seen a Tschaaa demonstrate Extreme Sorrow and Distress. Now he saw the waving, twitching and shaking of the tentacles, so unlike the smooth, flowing movements the Tschaaa normally exhibited. It was almost like he was sobbing.

"Yes, Your Lordship. We lost an eight year old female child to an Eater. And now I have a large favor to ask. Actually, a huge favor. I need to know how the Eater got from the West Coast to the East Coast in such a short time, with no sightings in-between. It seems impossible."

His Lordship paused, its Tentacles frozen in its signs of sorrow for a few moments. Then, he spoke.

"Unfortunately, I was afraid you would ask that question so quickly. There are times when I think a less cognitive able Director would make my job easier; less difficult questions. But then, we would be not be anywhere near where we are today."

The Tschaaa Lord paused. "And, unfortunately in some ways, I already have what I believe is the answer."

What looked like a Tschaaa version of a radar track, followed by an Eye in the Sky photo from above, showed the large unmistakable outline of a Falcon meeting with what looked like a large Go-fast boat off of the Florida Keys. The two vehicles stayed together for about ten minutes, then the Falcon disappeared in the blink of an eye. The Go-fast made its way to what looked like Tavernier cove.

"That, my good Director, was a Falcon from the Lord in control of Africa. I was only notified of this meeting by our surveillance system because I specifically asked for the information. We Tschaaa are supposedly not into what you humans call espionage against one another, so no one pays attention to our comings and goings, or the movements of air and space craft unless there is a danger of collision. Protocol dictates we contact each other when a Lord enters another Lords area. It has been followed in the past."

"But not now, Your Lordship,"

"No, Adam, not now. And, I am sure as you are sure that one or more Eaters were transported by that Falcon. Next week is scheduled a meeting of all the Earthbound Lords. This will cause a serious area of contention."

Adam paused, weighing how he was going to ask the same question. "So, if I may be so bold Your Lordship and ask.... Tschaaa rarely if ever lie, cheat and steal towards each other, practice spy craft against another Crèche, correct?"

The Tschaaa Lordship Neptune signed resignation with its tentacles, almost like a human sigh.

"Yes, my Director that is so. But now, it appears as if your human foibles are beginning to affect and infect some Tschaaa Lords. In the past, conflict involving areas and populations of food stock would be handled in what you humans call as 'straight up'. The subject of contention is brought up directly and dealt with. Worst case scenario would involve a duel between individual Tschaaa. No lies, no attempts to damage another's possessions by subterfuge."

Adam remained silent. Tschaaa interrelationships had just entered a new phase for them.

The Tschaaa Lord continued. "Rest assured, I will have an answer or a Duel. Maybe even both. This is the first time such a situation like this has happened in several millenniums. It nears what you humans would refer to as insanity."

Adam stayed silent. Then, he had to ask the question, results be damned.

"Sir, Lordship, I must ask. Why the distress over the loss of one of our children? Sorry if I am blunt, but are they not used like we use veal?"

"Because, my Director, as I have often said, you are not Meat Cattle. That is what the so called Dark Ones, the Darkies, those individuals rounded up in Cattle Country are for. I ask you, if a young canine, a puppy, died, would you not feel sorrow?"

"Yes, Your Lordship, I would. But I am a Western bred 'dog lover'. Prior to the Invasion, many people in the Chinese controlled parts of Asia ate puppies, dogs. They may feel sorrow about a personal pet, not puppies in general."

"Well, then, my Director, I guess I am beginning to look at your young, your children, as you look at puppies. So, you may be having an effect, may be affecting my feelings and beliefs. Is that good, or bad?"

"Your Lordship, with respect, I think it is a good thing."

"So do I, my Adam, so do I. And, hopefully, I can convince the other Lords that to embrace the idea that violent and deceitful parts of human nature is an aberration. But the love of puppies, of young non Cattle humans, is not. A good thing, Adam?"

"Yes Sir, I believe it is a good thing, Lord."

"Good." The Squid Lord signed fellowship and agreement with its tentacles. "Now, I will have what you call the Eye in the Sky present me with a workup as to where the human sea-craft went. Then, I will let you know. You may track them and the Eaters down. The humans will be Harvested. You may kill the Eaters. Agreed?"

"Yes Sir."

"Excellent. I will have Andrew give you the information once we have it all. Now, I must go. But please, extend my sorrow to the Birth Mother of the Young One. All Tschaaa grieve when our young are lost."

"Yes, Your Lordship, I will tell her."

Lord Neptune cut the connection. Andrew stowed his equipment in his secret nooks and crannies that were his Man Machine Interface.

"You will have the necessary information as soon as I have it, Director. Then, we go hunting."

"Thank You Andrew. May I ask a personal question?"

"I have no personal life. I am interfaced twenty-four hours a day. So, go ahead, ask anything."

"Did you have children before your....change into a Robocop?"

"No, I did not." Andrew paused in thought for a few moments. "But I would have liked some. That is almost impossible now, of course. But, though I am part man, part machine, totally interfaced to all Tschaaa information and power systems, I can still feel for the Young. Both the Tschaaa connected side of me and the human connected side of me agree...the Young, Children, are of primary importance."

"As events transpired in the Tschaaa controlled Reconstructed States of America, they did not go unnoticed by those outside the occupied areas. Nor did they distract or deter the citizens of the Unoccupied States of America and their Allies from their primary mission: Freeing the human species from the yoke of Tschaaa oppression."

From the Literary Works of Princess Akiko,
Free Japan Royal Family

MALMSTROM ARMED FORCES BASE, MONTANA

Lt. Yamamoto, the three Russian female officers, 'Pappy' Gunn, General Reed and Torbin were in a conference room at the Headquarters Building for a special ceremony. Only Torbin and the General knew what was about to happen. All four foreign national officers were dressed in their equivalent of dress uniforms, something that Torbin and his tailor buddies had obtained. Torbin had provided the photos of Russian and Japanese dress uniforms, the sizes of the four officers a week prior, when the General had told him to arrange all the foreign national officers to have dress uniforms befitting their station. Torbin, being a good Marine, said "Yes Sir" and got to work, no questions asked. Then, Madam President showed up out of the clear blue sky and he now knew the reason. All four officers had tried on the uniforms the day before, and with a couple minor alterations, soon all had dress uniforms their own countries could not provide them in a foreign land.

Of course, none of them held a candle to Marine Corps Dress Blues.

The officers snapped to attention when Madam President entered the conference room. Following her was one of the darkest, broadest, most muscular Black men that Torbin had ever seen. And when the term 'Black' was used, it meant 'Black' when applied to the gentleman. He was a bit over six feet, but his mass made him look much bigger. He looked like 99% was muscle.

"At Ease, Ladies and Gentlemen. I know we are all very busy, but sometimes a little recognition, pomp and circumstance is required. Then, I will be giving everyone in the room a little briefing about a project I need your help on."

"First, a quick introduction. The rather large African-American man behind me is former Chief Master Sergeant George Williams the Fourth. He now serves as my bodyguard, special assistant and troubleshooter when I need to insure something is done. You may think of him as a Special Assistant to the Office of the President. He was also an Air Force Judo Team Member who made the U.S Olympic Team a while back, when there WAS a U.S Olympic Team. In the heavy weight division, of course."

Madam President smiled. "He will be staying here, General, in order to insure you receive all the support you need. "

"Yes Ma'am." General Reed acknowledged. But he was also acknowledging that he knew Mr. Williams was also the Eyes and Ears of President to insure the General did what he was required. Or Else. Ichiro seemed to recognize Mr. Williams, and suddenly had a look in his eyes that Torbin had come to understand was one of utmost respect. Torbin would have to bug his friend later about how he knew one of the darkest surviving free Black Americans.

"Now, a little pomp and circumstance. Ladies First."

"Captain Aleksandra Smirnov, Lieutenants Afanasii Kozlov, Inna Popov, front and center."

The three Russian Officers marched up to the front of the room and formed a line, Captain Aleksandra saluting as ranking Officer. "Personnel reporting as ordered, Madam President."

The president glanced at Torbin." Have you been trying to turn them into hardass Marines, Captain Bender?"

Before he could answer, Aleksandra piped up. "Begging your pardon, Madam President. We are Russian. We were born hard."

The President chuckled. "Yes, I guess that is true. Captain, you and your comrades are hereby awarded the brand new U. S. of A Tschaaa Campaign

Medal for you efforts fighting our common enemy. Congratulations." She shook the hand of each of the Russian women, and then smartly saluted them. The Russian Officers stepped back and went to Parade Rest.

"Captain Yamamoto. Front and center."

Ichiro had a slight confused look in his eye. Should he correct the President about his rank? He smartly went to the front of the room and saluted. "Lieutenant Yamamoto reporting as ordered, Ma'am."

Madam President saluted back, and then added. "That's *Captain* Yamamoto. As of last week. I have here your promotion orders, as well as a Japanese Distinguished Service Medal. You should know better than to disagree with an older woman." She smiled as she said the last.

Ichiro registered shock, and then swelled with pride.

"In our tradition, Mothers and Wives quite often pin on our men folk's new rank. Would you mind if I filled in for them?"

Ichiro looked into the Presidents eyes. "I would be honored, Madam President."

After she had deftly pinned on the new rank, she then handed Ichiro two wrapped packages.

"Your Commander also asked me to deliver these packages from your Aunt. He said you would know what they are."

Ichiro took the soft packages reverently from Madam President. He touched them to his forehead as he bowed to the President. "You do my family honor, Madam President."

"You do our citizens honor by helping us free our country from an occupying enemy, Captain Yamamoto. It is an honor to stand in for your family. "

Captain Yamamoto came to attention, saluted, did an about face, then returned to his seat.

"Well, we just had the fun part. Now the serious part." Said President Sandra Paul. "Mr. Williams, the power point, please."

Soon images of an area map and a military base appeared on the screen.

"Ladies and Gentlemen, Key West Operations Base and new Capitol of the Occupied States of America. Home to Director Lloyd and his minions."

On the displayed map was Marquesas Keys. An image appeared, showing a huge installation

90 % under water. "Marquesas Keys, once a National Park. Now Home for His Tschaaa Lordship, who adopted the Earthly name of Neptune from our human mythology."

Madam President turned and looked at her small audience. "This is our target. We need to plan a strike at these nerve centers as soon as possible. After six years of occupation, resistance from the general population outside of the

Unoccupied States has all but disappeared. The only attempts at screwing with Tschaaa control has been breakouts from Cattle Country and failed attempts at assassination of Director Lloyd. We just lost five operatives. Director Lloyd has a very charmed life."

She continued. "Captain Torbin is putting together a very highly classified attempt at a major attack against Key West and the Tschaaa installation. You all will be involved. You will know only what you need to know. Captain Torbin will be the ONLY one with the complete picture. "

Madam President flicked to the next picture on the power point. A series of pictures of men and women appeared. "Here are photos of the Director, his right hand man Chief Hamilton, and various members of his inner circle. As you see, many of them are female. Adam Lloyd seems to have an extremely well developed libido. He also seems to be able to 'turn' all the female operatives we have slipped into the area. For you Russian Officers, General Reed thinks the Director is a modern day Rasputin."|

Aleksandra raised a respectful hand. "Yes, Captain."

"Madam President, it is commonly reported in Russian history archives that Rasputin was able to hypnotize, to take mental control of those around him. Do you and the General believe that the Director has such power?"

"Yes, Captain Smirnov. He either has some ability to exert mental control on all those around him, or he is just plain damn lucky."

The President suddenly displayed a small smile. "Now is as good a time to mention Mr. William's source of expertise of this subject. George, care to elaborate on the subject?"

George Williams stood up, and sighed. Then he spoke. "I, the Director, and Chief Hamilton all served together in the U.S. Air Force prior to the first Rock Strike. Both were commensurate professionals and Adam Lloyd was one of the nicest people you could meet. Not a racist bone in him."

For the second time in recent months, Torbin was in a room so still you could hear a pin drop. This was getting weird.

"And before someone asks, what happened, I do not know. I think he actually believes that he is insuring the survival of at least part of the humanity by sacrificing another part. Intelligence we have obtained is that Adam Lloyd and the Chief have personally saved dozens of people. And when I mean personally saved, I mean they have killed some real assholes, pardon my French, to save other humans. They have even taken out some Harvester Robs with no ill effects on them. His Tschaaa Lordship has given him unprecedented power and latitude under the so-called Protocols of Selected Survival. And, it has worked. Every day, the Director broadcasts over his reconstituted mass media new successes, new advances. They are about to launch a Tschaaa supported space launch from Cape Canaveral. Bottom line, he gets things done."

"But" George Williams continued "There has appeared a kink in the armor. This morning, while we were getting ready for this meeting, that Alien Life Form known as an Eater appeared on Key West and ate a child."

A sharp intake of breath came from the Russians.

"Yes, I know. The Eaters have already appeared in substantial numbers in East Russia, now Free Russia, after being dumped in China. But it is physically impossible for an Eater to make it from the last known location on the West Coast of the U.S., all the way to Key West in just over a week, without any sightings, unless it had help."

The former Chief clicked to a new screen. "We have some excellent computer and communications hackers, former Homeland Security and U.S. Customs Cyber Agents, who hacked this picture of a meet of a Falcon with a human Go-fast boat just off the Key Largo area. The hacked information points to a fact that another Lord is screwing with our so called Lord Neptune."

Madam President chuckled. "The fact is the Squids have no concept of communications and signal security. Only those systems that Director Lloyd has put in place have any security or anti-virus, anti-hacking software. However, the Tschaaa do talk over secure lines maintained by the new crop of Robocops, which are harder to hack."

The officers watched the short surveillance video. Next they watched Kathy Monroe broadcast the complete story, gory details and all, minus the secret meet between boat and craft. Seeing his brother's former fiancé broadcasting always made him do a double take. The last six years had been kind to her, or she was just very tough. She still looked great.

"The Eater killed a young eight year old girl before being killed by Major Jane Grant." Kathy said on the screen. "Major Grant did this using an improvised spear. To say she is a hero is an understatement." A woman identified as Professor Fassbinder was then on camera, talking.

"Major Grant saved my life and the lives of my other students. If the Medal of Honor still exists, she deserves it."

Back to Kathy. "Our Lordship, Lord Neptune, personally provided this reporter the following audio recording." A generic photo of a large Tschaaa was displayed as the Shakespearean Voice he had created for human contact spoke,

"To all the Humans in the Tschaaa controlled area of North America. Rest assured that the Eater Threat will not be allowed to continue. And, to the parents of the victim, the little Young One, it is a source of pain that I, with all my resources, was unable to prevent the death of this Young One. The Young are what are important, for both Tschaaa and Humans. My sorrow is great. But my resolve is greater. The Young will be protected." End of statement.

The video ended. Captain Torbin spoke up. "Is that statement from the Squid Lord for real, or just so much bull....pucky?"

Madam President looked towards George Williams. He answered. "Yes, Captain, believe it or not. The Squids have an extremely developed sense of duty towards their young. Now, this Lordship is apparently beginning to extend that sense of duty and protection towards human children associated with those under his direct control And, this may be a potential weakness that we may use against him."

"And how would that work?" General Reed asked.

"Threats of attacks on breeding areas may distract the Tschaaa, and get us a chance to hit them in their main command and control centers. Failing that, an actual capability to interfere with their breeding on a large scale basis might force them to deal with us an equals, rather than as chattel."

"Or," pointed out General Reed, "cause such a massive retaliation that all of us will be living in caves as they take breeding stock and leave."

"We have considered that. It is our assessment that the Tschaaa are becoming much too attached to our oceans. We think our planet is a bit younger than theirs, and our oceans are a reminder of younger, happier days that the Tschaaa will have difficulty leaving them behind. Or to destroy them."

General Reed grunted. "I sure hope you are right, Mr. Williams.'"

Madam President broke in. "Since everyone in this room has been cleared both by us and their respective countries, and the room secured from ease dropping, let me ut to the chase. We, and by 'we' I mean all resources of the U.S.A., have been working on every way to attack and expel the enemy from here, and eventually the entire Earth. This includes biological and chemical attacks." She paused a few seconds to let that sink in. "We have even looked at trying to replicate the disease that made the original prey creatures, the meat primates on their home world, poisonous and infect us with it. If it won't kill us too, that is."

She continued. "We are looking into chemical attacks against the Squids, to include the breeding Crèches. But that is taking time. We need to make a strike soon, to show the world that the human race has not just rolled over and acquiesced to being food for another species, an Alien species, on a daily basis. Inertia is beginning to set in, People. The idea that people of a darker pigment are just fine as sacrificial lambs is becoming commonplace."

"That is UNACCEPTABLE!" Madam President slammed her fist on the table. Torbin saw anger in her eyes that brought him a new level of respect. Given the chance, she would gut a Squid with a dull fish knife.

Madam President took a deep breath. "Sorry, but the idea of an Alien Invader occupying much of my ole America makes my blood boil. I am an old style Patriot. Death Before Dishonor. If anyone here isn't willing to buy a ticket for this ride, it's time to get off the train."

No one spoke. Then Ichiro slowly stood. "Madam President, if I may."

"Of Course Captain. You have definitely earned the right to be heard."

He began. "My Country, my people have accepted the possibility of Death since the first day the Tako, Squids, first arrived. Through an accident of history that resulted in high radiation levels in parts of my country, we were spared the Harvesting the rest of the world has suffered. Although we have had to work hard to feed our people, we have suffered only limited physical attacks. But, the Spirit of Bushido is now strong in our people. Not the Bushido depicted in your Hollywood. But what Bushido, the Way of the Warrior, was originally meant to be. Be Honorable. Protect the Weak, the Old, and the Young. And fight and die if necessary, for our Country, Our People."

Ichiro stood rod straight. "My government, my people, want all to know... this fight is also OUR fight. Everyone, every human, is now an Honorary Japanese. We will fight and die rather than let another person be used as a meal for a Tako."

The President looked at Ichiro. She was thinking what a fine young man he was, and that he reminded her of her son. But her son was dead. And she was the President, not just a Mother.

Finally, she spoke.

"Now I know why you were just honored by your countrymen, my new Captain. I think you just put into words what everyone has been thinking for a while. We are honored to be considered your countrymen and countrywomen."

Ichiro bowed. Madam President bowed in return. What she did not realize was that Ichiro had just adopted her in his mind as a Long Lost Aunt, now back in the Family to be honored... and protected.

"Now, back to brass tacks. As I said before, attack planning begins now, with each of you as representatives of your respective countries. Yes, this has all been coordinated with your respective leaders and commanders. Captain Torbin will work out more of the details with each of you. Please do not be offended, but as spies have operated in the past, much information will be compartmentalized, built into an organization of cells, each with a specific duty. As we reach D-Day, then everything will be put into the Big Picture and communicated in total. This extreme caution concerning specific details is because our so-called Lord Neptune seems to ferret out things even before we realize what we are about to do."

The president continued. "I will say two specific things about assignments now. Captain Yamamoto, you and Mister Gunn get to bring a Squid Delta up to flying status in record time. Just imagine that it needs to be done as of yesterday, because it does. The Japanese Government is transporting more pieces and a couple of fairly complete Delta's to us. Thanks to the numerous dogfights the Squids seem to be enjoying having with the Japanese Air Force, rather than just bomb it out of existence, quite a few Delta's have been lost over and around the Japanese islands, one credited to Captain Yamamoto. We need an operational Delta, to be flown by the good Captain here. Clear?"

"Hai." "Crystal, Madam President."

"Now, Captain Smirnov. You and your Lieutenants, all trained intelligence operatives, spies, yes, we knew all along why three attractive young females were sent as part of your original mission. You three ladies get to figure out how to successfully infiltrate Director Lloyd's inner sanctum. Preferably, by one of you three. If not, we need you to find a likely candidate, soonest. Mr. Williams can help with a lot of details about who Director Lloyd and the Chief really are, really believe."

She looked at Torbin. "I and the General have a bunch of details to share with you. Right now, start thinking about how you would go about attacking Key West and getting to the Director."

She paused, wishing she had a stiff drink right then. She knew she was going to send a bunch of people to their deaths, possibly the people in this room. Tough she was, but she was still human.

"As I said before, acceptance of the status quo is unacceptable, when the status quo means quotas of humans being sent to slaughter like beef cattle. We have to shake things up NOW. I know you have heard that the Tschaaa have moved most of their large generational star craft from Earth Orbit. Our scientists surmise they are going for an eventual Sun Dive maneuver to slingshot themselves out of the Solar System. Sounds like good news, right?"

She gave a wry grin. "The problem is they are leaving most of their brethren behind. Once they are gone, the Tschaaa wouldn't be able to leave, even if they wanted to. So, we have about four years, 'max' , to make Earth so uncomfortable, maybe even deadly, that they will want to leave on those ships. If not, it will be a species fight to the death. Now, time for me to go to the Generals office for a while."

She took a deep breath. "It is a pleasure to meet you all. It is an honor to serve with you. You are the future for humanity. Not this tough Old Broad. So, as we progress, go with Gods Speed. Thank You."

The sun was setting when Torbin headed back to his quarters. Aleksandra would meet him there later. He frowned. The concept of her being sent undercover was not a pleasant one. However, they were soldiers, and were paid to head to the sound of battle.

He heard a cry of greeting. It was Ichiro.

"Torbin-san. A moment please."

He stopped and waited for Ichiro to catch up, which didn't take long. Damn, he could move fast when he wanted to. Torbin realized his slender appearance hid a coiled spring of energy.

"What's up, my new Captain?"

Ichiro smiled a bit self-consciously. "I did not expect that, my friend. There are so many more qualified Japanese officers...."

"Oh, Bullsh*it. Ichiro, there are times when you are just too self-deprecating. You deserve whatever you get. If for no other reason than you are still sane after dealing with me and the other crazy Giajin."

Ichiro gave a short laugh, and then looked serious.

"Torbin-san, I have.... Something for you. From... my home."

Torbin was about to make a typical smart ass remark when he stopped. The look in Ichiro's eyes told him this was very important and serious to the young Japanese.

"Go ahead, Ichiro."

He handed one of the wrapped packages had been given by the President. "Please, Torbin-san. Open it."

Torbin carefully unwrapped the package instead of his usual rip and tear. In it was something he, being an amateur Military Historian, had read about but believed was a thing of the past.

"Ichiro, is this, a Thousand Stitch Belt?"

"Hai, Torbin-san. A senninbari - haramaki. A belt for eternal good luck in war, for protection. My Aunt had two... made. This one is for you. I am wearing mine already."

The Thousand Stitch Belt was literally, a cloth belt made up of one thousand French Knot stitches. But, not just stitched by one person. Ichiro's Aunt had one thousand different Japanese girls and women put a single stich in the belt, one at a time. She might have stood on a street corner, asking passersby to each sew one stitch in the belt, in the traditional way. Or maybe she took it to work. However she did it, this belt represented a way of life not seen in the West. Torbin touched the soft cloth of the six inch wide belt. The stitching was interlaced with red color, and what appeared to be human hair.

"Ichiro, I... can't take this. I am not Japanese and.... I am unworthy." He stammered the last part out. He was never a loss for words. But now he was.

Ichiro looked at him "Torbin-san, now it is time for me to tell you not to be so humble. First, as I said to Madam President, you are all Honorary Japanese. And, you are… my brother, from this day forward. No, do not argue. You have the Spirit of the Samurai in you. You must have been Japanese in a past life. There is no other explanation. You have shed blood and given your own blood as a warrior. You *are* worthy."

Torbin had an unfamiliar lump in his throat. Damn. No one had ever done something like this, other than his late brother William. Quickly, he unbuttoned his uniform blouse and his shirt, wrapped the belt around his stomach. It felt like it had always been there, like it belonged there.

He buttoned his uniform back up as a smiling Ichiro looked on. Then, from under his blouse, he removed his K-bar that he always carried, even when wearing his dress blues.

"Ichiro, some of our Native Indian Tribes had an ancient ritual that fell into disfavor in the age of AIDS and Hepatitis C. I don't think that's a problem anymore. "

He slit his left palm. "Ichiro, please do the same to your palm." Ichiro produced a tanto knife and slit his left palm. Torbin reached out and Ichiro, seeing what was needed, clasped his cut left palm to Torbin's left palm. "Ichiro, we are now Blood Brothers. Our blood has mixed. We are now brothers here, and in death, when we pass on to the next realm. This bond cannot be broken by other humans…or aliens."

Ichiro beamed. "Good. This has been a good day. We are now Brothers in Blood. We will now be invincible. We will slay the Takos in numbers that will be as numerous as grains of sand on the beach. Now, we need a drink, a toast. I have sake in my room."

"Okay, but just one drink. I need my rest. I have a sh*t load of things to do."

"Hai. Of Course… Brother."

A Combat Marine having "just one drink" is like being "just a Little Bit Pregnant"… it is impossible.

∽

Early the next morning, Aleksandra and Torbin were sharing breakfast in his quarters prior to setting out for another long day of work. She had chewed his ass in English and Russian when he had been delayed at Ichiro's for more than just one cup of sake. Then, she had thrown him down on the bed and began to ravish him. Well, he had actually assisted in the ravishing by making it mutual. They had then lain together in bed, Aleks snuggled up on his chest, gently running her nails across his body. And, as countless humans before had done, engaged in a little serious pillow talk.

"Torbin, did you know that Mr. Williams had him met his family, had him over for meals?" They knew who "he" was without mentioning the name.

"Well, Aleks, sometimes people change due to stress, due to seeing too much blood, being under constant threat of death and dismemberment."

"No, Tor, not this time. He seems to really believe he is helping most by watching some being sacrificed. He apparently is a very nice, helpful, even loving person."

Torbin grunted. "People say the same thing about psychopaths, sociopaths, serial killers. We had one here named Ted Bundy who everyone believed was the nicest boy. He worked on a suicide hot line and was apparently quite good at talking people out of slitting their wrists. Then, he raped and murdered, after torturing some, about a dozen young ladies. Tried to blame pornography just before he was fried in the electric chair. So, sorry if I don't propose a certain individual for a Citizen of the Year Award."

"Well, Torbin, my love, if he is a sociopath, is psychotic, he still is able to function without killing people other than in self-defense. And women just love and worship him."

Torbin chuckled. "Women always like the Bad Boys. Nice guys finish last."

Aleks pinched him. "Ouch, Woman."

"Is that why I love you, because you are a 'Bad Boy'?"

"The Baddest." Torbin answered.

Suddenly, Aleks rose up off his chest, and stared directly into his eyes, just inches away.

"My Captain, I love you because you are the nicest, most honorable man I have ever met. You are the one I desire to spend the rest of my life with....If you will have me."

Torbin had been feeling a warm glow for quite some time whenever he was near Aleksandra. Hell, whenever he thought of her. And it wasn't just sexual. He knew that, for probably the first time in his life, he was head over heels in love. As he looked into her eyes, he saw the look Kathy Monroe had given his brother William. He knew that he loved Aleks as much as his brother had loved Kathy.

Aleks brow furrowed. "A dark cloud just went past. What is it? Do you not want me?"

Torbin put his finger to her lips. "Hush. That is farthest from the truth. "

He took her face in his hands. "Aleksandra Smirnov, I love you more than you can imagine. I wake up every day, happy that it is another day where I will see you. Will you marry me? I don't have a ring; I can't ask your Father for your hand.....mmmmmf." Aleks shut him up with a deep passionate kiss.

After they stopped, he said "I guess that is a 'Yes', unless you were just trying to get me to shut...mmmfff." A minute later, Aleks moved her face back a few inches.

"Torbin Bender, of course I will marry you. And, after this war is over, I will give you many fine Russian Ukrainian babies."

"So, I take it, you do not want to be a member of a certain person's we were just talking about harem...Ouch! You bit me."

"And I will do worse things to you if you ever mention that idea again."

Aleks then gave him an evil little smile. "Besides, you are lucky. His "harem" already has a black haired woman, as well as blondes. We have decided he would be attracted to a bronze or red headed woman. So, you are stuck with me."

Torbin covered his eyes with the back of his arm and spoke in a falsetto voice. "Stuck with you. Such torture. ….Ouch! You bit me again." For the next hour, there was no more talk of biting.

Now, they were eating an American Style Breakfast Torbin had prepared. Ham, bacon, eggs and toast, with dark Russian Tea as the only concession to Aleks.

"You will make me fat, Torbin my love." Aleks protested.

"Then I will just have to work it off you, my dear." Torbin answered with a wink and a grin.

She smiled back. "Promises, Promises."

The secure line telephone rang. It was a recent addition to his quarters. It was still early, so Torbin knew they were not late for anything. He walked over and answered it.

"Captain Bender here."

It was the General.

"Well, I see you're up already. Good. I know you have some training plans in the works for the selection of the personnel you will need, but we have a real time problem that may be used as part of the selection process. Eaters have miraculously appeared near Montana and in Alaska, along with reports of so called Kraken humans. They may have been seeded like the one down south. So, start picking a team to take to the field for some real world action that will double as training and selection. Nothing like the actual fear of death to see how someone acts under pressure. Start thinking who you want to take to the field with you. In about a week. See you in the Training Section later."

"Yes Sir." He hung up the telephone, a grin on his face. He pumped his fist. "Yessss."

Aleks looked at him. "What is it, Torbin?"

"Action. A chance get to go to the field to hunt Eaters, and Krakens. It will be used as part of my selection process for assault team members. I won't be stuck in the Training Section." Then he noticed that Aleks face had gone a bit stony.

She stood up. "I am happy for you, Captain. It will free me and give my fellow officers more time to develop our on infiltration strategy." She stood up stiffly and began to take her dishes to the sink. He stepped over and grabbed her around her waist. "Sorry I sounded so excited about leaving the Base. It has nothing to do with you. I am just a field person first, staff second."

Aleks set the dishes down and turned in his arms to face him. She put her hands on his shoulders and looked into his eyes. "You American Men are just as stupid as Russian Men. You do not understand women at all. Of course I know it has nothing to do with trying to get away from me. I can tell by the way you look at me, touch me that you are, in the American vernacular, 'hooked'. Maybe 'smitten' would apply, though it is an older term." Then Torbin noticed her stony looking eyes were beginning to moisten with tears.

"But you men think you are indestructible. We women know different. So we are fearful that you will return hurt, injured from playing with your Man Toys." Her voice caught. "Maybe dead."

She looked into his eyes. "Torbin, you are first man I have truly loved. You are the first man I have allowed myself to care for since the Squids arrived. I have seen too many people killed, and then eaten, to not have developed a tough, steely shell. I am HARD." A tear rolled down her cheek. "And now you have softened that shell and I am feeling again. Damn You." She kissed him hard. He kissed her back. Then they stood hugging each other. Finally, they separated.

"Now I must touch up my makeup so that I look as a Female Russian Officer is expected." She looked into Torbin's eyes. "You have my Russian/Ukrainian heart. Please do not break it."

The next few days were even more hectic than usual, if that was possible. Torbin put together two teams of possible applicants for his Special Unit, twenty each, forty total. Not Counting Ichiro or himself, of course. He knew Ichiro was actually part of the Air Assets part of the mission, but in the back of his mind he was scheming to have him with the assault unit if that fell through. With the Son of Nippon's special abilities, he knew no one would question his presence.

As Torbin readied a trip to the field to go after the Eaters, Krakens, maybe Ferals, Ichiro demonstrated his abilities to everyone in a most unusual way.

Torbin had all forty applicants in the gym, busting their asses with calisthenics, sprints, pushups, trying to put as much pressure on them as possible. His years training to be a certified Physical Trainer as well as his SEAL experience gave him a one up on his personnel. You Train Like You Fight, You Fight Like You Train. That afternoon they would go to the Firing Range and Shoot House for Live Fire Drills. Thanks to some help from the base training technicians, he had come up with some realistic and very nasty simulations and manikins of Eaters. The film of Kathy Monroe's attack provided real world images of what Eaters were really like.

"All Right, Troops. Take a break. Get some water. I don't want anyone falling out due to dehydration. CLEAR?"

"CRYSTAL." As one, the forty applicants responded. He did not let on but the quick bonding they exhibited gave him a warm, feral feeling. Like a pack of wolves, they were quick to learn how to work as a close knit group of predators. Wolves. That was a good symbol, especially in Montana. Wolves were making a comeback, thanks to the reduction of human presence in their traditional hunting areas. And Man's Best Friend, the Dog, started as a Wolf. He had an idea for a special unit patch.

Just then Ichiro walked in. Instead of a combat fatigue uniform, Ichiro was wearing a traditional Judo Gi. He had no belt on yet, but was carrying something rolled up in his hand. Torbin knew he had the Thousand Stitch Belt on underneath, just as Torbin did. It was a bond that could not be removed. From the opposite end of the Gym came George Williams. He had a newer looking Gi on, with a slightly used Black Belt in his hand. He stopped short of some mats that had been set up for Combatives. He turned towards the 50 Star American Flag that still resided in a place of honor in the main entrance of the gym. He bowed, then quickly wrapped and tied his belt on in the traditional manned. Ichiro approached the mats. He knelt, bowed and touched what Torbin saw was a rolled up belt in his hand to his forehead. He quickly rose up on his knees and wrapped and tied the belt around his waist. His belt was not a commercial dye job to black. Torbin saw that it was once actually a white belt that was now very black from years of use. Torbin whistled to himself. He believed obtaining a "black belt" in the traditional manner was a thing of the past and old Hollywood epics.

Ichiro stood, approached the mats, and bowed before stepping on them. He then stepped forward and bowed to Mr. Williams who had also entered the mats. Torbin had asked Ichiro over cups of sake after he had received his Thousand Stitch Belt how the New Samurai knew Mr. Williams. Ichiro had smiled. "He and my Uncle competed against each other in the Olympics, in Judo. In the Heavy Weight Division. My Uncle had to, how you say, 'bulk up' to try and get closer to the American weights. Even then, Mr. William still was bigger, though with in standards."

Ichiro had smiled. "My Uncle told me during my training that Mr. Williams was as skilled as he. But his superior size, weight and muscle mass gave him an advantage. Judo, Jiu Jitsu are said to be able to allow the small to defeat the large. That only works if the large does not have the same skill as the small."

Now, looking at Ichiro, Torbin saw he had been trained in a very hard, traditional manner. No wonder he was so skilled and so focused. He had been raised to be a Samurai from childhood.

"Captain, Bender, may we borrow you for a few minutes?" Mr. Williams asked in a loud voice.

"Of course, Sir. As long as you don't mind my guys watching." Mr. Williams nodded in assent, and then motioned him over to the mats. "If you could please let us know when to begin and keep an eye on us so that if one of us misses the other one tapping out, you stop the match. We don't want anyone to be choked out unnecessarily."

"Will do, Sir." The two protagonists approached each other, and then bowed. They were standing arm's length apart, facing each other.

"Captain Yamamoto, are you ready?" "Hai."

"Mr. Williams, Are you ready?" "Yes Sir."

"Well, I am not going to waste my time asking two Black Belts if they know the rules. So, upon my mark, you will begin. Alright, Gentlemen ...Begin."

Both men grabbed each other's Gi, trying to get good grips. Both went for a hold towards the back of the judo Gi top collar, as well as trying to get a grip on a sleeve, belt, or front. At the same time, they slid on their feet, moving, shifting, and almost dancing with each other. Each man was trying to throw his opponent ever so slightly off balance, to gain an advantage so that he could get a good throwing technique applied. Suddenly, Mr. Williams went for a traditional Uki Otashi, Floating Hip Throw, the one often seen in movies. A man with superior muscular power could definitely make this throw look easy by literally overpowering his opponent. It looked like he had, as Ichiro began to be thrown over George's left hip. As Ichiro went over, he twisted in a blur of motion so that he literally landed on his feet before the throw seemed to be complete. Dropping down to his knees, he used some of the bigger man's momentum to pull him off balance, causing him to literally trip over Ichiro's now lower body. George went into a forward roll and was able to roll free, winding up in a standing position facing his opponent.

Ichiro rolled backwards, kicking out with his feet so that he rolled back on his hands. He literally did a hand stand, then a hand spring to his feet. Torbin's mouth dropped open. And he thought he was a prime physical specimen. He suddenly felt like a slug.

The large Black Man gave a broad grin. "Captain, I heard you were as fast as greased lightning and as flexible as a snake. Now I know there was no exaggeration."

Ichiro did a slight bow to acknowledge the compliment, and then reengaged his opponent. For the next ten minutes, the action seemed to repeat itself. Mr. Williams would seemingly have Ichiro in a foot sweep, a leg tripping throw, a stomach throw, a shoulder throw. In each case, Ichiro would either slide out of it, twist out of it, or go with the move and quickly flip onto his feet, then using the bigger man's momentum to push, trip or flip him towards the mat, making George roll out of his own technique. Torbin had never seen this type of Judo Play. He was used to clean throws, slaps to the mat, then some ground grappling as the opponents tried for a collar choke or submission hold. But Ichiro never had to break his fall, as he seemed to always land on his feet. And the older man, though in excellent shape, was beginning to breathe hard. Ichiro, on the other hand, had barely broken a sweat.

"Well now, I guess it's time to try something else." Mr. Williams said. As the two men closed, George went for a literal standing collar choke, grabbing the lapels of the Gi, crossing them and trying to twist the collar into the side of Ichiro's neck. Torbin guessed he was going to try and use his brute strength to overpower Ichiro and make him submit, since blows were not allowed in Judo. Ichiro, in a sudden move, looked like he was a Green Mutant Ninja Turtle as it appeared he had pulled his head and neck back into a non-existing shell. He had actually depressed his chin down to his chest between his shoulders, the Gi collar now sipping up towards the top of his head. He went limp, collapsing backwards and downwards while grabbing the sleeves of the bigger man's Gi sleeves. Ichiro seemed to roll his long, muscular body into a ball. In actuality, he was bringing his feet up into the large man's stomach as he rolled backwards. Caught by surprise and off balance, George tried to go into a forward roll in order to roll through the technique and out the other side. No such luck.

Two strong legs attached to the feet on his stomach sprang out like released coiled springs. The large black man was propelled like a rocket upwards. With Ichiro still holding on to his sleeves, he was rotated up and over the Japanese Warrior, being kicked so that he came crashing down on his muscular behind. A blur of motion followed and George Williams the Fourth found himself wrapped up by Ichiro's arms and legs. So wrapped up that he was sure that Ichiro had morphed into a Squid. He felt the Gi's collar pressing onto the side of his neck where the main artery carries blood to the brain. A few moments of pressure, and it would be Lights Out. The former Chief tapped out. Ichiro untangled himself in a blur of motion, stood up, and extended his hand to help the larger man up.

During the match, there had been a level of silence among the observing military men that was unusual in a gym setting. Now there was a roars of "OORAH," HOOAH" and Rebel Yells, followed by deafening applause.

Torbin had to yell "At Ease." several times as loud as he could to stop the display of exuberance. Finally he gained control.

"FALL IN, DAMMIT." He bellowed. All forty men fell into two twenty man groups, ten men to a rank.

"All Right. At Ease." He turned towards Ichiro. "Did I ask you to remind me to never piss you off?"

"Could you remind me also?" George Williams interjected. He reached out to shake Ichiro's hand, a huge grin on his face "Captain, you are definitely your Uncle's Nephew. And then some. Even at the height of my Judo career, I would never be able to move like you did. Did you study some new form of martial arts I don't know about?"

Ichiro gave him a shy smile. "No, Mr. Williams. I just studied with my Uncle and....I just do at you Americans call what comes naturally."

Tobin then interjected. "If I may be so bold to express an outside opinion, the reason that my friend Ichiro is blessed with his abilities is.... Karma, pure and simple."

George Williams looked at Torbin with a quizzical look on his face. "What do you mean by...Karma?"

"Easy. Captain Yamamoto was put on this Earth to kill Squids. His ability with a Katana is supernatural. He has reflexes that that are unbelievable. Thus, what we call God, the Great Spirit, First Cause, sent him here to take care of Squids. There is no other explanation that fits. He appears at just the right time, is trained just the right way. He is a meant to be here now." Torbin knew that they probably considered he was nuts. He didn't care.

George looked at Ichiro. "Son, I'm a God Fearing Christian, Southern Baptist type. I guess you could be an Old Testament Warrior of God. But in the greater scheme of things, whatever the reason, you have skills we need and can sure use. I am glad I have had a chance to meet you and compete with you."

Ichiro bowed to the large man. "You do me honor, Mr. Williams"

"Hell, Son, call me George. You're the first man to beat me in years."

Ichiro smiled. "Okay, George-san. If you wish to work out again, it would be my pleasure."

"I bet it would. Let this Old Man rest up a bit, then I'll take you up on it. Now, before I leave, I expect you two Captains to meet for drinks at the O'

Club at say, seven PM. Then I'll buy you each a steak dinner, if you wish. Women folk stay home, please, Torbin. Your Better Half will have to share you tonight."

"Yes Sir. See you at Seven."

He turned back to his forty troops. "All right, Gentlemen. Now that we have had our Entertainment for the day, two sprints around the inside track, shower, change, grab chow, then meet me at the Range in Full Battle Rattle at 1:00 PM. The rest of the day we get to bust a bunch of caps, one of my most favorite activities. Almost as good as Sex, but not quite."

" Are we CLEAR?" He Bellowed.

"CRYSTAL" they yelled back.

"Formation, Atten HUT. Fall Out." The forty men took off, running the two laps on the track as fast as they could. The faster they were done, the more time for chow. Eating, Fighting and Fucking. That summed up the favorite activities of a combat troop. Torbin knew he had a good core of volunteers. He would have to willow it down to a Twelve Man Assault Team, and two Security Rear Guards. He would have a Twelve Man Back-Up Team if something happened to the Primary prior to S-Day.

S-Day. Squid Day. His choice of terms. Screw D-Day, A-Day, whatever. The enemy were Squids. Everyone needed to remember that. They were not humans, though they would have to fight some humans along the way. Especially when he went in for the Director. He looked at his watch. Time to grab a sandwich at one of the Conch Roach Coaches, then change into is Battle Rattle.

∿

"As a trained scientist and medical professional, I should have seen the signs of what was being done much, much earlier. My failings may have led to permanent damage to our Species. I may not have tried to perform some of the perverted acts similar to those of Joseph Mengele, but I still bear the responsibility of blinding myself to realities. I was blinded by the promises of Tschaaa medical science. I thus ignored the signs of extreme dysfunction and damage. May God forgive me."

Excerpts from the "Great Compromise" by Princess Akiko of the Free Japan Royal Family.

Appendix 15, Recovered Notes from Doctor Brigitte Fredericks Private Diary, Key West, Florida

KEY WEST, FLORIDA.

While Bender was working hard to put an assault team together, Professor Joseph Fassbinder and his wife Sarah were taking a break in their duties by visiting a combination restaurant and bar in downtown Key West. Called the Admirals Cabin, it was owned by the Admiral and operated by many of his Daughters, although he stopped in often to insure everything was going well. Had anyone remembered his true name, they might have recognized him as the manager of one of the largest former resort hotels in the Keys. Thus, running a commercial establishment came second nature to him. His odd uniform and rough looking, sun bleached demeanor was an affection that had occurred since the Tschaaa occupied the Keys. His appearance may be a bit bizarre, but a quick mind still operated under his white, sun bleached hair. And today he made sure he was present when he heard that Joseph, soon to be a new class of Rocketman heading off into Space, the final frontier, was present. He had arranged a special table in a side enclave, with a waiter and hostess standing nearby to serve just the Fassbinder's and their young guides, the Olson Twins. Sandy and Samuel had led them here, espousing the charms and excellence of the establishment, especially the drinks. After being seated in their place of honor, surprised that they were expected, Joseph turned to the Olson Twins "Did you tell them we were coming, or made reservations or some such? I thought we came here to have a drink at the bar and admire the history of Old Key West. I did not expect a private table, private service staff. This is embarrassing."

Before the Olson twins could answer, the Admiral appeared form nowhere. "Professor. And Mrs. Professor. Or should I call you Professors One and Two as I understand both of you have doctorates well above my level of understanding."

He then laughed. The Admiral laughed and chuckled a lot. Even when he was angry.

"And to answer your questions, yes, I knew you were coming, and no, the Olson Twins did not tell me. You see, I have the most well developed intelligence establishment in North America, probably the World. The Conch Republic knows all, sees all. So I knew you were coming before you did."

Joseph did not know if he was joking or not, so he did not laugh, just smiled. Then the Admiral began to guffaw and slapped him on the back. "Relax, Professor One. You and Professor Two are here to have fun. You two are my guests. The two red heads can pay their own way. They've been here before."

The Admiral grabbed a menu. "Please allow me to order for you. I know what is good tonight. Garcon, Garcon. Attend please."

The dedicated wait staff hurried to the table. The Admiral soon ordered a Surf and Turf combination of seafood and beef, Long Island Ice Teas and Key Lime Pie for dessert (of course.). The Olson's ordered a stew and Boiler Makers. Joseph could tell by their demeanor that they had been here many times before.

After he left the area, Joseph asked Sandy. "Is he always so.....unusual?"

She laughed" Yes, for as long as we have been coming here, some three years almost. He IS the Conch Republic personified. Brash, independent, tough, but fun loving. And a bit eccentric. But he is extremely protective of his people, especially his Daughters. Don't ask me how many he 'adopted', but they must be in the dozens. So everyone seems to love him like the crazy Uncle that brings the fireworks for the Fourth of July."

Joseph noticed Sam was looking around, searching for something or someone. "Looking for something, Samuel?" Sam suddenly stopped and blushed.

"He is just looking for Jolene. She works here sometimes, and he still has a crush on her." Sam gave his sister the stink eye.

"She must be quite a woman if he is so smitten with her." Sarah interjected.

"The Professor has met her." Sandy said with a sly grin. "He can tell you about her."

"Oh Really?" Sarah said. "So, tell me about this Femme Fatale, Joseph. What makes her soooo special?" She cocked an eyebrow, a warning that Joseph had better give a good answer, or suffer the consequences. Before he could answer, Jolene appeared from the back of the establishment, making a bee line towards their table. Joseph started to stutter and blushed. He was still a bit of a blockhead when it came to interpersonal relationship.

"Uh, Honey, let me introduce ….."

Jolene did not even acknowledge the presence of Joseph and the Olsons. She went straight to Sarah, hugged her and kissed her on the cheek. Sarah began to sputter a bit until Jolene began to Talk. "Professor, I have a Niece in your class, Mary Ann Lane. You helped save her from that damned Eater. I owe you and Major Grant big time. Your money is no good when I am here. So put it away."

She turned to Joseph. "Hi, Professor. Glad you finally brought your wife here. And I see Sam and Sandy brought you here. Looks like you're up for a fun evening."

Sam managed to say "Hi Jolene" before she turned and hugged Sarah again.

"Jolene, it was Major Grant that killed that thing. I was just knocked on my ass." Sarah finally managed to sputter out.

Jolene brushed aside her protestations. "O Hush. You threw yourself on that thing. It distracted it so the Major could kill it. I have a big kiss and hug for her too. So, just accept my thanks. No. No more arguing."

Sarah, a bit teary eyed, finally said "Oh alright. You're welcome."

Jolene then turned Joseph. "You'd better treat her right, Professor. Or I'll take a dull fish knife to you." Joseph looked at her, and could see she was serious.

"Yes Ma'am."

Jolene patted Sarah's shoulder. "Got to go now. See you later. If the Admiral doesn't get you good service, come see me in the main bar and I'll fix you up." Then, like a force of Nature, she bee-lined back the way she came. Joseph turned and looked at Sarah, who was dabbing her eyes with a napkin. "You okay, Honey?"

"'Its just my waterworks seem a bit sensitive lately. You'd think I'd get used to this show of....gratitude. But. Damnit. Jane did all the heavy lifting. I was just knocked on my ass."

Joseph put his arm around her. "Darling, I love you. Just accept the fact that people care that you even tried. A lot of people would have run screaming. Now, I see our drinks are coming. That should help."

The Long Island Iced Teas helped to lubricate Joseph and Sarah, as Sam and Sandy's drinks helped relax them. They were soon involved in small talk.

"Professor, I am jealous." Sam Interjected, "Here Jolene kissed you the first time you met. It took me a month to get to first base."

His sister slapped his arm. "Quit talking about your sexual frustration. You have women hanging all over you."

"Yes, but not Jolene." He shot back.

"She seemed quite the woman." Sarah interjected "How did you meet her, Joseph?"

He took a drink of his cocktail. "I met her my first day of work. She was running the Conch Roach Coach outside my building. She knew who I was already." He paused and looked at Sarah

"She gave me the beers I brought back to our room. She said I had to go home and make up."

Sarah suddenly kissed him, her tongue a quick probe of his mouth.

"I guess I owe her, too." Joseph and Sarah then both felt like High Schoolers at the Prom. Sandy interrupted the moment.

"I'm going to the Ladies Room. Would you like to show me where it's at, Sarah?"

"Yes, that would be a good idea." Sarah answered. She kissed her husband on the cheek.

"Don't be going and flirting while I'm gone." '

"Don't worry. Jolene would cut my balls off."

Everyone laughed and the two women headed to the restroom. Joseph watched Sarah walk away. He felt a stirring in his loins as he watched his wife's nice ass move in the black cocktail dress she had found. He noticed that she looked and acted years younger. And, her body seemed firmer, like she had received a rejuvenation treatment. Her five foot six frame had always been nice, with firm fairly large breasts. He knew all she had on under the dress was a pair of bikini panties and a shear nylon bra. He had a strong urge to run after her, drag her in the corner and take her underwear off so he could squeeze and fondle her female form. Joesph shook himself out of the reverie.

"Professor, don't be pissed, but your wife is hot. You are one lucky man."

Joseph looked at Sam. "Yes, I know. So where are all these young women who are throwing themselves at you?"

Sam laughed. "A couple are in the bar as we speak. BUT, I really wished Jolene wouldn't be so hard to get." They both laughed.

"Well, young sir, you have lots of time ahead of you. Enjoy the attention you get now. As you age, the people desiring you decreases."

Sam laughed. "Let me warn you, Professor. My sister has the hots for you. So in your case, you must be like fine wine. Better with age."

Joseph laughed the comment off, but knew it was true. Sandy sometimes would bump her firm body into him. He was sure she was doing it on purpose. So, he made sure she did not get him cornered alone. He didn't need any problems, now that Sarah and he were acting like newlyweds again.

Sarah was touching up her makeup in the Ladies Room. She thought to herself that she seemed to look younger. "This is weird," she mumbled to herself. She smiled. Must be because she felt like a young schoolgirl with Joseph these days. She felt a warm feeling in her loins.

"You have a great looking Husband, Sarah." Sandy was standing next to her. She was about an inch shorter than her but was just as shapely. Sarah had noticed her nice legs, and she could swear she had no panties on under her shapely night dress.

"Yes, I know. I'm lucky. To be honest, I almost lost him."

Sandy then said something that was completely from left field. "Would you fight for him?"

Sarah sputtered a bit. "Wha... what do you mean?"

"You know, Fight. Bite, scratch, pull hair, kick slap, punch. Rip the other woman's clothes off." Sandy had an intense look in her eyes, and seemed to be breathing a bit harder. But then, Sarah felt an odd, almost feral feeling. She began sizing up Sandy. She was younger, but no bigger or stronger looking than Sarah. A momentary flash of her yanking on Sandy's auburn hair flashed thru her mind.

"Yes, I would." She suddenly answered.

"Would you fight me?" Sandy asked, staring into her eyes.

"Yes, I would." Where that answer came from, Sarah had no idea. Other than a couple of school yard scraps in Junior High, she had been decidedly non-violent. Now, she was thinking she had nice manicured sharp nails, and could do a number on Sandy's face and body. The two women started to close.

Jolene chose that moment to walk in. "Evening Ladies. Hope everything is nice and clean in here."

It broke the moment. A few more seconds, and they would have been rolling on the bathroom floor.

"Just fine, Jolene." Sandy answered.

Sarah suddenly turned towards Jolene and kissed her cheek. "Thanks for sending my Husband home with the beer that day. I owe you."

Jolene broke into a big grin. "Just did what was right, Professor.

"My friends call me Sarah, Jolene. I think we're friends now." Sarah noticed the large scar on the left side of Jolene's face that had been covered by her long hair and paused.

Jolene said. "Okay, Sarah, It's a deal. And my scar is thanks to an assh*le that was trying to kill me. The Director saved me. So, I owe him too."

Sarah blushed a bit. "I didn't mean to stare...."

Jolene waved her off. "The Director offered to have it fixed with Tschaaa nannite technology, but I turned it down. I think it gives me character."

Sandy took this moment to leave. "Excuse me, Ladies, see you back at the table" Sarah glared a bit at her as she moved her hips more than normal. Jolene grinned after she had exited the Ladies Room.

"You two were about to get into it with each other, weren't you?"

Sarah looked at Jolene. "How could you tell?"

Jolene laughed. "It's been happening with increased regularity. Almost every night, two girls get into a hair pulling contest. Unless it's broken up, they wind up like two alley cats, all scratched, bruised, and bitten, usually sans most of their clothes."

"Any idea why?" The scientist in her asked.

"No, nada." Jolene answered. "I think it's something in the water. Or some other substance that women are exposed to".

Sarah looked at Jolene. "Any desire to scratch my eyes out? "

"Hell No.!" Jolene answered. "I have no desire to fight anyone. I'm looking for loving, not fighting."

The Gathering Storm

Both women laughed. "I'd better get back to my table before that red haired Bitch tries to screw my Husband. See you later, Jolene." Jolene laughed some more and waved goodbye.

Sarah went back to the table. Sandy had not arrived yet. Sarah then saw her at the bar, chatting up a couple of good looking young men. Sarah made a beeline back and sat down next to her husband, grabbed him and kissed him. "My, aren't you feisty tonight." Joseph chuckled. Sarah leaned close and whispered into his ear.

"When we get home, I am going to f*ck your socks off."

She reached under the table and began to rub his crotch under the table. Joseph soon had the proverbial raging hard on. Their food arrived at that time, giving his genitals a reprieve. Sandy came back to the table with her brother and sat down. For the rest of the evening, Joseph noticed a noticed an odd chemistry between Sandy and Sarah. They kept giving each other little smirks, twisting their bodies to display their breasts and bottoms in some type of weird competition. Once, Sandy flashed them both with spread legs, revealing she had no panties on. And, that she was a natural redhead.

Eventually, he whispered to his wife, "Darling, what is going on?"

His wife squeezed his male genitalia under the table. "I'll tell you at home, after you pork me."

During the evening, conversation did include talk about "the good old days", before the Tschaaa appeared. Sam made a rather controversial statement. "Sometimes, I think the Squids coming are going to be a Godsend."

Both Joseph and Sarah stared at him. "How can you say that with the amount of humans that were killed? And the People of Color being turned into menu items?" Sarah was quick to question. She may have controlled her old radicalism, but she wasn't dead.

Sam looked at her in defiance. "How can I say that? Easy. We had a Black President who did more to institute class warfare and divide the nation, after claiming he was the great unifier, than anybody in history. Africans practiced genocide on their own people just because they are of a different tribe. The Cambodians slaughtered a million of their own people in the name of Communism. And I and other so called "white people" lost out on education and jobs due to Affirmative Action because we were blamed for Slavery and Segregation. Hell, I wasn't even born until the Millennium. But somehow it was my fault." He took a slug of his alcoholic drink.

"All of the secularist socialists and atheists were promoting Darwinism and Evolution. Well guess what. The Tschaaa are proof of Darwin's Theory of the Survival of the Fittest, Top of the Food Chain. It's not my fault that the People of Color lost out in the cosmic crap shoot of Evolution, in which the Tschaaa find them tastier than us."

Sarah broke in again." But you lost family and friends. Don't you wish them back?"

Samuel Laughed. "If wishes were horses beggars would ride. Of course I miss my parents, my cousins, my friends. But Darwin won out. Now, we have to make the best of it, and climb back towards the top. Hell, our early ancestors were meals for leopards and hyenas. But we worked past that, began to top them in the 'food chain'. And we will eventually be equal to or on top of the Squids in the food chain again, just as we beat out the all the other predators."

Samuels face was flushed by the end of his speech. Joseph could tell the fresh faced student he had known years ago was long gone.

"Pardon my Brother." Sandy interjected. "He wonders why Jolene and some other women tend to shy away from him. It's because he always carries a soap box around with him."

Samuel waved at his sister in a sign of exasperation and dismissal. "You're like most of the other women. You don't want to admit the unpleasant truth. I need another drink." He stood up and headed towards the bar Jolene was running.

"He is a bit angry, isn't he? "Joseph asked.

Sandy gave a short laugh. "He's just frustrated and self-centered. He is my Twin and I love him, but he seems to want what he can't have. Primarily Jolene. And to change the past to what HE wants." Sandy gave Joseph a bit of a smoldering look. "I know what is obtainable, what isn't. Thus, I'm less frustrated."

Sarah gave Sandy a bit of a glare. "Well, Sandy, sometimes there are obstacles that are greater than you realize."

Both women began to lean in towards each other. Joseph jumped in. "Hey, Sandy, can you suggest some other establishments to visit in the future? My wife and I have some fun time to catch up on." He squeezed his wife's hand.

Sandy saw that and sighed. "Yes Professor. Let me write on this napkin....."

The evening was becoming curiouser and curiouser. Finally, they had eaten, drank and laughed enough. Various men and women kept coming over to strike up a conversation with the Olson twins, all unattached singles. Two young ladies kept glaring at each other as they vied for Sam's attention.

Joseph looked at his watch. "Come on, time to go. I'm about to turn into a pumpkin."

He and Sarah got up to excuse themselves. Surprisingly Sarah and Sandy hugged each other. But then he noticed that they purposefully pressed their breasts together and squeezed each other in a short bear hug, as if checking out the strength of the others body.

After tipping the serving staff handsomely, they left the establishment, waving at the Admiral as he was coordinating something with his staff. Outside they jumped on a Conch Trolley, the most efficient transportation system around. The one addition was two armed guards, one Base personnel, one Conch Republican. They were the result of the Eater Threat. Unfortunately, the Director's Security Forces had been unable to locate any of the other Eaters that had been transported into the mangroves. Then, thanks to their voracious appetite, they had begun to eat the local flora and fauna, and were soon reproducing like rabbits. At least a couple of the Aliens, close to giving birth, had apparently been released. Within a day, there were four young. Then, within a week, four more, with four more on the way. There were few 'gators where they had been dropped, so there were no large predators to compete. The local manatee population, having made a big comeback because of few humans in boats to run over them, began to suffer. More food, more births. Sightings began in the mangroves, and a few were shot and killed. Then a couple of the creatures arrived during the night in downtown Key West, eating a dog and its owner. All Hell broke loose.The two were quickly tracked down and shot, but the damage had been done. No outside security presence meant that few people ventured out. Soon most of the population had a gun, leading to some shooting at shadows and one death from gunshot. The next day, armed trained personnel appeared on the trolleys, as well as on walking patrols and on a couple of jeeps running around.

Joseph and Sarah found a seat towards the back of the trolley in order to be alone. Sarah began messaging Joseph's manhood, and Joseph slid his hand up under her dress. Her panties were already wet with womanly lubrication and she began to moan as he touched her. They kissed deeply, tongues gently dueling. The fifteen minute trip to their quarters seemed to pass in a few moments. The Trolley driver dinged the bell when they reached their quarters, the trolleys allowed on the base with no restrictions. Joseph slipped a tip to him as they exited, the two guards having purposefully ignored he two lovers in the back. They had first floor quarters in what was basically a two bedroom duplex. After some six years living either in a cabin or modified offices on a college campus, this was like a palace. Joseph did not let Sarah reach their bedroom. He unzipped her dress, pulling it over her head. She had a shear black bra holding her 34C breasts. With practiced ease, he unclipped the back bra clasp, and let her bra slip off. She giggled. "You always were good with clasps and hooks."

"It must be my engineering background." her husband said, just before feeding her breast's left nipple into his mouth. As he suckled her breast, she moaned and began to gently scratch the back of his neck.

"Darling, please. Do Me. Now." He scooped her up into his arms and carried her to the marital bed.

∿∿

An hour later, Joseph was spooned up against his wife's luscious backside. Already, the contact was causing warmness in his loins and he began to have another reaction. Damn. It must have been the years of sexual drought that was causing his horniness. Sarah made a nice humming sound of satisfaction as she felt his manhood. She reached back and grabbed his erection, guiding it to just the right spot. Soon, he was gently rocking against his wife s body.

"I love you, Sarah. I always have, I always will." He whispered into her ear.

"I love you, Joseph, my husband." She whispered back. "And, I will tell you now that after tonight, I may be pregnant. My cycle should be in just the right time."

Joseph had thought that might be the case when she refused him the time to put on a condom. Suddenly, he wanted a child by her. He rocked in and out of her, Sarah using her muscles to massage his hard manhood. But she seemed to be slowing the rhythm, to make it last.

"While I have your complete attention, you gorgeous creature, what was going on between you and Sandy?"

"Oh, That. She wanted to fight me for you."

He stopped in mid-motion "What?"

Sarah answered, "I said, and don't stop screwing me, it feels too good, she asked me if I would fight her for you. I said I would. Jolene came in and interrupted the moment. Keep moving, Dearest, I am enjoying the Hell out of this."

Joseph started to move but stopped. "But, you've never had a fight since a couple junior high tussles. Unless you have a secret life."

Sarah moved, quickly turned and pushed him over onto his back. Then she mounted him in a superior position. She began to move, controlling the action.

"There, that's better. Now you can't stop the action. Of course I would fight for you, now. Not only because I love you madly, but something clicked. I wanted to scratch her face, pull her hair, and beat her ass. No red haired Bitch is going to take my man. I'd strip her naked and sit on her until she gave up, maybe pinching her nipples to help her decide."

Joseph saw an odd look in her eye he had never seen before. It was fleeting, but a bit feral. She started to move at a faster rhythm.

"And, if I catch her sniffing around you, I'll punch her in the nose. Now, no more talking unless it's about what I'm doing to you right now. OOOOOooooo, You feel so nice." She leaned over, taking his face in her hands. "I need to make up for all that lost time when I wouldn't f*ck you, Professor. I Love You. Now, let's get going... I mean coming...

∿∿

They laid in each other's arms, finally satiated. Joseph had to admit the image of wife fighting Sandy, naked, was a surprising turn on. He could tell she was getting firm and fit. Sandy's young age would not be an advantage. Sarah, squished up next to Sandy, scratching, clawing, and Sandy screaming in pain....

"Something is growing again. Is there something in the water, Joseph?"

"Could be, my love. Come here one more time....."

Joseph was glad today was Saturday, a day off. He literally screwed himself silly, and his lower regions ached a bit from an unknown number of orgasms. He heard the toilet flush. A moment later a nude Sarah walked from the bathroom, heading back to the bed.

"Hungry?" She asked. Joseph looked at her. Her 34C-24-35, five foot six body was back to its firm, sensual form that had been his wife during their college and early marriage days. His six foot plus lanky frame seemed to offer a unique challenge to her, as she was always trying to climb him like a tree.

He gently smiled.

"Well, are you? A smile is not an answer. I'm famished. Want to join me in the kitchen?"

He stood up silently and walked to her. He bent over and took her face in his hands. "Sarah Ann Broadmore Fassbinder, I love you. Would you marry me? "

She gently removed his right hand and kissed it. "Silly, we are already married. I think I have a copy in the stuff we saved after the Rocks hit."

He looked into her eyes. "No, I want to marry you again. I want to take the vows again. I almost lost you. I want you to know how much I love and need you, especially as we are about to start a family. Please, it can be a small service if you want, just ……"

Sarah began to cry. She threw a bear hug around him and squeezed so hard he was wondering if some of his stuffing would pop out. She kept crying, and he just held on to her, gently stroking her hair. Finally, she stopped. She tried to wipe his eyes with her hands, then turned and found some napkins they had appropriated from the chow hall. She blew her nose, wiped her eyes. "Sorry, those damned waterworks again." She looked up into his eyes. "Joseph

Fassbinder, I will marry you again, anyplace, anytime. I almost lost you. At the time, I didn't know what I had. Now I do. I am alive today because of you. When all those other pinheads friends of mine were arguing about an esoteric point about existence, fairness, and justice, you went out and found food and supplies that kept us alive. No, don't interrupt. I need to finish this."

She took a deep breath. "Just before the Invasion, I was thinking Divorce. I was a goddamned snob, thought you were a dolt holding me back. The Rocks hit, and I went numb. Then I went bitter. I believed the whole Invasion was just to screw up my life, my career. Next the Chief shows up, we come here, I make an ass of myself to the Director, and you leave." A tear ran down her cheek. "I still need to apologize to the Chief. Right now, I need to apologize to you, my dearest. Can you forgive me?"

Joseph thought how lucky he was to get a second chance. He kissed her gently. "Sarah, if you want me to formally accept your apology, then consider it accepted. But it isn't necessary. We have been through Hell. I love you more than life itself. When I heard about the Eater, I realized how close I had come to losing you forever. There is a part of me that only you can fill. So, are you going to marry me, again, or not?"

Sarah kissed him gently. "Yes, my love. I will marry you nude in the town square if you want me to."

Joseph laughed. "That would be interesting, but I want to keep this gorgeous body to myself." Then they were quiet. They kissed long and slowly. Sarah whispered in his ear, "Please make love to me, Joseph. I know I've probably worn you out last night. But, please."

"You are the ultimate aphrodisiac, Dearest Sarah. See?"

She looked at a specific part of his body. "Yes, I see."

He made slow love to her there on the carpet in front of the bed. If asked, they could not answer as to why they did not go back to the marital bed. It just seemed right to do it on the carpet. They reached orgasms at the same time, as they often did, their bodies attuned to each other. Sarah gave a little cry, he a deep guttural moan. Then, they were lying on their sides,. They gently kissed again. "Still want some food, Sarah?" Joseph finally asked.

"Yes, I'll fix it."

"No, you won't. You will take a nice warm shower, or bath, which ever you want. I will then wait on you. I think I may have just given you a child. You need to rest and relax." He gently untangled himself from her and went to the kitchen. Sarah laid there for a few moments. Then, her face broke into a broad grin. "Twins. I will have twins."

"Space, the Final Frontier" Copyright *STAR TREK, the Series.* Gene Rodenberry
Footnote, Chapter Five, "The Great Compromise" by Royal Princess,
Akiko, Free Japan Royal Family.

THE CAPE, FLORIDA

The Space Shot had been postponed a couple of weeks after the first Eater death. Now the launch time was rapidly approaching. A few days after 'The Night', Joseph was up at The Cape, going over last minute details and checks. Andrew had taken on the job of zipping him back and forth on his Falcon. Joseph had asked him why, when the Director had dedicated aircraft.

"My independent evaluation is that it is safer and faster," answered Andrew. "The Director is hard-headed about his autonomy, his independence. He does not like to depend on anyone more than absolutely necessary. Unfortunately, his idea as to what is necessary is not always in congruence with the facts of the situation. I have been directed to let him do what he wants, unless he is about to get himself killed. With you, I have complete autonomy. Thus, you travel with me."

Joseph had to admit that he was getting spoiled flying in the Falcon. He sat in the supposed copilot's seat and watched Andrew fly. The Cyborg had a direct interface with the controls, so he did not need to touch the controls, which had a hand shaped recess where a joystick would have been. A so called normal humanoid would put its hand into the recess. Sensors interfaced with the hand and enabled the pilot to operate the craft based on finger and arm movements. By watching Andrew, he believed he could figure out how to use the hand recess to fly the craft, as long as the craft would interface with his hand.

Before you knew it, they were there. Andrew landed within walking distance of the launch control building. Joseph walked down the small entrance ramp and was met by the Olson Twins. Their genius had been indispensable to getting the so called Space plane ready for launch. Now, it was just seven days until launch. Seven Days. Just seven months ago Joseph was worried about where Sarah and he would find for their next meal. Now, he had finally begun to fill out with lots of good food and exercise. And he was about to take Mans next step into Space.

He had asked Andrew why it was so important that humans used their outdated technology to launch into Space once again. Why not use a Delta or a Falcon?

"Humans must prove to the other Lords that they can be more than just meat. They must do it on their own, with only limited support from Tschaaa or the other species technology. Some Tschaaa think you are the equivalent of a fairly smart parrot. Able to copy what others say and do, but with limited problem solving capabilities."

Joseph had been surprised. "Where did they think we got our aircraft and other machines from? I realize they may seem crude compared to Your Falcons, but they still work."

Andrew answered. "They do not care where your technology came from. Someone else could have left the items. As the Tschaaa discovered on a couple of ruined planets not long after traveling outside their solar system. Everyone is automatically assumed to be inferior to the Tschaaa. Your worth must be proven positively, rather than demonstrated by existing products. Once the Tschaaa get an idea in their heads, it is hard to remove it."

Soon he was in the Launch Control Room, looking over the final plans and details.

"Well, Sam and Sandy, it looks like everything is ready to go. Let's go up the Gantry and check our transportation."

Thankfully, Sam and Sandy were wearing jumpsuits, so Sandy would not be flashing him with her vagina. Even after the night at the restaurant, whenever possible, Sandy wore a dress with no underwear. She seemed extremely over sexed, but her brilliance was such he did not want to force her out of the project. She and her brother were part of his crew, with one former astronaut rounding it out. Former lieutenant Colonel Bettie Bardun had trained in the old Space Shuttle Program When it was cancelled, she managed to finagle a trip on a Russian Space Capsule to the International Space Station, then began training on the Commercial Spaceplane project. The Tschaaa came, and everything went to hell in a handbasket. Bardun had actually survived at the Cape, had been visiting when the Rocks fell. She, some technicians and security personnel had barricaded themselves in the administrative offices, living off of Hurricane Supplies. They made a few forays into the surrounding communities and managed to stay alive and in control of most of the Launch Area. Until Director Lloyd showed up some four years ago. Cape Canaveral was one of the first places he and the Chief had established control over after the Florida Keyes and Miami. A nearby Tschaaa breeding area had been established along the shallows, but they had ignored the Launch Area after a short penetration by a bunch of young Warriors. They harvested a couple of humans, and then took the meat back to the newborns. They never returned. Cattle Country had been established by that time.

Colonel Bardun could have been a sister to the tall female lead in series of sci-fi movies involving a nasty species of aliens with acid for blood. She had been nicknamed "Rip" after the name of the protagonist, but she had never gotten angry over it. A good sense of humor helped keep her alive and relatively sane. And now, she was going back into space.

"Ready for a final interior check before we SEAL her up?" The Colonel asked Joseph.

"Might as well do it. In seven days we make history. Humans...In... Spaaaace..." Joseph was trying to copy the intro to a famous "Muppet" vignette called Pigs in Space, with Miss Piggy and her porcine relatives the astronauts. The Olson twins looked at him with a confused look, Bettie Bardun was old enough to remember and laughed. "I hope you don't think I'm Miss Piggy, Professor."

"Of course not, Colonel. Not only are you not built like her, but she was never a pilot."

"You can say that again." Sandy chimed in. She had been giving the Colonel some once overs lately, almost like she was imagining what was underneath her flight suit, and not bothering Joseph. He wished she would calm her lust. He knew she already had a string of "conquests" among the young males at the Cape. Which was why he was a bit surprised that she was suddenly paying close attention to Colonel Bardun.

They took the elevator up to the Spaceplane perched on top of the equivalent of a giant roman candle. A conventional looking delta winged large aircraft; two new engines perched on top of one another would boost them into orbit after the original large rocket booster kicked them up to the edge of space. The new engines made use of a very dense organic fuel the Tschaaa had literally grown in some of their vats. The energy available was immense compared to human fuel types. This enabled the Space Plane to make do with less on board fuel and thus more space for cargo, in a smaller craft than the Shuttle. Two hours later, after going over the craft with a fine toothed comb, Colonel Bardun had the Launch Technicians SEAL the Spaceplane.

"Well, Lady and Gentlemen, seven days from now we launch. What are you plans, Professor?" The Colonel asked.

"Andrew offered to give me a ride back to Key West for tonight and tomorrow. Anybody else need a lift? I can probably convince Andrew to find space aboard his Falcon."

Bettie Bardun smiled. "Thanks, Professor, but I have no people there, so it would be a wasted trip. I think I'll stay here and relax, review a few procedures for launch."

Sandy piped up. "I'll second that. Care to join me for dinner, Colonel, a girl's night out?"

The tall woman paused, and then answered. "Sure. I haven't been able to do that in years."

Sam frowned at his sister. "Well. I guess I'll find my own entertainment for tonight. Don't keep the Colonel out too late, Sis."

"Don't worry, Brother, we'll be back in quarters at a reasonable time." She gave Bettie a wink and a smile that was a bit confusing. But Bettie shrugged it off. A little bit of relaxation would do her good.

"Okay" said the Professor. "I'll see you all day after tomorrow" He headed out to meet Andrew.

"Well, Colonel, I'm going to change into something a bit more comfortable and frilly. How about you? "

Bettie had to think for a moment. She had a black cocktail dress she had picked up someplace in the last few months, with a few other odds and ends. She wore flight suits or a former USAF Uniform most of the time. Social time was not something she experienced very often these days.

"I have a basic black number that will suffice, I think. We can eat at the All Ranks Club, if that's okay."

"Fine by me." Sandy flashed a big grin. "Meet you at the Club in an hour."

∿∿

An hour later, Bettie was just getting the hang of her high heels after near six years of non-use. She had felt an unusual desire to be as feminine as possible, so that even though she now towered over most men, she wore her black four inch heels. Her smooth, fit and long legs did not need nylons to be attractive. A sheer black bra and matching underwear, items she had forgotten she owned, completed her ensemble. She now felt very desirable and a little bit horny. Bettie then saw Sandy approaching, wearing a dark blue cocktail dress and matching high heels. Her long auburn hair shone from a healthy brushing. Even without the looks of the men, Bettie could see she was classified as 'hot'.

"Well, look at you, Colonel. Aren't you the hot one?" Sandy smiled at her. Bettie blushed a bit.

"This is the first time in ages that I've dressed up in ages. I guess I'm old enough to have been classified as a "Cougar" Pre Strike."

Sandy giggled. "That is an understatement, Colonel. Since it is Girls Night Out, can I call you Bettie?"

"Of course. You're a civilian, so Rank doesn't really apply to you. Just remember whose boss when we are under way."

"Aye aye, Sir." Sandy giggled again and gave her a sharp salute, which surprised Bettie. "Come on, let's hit the bar for a quick drink."

They found a table in the cocktail lounge, turning the heads of the men there. A little feeling of power went through Bettie's mind. She had been so busy, any idea of sex had been suppressed. Now she knew she was still desirable. At the table, a waitress came and got their drink order, giving the two women a sizing once over. As she walked away, Bettie noticed that Sandy was admiring her backside. Sandy saw that Bettie had seen her looking.

"To answer the unasked questions, I like women also, though I usually prefer men."

Bettie shrugged. "Sexual identification didn't matter in the Air Force after they did away with 'Don't Ask, Don't tell'. Just don't get caught screwing a subordinate."

The drinks arrived and they relaxed. They began a little small talk about the Cape, Key West, and recent history. Most people tended steer away from in-depth conversation of Pre-Strike /Pre-Invasion Days, as most had lost family and friends. Sandy and slid her chair out to the near side of the table. She crossed and uncrossed her shapely legs towards Bettie. She looked at Sandy's glorious gams and noticed when Sandy flashed her that she had no panties on.

"Caught you Looking." Sandy said with a sly smile. Then, before Bettie he could respond, Sandy reached out and caressed her thigh. An electric shock went through Bettie. Then she surprised herself by reaching her hand out to Sandy's bare knee.

The younger women smiled at her. "What say we get dinner to go and head to my place?"

"Yes." Which was all that Bettie could answer.

∽∽

Two women wrestled and grappled on the queen-sized bed of the suite. Sandy let out squeals of frustration as Bettie Bardun kept overpowering her nude body. Finally, Bettie was straddling the redhead, pinning her hands near her head. Sandy, breathing hard, glared up at the just under six foot tall woman. "You have to be so Goddamned strong. It's not fair. Are you sure you aren't really a Man?"

Bettie laughed., then bent down and kissed Sandy. Sandy did nothing to resist. She was soon making little noises of pleasure at the back of her throat.

Bettie let go of Sandy's wrists and began to caress Sandy's rather large breasts. Sandy caressed Bettie's firm ass cheeks, running her fingers in between shapely buttocks, Now Bettie moaned.

"You have talented hands, Red." The Colonel said as she felt Sandy's caress her most private parts. "But you can tell I am definitely female."

Sandy giggled. "You're wet. You must like something about me."

"You could say so...." Bettie took Sandy's face in her hands and kissed her deeply, their tongues slowly wrestling with each other. Their mouths finally parted. Sandy looked up into Bettie's eyes. "Screw me, Colonel. Do me any way you can." And Bettie did.

∽∽

An hour later, tall Bettie lay on her back. Her body smelled of sex and sweat, or sex sweat, depending how you looked at it. Sandy was snuggled up against Bettie, her head on Bettie's left shoulder. She was caressing Bettie's left 34C breast with her left hand, turning her nipple into a rock hard pebble.

"So, Colonel. How do I compare with other women you have had?"

Bettie looked down at her. "Honestly, I fooled around once at a sorority function in College. We played a bit of drunken feeling each other up. Nothing was mentioned after that night."

Sandy laughed. "Well, I guess making love to another woman must come naturally to you."

"So, Sandy, how many women have you...slept with."

"Quite a few since coming to Key West. There must be something in the water as I have discovered I am an equal opportunity sex partner. Man, woman doesn't matter, as long as you attract me."

Bettie kissed Sandy's forehead. "So I attract you? Well, you definitely turn me on, the first time a woman has to this extent."

'"Previous love affairs with men, then"

Bettie's face got serious looking. Sandy noticed the change and rose up on her arm so she could look down at her.

"Hey, sorry if I said something wrong. I don't want to ruin the moment."

Bettie smiled at her, then rose up and kissed her. She pushed Sandy onto her back. Before Sandy knew it, Bettie's face was between her thighs. Lips and tongue quickly brought her to an orgasm she had not expected. Bettie leaned over Sandy and took the redhead in her arms. She kissed her, and Sandy wrapped her arms around her and hugged her tight.

"I could love you, Bettie. I hope that doesn't bother you."

Bettie hugged the other woman and kissed her neck. "Sandy, I was in love with a Man, a pilot, when the Squids attacked. He was a Colonel Clifton Hunter. Neither one of us were spring chickens, he had a previous wife and kids. I had put my career first, so my lovers I had were not serious....Until Cliff." She sighed. "He was sent to Area 51 during the first days of the Invasion. That is the last time I heard from him. I assume he is dead, since I imagine he would have tried to contact me by now. My face has been on the boob tube for over a month."

Sandy looked into her eyes. "So why me, then? A big boobed woman, years your junior?"

"Hell, I don't know. Maybe there is something in the air and water. Look it, I can't make promises. This is new to me. To put it bluntly and crudely, I'm used to a large stiff male member between my thighs, not a woman's face."

They kissed passionately. Hands began to squeeze and caress breasts, tongues wrestled for dominance. Bettie was lying between Sandy's thighs before she knew it. She began to thrust against the other woman, with Sandy returning the action

"You play me long time, G.I." Sandy playfully uttered, then bit Bettie's shoulder. Bettie moaned, then bit back…..

Bettie slid up to lay head to head next to her lover. Then, she spoke. "I don't know why, but you do something to me that needed to be done. We have to fly a mission together with me as the Command Pilot. I won't have time to love you. And, you cannot treat me any different. If you can't accept that, you stay behind."

Sandy answered. "You are tough, aren't you? Good. I like strong people, not pushovers. Just do not expect me to ignore it if some dyke starts sniffing around you. I'll mess that woman up."

Bettie, moving quickly, had Sandy pinned to the bed, hands on Sandy's wrists. "This is how we started. Two falls out of three?"

"Oooo, Bettie, you are too damn strong. Sure you aren't transgendered.... OUCH! You bit me!"

KEY WEST, FLORIDA.

Adam Lloyd sat at his office desk, watching the live feed from the Cape. Launch Day. Now, humans made one more relatively crude attempt at spaceflight to Platform One. Buried in it were the remains of the International Space Station. The launch was being broadcast all over North America, and parts of the rest of the world. Ever since they began broadcasting the accomplishments of his Occupation Administration, especially the Space Program, a steady stream of people from the so called Feral Areas, those areas not Occupied or part of the Rebel areas, had begun to move to the Occupied Areas. After some six years of hand to mouth existence, the medical care, food, power, shelter, and amenities like television and the Internet were a huge incentive to "reconnect" with the coastal areas. More ex-technical people, aircraft mechanics, pilots, police, EMTs, you name it, were checking into the major ports up and down both coasts. The Vigilance Committees, small groups of humans under watch by a Robocop that Adam had been setting up the last three years to provide some semblance of control, were now tasked with the inserting and inclusion of the new arrivals into the existing framework, especially categorizing their skills. Already, a dozen pilots and two dozen maintenance types were up at the Former Eglin Air Force Base, working on getting an air fleet together. Other maintenance types were working on vehicles, tanks, heavy equipment, power stations, you name it. A half dozen new medical centers were being brought online. Agricultural crops were being grown in the fertile valleys of Southern California, fruit crops in Florida. Other groups of humans were going along the Gulf of Mexico and salvaging the remains of crops and fruits that had gone wild but still existed. Small areas of Mexico and Central America were also being re-farmed.

With the help of the Tschaaa, manufacturing plants were being set up around San Diego and Los Angeles to produce traditional consumer goods. Others were popping up in Florida, Louisiana, and Texas. And, because of this, people had real jobs again, instead of subsistence living and scavenging. Recycling of usable goods had been increasing during the last three years, adding a basis for expansion. This recycling also helped provide raw materials for new goods to be manufactured. Adam was trying to reopen mines in Mexico, and in small areas in Nevada and Arizona with the help of the Lizards, who thrived in the hot, dry climates. Yuma, Arizona and 29 Palms, California, as well as Area 51 in Nevada, were now the home of Lizard settlements. They were now breeding another generation.

He stretched, and then rubbed his eyes. He had been working long hours the last week, waiting for the Launch. As he took a short break, pouring himself a scotch on the rocks, his thoughts went back to a secure teleconference meeting he had with Lord Neptune some two weeks after the Eater attack on the Base. He had asked His Lordship what had happened at the then recent meeting of all the Lords. His Lordship tentacles seemed to indicate a bit of agitation before he answered.

"My Director, to be honest, the Lord of Africa is…..no more."

"No More? Is that means what I think it means, Your Lordship?"

"I believe so, in that he is now lifeless, recycled into Mother Ocean."

Adam paused, a bit shocked. He did not see the Tschaaa as having Mafia like sensibilities.

"I sense surprise, My Adam. "

"Yes Sir. I did not think that you....summarily executed your own kind."

Lord Neptune gestured resignation. "The first time in centuries, and we have had to terminate the life of a senior Tschaaa. Usually, someone conducting such aberrant behavior would become catatonic after being forced to acknowledge what they have done. Our species does not have a history of lying or espionage. By smuggling those Eaters into your area, he not only committed a form of humanlike spy-craft, he also endangered young Tschaaa. An Eater can be dangerous to an adult, and have preyed on our Young since we first migrated to land on our Home World."

His Lordship displayed rage. His body changed to a dark camouflage, the digits on his social tentacles clenching and unclenching like a human's hand would.

"He endangered the YOUNG. Just to get back at me and my so called' pet' humans. He was either insane or evil. Maybe both." The artificial voice did a bang up job registering humanlike emotion.

His Lordship's body began to shift back to its normal color, a light aqua. He was calming down. "Sorry for the anger, My Director. But to threaten our Young is the ultimate crime."

"Are we affected here, Your Lordship?"

"Actually, the situation and you humans reactions to the loss of a Young One to an Eater forced my fellow Lords to admit that at least Non-Cattle may have Tschaaa like sensibilities and intellect. Your Space Launch will make them recognize your useful abilities even more."

Joseph paused. "Well, Your Lordship, I hope that soon we can have a relationship with the other Lords similar to the one we enjoy with you. But, I must ask.....who takes over Africa?"

"One of my distant Crèche members, Director. I have been tasked with trying to reorganize what is left of the Meat Resources. And, to be completely honest, thanks in part to your efforts of showing what Tschaaa / Human coordinated actions can accomplish, I am now considered what you humans would call the Senior Lord here on Earth."

Joseph smiled. "Congratulations, Your Lordship. But, won't this limit your time you can spend directly with us here on North America?"

"Never, My Director. I have become an expert in what you humans call "delegating authority and responsibility. I am also grooming the Tschaaa you know as El Segundo for additional duties. So, in the very near future, you will also be dealing with him."

"He will have a distinctive Human Voice?"

"Yes, he will create one much as I have. Your vocal chords cannot do our language justice, so it is easier to mechanically synthesize our language into yours in a voice that is understandable and pleasant. I will help him chose a voice that matches his Tschaaa personality. But, I will still spend much time with you, if for no other reason that I obtain a level of intellectual stimulation I have trouble finding with my fellow Tschaaa. Part of that is due to your Alien outlook on things. Part of it due to my outlook having been changed by my contact with you Humans, especially you, My Director."

Adam paused for a moment, thinking. "So, you believe we, an Alien species, are affecting how you think?"

"You, specifically Director, you affect me. Our conversations have enabled me to see an Alien viewpoint. The Lizards did not have that effect on any individual Tschaaa, nor any other race or species we came in contact with. Maybe it is because, on one hand, you are prey. On the other, you are entering into a cooperative relationship, where you assist us and we assist you. Your relationships with your dogs are one of profound affections as well as a symbiotic relationship that is mutually beneficial. That relationship developed over thousands of years. Possibly because our intellects are so much closer to equality, a similar relationship is developing many times faster."

His Lordship signed the Tschaaa equivalent of a shrug. "As some of your Humans say, it is what it is. Now, we must get back to the business at hand. Tell me about how close you are to launching..."

Now, Adam was watching the real-time broadcast from the Cape, listening to Kathy Munroe's commentary.

"In less than fifteen minutes, the first Humans to be launched into Space in quite some time will be headed towards Platform One, a supersized space station. Colonel Bettie Bardun, Commander and Pilot, will guide the Spaceplane to docking with the Platform. Professor Fassbinder has been trained as a Co-Pilot should the Colonel become incapacitated. Mission Specialist Sandy and Samuel Olson round out the crew, and will remain on Platform One for at least a month, assisting in some ongoing projects."

The cameras cut away from the Launch Gantry and focused on Kathy. The sight of her gorgeous face and blonde hair caused a familiar stirring in his loins. Damn, she was pretty. And her sex appeal seemed to reach over the television airways. At least it did to him. Kathy had become The Symbol, the Face of The Future. Even bad things, like the Eaters, seemed less of a problem after she had explained the situation. Her calm demeanor and signature perky smile communicated "Hey, don't worry. Things will be all right. We'll work this out together." The Together was her, the people, Adam as Director, and a behind the scenes Tschaaa Lordship.

Kathy continued. "Twelve other humans, including four Chinese Nationals, are currently residing on Platform One. The Chinese Astronauts have been there since when the Tschaaa first arrived."

No mention of Invasion. That was unspoken. Rather, it was an Arrival, like a train or plane fight. "The Chinese will be returned to Earth when Colonel Barden and Professor Fassbinder bring the Space Plane back to Earth, in about a week or so. They are waiting to be reunited with their Countrymen at the first opportunity."

Actually, it looked like they would stay in Key West and raise families, if they hadn't been dosed with too much radiation. Former Communist China had been broken up into warring municipalities ruled by Warlords. Thus, the chance the Chinese Astronauts could locate any surviving relatives and get to them in one piece was very remote. The huge nuke that had been used to destroy a Chinese Army had irradiated a substantial portion of the Mainland. This, plus the fact their pigment was not that dark, had limited the Harvesting. However, internal strife, Nuclear Winter brought on by the Rocks, as well as the breakdown of central control within a month of the Invasion had reduced to Chinese population down to 500 Million. Still a lot of Chinese, but nowhere near the one and a half Billion former residents of the Celestial Kingdom.

Kathy continued. "The voice in my ear says we are going to cut to live audio feed from Launch Control and the Space Plane Crew."

What followed was an exchange that was fairly mundane in Pre-Strike and Invasion days. But with over six years since the last launch of any spacecraft or satellite, it was like a new experience. Then, the final Countdown began. "20, 19, 18, 17, 16......." Interspaced with comments from both Colonel Bardun and the Launch Control crew notifying each other of actions taken, equipment status. It was "0" and the main thrusters began boosting the whole shebang skyward. The Tschaaa fuel in the pocket boosters led to a quicker and more powerful burn rate, so the complete launch vehicle looked like it had been fast forwarded on a VCR tape or DVD. It appeared as if some of the launch gantry had been damaged due to this additional power and Adam held his breath when he expected to see pieces start flying all over the local area. The structure held together for the most part and Adam began breathing again.

What Adam couldn't know was that Bettie Bardun was trying to adjust to what felt like being hit by a giant fist while on a bucking bronco. "F**K."

She exclaimed, as she tried to adjust to the unexpected thrust and G's. She had visions of the Human designed Spacecraft breaking apart under the extra acceleration. However, as any good engineer will tell you, a "fudge factor" is often built into any design to take into account unforeseen forces and Murphy's Law. The Space Plane and Rocket Boosters held together. Before she knew it, she felt and heard the "Bang" that indicated the first stage had separated off. Much faster than expected, the small second stage booster kicked in, then quickly expended itself. Bettie was on her own now. The unexpected acceleration kicked them into the beginnings of a low orbit without any use of the Space Plane engines. Bettie, recognizing the change in the flight characteristics, quickly overrode the automatic activation of the engines.

The G forces had been reduced so Joseph could now pay attention to what Bettie was doing. Bettie looked like a one legged man in an ass kicking contest, flipping switches, checking gauges, talking to Mission Control. Joseph heard the rising fear in the Mission Control specialist voice when he realized that things were happening a lot faster than planned. Colonel Bardun's voice was cool and calm, like she was in a class room rather in a speeding craft. She turned her head slightly towards Joseph.

"Professor, keep an eye out. We are travelling a lot faster than was expected and I do not want to smash into something we were supposed to be well away from."

She began to use the attitude and steering jets, making sure the craft was adjusted to the correct attitude. Then, they had completed almost a full orbit and could see Platform One.

"Station Control, OSA Spacecraft HOPE approaching from course 100. Do you have me on scope?"

The calm, mostly monotone voice with a slight, odd accent came back. "I have you, Colonel Bardun. Please release control of the craft. I have it." Joseph recognized it as one of the Original Robocops, which had learned modern human Language recently. Grown from proto human DNA, they definitely were very different. They felt a thump, and then the craft seemed to be pulled towards the space station at a leisurely yet straight plot. "Shades of Captain Kirk. A tractor- beam." Bettie exclaimed. Joseph checked on the Olson Twins, located in seats behind them.

"Fine, Professor." Sandy answered. "Are we about to dock with the platform, Professor?" Samuel asked. "Yes, we are. We made the trip a lot faster than expected. That Tschaaa fuel was a Hell of a lot more efficient than anything we have."

The Robocop used the so called tractor-beam to bring the Space Plane into a large docking bay as effortlessly as placing a plate on a table. It seemed so

The Gathering Storm

anti-climactic. Joseph turned to Bettie. "Thanks for saving our asses in the first part of the flight. A lot of pilots would not have reacted so surely."

She shrugged inside her protective suit. "I was just doing my job. It was no big deal."

"Colonel, do not bullsh*t a billsh*tter. It was far from normal. And you handled it just fine."

She smiled. "Oh, all right. I'll accept a complement, Professor. By the way, notice that we have a bit of gravity on board?" At that, Joseph tried moving his arms and noticed the difference from weightlessness.

"By Damn, You're right. So soon."

"They can generate a gravity field, but if you remember our briefings, the Platform has a slight spin on it also." Colonel Bardun hit her intercom connection with the Olson Twins. "Just as a reminder, we have a substantial gravity field as of now. Don't trip and fall, it may hurt. Keep you helmets secured until me make sure the docking bay is pressurized"

About five minutes later, someone knocked on their small airlock door. Sam went in, locked the inner door, and then opened the outer. It was a Gray. The large expressionless eyes scanned Sam. "Humans...please follow. There is air and pressure."

Five minutes later, after letting Mission Control know they had arrived safely and would broadcast more details once they were officially received, the four humans followed the Gray out of the docking area. They had been told one of the Humans would meet them and take them to the so-called "Head Office "to meet the Senior Tschaaa in charge of the Platform. As they proceeded into one of the main corridors that ran thru one of the large "spokes" running from outer to the center of the superstation, Bettie saw a figure approach from the distance. From the outer hull to the center pod area of the Platform was a shade over an American mile. The whole structure looked like the classic Sci Fi Space Station, a huge wheel slowly turning, but had been given a shot of steroids. Over two miles in diameter, with each of the eight spokes having three stories, the available space was stupendous. Slowly the figure approached. An odd and un-expectant feeling of both excitement and fear went through Bettie as she realized who the approaching figure looked like.

"Un-fricking-possible." she said under her breath. Then she heard a voice she had not heard for over six years.

"Welcome Aboard, Bettie Bardun. It is about time you got here."

It was Cliff Hunter. DEAD Cliff Hunter, apparently very much alive. Bettie stopped and froze. Her crewmates almost ran into her, looking at her quizzically. "Anything wrong, Colonel?" Joseph asked.

"Its okay, Professor. She is just trying to get used to seeing a ghost." Cliff

Hunter said.

"Come here and give me hug, Bettie. To Hell with protocol." In one quick motion, she was in his arms. He was only about an inch taller than she, but with huge broad shoulders and chest. Bettie used to kid him about looking like a cartoon character, with huge v shaped chest, chiseled chin and face, slender waist and then a normal set of legs.

Bettie began to tear up. "You Son of a Bitch! You're supposed to be dead."

He laughed. "The stories of my demise have been greatly exaggerated, my dear."

She pulled back enough to look at his face. A few more lines, some hair now white, it was still Cliff.

"Why didn't you tell someone?" Bettie demanded. "You're not even listed among the Human Staff up here."

"Sorry, Darling, I couldn't. I was put on ice, and told that if I pissed off the Lordship in charge here, I would have a quick trip out the airlock. I guessed I got some beings pissed off about how I got here."

He looked at the Professor and the Olson Twins. "Pardon me why I completely destroy any semblance of Good Order and Discipline and kiss the woman who was 'supposed' to be my fiancé." He kissed her deeply, and she automatically responded. It was like they had been apart for six days, not six years.

"Oh shit." Sandy said just loud enough for her brother to hear. Sam smirked. "That's what you get for being the horniest female in the Solar System. Is there anybody you haven't tried to sleep with, Sister?"

She glared at him. "I can't help it. It must something in the damn water."

Sam looked at her, a serious look on his face. "I just worry, Sandy. You were not like this about six months ago."

Sandy took a deep breath, and then let it out. "I'll be okay. I guess I use sex and affection too much as a stress reliever." Sandy pouted. "Another woman, I could deal with. Her old male partner, forget it. I sure hope there is someone on board that wants some variety."

Joseph was purposely trying to not hear that conversation. Everything was way too sexually charged these days.

Bettie and Cliff finally stopped clinching. Bettie tried to wipe her eyes and Cliff provided a clean cloth for her to use. Then, she froze. "Did I hear the word "Fiancé"?

"Oh, almost forgot. I've been carrying this around for some six years." Cliff pulled a small beat up ring case with what looked like dried blood on it from his patched up flight suit. "Here, it's been too long for me to get down on one knee. You can't say no to marrying me."

She glared at him. "How do you know I'm not already hitched, you conceited bastard."

"Good Intelligence. Now, are you going to say Yes, or am I going to have to take this thing back to where I bought it."

It was gorgeous. A huge central rock surrounded by a starburst of others. A ring like this had not been manufactured since the first Rock hit.

She started to cry. "Damn You. I'm in uniform." She heard her shipmates begin to clap. "Congratulations, Colonel." Joseph said. "Now, I hate to be a party poop, but please. Say yes, kiss him, and let's go check in with the powers to be. I have a Broadcast to make." And Bettie did just that.

They slowed their walk to the Central Control Room so that Cliff could explain to Bettie and company how he got to be on Platform One but not be listed officially.

"Well, it started with a launch of our one and only Space Interceptor from Area 51."

He chuckled. "I had been helping test various systems on that craft when the 'balloon went up'. Actually, the Rocks came down." He squeezed his new fiancé's hand. "I couldn't even tell the good Colonel here what I was doing. Need to know crap and all. Anyways, they managed to get what looked like a cross between an SR-71 and one of those spacecraft from a Saturday Morning Cartoon shows up and running. It was Day Seven of the Invasion." A serious look appeared on his face. "It had an experimental pulse generator engine, two to be exact, and we cobbled some weapons onto it. A 30 millimeter cannon from an A-10, two Sidewinders and two AMRAAM air to air missiles, and a tactical suitcase nuke hooked up to a small cruise missile. "

He sighed. "Man, were we rushing around like a Chinese Fire-drill. Before I knew it, I was strapped in doing some half assed systems checks. Then, they told me I had to act as a Delta was approaching the area. We didn't know it was just running a recon flight. They launched me using some Jato rockets, so I got off the ground. Then, a thousand feet up, I fired the engines." He laughed once.

"What a kick in the ass. I managed to get the interceptor pointed straight up and away I went. I was slammed into my seat with I don't know how many G's. Somehow, I managed to shut the engines off after a few moments before I blacked out. After that, I restarted them and used them in small bursts of power by throttling up and down. The engineers had built one Hell of a strong craft or I would have broken apart due to the unexpected power of the two experimental engines."

"Before you knew it, I was in Near Space Orbit. I saw the huge Asteroid that is Base One and decided it made a Hell of a good target because, it was so big even, I would have difficulty in missing it. I used the gyros and maneuver rockets to line up my nose on the target, and then hit my main engines."

"Were you scared?" Samuel interjected.

"Frack Yes. Oops, sorry about my language. Anybody who says that they don't get scared is either a huge liar or else is psychotic. Anyways, there I was hundreds of thousands of feet in altitude, flat on my back, heading towards the Target, No Sh*t."

Bettie jabbed him in his ribs. "Please stay focused. This may be fun for you; it's a shock to me."

"Sorry, Bettie. I haven't had a new audience in years. Anyways, I was lining up, accelerating towards this huge rock when suddenly, some Deltas are in my flight path. They must have launched from Base One as they were crossing my flight path at a near right angle, and did not even see me. Well, I knew it was only a matter of time measured in seconds before someone noticed me. So, I started shooting."

His eyes got a little faraway look to them as he continued. "I hit the thirty mike-mike first as in outer space, there is no air friction to affect the trajectory, just Earth's Gravity, which at my altitude was reduced. I was basically weightless, so the rounds were too. Straight line of shot, over a mile away I hit the first one. Nice, satisfying plume of water shot out as the cockpit was penetrated. Then, the cockpit itself disintegrated, and pieces of craft and Squid are joining the rest of the Space Junk orbiting the Earth."

His voice took on a new intensity. "Other Deltas then began to notice something new was in orbit with them. I was soon the proverbial one Legged Man in an Ass Kicking Contest as I quickly had a target rich environment."

He took in a deep breath, and then let it out. "The Squids had more experience in their craft maneuvering in Space and I was definitely learning as I went. Maneuver jets, vectoring the main engines, using the gyros, I was trying to twist and turn and shoot all at once. I hit two more Deltas with the Thirty, watched as they turned into Space Junk. I hit the gun one more time and it fired a couple of rounds and quit. I hit a Delta with at least one round as it started to leak water from the cockpit system into space. It broke off the attack on me, but was quickly replaced with another, that started firing rounds at me."

He squeezed Bettie's hand again. "I cooked off one of the sidewinders and the damn Delta started tracking it instead of me. Found out later that the Squids and their systems latch on to whatever is travelling fastest or maneuvering sharpest, as predators like T-Rex apparently did. So, I cooked off the second Sidewinder, that tried to track the ambient heat the Delta still had from its maneuvering rockets and from its recent launch from a heated launch pad. Its maneuver fins were worthless in airless space, but its gyro and the missile vectoring engine trying to jerk it around caused it to kind of skid towards the Delta. Once its internal brain said, 'Oops going to miss,' it self-

The Gathering Storm

detonated. That peppered the Delta with some debris, but also threw some in my direction also. So, I almost shot myself down. One decent chunk cracked the Deltas cockpit, releasing more frozen water in Earth Orbit."

"The Squid Pilot must have been pissed as he turned towards me and started shooting. So I launched an AMRAAM Missile at him. They have directional engine thrust so it was able to maneuver towards the Delta after I skidded my nose to point in the general direction. The Delta fired at it at point blank range, so when the warhead exploded, it shattered the cockpit and nose cone. I saw the Squid in its cockpit seat zip by me. Then I took more hits from shrapnel. My cockpit was holed, but since I was in a suit, I still had pressure and oxygen. The straps in my seat held me in. The Interceptor held together, and I tried to line up on the Asteroid again."

He paused and swallowed. "I could use a beer right now. Well, more Deltas' came at me. I fired my last missile, armed the cruise missile with the nuke, and pushed the throttles forward."

Cliff paused. Everyone kept slowly walking.

"Something hit my spacecraft and it came apart. I remember trying to eject, blacked out, then was floating in space. I saw a Delta tumbling end over end nearby, spewing the water atmosphere of the cockpit out in every direction, then it smashed into another one and they both started tumbling towards Earth's atmosphere. I said a prayer and began to enjoy the view as I knew my air would run out before I was pulled into the atmosphere. And swore because I couldn't leave Bettie here a note that 'I Love You."

Bettie swallowed hard and tried not to tear up.

"What happened?" Sandy asked.

"A large Falcon spacecraft latched onto me and pulled me in. The Robocop piloting the Falcon was one belonging to his Lordship Neptune. He grabbed me and pulled me in on direct orders of the Lordship. I wound up on board of Base One with the Four Chinese Astronauts. And, because I had destroyed at least five Deltas, my existence was hushed up. His Lordship, being a student of human nature, knew he needed another hero like Captain Bender stirring up resistance like he needed four more arms."

"Captain Bender?" Joseph asked.

"A young pilot who took down three Tschaaa craft, including a Falcon, near San Diego and died." Cliff answered. Then he continued.

"The nuke warhead on the missile did not go off, so no major damage was done to Base One. I and the Chinese were told, after over a week of isolation, we could cooperate, not cause problems, or be slaughtered and eaten."

He took another deep breath of air and let it out. "I figured if I stayed alive long enough, I might be able to help with human survival. So, here I am, six years later. "

Bettie squeezed his hand. "Glad you are."

"Well," Joseph said, "I've learned that the Tschaaa rarely do things without a reason. So, I bet you I will get some special directions when I talk to the Director about you, Colonel Hunter. Let's head into the main control room and have a talk with the powers that be and the Director, shall we?"

Bettie looked at Cliff. "If you can't come back to Earth, I'm staying here. I take it you have been exercising under Earth G in case you can go back?"

"Affirmative. Between the slow spin and the artificial gravity field on most of this station, I think I've been able to keep my bone and muscle mass up. But like they say, nothing is like the real thing."

He put his arms around Bettie one more time and gave her one more a hug. "Damn, you feel good. Now, let's go meet the Wizard."

The Tschaaa Lord in charge of the station was younger than Lord Neptune. Cliff had called him the Wizard, after the character in the Oz books, a nickname he had come up with because he was always behind a curtain of bulkheads and doorways in the central section of Platform One. He communicated through Grays and Robos, or occasionally as a disembodied voice. Like his Lordship in Key West, he had created a human sounding voice to emanate from his translator. This voice sounded like a plain Mid West Talking Head Broadcasters voice from the 1980's. Plain, clear, easy to understand. No apparent emotion. But, surprise of surprises, the Wizard came from behind his curtain. He lounged in a large sling like hammock affair, his eight arms hanging down loose, suspended about twelve feet in the air so the Humans had to look up at him. He was of average size, and the Humans would be hard pressed to differentiate him from other Squids.

"Welcome Aboard, Humans. Colonel Bardun? You are female, yes? You have definitely accomplished a great achievement for other Human Females to follow. His Lordship in Key West sends his congratulations. I add my congratulations. The idea of piloting such a crude craft from the atmosphere into space gives me a feeling of consternation."

"Professor Joseph, I have a direct secure line to your Lordship. Just go to that large console the Gray is standing at."

"Thank You, Lordship." A nervous Joseph said. He still felt very uneasy anywhere near a Squid. He walked towards the console."

"Colonel Hunter, I will tell you one thing the Lordship in Key West will tell the Professor. You will be headed back on the Spaceplane in about one Earth week. To say that I will be sorry that you are leaving would be a falsehood, something we Tschaaa, unlike Humans, have trouble uttering." The Wizard paused, then continued. He held his tentacles loose, not using them to sign any emotions or message. "One of the Tschaaa pilots you destroyed six years ago shared both Birth Mother and Sire with me, though a more recent birth group. That did not make me happy."

Cliff replied "Well, your Lordship, I would be lying if I said I was sorry that I sent your relative to the Great Ocean for disposal."

Bettie froze. What the Hell was he trying to do? Get himself Spaced, now, after seeing her?

But the Tschaaa lord did not react at all. "I respect you as a Warrior, Colonel. That is why you were not Harvested and Eaten. Though, I have heard you would be tough and bitter tasting had I eaten you."

The Tschaaa paused, and then continued. "The two Olson Twins will remain here for at least one Earth month to help the human scientists, as well as our own, on various space engineering related projects. I expect good things from you. Please do not waste time, air or resources here on Platform One."

"Yes, your Lordship" Sandy and Samuel answered in unison.

"I see the Professor is done with his conversation with Earth. So, the Colonel is returning with the Space Plane, yes?"

"Yes, your Lordship. And I will be helping you with the examination of a couple of craft you have here. After we get the study set up, Sandy and Samuel Olson will be doing most of the hard work on this project. I expect they will learn and accomplish much."

The Tschaaa Lord shifted his body slightly. "Good. Now, I will allow you humans to depart to you living quarters. Tomorrow, you will all begin helping the personnel on this station. "

Joseph saw Cliff give him a slight tilt of his head towards a side exit, guessed they had just been dismissed.

"Thank you, Lordship." He turned and walked towards where Cliff had indicated, the other Humans quickly catching on.

The exit led directly into what had been the International Space Station, with a couple of large compartments added. Cliff began giving them the Cooks Tour. "Here is where we sleep, bathe, eat, crap, and do whatever we Humans do when not working with the Tschaaa."

Joseph interjected. "Is the ....Wizard always so... vibrant? "

Cliff laughed. "To say he exudes the enthusiasm of a rock is an overstatement. Just imagine having to put up with this for six years. Anyways, over there in that added compartment are sleeping quarters for you. There is functioning airplane type toilets thanks to the gravity provided. The other large added compartment is the kitchen, dining and social recreation area. We are provided with an odd assortment of food, whatever an occasional Falcon brings up, plus a food synthesizer that produces soup- like and tofu- like foods. The soups are not bad; the fake tofu is not edible in my humble opinion. But, it will keep you alive."

He then took them into a part of the original Space Station. "That area is my crib. It's cozy enough for me. I've managed to scrounge a lot of stuff, including a few books that somehow made it up the Gravity Well. And a Tschaaa version of a Laptop, which is actually quite fun to use."

"So, Cliff, just how is this place set up, Vis a Vis the other Humans and the Tschaaa?" Joseph asked.

"Well, Professor, we work primarily with Lizards, Grays, an occasional Robo and on line with the Tschaaa. The Tschaaa give us general instructions, or a project or idea they want us to work on. We then run with it. The Tschaaa soon realized that we could come up with a lot more original ideas than they could. The Lizards are brilliant, but slow and methodical. The Grays are just plain weird."

He shook his head. "If they are told to do something, they will do it or die trying. I do not know if they have a true sense of individual self. They can talk and reason, but sometimes it seems like they are working off a collective type brain. They do not show emotions. Believe it or not, Lizards show emotion, once you know how to read their expressions and body language. They have a very droll sense of humor."

"We humans are divided into two groups. Us Old Hands , the Originals, the four Chinese Astronauts and myself, all taken into captivity within the first couple of weeks. The four Chinese are pair bounded, two women, and two men. Then, two years ago, fourteen volunteers showed up. Director Lloyd and the Tschaaa selected these people out of a group scientists that had jumped at the chance to go into Space, Tschaaa control or no Tschaaa control. Twelve still remain alive."

What do you mean, still alive?" Bettie interjected.

"Well, Honey, one committed suicide two months after getting up here to Platform One. This was built in the first year post Strike, with me and the Chinese helping with the design. We lived on the Asteroid Base before that, with the families that produce Robocops; modified Gigantopithicus and Homo erectus that are Near Human. And I emphasize the word "Near". They sometimes seem to think a bit differently than we do, though it is hard to explain. "

"Anyways, back to the two casualties... one, a man, committed suicide by a large overdose of a synthetic painkiller he was working on. Apparently the stress got to him. The other, a woman, died a year ago. She was caught trying to sabotage the Tschaaa living quarters with some biological agent. The Wizard had her hacked to death by a couple Young Warriors as we humans watched."

There were sharp intakes of breaths from the four new arrivals.

Cliff shrugged. "Hey, this may sound crass, but we are still basically at war. You get caught as a saboteur or as a spy, you die, just like in past human wars. Her death let us know that if we got caught, screwing something up on purpose, we were next."

Bettie stared at him "Then why were you baiting that Tschaaa Lord? Arguing with them like that seems like a good way to get a quick trip out the airlock."

Cliff laughed "Oh, That. We have been talking like that for almost six years. I am like a spirited horse or dog to him. He likes the fact that I make him think sometimes." A serious look appeared on his face. "But while we are on a serious subject, do not forget one important fact. To His Lordship in Key West and the Tschaaa he has influence over, we are seen as pets or useful beasts of burden, maybe even the equivalent of a Military Working Dog. But, no matter what we are seen as, the bottom line is that we are expendable. Cause too many problems straight up, you wind up as Meat. Thus, all of us here do enough to stay alive, and try not to do anything that may hurt another human. The Tschaaa do not seem to worry about us plotting a revolution. I know they listen in on us periodically, even when we are cursing them. But they seem so sure of their position of power that short of trying to build a secret nuke; they let us accomplish our assigned tasks in whatever way we want."

Cliff sighed. "It is not easy for an old soldier like me *not* to fight them, to go out with a blaze of glory. But I decided after seeing what happened the first month or so, that I could be cannon fodder now, or work to help humans survive until things get better. Until the day a Moses comes, says 'Let My People Go,' splits the Red Sea, and leads us out of bondage. As unrealistic as it may seem, I chose the latter."

"Hope." Bettie said.

"Come again?" Joseph asked.

"Hope. That is how our Space Plane got its name. Hope for a better future for us, and maybe later those Humans classified as Cattle. I came up with the name. The Director approved it."

Cliff smiled at her warmly. "That's why I love you. You're definitely a thinker and a romantic, all rolled up into one."

"One last little set of factoids." Cliff continued. "Over the last six years, the Squids have been sweeping the various Earth Orbits of all the Space Junk. Dead satellites, pieces of rocket boosters, dropped wrenches and hammers from various space walks, pieces of asteroids caught in Earth's gravity well. Guess what they did to all that stuff?"

"Boosted it towards the Sun?" Asked Sandy.

"Naw, that would be a waste of a resource. Any others? Okay, they brought them to Base One, melted and welded them together, and have these objects sitting by the Mass Drivers on Base One. So, if they want to, the Tschaaa have a batch of Rocks to sling at us. We have another Nuclear Winter if they ever do it. I don't think they would do that because it would affect their Breeding Crèches. But they could sure smash a few population centers as a reminder to not piss them off. So, we have a Sword of Damocles above our heads. Well, not our heads, because we are up here, but everyone else's."

Cliff then flashed a smile. "Come on, let's get you settled."

Some three hours later, the four new arrivals had their cubicles and sleeping areas set up. Sandy and Samuel took a little more time getting settled in as they would be remaining for at least a month. Cliff grabbed Bettie's gear and stowed in his quarters.

"I can rig another hammock for you, or we sleep on the floor. On the floor, we can wrap around each other, though I don't have a lot of padding."

Bettie slyly smiled at him. "You forget I'm a pilot also. And what are aircrew good at? Scrounging."

She quickly pulled two plastic wrapped bundles out of her equipment bag, and threw on to Cliff.

"Air mattresses. How did you think about packing two? Plan on finding a boyfriend?"

Bettie blushed a bit. "Actually, since we are alone, I and Sandy had a little.... something going on Very recently. I know, don't screw in the office pool. It just...happened. And, a lot of women seem to be at a level of horniness only seen in cheap porn movies."

Cliff looked at her. "I didn't realize you were, you know, interested in other women."

"I wasn't. It just happened. Literally. One minute, I am straighter than straight, trying to remember what your male member looked like, then I'm playing around with her naughty bits."

Cliff's brow furrowed. "Hmmm. I have something to show you in the labs later. The Tschaaa have us working on some human biology experiments that seem fairly benign. Now, I wonder..."

Bettie blushed more. "Are you...angry?"

Cliff stepped forward and kissed her "I can tell you still find me hot. And you love me. And I love you. We were supposed to both be dead. We are not. Now, we can at least try to start where we left off. Though it will be on an air mattress rather than a Queen-sized bed."

Bettie grabbed him and hugged him as tightly as she could. "Damn, woman. What have you been doing, power lifting?" Cliff hugged her back, but definitely not as tightly.

The Gathering Storm

Bettie slowly let up on her squeeze. Then, she looked him in the face. "I thought I was dreaming when I saw you. I grieved when, after a year, I had not heard about you. I was sure you were dead. And I was surviving hand to mouth until about two years ago, when the Director and his people first showed up at the Cape. We have been slowly building ever since. Now, I am here."

She kissed him slowly, nibbling on his mouth. He kissed her back, and then kissed her throat, her neck. Bettie began to breathe harder. She ran her long fingers through his hair as he kissed and nuzzled her like he had done six years ago. Finally, she slowly pushed him back.

"One moment, please darling. I think we have a little while for personal time."

With practiced ease she unzipped her flight suit. Underneath were OD green panties and bra. Nor exactly Victoria's Secrets, but to Cliff they were the sexist things he had ever seen,

"Still remember how to unhook a bra?"

"I think so, Bettie. If not I know you will help me."

"Darling Cliff, I will help you with anything you want."

"Anything?" He said with a bit of a leer.

Before he knew it, she had shucked her bra, her still firm breasts and hard nipples pointing at him.

"Guess." She answered.

About a half hour later, they were laying on their flight suits on the hard floor. Bettie had her head on Cliff's large chest. She felt like she was in a dream, She suddenly pinched herself, hard. "Ouch." Bettie Exclaimed.

"What are you doing?" Cliff asked.

"Pinching myself." Bettie answered. "I had to make sure this wasn't just a dream. '

"It's real enough, alright. What is going to be dreamlike is when I travel back to Earth with you."

Bettie kissed his chest. "I'll get you there. And I am sure I can help you find something to do."

Cliff frowned a bit. "What if I want to go to the Unoccupied States?"

Bettie raised herself up on her left arm. "I don't know. The Director says everyone is free to leave within the first 24 hours after they arrive. After that, he reserves veto power, though I have not heard of him stopping anybody. "

"Would he tell people if someone left?"

"I think so. The odd thing is that neither the Tschaaa Lordship nor he makes any attempt to hide things from us. He allows people outside the Tschaaa Controlled areas to hack into the New Internet. He has provided medical treatment to people who just showed up from the Feral Areas, then let them leave. I saw that happen more than once when he took control of the Cape."

"He hasn't tried to take out the Unoccupied States?"

"No, Cliff. Even after quite a few assassination attempts. The last one was close, too. "

Cliff looked at her. "What about Cattle Country? "

Bettie sighed. "Yes, he helps keep the people designated as Meat contained. I know that he looks at it as the lesser of two evils. The alternative is that everyone is put on the menu. "

"What do you think, Bettie?"

She paused. She had to admit to herself that this was a subject she tried not to think about.

"Cliff, the idea that another Human Being is being eaten makes me ill. But, I will have to admit that I am not ready to try a suicide mission to stop it. Because that is what it would be, a suicide mission. I know that as a military member, I should have resisted to the end. But, after everything fell apart, and I had no real way to carry on a war against occupation, I was just trying to stay alive. The Director showed up, figured out who I was, and offered me a job and a chance to travel back into Space. I took it. Is that selfish? Yes. But, someday I hope I am in a position to help those people who are still menu items."

Cliff looked at her. Then kissed her. "Well, I guess all we can do is what I have been doing for the last six years. One Day At A time."

He stood up. "Come on, I think we need to get back with the others and try to put a meal together. Then some good sleep. Ole Mr. Wizard is a hard task master. He'll keep us busy until we leave. I just hope the Olson's know what they are getting into by volunteering to stay here for at least a month."

KEY WEST, FLORIDA

Adam Lloyd had sat quietly after talking with Professor Fassbinder. The short conversation after the arrival of the Spaceplane at its destination had been broadcast live, with Kathy doing the Intro and Exit. He had congratulated the crew on their achievement, mentioned in passing that one of the more permanent human occupants of the Platform would be returning to Earth, swapping out with the Olson Twins. But he mentioned no name. Adam had been told by his Lordship the week before about Cliff Hunter and how he got there. He was beginning to realize that, although the Tschaaa had a cultural aversion against outright lying, his Lordship had developed a good ability to remain silent about something until he was ready to reveal it. Almost like a form of purposeful ignorance. If he did not admit to it, it did not exist yet.

Adam stood and stretched. He was going to head to the gym in about an hour for a work out with Heidi Faust, the former Coastie. She definitely demonstrated an excellent working knowledge's of all things that were martial arts. She had begun giving him quite the work out in Filipino Knife Fighting, Eskrima. He had soon found that Heidi had a level of aggressiveness and strength beyond any normal human her size, especially most women he had known. She had shown him some tricks with a balisong folding knife that were a blur when she did them.

His radiophone pinged. "Director here."

"Director Lloyd" It was Andrew. "I will be in your office in ten minutes. The Lordship wishes to speak to you on a secure line. "

"Fine, I'll be here."

The Tschaaa Lord had provided a recorded message for the successful Spaceplane mission that was played as if it were live at the end of the live broadcast between Adam and Professor Fassbinder's. Now, he wanted to talk to Adam, subject unknown. He sighed. Dealing with the subject of Colonel Hunter was enough of a pain in the ass; Adam did not need any further unforeseen complications.

Right at the ten minute mark, he heard Andrew saying hello to Mary Lou in the outer office. She did not bother to buzz Adam as she knew that if Andrew showed up, Adam was expecting him.

The very large Cyborg, part man part mechanical entity called a Robocop by most, walked effortlessly into the office. The original movie character thumped around. Andrew could walk stealthily in a gliding fashion that belied his 400 pound weight.

"Good Day, Director"

"Good Day, Andrew."

Andrew produced the well- known combination handset and screen from a concealed location in his frame. Adam took it and said, "Adam here."

"My Director. How are you today? And such a glorious day it is." His Lordship was in one of his very enthusiastic moods. "The Spaceplane mission has shown what humans can do, after recovering from much destruction some six years ago. My fellow Lordships are pleasantly surprised. And, since the unfortunate forced demise of the African Lordship, I have been able to convince them to follow my lead more each day. Much of this is due to your direct efforts."

"Thank You, Sir, but I am your simple servant just doing what you wish."

"Oh pashaw, as some of your old movie characters would say." Lordship Neptune answered.

"You have taken a small idea from me and woven it into a successful mission. There are positive results from your efforts and successful space project. I have been given complete control of all manufacturing resources. My new Soldier class individuals will be grown in large vats at the San Diego/Baja California Complex, at least one being delivered for service each day, with new weapons to match. Other vats are being set up around Earth. And, I have been given control of the manufacturing and organic growth resources aboard Base One. Six new Robocops, as you call them, are being finished from some human stock from Europe, and six from America. Finally, new Deltas and Falcons are being scheduled for manufacture, along with new weapons that have been developed. With the help of you humans, new interstellar craft will be developed and built to replace the inefficient Generational Ships we use now." Adam could tell by the actions of Lord Neptune's tentacles that he was very happy.

"Our participation has that much of an effect, Your Lordship?"

The Tschaaa Lord did the equivalent of a chortle. "Yes. As I have said before, many of my fellow Tschaaa have become lazy and stagnant in their thinking. Because of my success, and you humans continuing success, and because many Lords are so lazy, they are willing to let me, with you hHumans, perform what you, my Director, would refer to as the 'heavy lifting'."

Adam smiled. "I hope this will help in the continual survival of my fellow Humans."

"Of Course, Director Lloyd. You and your fellows are rapidly becoming an essential part of the continual healthy existence of the Tschaaa species on this planet. There is an increasing belief that the Earth Mother Ocean is somehow directly connected with our original Mother Ocean at our home world. I do not concern myself with such theological discussions, and I do not see how here could be an actual connection. But, I have to admit that I have no explanation as to how your giant squid creatures developed so closely parallel to us, and even larger in size. As well, your seas and oceans seem to support our way of life even better than our original Mother Ocean. This despite the so-called pollution and abuse you humans did to the liquid environment."

Adam stopped and thought for a moment. His Lordship, having known Adam for some five years, could tell he was considering whether to ask something.

"Go ahead and ask your question, my Director. You cannot anger or offend me. Thanks to our relationship, I am on the top of the world."

Well, here goes. "Your Lordship, with the increases in technology and biological sciences since your arrival, is there a chance that.... someday; you may be able to produce sufficient Dark Meat artificially, in tanks and vats, of sufficient quality that another human will not be Harvested?"

His Lordship signed compassion. "Your concern for your yet unborn Young does credit to your species. There is always that possibility. Some of your human scientists on Platform One are involved in some experiments that may bear results helpful to achieving that result. But, I must be truthful. My fellow Tschaaa have been addicted to fresh meat for millennia and may not accept a replacement, unless it is indistinguishable from the original."

Adam continued. "Speaking of the Humans on Platform One, are there any... restrictions concerning Colonel Hunter?"

His Lordship paused. "I am sorry I could not inform you about him before. Colonel Hunter was almost successful in attacking Base One some six years ago, shooting down several of our Deltas. One was piloted by an offspring of mine"

"Please accept my condolences, Lord Neptune."

The Tschaaa waved his tentacle in dismissal. "She died as a Warrior, one of a minority of female Tschaaa that became a successful warrior. She served and died with honor. And the Colonel Hunter was a worthy opponent. Now, that is what you humans call 'ancient history'. And, to answer your question, you may utilize the Colonel in any way that is productive in achieving your aims. But, with one restriction.......please keep him away from any armed Space Interceptors you may have hidden away."

Adam laughed, and his Lordship signed amusement. "Of Course, Your Lordship. "

"But, my Director, Colonel Hunter may be....distracted from doing anything complicated. You see, he is a Pair Mate with your Spaceplane pilot, Colonel Bardun. "

Adam was surprised. "They are... a couple, as we humans would say? How did you discover that when he has been incommunicado for some six years?"

"Ah, I must keep my secrets. And now, Adam, I must go. With my new power and authority come new responsibilities. Again, congratulations and thank you for your efforts. I will talk to you later."

Adam signed off and handed the communicator back to Andrew. "Well, Andrew, I must ask.... did you know about the Colonel?"

"Yes. He is in the Tschaaa data bases. But no mention has been made over clear air communication."

"Hmmmm... Now I must find a position for him."

"If I may suggest, Director, how about Space Plane Pilot? You really only have one experienced one. And, a mated pair will work hard for their continued survival."

"Very true, Andrew. "

"Now, please excuse me, Director. His Lordship has some other tasks for me."

"One of the concepts that seems to attract and fascinate historians of all types, from armchair to Chairs of University Departments, is the apparent congruence and confluence of many of the main characters and participants in what we now call the Infestation and the Great Compromise. By some trick or quirk of fate, the working of the Universe, or some invisible hand we have yet to discover, individuals with positions of extreme importance in how things progressed seemed to be destined to come in contact with each other at just the right time, under just the right circumstances. For this was destined to be their future, but is now our realty. One such incident involved two of the central characters instrumental in the future Great Compromise. Who could have foreseen the wide reaching ramifications from the meeting of Torbin Bender and the then Abigail Young, the Avenging Angel, my dear friend?"

Excerpts from the Literary Works of Princess Akiko,
Free Japan Royal Family.

UNOCCUPIED STATES OF AMERICA, WYOMING/UTAH BORDER

While the Director et al were dealing with the Space Shot and its aftermath, Torbin Bender was dealing with a dangerous situation that was rapidly turning to shit. He was with 40 Assault troops he was training for S Day. Malmstrom Operations Base had gotten a panicked hotline telephone call from Evanston, Wyoming near the Utah/Wyoming border that they were under attack. Then, dead silence. Torbin and his unit had been patrolling for Eaters and Krakens around the Montana/Idaho Border, using the limited mission as a way to shake out the Assault Unit Members, see who worked together the best for the final Twelve plus Two. The Base called them and directed them to respond to the town. The Unit had already intercepted three Krakens trying to use motorcycles on backroads to infiltrate. A short chase and about a dozen rounds fired, there were three dead Krakens. Then they had received the relayed cry for help, "Eaters", and they responded.

They hauled ass down the roads and highways in their Humvees to Evanston and found..... No one. According to information based on a limited census conducted some five years ago, there should have been some one thousand men, women, and children. They had guns and other arms, so they were not push overs. However as Torbin and his personnel entered the town, they found nothing moving. They slowly drove down a main street, scanning the sides. Nothing moved, not even a dog, a cat or a rat. Information from the Tschaaa said that Eaters very rarely attacked in anything larger than a pair. Yet, where was everyone?

Just after they stopped, turned off engines to listen and dismounted, they heard a large scrabbling, running sound, like a bunch of goats hauling ass on pavement.

"What the...." Torbin began to say.

The Eaters seemed to come from every direction. None had the distended stomach of a recent meal; some had the beginnings of the two buds that signaled that two more creatures were on the way. There were dozens.

"360 perimeter. FIRE AT WILL." Torbin yelled, and began firing his assault weapon at one target after another. A couple of Ma Deuces opened up, as well as a M240 Medium Machine Gun. A Mark 19 began shooting 40 Mike Mike grenades into the buildings along the side of the street from which the Eaters were exploding. Torbin fired at one rushing at him, stitching rounds thru both large eyes. The Eaters legs collapsed and the creature pancaked as rounds penetrated to what passed as a brain. He fired at the second Eater that passed into his sight area, putting it down like the first. Next a third. Then a fourth. His weapon went dry.

"Reloading." He yelled, swapping for a new mag. Another Eater was almost on top of him.

Several Shotgun blasts from a drum fed Saiga semi auto twelve gauge, courtesy of the Russians, tore the guts and so called brains from the Eater. It collapsed sideways, and Torbin jumped back, managed to dodge the corrosive stomach acids which were splashed from the ripped intestines.

"Thanks, Sergeant Washington."

"Aim to Please, Captain." Sergeant Washington was the only African American going through the training. Thanks to the Protocols of Survival Harvesting, there just were not many People of Color who made it to the USA. Not to mention with the physical attributes and experience to have made the first cut.

Torbin heard some screams that told him they were taking casualties. He kept firing.

He cut the legs out from under another Eater, which then tried to use its arms to crawl towards him. Torbin fired a single round through each eye, and it finally stopped. The Mad Minute was over. It was quiet, except for the sound of moaning and cries of pain from the troops.

"Gunny. Status Report!" Torbin commanded.

Gunnery Sergeant Greg Smith, late of the U.S. Marine Corps, began a head count. Right then Corporal Black, manning a Ma Deuce on the front Humvee, called out. "Contact, twelve o'clock, 100 meters."

"What've got?" Torbin asked.

"Two Eaters just entered the street, look like they're facing this way. Wait, now one is taking off. The other is headed straight towards us."

"Take it out, Corporal."

"Yes Sir" A couple moments later, a single round of fifty caliber between the eyes flattened the Eater.

"Well Done, Corporal Black."

"Thank You, Sir."

"Gunny. Got the numbers?"

"Yes, Captain. 10 casualties, seven minor, one serious..... Two dead, Sir. Sorry."

'F&*k', Torbin thought. He had lost men before, which could happen when going into Harm's Way. But this had been entirely unexpected. He had lost men to wild animals.

"All Right Troops, Listen Up. I screwed up, underestimated the enemy. That ends now. Everything gets checked out by the numbers. Stay Frosty. Understand?"

"OORAH." Was the response. They realized lessons of the deaths would ensure it did not happen again. Just then, Torbin could have sworn he heard a cry for help.

"Captain. Up there. The steeple of that church, where the bell is."

He looked up, and then grabbed his binocs. "Well I'll be damned. Survivors."

Torbin saw thru his binocs a single adult female, and what appeared to be three children.

"Corporal Tatupu, take a squad and rescue those civilians."

"Yes Sir." Corporal Tapua Tatupu was a huge American Samoan, noted for his unnatural strength. He took a look at his rifle, which looked small in his hands. He laid it in the back of a Humvee, and grabbed the M60E1 they had brought along as spare firepower. He threw a couple of ammunition belts across his chest, al la Pancho Villa style, then yelled out.

"Squad One. On Me. Assault formation. Let's go."

The Corporal and Ten Troops quickly made their way to the large double door entrance of the church. A large building, the Church was also fairly old, apparently having been part of the original town. The Troops lined up, breached the doors, and went in by the numbers, the Corporal in front. The M60 boomed. Then silence.

"One Eater Down. You and You. Get up those stairs and get the civilians."

"Yes, Corporal."

In five minutes, the woman and three children were down in front of the Church, the EMT checking them for injury. The soldiers also brought out a very injured male, his right arm severely burned from what looked like Eater stomach juices.

"Sir, the Lady said the man here was jumped by an Eater that tried to eat his arm. He managed to blow its brains out, but received some stomach acid for his efforts." Corporal Tatupu reported.

"I think this is a good time for a chopper dust off." Torbin replied.

"Private Hagel. I need the Tactical Radio."

"Here Sir." Torbin took the handset of the backpack radio, a modification that tried to bounce waves off of both cell towers, of which some had been repaired, as well as bounce messages off of the ionosphere.

Torbin soon had Malmstrom Security Control on the line.

"Yes, that's affirmative. Need chopper support for four civilian survivors, one serious injury civilian, one serious military, and one moderate military. Yes, ASAP. Roger. Over and out. "

He walked up the civilian woman, a 30 something five foot and a half frontier type that was still attractive in her disheveled state. Her hair was pulled back in a ponytail, and she was helping the three children, ages six to twelve, drink from water canteens.

"Ma'am, excuse me "

She looked at Torbin and smiled. "No need to stand on ceremony, Captain. Just tell me what I need to do. You just saved me and three children."

She continued. "My name is Heather O'Hara, Teacher and Librarian of this town. Anything I need to do, just tell me."

Torbin saw she had the frontier toughness of two centuries ago, when the American People were expanding Westward. She also had a lever action rifle in her left hand.

"Well, Ms. O'Hara...oh, okay, Heather, two helicopters should be here in about an hour to airlift you, the children and the gentleman to Malmstrom Operations Base. You'll get food, quarters, medical aid. Right now, this town is not secure. Can you tell me what happened?"

Heather paused. "Yes, I can. Hell visited us here. Pure and simple."

It seemed that about two weeks ago a large herd of feral pigs, well known by the townspeople who used to hunt them for fresh meat and sport, had suddenly disappeared. An unofficial dump about two miles out from the town had been used as an additional food source for the pigs in order to fatten them up. Then, no pigs. A hunting party went out and saw the first Eater, which they promptly shot. It was decided that the Eater and maybe a sibling or two had scared off the pigs, and would come back once the Eaters left the area. So, the Townsman started sending out hunting parties to get rid of any Eaters ASAP. Being an independent and self- sufficient lot, made even more so by the Invasion, they told no one. They went out near a farmers feed lot where a calf had turned up missing. Two hunters were jumped by an Eater and injured before they shot it. One of the men was bitten and burnt by regurgitated digestive juices of the creature, an unpleasant characteristic of contacts with Eaters.

The badly injured man was recuperating in his home near the edge of town three days later when Eaters broke in and drug off him and his wife, his dog and his cat. People responded to their screams but it was too late. Tracks looked like at least four Eaters. Current information was that Eaters sometimes attacked in pairs, nothing more numerous. A good old fashioned Posse was formed, some two dozen armed men folk, some with military combat experience. A couple of good old bloodhounds were used to help track, it soon being established that dogs HATED Eaters, would attack them on sight. A few hours later, about a dozen shots were heard. Then, nothing. No one returned. No one answered the radio calls.

They had a Town Hall Meeting. It was decided to start moving everyone to the Town Hall and the Church area on the main thoroughfare. A three man recon team went out, never to return.

Just as everyone was moving into the Town Hall and the Church, some two dozen Eaters attacked. Once again, no one expected such pack behavior. The creatures grabbed and chomped on anything and anyone they could latch onto. Crossfire also hit a few town residents, adding to the confusion.

Heather grabbed three kids she knew, having lost her family in the first days of the Invasion and Harvesting. She took them to the Church, where the Assistant Pastor Randolph, the injured civilian, was trying to get as many people in as possible. Then, another group of Eaters, about a half dozen, struck from the other end of the main street, making a beeline to the moving figures in and around the Church. They came in through a back door of the Church. Randolph shot a couple before he had his arm almost taken off. Everyone scattered. Heather grabbed the kids and headed up the steeple to the church bell tower. Somehow, the Pastor followed before he collapsed at the bottom of the steeple stairs and ladder. Heather went back down and managed to get the access door locked. She had her own rifle, a Marlin 30-30, that she fired through the door when one Eater began smacking and tearing to get to the Pastor.

She said she believed the Eaters were attracted to people whom they had wounded due to the digestive juice/saliva smell the Eaters left on the wounded, not to mention the smell of fresh blood. Torbin believed that jived with reports

The Gathering Storm

he had gleaned. It was much like Komodo Dragons in the Southwest Pacific. She heard shots and screams coming from all over town. After binding Randolph's wounds as best she could, she made sure the access door was barricaded with a bunch of boxes of Church Bibles. She then joined the children at the top of the steeple. From there she watched the surreal Tableau.

Eaters were being shot and killed, but were replaced with others. Panic set in, and people began fleeing from the center of town. A fire somehow started in the basement of the Town Hall, adding to the fear and confusion. Heather watched as people tried to get into vehicles and flee, only to have some of the vehicles mobbed by Eaters. Eventually, a window would be smashed in and the occupants mauled. Within about a half hour there were no living humans moving within sight of the Church. Heather made quick trip to the Church kitchen and grabbed as much water and canned goods as she could, as well as a couple of fresh loaves of bread. She went back to the Steeple and secured the door. Somebody must have made the telephone call from the Town Hall to Malmstrom just before the fire started, as it had been about an hour later when Torbin was contacted and told to respond. It took Torbin and his Unit just under 24 hours to finish the Patrols they were on in Western Montana and haul ass to Evanston. And now, they were here, with dozens of dead alien bodies need tending to.

"Well, Heather, we'll take you to Malmstrom with the children and the Pastor. When this area is secure, we'll bring you back."

Heather looked at him. "Thank You Captain. But I think it will be a while before I'll want to come back. Think they can find me something to do near the Base?"

"I'm sure of it. If nothing else, you have a lot of hands-on experience in pure survival."

Just then, he heard a single shot. It came from a large caliber firearm from the sound of it.

"Anybody see where that came from?" He yelled out.

"Out to the south of town, Captain." Someone yelled back.

"Gunny. Take a squad out and sweep the area south of town. "

"Aye Aye, Sir." The Gunnery Sergeant began yelling for Squad Two to fall in on him. Within a couple of minutes, the troops were moving out in loose column formation.

"Ma'am, please stay behind cover with the kids until we figure this out. "

Corporal Black manning the Ma Deuce on the forward Humvee yelled out.

"People approaching from Twelve O'clock Sir."

Torbin jogged up to the Humvee and looked through his binoculars. He saw three smallish adult sized figures in some kind of camouflaged uniform approaching in a loose diamond formation. They all had long arms slung, but were pushing two ragged looking figures along. The front figure held its hands out, palms up, to show that they were empty. Torbin unslung his rifle and placed it on the hood of the Humvee. "Got me covered, Corporal?"

"Of Course, Sir. This is close range for my Deuce."

"Don't fire unless I go down. Clear?"

"Crystal, Sir."

Torbin walked out to meet the three humans. About thirty yards out, Torbin noticed two of the figures had feminine curves that the camo pants could not conceal.

"Captain Torbin Bender of the Unoccupied States at your service. With whom am I speaking? "

"Avenging Angel Abigail Young, Nauvoo Legion, State of Deseret, formerly Utah."

It was a young feminine voice, but one which spoke with authority. Sixteen, Seventeen? The figure to her right was definitely a female also. The one figure to the left rear looked like a young male.

"So, how do I address you, Ma'am?"

She was close enough to speak in a normal voice. She took off her Fritz Helmet that was adorned with a large set of painted on wings. She had natural blonde hair, braided up into a bun, and flashed a genuine smile. "You can call me Abigail, Sir, being my Senior."

He chuckled. "Hey, I'm not that old. Call me Torbin. I take it you are in command of this small Unit.

"Yes Sir...Torbin. I am An Avenger First Class. To my right is Ruth Young, Second Class. The young man is Mathew Young, Third Class."

"You all related?"

She shook her head. "No. We Avenging Angels all take the Prophet Brigham Young's name to show we operate in His Name and Spirit."

"Is this it? Kind of sparse in the numbers department to be leaving your borders. And I see you have a couple of prisoners."

Abigail frowned. "We started with six. Two are dead, Passed On To Glory. One is wounded in a cave a few miles away. That is why I am approaching you. Can you provide us with some medical help? He is bitten and burned. Plus, we have these two...scum." The one called Mathew had made the two handcuffed miscreants knell during the conversation

Torbin looked at her. Five foot seven or so, a hundred thirty pounds on a good day. Yet, she had the air of an efficient soldier and killer.

"Would you consider Air Evac? I have two Choppers in route."

She glanced back at her fellow Avengers. They each gave a slight nod. "I

The Gathering Storm |||223

believe, given the circumstances, that would be a good idea. You are Non-believers, but not Heathens as the Ferals are. Or Evil Ones like these Krakens." Abigail spat the name out as she spoke it.

Torbin Chuckled again. "No Ma'am. I may be a bit rowdy at times, but I definitely not like a Feral."

Ferals to the Tschaaa meant all humans not Under Control. Ferals to everyone else meant humans that had basically reverted back to a primitive concept of behavior; anyone not part of the Group was potential Prey, in every sense of the word.

"Where is he, Abigail?"

She pointed due South. "We came straight north the last few miles. We crossed our border over a day ago, tracking Demons that had killed some of our people."

"Demons? You mean Eaters?"

"Yes, I guess that is what you call them on your broadcasts. They are Demons to us, brought here by the Antichrist and the Evil One."

It took a moment for Torbin to translate. "Director Lloyd and the Tschaaa Lord."

Abigail spat in a very unladylike fashion. "Yes. His name is a Curse. The Evil One the Curser."

"CHUTHULU, the Ancient Evil One." Mathew suddenly spurt out.

"Stop That." Abigail yelled at him. "This is not one of your fantasy books you read. "

"Shades of H.P. Lovecraft." Torbin exclaimed.

Mathew's eyes widened. "You have read his stories?"

"Yes, young man, at about your age. I looked them up recently. Funny how they match much of what is happening today. An evil in the form of a Kraken like species. Go figure."

Abigail looked back at him. "Whatever his name, you agree as to his basic evilness. Our mission is to Destroy His Minions, send them back to HELL."

Torbin thought how sick this was. A young Girl coming to womanhood killing creatures from Hell instead of going to the Senior Prom like he did. He had to keep himself from going into a slow burn. He was going to mutilate the Tschaaa Lords the first chance he got.

"If you three will walk back with me, I will introduce you to the men and I'll make arrangements to get your fellow soldier." As they walked back, Torbin noticed that the three literal Teenagers were on a Relaxed Alert Status, walking loose but not missing anything. Some of the men took a break from dragging Eater bodies into a large pile for burning and walked up to get a look at the three newcomers. The female form even in a uniform attracts males like honey attracts flies. Soon, several troops were buzzing around Abigail and Ruth.

"Alright, At Ease, Troops. These soldiers are from the Former State of Utah. They are military members so treat them with the commensurate respect." A little bit of grousing, but everyone kept a respectful distance. Torbin walked over to the lead Humvee.

"Ready for a little trip, Corporal Black?"

The young black haired soldier gave a slight smile. "Of Course, Sir."

Torbin went back to Abigail and the others. "You can jump in the Humvee there with me. I'll drive, the Private will man the Fifty. We should be able to get close to the cave and recover your teammate. Sound good?"

"Yes, Captain Bender. Thank You."

He walked towards Gunnery Sergeant. "Gunny, get the people ready for the medivac. We'll take the prisoners with us in the HUMVEES unless Abigail disagrees. I'm going to take a little trip."

Large, broad shouldered and deep chested Gunny Smith walked up to Torbin. "Sir, if something happens to you, the General will have my balls."

"True, Gunny. But I'll not put anybody into a risk that I am not willing to face. I underestimated the Eaters here. I owe the men not to do it again until I figure out what is going on." He handed the NCO his Assault Rifle. "Hang on to this. I'll take the 1897 Pump Twelve Gauge we found. I don't want to give someone an extra full auto weapon if appearances are deceiving. And, I have my pistol also."

"You're the Boss, Sir. Just please get back in one piece."

"Don't worry, Gunny, I'll be careful."

He walked back to the three Avenging Angels. "Mount up. Let's do this quick."

The three had apparently ridden in a Humvee before as they quickly found seats and belts. Torbin started the engine, pulled out the line of vehicles, and then made a ninety degree turn to Due South. "Point out where we need to go, Abigail. You're the navigator."

"Yes, Sir," was the reply.

Abigail was soon giving clear and concise directions. Torbin had noticed that Abigail carried a Remington Pump .308 rifle with an extended ten round magazine. Ruth had an M-16 clone, and Mathew had a bolt action scoped .308 Remington. The two ladies had sawed off double barreled shotguns shoved in the pack on their backs, with Mathew having a Hipoint 9mm Carbine slung there.

"Need some ammo later, Abigail?"

"If you have some to spare, yes.....Torbin. We have only a dozen or so rounds left per weapon."

"Well, the Corporal up top should have more than enough firepower if we need to bug out fast. I have to ask how all three of you young people got this job."

"We all came down from Idaho. We were irradiated when the Hanford Nuclear Plant Complex blew and we fled South through the fallout area to Salt Lake City, as some of my family was Mormon. The Church decided it would not be a good idea if we found husbands or wives, too much chance of serious birth defects from damaged DNA. So, we serve the Prophet and God the best way we can; killing Demons, Evil Ones, Ferals so that others may live."

Torbin glanced at her. Mature beyond her years, but not by choice. The Tschaaa had a lot to pay for.

"You are betrothed, are you not, Torbin?"

"Why, yes. Who told you?"

Abigail shrugged. "It is a gift from God. I can see into a person, feel what is inside. You have a love inside your rough exterior that is connected to another. I hope your children are all healthy."

Children? How in the Hell did she know that he and Aleks just started trying to get her With Child?

"Thank You. Abigail. Looks like we are about a couple hundred yards from where you said the cave is. Time to stop and go on foot."

Torbin told Abigail to leave her rifle here, just take her sawed off. "If we have to shoot our way in it's going to be time to leave. I have this pump and my pistol to slow them up if we have to run from the Eaters. Do you have a pistol?"

"Yes." Abigail pulled a little top break .32 revolver. Torbin frowned. "Kind of small, isn't it?"

"I carry it for two legged Demons passing as Men who try to abuse me. Nothing more."

"Well. Abigail, it will mess a man's plumbing up at point blank. Since we don't plan on a firefight, we should have enough firepower. "

Torbin looked at Corporal Black. "Keep your hands on that Ma Deuce. our job is to keep the other two Avengers here in one piece, and be ready to cover our retreat. Clear?"

The Private grinned. "Crystal, Captain."

Torbin signaled to Abigail and they began a quick walk down an animal trail that Abigail said led to the small cave in which her comrade was hidden. It took them just a few minutes to travel some 200 yards to a small clearing. A fairly substantial brush and small tree covered hill rose near the small clearing in the light forest. Abigail pointed to a spot that looked like every other. Torbin was impressed when she deftly moved some strategically placed brush and revealed a small opening. She went in and Torbin followed. He had a small LED flashlight that revealed the injured man. The man looked a bit older, maybe twenty years of age, and was very pale. His left arm and side were heavily bandaged, with signs of blood seeping through.

"Here is some help, Peter." Abigail whispered.

"You came…back." The man named Peter whispered. He looked at Torbin. "Heathen?"

"No," Abigail answered. "Just a Non Believer from the Armed Forces of the Unoccupied States.'

"Captain Torbin at your service. I am now going to pick you up onto my shoulders in a fireman's carry. It may hurt, but we have to move. Understand?"

Peter nodded yes at Torbin. "Good, here goes." Torbin easily positioned the wounded man on his shoulders. "Abigail, grab his rifle, and let's go."

As they started to exit, an Eater began to enter. Before Torbin could react, Abigail raised the lever action she had retrieved from Peter and fired a round right between the large eyes of the alien. The rifle round did a number on what passed as a brain in the Eater, the creature collapsing where it had stood. Quickly, Torbin passed the body and started striding up the trail. ' Torbin thought how fast that reaction had been. These young teenagers were full of surprises, he'd bet on it. Fifty yards up, an Eater came rushing up from behind them. Abigail turned and tried to lever a fresh round and fire. The round she had just fired had apparently split, bulged and jammed itself in the chamber. Abigail reefed on the lever action and ripped the case head off the expended round. "Sh*t." A much unexpected curse from the devoted Mormon caused Torbin to look back and saw the rushing Eater. In one smooth motion, he turned and fired from the hip with his pump shotgun past Abigail. The heavy shot struck the alien in its eyes, at least one buckshot penetrating to its brain. It collapsed on the trail.

"Ditch the rifle, Troop. Here, take my shotgun." Abigail reacted to the orders automatically, easily bowing to his seniority. She grabbed the shotgun, ejected the spent shell and chambered another twelve gauge, the rifle forgotten on the trail. Torbin began jogging easily with the extra load. The man was a bit slender, probably no more than 150 pounds. Torbin was strong for his size and weight, easily moved along the trail towards the Humvee.

"Eaters moving in the brush." Abigail called out. "Thanks." Torbin replied as he tried to go to a full run. He had to be careful that he did not trip on the rough ground. But he did not want to get into a firefight, even a one sided one, with an unknown number of Eaters.

Moments later, they neared the Humvee thru the brush. Torbin saw the looks of relief on Ruth and Mathews faces as he brought the injured Peter up to the vehicle, just as the Fifty Caliber spoke. Torbin glanced in the direction they had just come from in time to see some three Eaters be dissected by the heavy machine gun rounds.

"Have some Eaters still in the bush, Captain. And I thought I saw a human figure take off. Couldn't get a shot."

Abigail looked in fury towards the underbrush and trees.

"Kraken Scum and garbage. I know they are inserting the Demons into this area. I feel it in my bones."

Torbin nodded in ascent as he placed the wounded Peter on a stretcher they had assembled

"That fits what we know. I guess the Director and the Tschaaa Lord in Key West have decided to start harassing us"

"I know of only one True Lord, and that is Jesus Christ," said Abigail.

They strapped Peter in the stretcher, then strapped the entire stretcher to the top of the Humvee, near Corporal Black's position.

"If you have to fire, Corporal, just watch where you are aiming that Fifty Cal. We don't want to injure our patient.

"Aye Aye, Captain." Black said with a slight grin. Torbin Chuckled. That man sure enjoyed his work.

"All aboard. Let's head out." They were drove back towards the town within a minute. Abigail turned towards Torbin. "Thank You, Captain. I am forever in your debt. I couldn't stand to lose another."

"Like they say on the Southwest Border, Abigail, De Nada. I'm just doing my job required of me by helping my fellow humans. "

Abigail looked at him with appreciation. In an hour, Torbin had acted in a more humane and Christian Way than many of her fellow Mormons had. She would always remember this day.

Torbin noticed her looking at him. He reached into his right fatigue shirt pocket and pulled out a hand calligraphy business card while he kept his eyes on the road. Aleks had made him a couple of dozen of these handmade cards, each beautifully drawn and lettered. His "wife" in all but formal license had many astounding skills, including the ability to produce detailed drawings and stylized printing. Torbin was lucky if he could draw recognizable stick figures, and he flunked handwriting in grade school.

"Here, Abigail. On this card my betrothed made me are a couple of telephone numbers and a radio frequency you can use to contact me at Malmstrom Base. We have a cell phone system that is up and running through most of our States using microwave cell towers and connections with a couple of satellites the Tschaaa left up. Funny, they don't try to block us. It's like we are gnats buzzing around that they ignore."

Abigail took the card.

"Thank you. I will keep this safe. I can sense the love that went into its making. And I will tell my superiors of the help you provided."

"Please do. We would like to establish regular contact with your people. So far, it has been very much hit and miss."

Abigail sighed. "They shut the borders of Deseret, your Utah, in the first year. That enabled them to completely organize a rebuilding effort, even while we suffered The Long Winter. But our religion always had us prepare, with extra food, supplies in every Latter Day Saints Home. We lost almost none to hunger, few to sickness. Since then, they have been very hesitant on opening up. Especially after some Heathens, your Feral, tried to take by force what was not theirs, including some women folk. That is when we Avenging Angels were created. No one is allowed to hurt one of our people and get away with it, no matter where they flee."

"How about Squids? Do you go after them?"

Abigail frowned. "I was told they tried to Harvest our State in a couple of locations early on. Then they stopped. Our Living Prophet said it was our strong faith that made the Tschaaa leave us alone. Other than this answer, I have no other."

Torbin did not tell her that his people had it on good authority (I.E Intel) that the Mormons had rounded up all the People of Color they could find and sent them out along Interstate Highway 70 into Colorado. Some had made it to the bases and population centers being set up as The Unoccupied States by the end of the first year. Many died due to the Long Winter, others had been Harvested by roving Falcons. No one would know for sure the numbers involved. What was known was the Tschaaa left Utah alone after a couple of months. Random Harvesting was being done in the so-called Feral Areas and what would become the Unoccupied States of American during the first year, when the Nuclear or Long Winter had set in. Not so Utah. The borders were quickly closed, and the state now called Deseret by its populace became a country unto itself. Torbin had reports from reliable Sources that the Director was told to ignore the former state of Utah, not to worry about it.

They arrived back at the town, just as the two choppers called in and said they were a half hour out. Torbin checked with the Gunny, who reported they had set up a landing zone in a field on the outskirts of the town. The wounded and the surviving town residents were waiting, under the protection of a squad of troops. The one seriously wounded troop, plus one with a foot injury, were to be loaded with the badly wounded Pastor and flown back ASAP, aboard a Blackhawk Copper set up as a Medevac Bird. A ubiquitous Huey would transport Heather and the children at a slower pace. Torbin and his men would transport their dead. And the two prisoners.

"As usual, Gunny, you needed me about as much as a boar hog needs tits."

The Gunny smiled nervously. "Sir, you get the 'big bucks' to make all the decisions and get your ass chewed by the General. I just do what I'm told."

Torbin laughed. "That may be true to an extent, but NCOs like you still really run the military."

"By the way, Captain, there is a set of SEALed orders onboard one of the choppers. They are from the General."

"Oh fun. Well, I guess he has something else he wants me to do. Carry on, Gunny."

"Aye Aye, Sir."

Torbin went back to his original Humvee. Out of his ditty bag, he grabbed a small twenty round box of .223 and a five shot box of double ought buck. He also grabbed three MREs. He next went over to the Humvee with the MG 240 attached in its gun position. He took two twenty round belts of 7.62 ammunition and slung them over his shoulder. He walked back to Abigail.

"Here, Ma'am. This should help out. But I would like to talk you into coming with us."

Abigail smiled and shook her head. "I am sorry, but I have my orders. We will ask you to take the two Kraken scum with you as we have already... obtained information from them. We will stay here for a couple more days and kill as many Demons as we can find. Then, we will travel back the way we came, Home."

Torbin knew about Orders, so he did not argue. He noticed the Kraken had signs of "questioning" displayed on their bodies, and they were very quiet. He hoped he never caused this Avenging Angel to become angry at him.

He called to Corporal Tatupu. "Corporal, take a couple of men and check out that General Store. See if they have some canned goods or local produce for the Avengers here. Some water also."

"Yes Sir." The huge Corporal glommed onto two troops and headed out, weapons at a ready in case an Eater was hiding out. Torbin turned to Mathew. "I see a cap and ball pistol in your shoulder holster. Need some black powder?"

Mathew perked up. "Yes Sir. I have spare caps and balls, but no powder."

Torbin reached into one of his pockets and produced a cylindrical object the same size as a toilet paper roll, because that was its basis. "Here. Being the strange person I am, I made a couple of overgrown firecrackers as homemade flashbangs. Here's one. The center is black powder. Keep it from a flame, of course."

"Thank You, Captain. I can surely use this."

Torbin made some small talk until he heard the sound of choppers.

"Well, Abigail, I need to meet those Choppers. The Corporal will give you some food supplies when he gets back. I suggest you use that church and it's steeple to keep a look out for the Eaters. And, give me a call when you get a chance, please."

Abigail smiled again and stuck out her hand. Torbin took it, feeling her firm handshake. A connection only two warriors who have experienced combat, faced Death together, passed between them.

"Thank You, Captain. I will keep you in my prayers."

Torbin looked at her. "Thank You. I'd like that." He released her hand and stepped back.

Abigail came to attention and snapped a salute an Honor Guard member would have been proud of. Torbin saluted back.

"Vaya Con Dios, Angel."

"Thank You, Captain. May God go with you also." She turned and walked towards the approaching Corporal with a wheelbarrow full of food and drink supplies.

Torbin walked to his Humvee, his driver, Private Martinez, starting it before Torbin said anything.

"Heading towards the Choppers, Sir."

"That's what I like about you, Private. You can read my mind."

A few minutes later, the wounded and civilians were being loaded aboard. Torbin used his K-Bar to open the heavily sealed envelope. A quick glance over the terse message elicited a small curse from him. S Day had to be moved up. The success of the recent space shots and all the other material improvements the Director had overseen was causing more and more humans to flock to the Tschaaa Controlled areas, like so many sheep. Time was running out. At a certain point, much like Occupied France and some Communist Countries, the populace was more apt to shrug their shoulders and say "Well, it could be worse" as an extreme inertia sets in. Then, the populace becomes almost as much of a problem as the Occupiers.

"Gunny." Torbin yelled. "Get everybody mounted up. We are going Home."

∽∫∽

As they watched Torbin and his unit depart, Ruth turned towards Abigail. "They are fine men. As fine as any man in Deseret. It is a shame they are Non-Believers."

Abigail sighed. "Yes, it is a shame. They would also put to shame some of our males who claim to be men of faith, warriors of virtue."

Ruth spoke again. "Abigail, have you ever thought of leaving Deseret, going to the U.S.A. so you could marry?"

Abigail paused. Then answered. "Yes, truthfully. I've often thought of being able to marry. But right now, God, Jesus Christ and the Prophets have a different path for me. I know God will let me know when I have fulfilled my Mission as an Avenging Angel. Then, I will decide, with God and Jesus' council, what path I will take."

She turned to the others. "Come, let us take our food supplies to the Church. I agree with the Captain that the steeple is a perfect look out post."

"And a perfect sniper perch." Mathew said with a smile.

Abigail laughed. "Yes, Young Man, you will have ample opportunity to demonstrate your shooting skills, I am sure of it." The three young humans, mature beyond their years, began to move their supplies into the Church.

∿

"Once humans fall into a pit of depravity and degradation, even without Alien help, it is often near impossible for them to crawl out unless helped by outside people and forces. What happened in Atlanta, Georgia, Cattle Country, is a horrible example of the concept."

Excerpts from the Literary Works of Princess Akiko,
Free Japan Royal Family.

ATLANTA, CATTLE COUNTRY

It was Fight Night again. So, Mayor Luther was happy. Very Happy.

Extremely happy as, due to the reported successes of the Crackers Space Program, they were providing him with a whole boat load of extra food and drink as a way of saying "Thanks for staying out of the way. Don't screw it up." So, he, with Joe's help and contacts, had turned tonight into another extravaganza.

The first fight had just ended. And a memorable one it was. Blue, he never did find out her real full name, had fought a young Filipina of the same size and weight. Blue had asked to Fight to gain some more favors like the ones she had earned the first go around. But, alas, her wish was not fulfilled. In a climax to the fight that would not be forgotten, the Filipina had wrapped her strong brown legs around Blues waist from behind, squeezing with all her might. Then, she had wrapped her arms around her rival's body, using her sharp fingernails and strong fingers to claw and maul Blues large breasts. The pies de résistance was when The Filipina sank her teeth into the neck muscles of Blue, drawing blood.

Blue, shocked and beaten, had screamed for mercy, admitted defeat.

The Mayor had taken a chance of inciting interracial rioting by having a Filipina fight an East Indian. But he did not care now. The results had been fantastic, the crowds yelling for more. And now, Blue was going to receive what all losers received. A good porking. But this would be a bit different. Sitting in a chair facing Mayor Luther was Red, the Mayors Main and Only Squeeze and the loser to Blue previously. Now, she was clad in a bustier and domitrix outfit. Next to her were a bag of sex toys, ready for use on the loser.

"Hey, Joe, are they coming up?" The Mayor asked his Bodyguard and Right Hand Man.

"Yes, Boss. Just got the radio call they are in route."

Mayor Martin Luther looked at Red. "Are you ready for this, Honey?"

She gave him a big smile. "Yes, Dearest, I am. I have waited for this for a while. Now, I will enjoy her writhing underneath me as I mount and abuse her."

The Mayor gave a big belly laugh. "Remind me never to piss you off."

Just then, the Mayor heard a shout cut short at the outer door to his office suite. Next there was a gunshot, followed immediately by the door being smashed in. Joe leapt to his defense, his signature Bowie in his hand. The Mayor started to reach for the Luger he kept loaded in his desk side drawer.

"Don't even think about it." A loud voice commanded. It was Malcom, whatever his last name was.

He had a silenced .45 aimed at the Mayor, two other ski masked men appearing, sawed offs in their hands.

"Sorry about the noise, Mayor. One of your guys got off a shot before I blew his brains out. Now, nice and slow, hands on the table. JOE. Don't be stupid. Buckshot in the gut will do you no good. Now, please, put you knife away and raise your hands."

Joe grudgingly complied. Another large man with a well- used but well-kept Winchester lever action came in.

"Sir, our other men are securing the other Guards. A couple have had to be knifed. But we should have everything under control on the auditorium floor in just a minute. We have the communications booth already. So, in about ten minutes, you should be able to broadcast your message."

"Excellent, Tyrone. I am glad casualties have been kept to a minimum."

Malcom stared at the Mayor, then spoke. "Consider this a Recall Election

The Gathering Storm

that you just lost. Sending those seven men to Talbot as sacrificial lambs was the straw that broke the camel's back. Especially since you picked ones you personally disliked. Sorry, but you will not be allowed to remain here." He looked at Red. "You can stay or leave. I have nothing against the Big House help. We are all in the same leaky boat. So, what do you wish?"

Red looked at Martin Luther, then at Malcom. She stood slowly and began to remove the strap on dildo. "I would like to stay, in one piece, if there is….. something I can do …for you."

"RED!" The Mayor yelled and lunged upwards and across the desk. Malcom shot him through his right eye, the large round blowing the back of his head off. He toppled, slid and fell behind his former desk.

A second after the shot, Malcom was covering Joe. "Same deal for you, Joe. I could use someone with your connections and abilities. But you will *not* be my pimp. However, do not think you can be some an avenging angel, waiting to take me out. Because if you do, I have a few very loyal people who will draw and quarter you on general principles, and do it very slowly, whether I live or not. Get Me?"

"Yes, Sir. I understand." Joe did not look at the former Mayors body.

"Red, is that your name? Well, let's just keep it that way for the time being. Do you have any office or management skills, other than porking the boss that is?"

She looked at her feet. "I was attending business college and working part time at an import/export broker in Savannah when the…Squids attacked. "

"Good. Office skills, some brains and knowledge of Savannah. Hey, look at me…I said LOOK AT ME." Red quickly met his eyes. "No more of this looking down like you have something to be ashamed about. We all had to do some nasty things to stay alive. But same deal as with Joe. If you think you can stab me in my sleep, forget it. You'll be sliced up by my people just like anyone else. Understand?"

"Yes…Mayor. I Understand. But please understand also. Mayor JLuther was nice to me. Treated me like he…cared. So please do not think I will degrade him to you. If that is what you want, you need to shoot me now."

Malcom looked at her, finally spoke. "You have some fire in you. I like that. And you aren't willing to speak ill of the dead. But, being as you chose to stay, you are pragmatic also. Good. I can definitely use you. You can remain in this Suite, as I know you have nowhere else to go. But, you are not my piece of ass. Okay?' She nodded yes.

"Now, how do you get a hold of the Squids to pick up bodies?"

Joe spoke. "There is a large spotlight on top of this building. We shine it upwards, towards the clouds. A Falcon shows up, picks up the…meat."

Malcom guffawed. "A Bat Signal. Some Squid has a sense of humor, and I bet I know who. His Lordship in Key West. Well, Joe, show Tyrone what needs to be done. I don't want to start off on the wrong foot."

A small radio that Malcom crackled to life. He held it to his ear as he had the volume turned down. A smile lit his very dark face.

"Okay, I'm off to the control room. Joe, you need to get Mr. Ex-Mayor's body out of here and have someone clean up the mess. Okay?"

"Yes, Mayor."

"Okay, I'm off."

Ten minutes later, he was broadcasting inside the Arena and outside into Greater Atlanta.

"Ladies and Gentlemen. There has been a change in Management here in Atlanta. My name is Malcom Carver. I am the new Mayor. Now, before everyone starts rioting, fussing and fuming, Tonight, The Show Goes On. And, we will have future entertainment. BUT. And this is a big but. Just like ones on some of those women you Brothers like to look at. I will be asking everyone to start doing some things for me. Call it having a 'job'. That's right, a J...O...B. You want some fun and entertainment; you will have to do some WORK. I'll give you a while to think about that. Right now, enjoy the next Fight." With that, Malcom stopped broadcasting.

"Well, let's see how long before some Brother starts breaking windows and acting the fool."

ᴧᴧ

The rest of the Fights went well. All the Winners and Losers went to the Mayors suite as before. The one difference was that the Losers were not porked. They were told they had to work it off some other way, to be determined. And were told to report back in two days.

Sure enough, the next day, when things began to sink in, a bunch of people, mostly young, began to mill around in the streets. Soon, rocks were thrown. Then, a few Molotov Cocktails. Since so many buildings were vacant, it was hard to really see any damage. Malcom sent out his trained personnel with some edged weapons gleaned from the local museums and one intact hardware store. A bunch of people were "Harvested", and a point was made. When one of his personnel was shot during a demonstration, he retaliated within the minute by having ten of the participants shot. Within another minute a Falcon showed up overhead, and began lifting the bodies up with its well-known articulating tentacles. One dark skinned Mexican American young male was still alive, having been hit in the leg. He began to scream. Suspended some fifty feet in the air, a tentacle with a blade attachment eviscerated him, allowing his intestines and other internal organs to shower down on the streets and buildings below.

Malcom was watching the scene via live video feed. He chuckled and turned to Red and Joe, who were with him in his office suite. "The Squids learned something that the Klu Klux Klan knew. When an uppity Nigga resisted, terrorize everyone by brutalizing him publically. Burn him, whip him, lynch him. Since minorities in the South had their access to firearms restricted through Jim Crow laws, they couldn't resist efficiently anyways. Throw terroristic violence at them and you soon have a pliable populace. They may hide when possible but accept violence done to others, 'the Troublemakers'." Malcom cracked his knuckles.

"Now, Joe. Use your contacts to get representatives from the various ethnic groups and organized neighborhoods here for a meeting the day after next. I am going to lay out what will be expected of them. They will be given the choice in helping me form a Resistance Movement, or they will be sent to Savannah for Harvesting. "

The New Mayor continued. "While on the subject of Harvesting, we will not be filling our quota for slaughter. To achieve this, we must have sufficient hardened shelters, hidey holes, as well as food and water supplies stashed for our city populace to survive. We also have to collect as well as build weapons to resist. Yes, we can develop weapons to take on Falcons and Deltas."

Malcom cracked his knuckles again. "Initially, Talbot and his Cracker Krakens will be sent. We will wipe them out and take their weapons. Falcons and Deltas will show up next, with some Robocops on the ground. They will try to terrorize us by tearing open buildings and yanking people out, slaughtering them in public. We will not give in. The other population areas in so called Cattle Country will be given the chance to join us. If not, they may be expected by the Squids to make up the losses in Harvesting. So, they either help us, or suffer the consequences."

Malcom turned and looked out the window onto the bare street. "We will be like the Polish Jews in the Warsaw Ghetto. We will fight with whatever we can. And, yes, most of us may die. But we are a populace of Walking Dead anyways. Each of us eventually facing the butchers block. However, since we are a necessary food supply, I think the Squids will have difficulty in trying to wipe us out completely. Killing off your breeding population is like killing the goose that laid the golden egg. No goose, no eggs."

Malcom turned back. He knew that Joe and Red thought he was nuts. Too bad. He was the Head Nigga What's in Charge.

"I know you think that we have as much of a chance as there is in finding an ice cube in Hell. Well, I think when harvesting us, fighting organized resistance, becomes too expensive in resources, the Squids will go back to hitting the Whites in the Occupied Areas as well as the Ferals, as they have been left alone for the last couple of years. Then, those Cracker Mothas will be forced to fight again. Instead of selling us People of Color as sacrificial lambs, they will either start resisting or they will be marched off to the butcher block like the rest of us." Malcom realized he was becoming agitated. He took a deep breath and centered himself.

"Mayor, what about Rocks?" Joe asked. "What's to stop the Squids from bombing us again?"

"They have too many Young developing in our oceans, Joe. Creating another Long Winter, or some other climate change, not to mention the chance of an errant missile hitting one of their Breeding Areas, I believe will limit those types of attacks. Who knows, maybe we can find a way to attack those Breeding Areas. See how they like it when it's their babies are dying, being used as feed for other species. The more we hurt them, the more they will have to think, is it worth the cost?"

He stopped. He saw that Joe and Red understood what he was saying. They just did not have the confidence that he could succeed. Well, he had the confidence of a hundred Joes and Reds.

"That's enough ranting for now. Red, the Losers from Fight Night will be here. You need to find tasks and jobs for all of them. We will house them here, so find some usable rooms in this former hotel. They will be fed and provided for a long as they work. Others who commit crimes in the streets will be given the same chance. Work it off, or wind up as a filet for a Squid whelp. Got it?"

"Yes, Sir. I will take care of what you wish."

Malcom beamed. "Excellent. Now, excuse me while I go to the Men's Room. I've been drinking up our coffee supplies." He went to now his, as Mayor, private bathroom.

Joe looked at Red. In a low tone he asked. "What do you think?"

Red looked back. "I think I will do what I am told. I think I may have a chance of a better life with him. I will do anything to prevent me from having to give birth and having my child taken off to be slaughtered."

Joe nodded his head in agreement. "I guess you're right. I was always careful in my younger years in football not to get some girl pregnant. I am even gladder now that I did not. I would kill anybody who tried to take one of my kids away, to be used as fancy fish food."

Red smiled. "This will not be easy. But is better than the current living death we are in."

KEY WEST, FLORIDA

Kathy headed for the Ladies Room as fast as she could. The Major had been keeping her so busy preparing for the necessary follow up broadcasts to the Cape Canaveral Missions, Eater Threat and updates on rebuilding the infrastructure of the former U.S.A that she barely had time to pee. She went in, grabbed a stall, pulled her panties down and let it flow. "Ahhh." She had heard from many men about the good feeling they had taking a good, long piss. Now she could readily understand. She had checked out the janitorial support in the broadcast building weeks ago, slipped the young woman who cleaned it some cash and asked her to "pulleease" spend as much time as possible keeping the women's toilets clean. And since that time, she had kept a steady flow of little "tips" to the woman and her sister. You could eat off the commodes now. Kathy thought it must have been a cosmic joke of God that Men had the ability to stand up and urinate, no danger of infection, irritation, etc. and it was Women who had the complicated plumbing that lent itself to these problems, yet had to sit down, placing ass and vagina close to potential sources of trouble.

She finished and stood up. As she pulled her panties up, then started to open the stall door, another women entered the bathroom in a hurry, and tried to enter her stall just as she was leaving. It was Mary Lou. They bumped, did the little Dance of Pedestrians, each trying to get around the other, but kept going to the same side.

"Kathy, if you don't move, I'm going to pee on you." Mary Lou snapped.

"Promises, Promises." She quipped back, and then squeezed around Mary Lou.

Mary Lou, sat down and began to relieve herself without shutting the stall door. Kathy, feeling a little nasty, stood and watched.

"What are you doing?" Mary Lou demanded.

"Watching you pee. I just wanted to see if you are as human as the rest of us."

Mary Lou finished, glaring at Kathy as she stood up and pulled her panties back up.

"Should have brought a camera and taken a picture. It would last longer."

Kathy chuckled. "I will admit you are definitely put together nice. But, I prefer men, like Adam."

She knew she was being Bitchy, but for some reason, could not help herself.

She suddenly had a desire to really irritate Mary Lou. She succeeded.

"Are you trying to be rude, crude, and piss me off?" Mary Lou demanded.

"What's rude about stating my preference? Or, did you want me to make a pass at you? I told you before, I prefer large male members, like Adam's."

Mary Lou's face flushed with anger. "Look, I know you f*%$ Adam. We both do. We have a truce about screwing around with this situation and causing Adam problems. Now, you seem to want to piss me off. What's your problem?"

"Hey, lighten up, Mary Lou. I'm just joking. "

"Yea, right. You're just a comedian. Well, you were on your back so much, I know you never developed a descent stand -up routine."

Suddenly, Kathy was angry. She got so tired having to defend her past as a porn star. Hell, she made a lot more money than Mary Lou had, and probably had more fun doing it.

"I said, I was just joking."

"Yea, sure. You're just one big joke. Now, move so I can wash up."

"You're going to need more than a sink to wash that smell off of your tw*t," A now angry Kathy hissed.

"Take that back!." Mary Lou Yelled.

"F%$# You, C&*T." Kathy turned to her heel to exit. It was a mistake to turn her back on an enraged Mary Lou.

Two hands grabbed handfuls of her blonde hair and yanked back. Hard. She squealed in pain and surprise, then felt herself being pulled backwards and twisted back towards the stall she had just exited

"You're the C$%T." Mary Lou yelled in her ear.

The fight was on.

Mary Lou tried to force her down into the stall. Kathy grit her teeth to the pain in her scalp and reached back low with her right hand, finding Mary Lou's crotch under her skirt. She dug her sharp fingernails into Mary Lou's soft woman flesh, the panties she was wearing providing little protection. Her fingers clawed, pinched, and then worked through the panty crotch material into the sensitive flesh of the other woman. Although Mary Lou shared her bed with two other women, having another woman suddenly claw at her genitalia was as shocking as it was painful. She let go of Kathy's hair with her right hand, grabbed at the woman's wrist to stop the nasty attack, and went into a Virgin Clutch. Kathy twisted around, jamming the nails of her left hand into Mary Lou's face. The participant in many a nasty porn catfight, she fought instinctively, no fancy martial arts moves. She managed to push her way back out of the stall, as she felt some of her blonde hair being pulled painfully from her scalp by Mary Lou's left hand. Both women began to curse and spit at each other, bumping into the bathroom wall as they now tried to knee each other's groin. Shapely legs became intertwined, tripping each other. They slipped and fell to the bathroom floor.

Mary Lou bit Kathy's left thumb, causing her to stop clawing at her face. Kathy managed to free her thumb before serious damage was done, then it was her turn to grab a handful of Mary Lou's jet dark hair and hank hard. The brunette squealed as she felt some strands of hair being yanked from her scalp. Then Kathy squealed as Mary Lou stopped trying to free Kathy's fingers from her crotch and instead returned the favor, jamming her hand right hand into Kathy's pubic area, clawing and scratching. For a moment, on the floor face to face, their eyes met, each seeing anger and pain.

"Ladies, WHAT are you doing?"

It took a moment to recognize the voice. It was Major Jane Grant. They froze.

A strong hand grabbed an ear on each of their heads, twisting it painfully like a Nun in a Catholic school. They both yowled in pain as Jane forced them to stand up, or have their respective ears seriously damaged. Neither woman thought of striking the Major.

"What type of childish bullsh*t is this?' scolded Jane. "Two grown women fighting in the girl's room like a couple of spoiled cheerleaders? Do you think this helps anybody or accomplishes anything? Other than maybe working out spite and anger towards each other, I sure as Hell cannot think of anything!"

"Now look, Jane..." Mary Lou began.

"Shut Up. That's MAJOR to you. You may be a glorified assistant to the Director but that doesn't cut the mustard with anyone who has gone In Harm's Way. "

"And You." Jane Yelled at Kathy." Do you think school aged kids who are sending you homemade cards and hand written letters on scrap paper want to see you with your hand buried in some other woman's crotch? Fighting over some guys cock?"

Kathy stood, stunned. She realized then that her old adult entertainment frame of mind about being sexy on camera did nothing for a whole new audience.

As if she could read her mind, Jane said "That's right. There is a whole bunch of younger kids

who haven't been exposed to the superheated sexuality that we were, thanks to the lack of Cable Television and the Internet. They look at you like the old Saturday Morning Kids Show Host, hawking toys and sugary cereal in between cartoons and cream pies to the face.

"In other words, Ms. Monroe, you've turned into a F@!%Iing Role Model."

Kathy almost cried. She was messing up a good thing and was too stupid to realize it.

"And I'm not done with you, Mary Lou. You're supposed to be helping the Director, not just porking him. Unless your goal in life was to be some expensive concubine."

Mary Lou's rage got the better of her, and she tried to shove Jane away. She was quickly on the bathroom floor, a painful wrist lock holding her right arm up, and Jane's shoe on the back of her neck.

"Want to try that again, Bitch?" Jane hissed. "I don't Catfight. I Street Fight."

Jane let a subdued Mary Lou back up, then glared at both of them. "I expected that from you, Kathy, not her. I guess I'm as guilty of stereotypes concerning Porn Stars as some others."

Jane let out an exasperated sigh. "I don't know why I put up with this sh*t. I could be a General in the Resistance, in the Unoccupied States. Not having to think about the people being slaughtered in Savannah each week as part of a deal with the Squids. "

"And not having to catch two prima donna assh*les hair pulling and scratching next to the commode."

"Especially after the death of a little girl."

There was silence for a few moments, only the breathing of the three women being heard.

Then Major Grant spoke. "This stays between the three of us. The Director needs another problem like this like he needs a bottle of Viagra. "

"But!" Jane stared in each of the women's eyes. "If I hear of anymore c*&©t like behavior such as this, I am going to track you down, kick your asses and leave you hogtied naked in the Director's Office. Are we CLEAR?"

"Crystal" Kathy replied.

"Yes, Ma'am." Mary Lou said, rubbing her wrist.

"Good. Get back to work.'"

The two women hastily did some damage control to clothes and makeup. Kathy wanted to say something, to try and apologize for her behavior but she saw Mary Lou was seething. They left the Ladies Room at different times.

KEY WEST, FLORIDA, DAYS LATER

The work out with Heidi was kicking his ass. She had already helped Adam lose ten pounds of fat and tone up muscles that were getting soft. She did not go into the martial arts and weapons training, Eskrima specifically, until after she had given him one Hell of a work out. He stood breathing hard, thinking he was getting too old for this sh*t. Heidi was sweating also, but had a big grin on her face. "Ready for another round, Director?"

He looked at her. "You're getting a sadistic glee out of kicking my ass, aren't you?'

Heidi laughed. "I just like to smell your man sweat. But seriously, you need to train like you fight. Otherwise, you are just playing and wasting time. "

Adam began to control his breathing. "I think I need to get some of my female staff in contact with you. Not only will they get a great work out, but they will learn some fighting skills also. "

Heidi had a wry expression on her face. "I don't know if they need any more push in the direction of fighting, Director. Not from what I've seen and heard recently, involving members of my gender."

Adams brow furrowed. "What do you mean, Heidi?"

The Coasty hesitated. "I don't want to cause problems or be a Rat, but, well, not only are many of my fellow females getting into it with each other in a nasty way, but…two of your so called Ladies got into it recently."

Adam stood quietly. Heidi thought she had just stepped in it. Finally, he spoke.

"Petty Officer Faust, sorry to put you on the spot, but I need to know, now, Exactly what happened."

"Well, Director, from several sources, it was like this.…"

After he had received the full story, Adam had Heidi run him through a series of doble daga and doble baston exercises, both against her and the large fighting dummy she had managed to have produced. For the first time, using live blades in doble daga, Adam had no nicks. In double baston, stick technique, he laid a couple of nasty hits on Heidi that he apologized for.

Heidi shrugged it off. "Hey. I'm the Instructor. If I am doing my job right, eventually you get good enough to smack me once in a while. So, I guess I am doing something right as you are getting better."

Adam let a small grin show. "My anger is getting the best of me, Heidi. No, do not feel like you did something wrong by telling me about that.….catfight. It has been building and I thought I had nipped it in the bud. Apparently, not."

"Well, in their defense, many women are suddenly throwing down on each other. Someone said it was like something was in the air or water, making them not only horny as Hell, but 'extremely' competitive and aggressive towards other women. "

"Well, Heidi, why not you?"

"Honestly, I think it's because you and I have been working out, sparring a lot lately. It seems to help me work out any feeling of aggression towards others. And, of course, my Martial Arts based spiritual training helps me keep my feelings centered, controlled"

Adam shook his head. "I'd like to accept your concept, but, since I already dealt with it, out in the open, they knew what was at stake. Now, I have to deal with this problem in more finality."

He took a deep breath, and then let it out slowly. "One more short spar, okay? Then it is time to get back to work. "

The next day, Kathy got a call on her Radio Phone. "Yes, Boss."

"Kathy, could you come to my office? There is something I need to discuss."

"Sure Boss". Kathy had been so busy she'd hardly seen Adam. She sighed. It was unfair that Bitch Mary Lou slept with him almost every night. Oh well, she couldn't complain. He had offered to make it a foursome. She walked up the Stairs to Adam's office entrance door and met Mary Lou as she arrived at the same time.

"Kathy." Ice.

"Mary Lou." Ice right back. The last attempt at a tussle with Mary Lou in the ladies room was just a short while ago. But no passage of time, no matter how long, would ever really help things between them.

She let Mary Lou knock and announce the both of them. Kathy frowned. Why both at once?

"Come in, Ladies."

"Director." "Boss"

They both walked in and stood several feet apart in front of Adam's desk.

"Both take your clothes off."

Mary Lou's mouth dropped. "Excuse me?"

'You heard me. Both of you take your clothes off. Strip. Now."

"Director......"

"Take- your -f#$@ing- clothes-off. NOW."

Kathy had no idea he had this level of red rage in him, nor a cold, steely capability for violence.

Kathy began to strip as if she was getting ready for another day in the Adult Film industry. Mary was still frozen. Until Adam rounded the desk and stood an inch from her face. In an icy whisper, the Director said. "Now. Or I will do it for you." Mary Lou began undressing.

Within five minutes, both women were totally nude where they stood. Adam had them hand him their clothes, which he unceremoniously bundled up together and threw behind his desk.

"Do you think you can hide things from me? Do you think I have a big Red S on my face for 'Stupid"?

"Boss...."

"Shut...Up."

"You two so called Ladies have embarrassed me for the last time. A Catfight in the Ladies Room? No. I don't care who started it. The Squids think we as a Species are already too violent to our own kind, too uncontrolled without two of my closest associates rolling around on a bathroom floor. I need two of my personal staff fighting like five year olds like I need a hole in the head."

"So, we are going to adopt some Tschaaa concepts here that right now seem a little more civilized."

"You two, today, Personal Duel. Here, Nude. No weapons but your own bodies."

"Rules? Squid Duels are not to the death, so no Eye Gouging, no fists to the face, no karate kicks, throat strikes, rabbit punches."

"Instead, you two will use you God given female talents to scratch, claw, bite, rip hair , slap, choke to submission only. Oh, biting like I said is okay. No biting off of nipples, fingers, ears, or chunks of flesh. Start doing that and we start the fight all over again. A little blood is okay. You want a Bitch fight, you have one. This timer goes off in three minutes. Better start stretching and loosening up now. The timer goes off, the fight begins. And, this is all being filmed for posterity.

Winner decides what happens to Loser. Do they stay, or hit the road. Submission only, unless someone is unconscious. Start warming up."

As the two women began to stretch and loosen up, Adam noticed for the first time just how close in size and shape they were. Was that why he had chosen them both? He also knew that leaving here would be a devastating. He grit his teeth. They chose this path, not him.

Both women finished their warm-ups just seconds before the timer went off. They had taken Adam's directions to heart. Both exploded, lunging at their opponent with nails and teeth, slamming together, breast to breast. Adam had never seen two women clawed tear at each other like this. The pent up anger must have been huge. They dug fingernails into each other's faces, breasts. They rolled on the floor, kneeing each other, trying for the pubis. Adam thought Mary Lou was going to win as she went for a school yard pin but Kathy jammed a thumbnail up a nostril, drawing blood and forcing Mary Lou off her. Kathy then bit Mary Lou's left nipple, drawing blood just short of taking it off. Mary Lou clawed Kathy's large shapely breasts, leaving red and bloody scratch marks. Both yanked at head hair and pubic hair, strands evident on the carpet. They attacked each other's genitalia and buttocks, trying like animals to do as much painful damage as possible. Sharp nails left mute evidence of the attempts.

With a sudden move, Kathy jammed stiffened fingers into Mary Lou's crotch and clamped down with perfect aim.

Mary Lou's eyes bugged out, and she screamed.

Kathy clamped down harder, putting a vice grip on Mary Lou's crotch. She began to try to pull and push Mary Lou around the floor by that grip. Her left hand clamped on her rival's throat.

Mary Lou tried to kick and scratch herself free. Kathy sank teeth into Mary Lou's left breast, tasted blood. She moved her left hand and bit Mary Lou's throat. Mary Lou screamed louder.

Before Adam realized it, Kathy was straddling Mary Lou, choking her with both hands. Mary Lou's heels drummed on the carpet helplessly. Kathy ignored Mary Lou's fingernails digging into her breasts, and her wrists, now bloodied.

Spit from Kathy's mouth drooled onto Mary Lou's Face.

Somehow Mary Lou managed to croak out "I Give."

Kathy rolled off of Mary Lou. After struggling for breath, Mary Lou began to bawl and sob.

Kathy laid, exhausted, bloody scratch marks adorning her body. She began to cry also.

"Chief" Adam radio phoned.

"Yes Boss."

"Could you have Dr. Fredericks, our senior surgeon come to my office? I have a special project for her. And have her bring that Tschaaa medical and nannite technology we recently received."

"Will Do"

Adam walked over to Kathy. "Well, you won. Decide."

Kathy sobbed "She stays."

"Excuse me?"

"She stays! It's just as much yours as my fault it got to this level."

Adam paused. She had a point. Adam had never dissuaded competition for his attention since he became Director. He had picked and chosen his bed partners with little consequence. Now things had blown up.

"Fine. But you two live together, from this point forward"

"Work it out or leave. Kat, you and Mary Lou will move into the spare suite bedroom. Tonight."

"Jamey, Jeanie."

They had been quietly watching the fight, unnoticed by Kathy and Mary Lou. The looks on their faces said "Wow", what the Hell just happened?"

"Take Kathy and May Lou to the spare suite. Clean them up. Help them move their stuff in. Medical attention will be there shortly." When they didn't react, he yelled "MOVE". They moved, each taking a woman in tow.

The Gathering Storm

Approximately two hours later, Dr., Fredericks called him.

"Director, may I come and speak with you?"

"Sure Doctor. Come up to my office"

About twenty minutes later, an attractive middle-aged red headed woman was standing in front of Adam. The Doctor, Brigitte (Gitte) Fredericks was a zaftig fifty something with still a slight German accent. When Adam had found out that the developer of new plastic surgery techniques was still alive three years ago, he had the Chief literally kidnap her from one of the few operating hospitals. She had large, natural breasts that had never needed a scalpel to turn heads, not to mention her nice posterior. Adam had a fleeting thought that maybe he was becoming way too sexually obsessed.

Dr. Fredricks came in closed the door, ad literally marched up to in front of Adams large desk.

'Mr. Director, I must be blunt. I do not know what you believed you were doing, but those two Ladies were in extremely bad shape. A Bitch Fight like that.... I only saw one that nasty was in a whore house in Zambia. *What* were you doing? Are you having a breakdown? Is this a new sport? Because, let me tell you......"

"Halten Sie, Bitte."

His use of his limited German made her stop.

"First, Herr Doktor, I did not start this fight, they did. I just finished it.

"Second, did the nannites and other things work?"

"Why yes, they did. Quite fantastic. The nannites are healing all the bites, scratches even old scars as we speak. They should be healthier than they were a week ago.""

"So, Third, this was the perfect test case, as you say, nicht wahr?"

"Yes, Herr Director. It was. "

He stood up, walked around the desk, shook Dr. Frederick's hand, and bussed her on the lips.

"Thank You. You are a miracle worker. Please return to your clinic and write an in-depth report on this. Now, if you excuse me, I have something else that has to be taken care of."

Dr. Fredericks left, convinced that Adam was having a breakdown. But now it was not her business.

About 8:00 PM that evening Kathy woke up in her double bed in the spare suite. She looked over and saw that Mary Lou was waking up also. Kathy. Now Kat, since Adam had called her that, sat up. The nannites made her feel like she had been infused with some magical potion. A quick check of her breast revealed that her old scar was gone, like it had never happened.

That was a good concept. It came to Kat all at once

"Mary it never happened."

She refused to answer.

"Look at your body. It's like it never happened."

"But it did. You kicked my ass, humiliated me in front of Adam. How can I ignore that?"

"Because, dear Mary, you have to. We are in this together, now, thanks to our own bitchiness.

"We are both less in Adam's eyes than before. At least for me, I may be working in the kitchen tomorrow. He needs your organizational skills. I'm just a pretty face."

Mary Lou sat up, and then stood up. Kat saw she was naked, and again realized she was also. Kat stood up, and looked more closely at her and Mary Lou's bodies.

"Correct if I'm wrong, Mary but.... isn't everything just a little bit.... tighter? Less sagging. Less wrinkles. Hell, I'm a new woman, like a virgin. "

Kat began to giggle. Finally, Mary Lou did also. The nannites and other Squid medical technology might have even helped their mental health.

"You keep calling me Mary, not Mary Lou, my full name."

"Adam called me Kat. New name for a new beginning. Likewise, Mary, instead of Mary Lou. We are different now."

Kat walked over and took Mary's hands in hers.

"Truth be told, Mary, I only beat you because former porn stars have more experience in good old nasty cat fights and by pure luck. Straight up fight in the gym, you'd have knocked me out.

"Now please. Truce. I need your help. If we do not make this work, we are both gone. Then he's left with the Barbie Twins."

Mary began to laugh, hard, at that thought. Jamey and Jeanie taking over? Forget it.

They unexpectedly hugged. Kat kissed May Lou on the lips.

Mary had shared a bed with two other women who seemed to like women a bit more than men. Kissing another woman could be enjoyable, exciting. In a moment, they were on Mary's' double bed. Kissing, tongue wrestling, rubbing each other's nude body against the other. Whether it was the side effect of the nannites, or just an aftermath of the fight, but within a minute, both women had an explosive climax. Mary rolled off of Kat, shaking with the aftermath of the climax. They laid next to each other, trying to regain their composure.

"Mary, what brought that on?"

"The nannites? Or, Kat, you always wanted me"

"Could be........Truce, Please? I'm serious."

Mary sighed "I agree we seem to be new women. Hell, we can start over. We have to if we are going to make it work with Adam."

"Thank You."

Kat lay her head next to Mary's shoulder.

"So, Mary, since we are starting over, history time. How did you and Adam meet?"

"He saved my ass, literally. Twice in one day.'".

"How so?"

"About three years ago, I was trying to stay alive in San Diego. Food was still scarce, various gangs were trying to run the city, and there was no governmental control to speak of."

"There were also groups of scavengers who were grabbing attractive women, boys, and girls off the street and basically selling them for sex meat or as food meat. Yes, a certain segment of the population decided that if the conqueror can eat human flesh, why not the conquered. Some sick assh**es began to tattoo images of Tschaaa on their bodies and tried to emulate what they thought alien society was. Usually they dumbed it down to treating other humans as sex cattle and meat cattle. The fact that there was a food shortage didn't help."

Mary shivered. "I got grabbed. Drugged, woke up in some crap hole former hotel. Nude. Not only were there live nude humans there, there were the human equivalent of sides of beef hanging from hooks. All 'white meat', of course, so as not to unduly attract the attention of the local Robocops. I was just about to begin the life as a human sex toy by various men and women, when someone kicked in the door. This was just as a debate beginning as to whether I should be slaughtered instead. It was Andrew, our Cyborg Robocop, Adam, the Chief, and their Security team. Adam and the Chief shot a few, the Security Team smashed a few, and the bodies were Harvested, every one of the assh**es. They tried to take me to a security convoy. Seemed Adam had convinced the Lordship that this lack of local control in Tschaaa controlled areas was leading to disintegrating human populations. If our Lordship really wanted a productive client species, members can't be allowed to indiscriminately abuse each other. Bad for business. I tried to flee, and was almost Harvested by one of those ATV looking Robots attached to Harvesters. Did you know His Lordship developed them in transit to Earth? Any ways, Adam whacked the Robot before I was drug away."

"Why did you run Mary?"

Tears began to run down Mary's cheeks. She sat up "I had a boy, a girl, and a husband waiting for me in a small compound we had secured with some friends. They were gone when I got there. Just blood, no other trace. Could have been Harvested. A couple of our friends were Mixed Race, darker skin. That's why I did a lot of the scrounging, I look the palest. That's what I was doing when I was grabbed."

Kat got up on her knees; she looked at Mary, then took Mary's face in her hands and looked in her eyes.

"Mary, I owe you an apology. Here I thought I had it so rough. The only person I had to worry about after the first thirty days was me, myself and I. And, being very experienced in how to use sex to wrap people around my finger, to be the center of attention, I obtained a lot of bennies the past few years others didn't. Like.....Adam."

Mary took Kat's hands in her hers, and kissed them gently.

"That's why I didn't want you here. I thought I was going to lose Adam. I know, I and Jeanie and Jamey are bed partners to him. But ... he saved me when I lost everything. He brought me back here, gave me a reason to live, to start over. He could have kicked me out of bed for the proverbial eating crackers, but he didn't."

"So, you ate crackers in bed?" Kat said with a slight giggle.

Mary looked at Kat. "You have a way of relaxing tense situations. I wished I was able to do that. To use a term from old movies, I am Adam's Girl Friday, that's it."

"You're more than that. Mary. Adam told me he was careful who he selected for important matters. And, I can tell by the way he looks at you. He wouldn't want to lose you."

"Then why did he put our fates in each other's hands? Do you think I would have hesitated having you deep sixed if I had won our bitchfight?"

"Yes, I think you would have."

Both women paused, looking at each other. Finally, Mary said "I wanted you gone. But, not dead."

"And now?"

Mary sighed. "I realize that I do not own Adam. It is just that I have everything vested in him. IF he failed horribly and was gone tomorrow, I'd go with him. I have no one else."

Kat put her arms around Mary, gently hugging her. "I think we have each other also. I think we need each other. To use an old hackneyed saying, us women have to stick together."

"Do you need, want Adam, Kat?"

"I want him as a man. Crassly, I want his cock, his manliness. I also know that if anyone can pull his weird balancing act off, between Alien and Human, it's him.

"And," Kat continued; "Now I want and need you. Not in a sexual way. I have loved women before, though I prefer men. But, I need you to help make Adam succeed. "

Mary gently pushed herself away from Kat, and then stood up.

"Kat, please stand up"" Kat did, then stood so close to Mary that their breasts brushed each other. Mary shivered a bit. "Dammit, you know all the moves, know how to use sex to get everything. I don't want to be manipulated. If you really believe in Adam, then I need to trust you."

Mary and Kat each felt and smelled each other's warm breath. They stood, barely touching.

Finally Kat asked the big question;

"Can you share Adam?"

"With you, yes. As long as you share 'you' with me. I need to know what you are thinking"

Kat began to gently stroke Mary's hair.

"You can have a personal part of me anytime you want. And I do not mean sex. You and I need a formal relationship that includes Adam. The two of us together can make this work. As long as Adam does what he does so well.... somehow keep us all from being just slabs of meat, give us a Future beyond Earth. If we are stuck here, with the Squids that will be left here when their ships move on, we are screwed. Eventually it will degenerate into a small group of humans watching the rest get eaten."

Kat sighed. "So called Lord Neptune won't live forever, or could lose his position tomorrow. Having to depend on someone who may decide to cook you and eat you tomorrow is no future."

Mary put her arms around Kat, pulled her closer. Kat felt the strength in her arms. Mary looked into her eyes and then whispered s softly into her ear "I hate Squids. They killed my family."

Kat whispered back "I hate them too. They killed my fiancé, and my chances of a normal life."

"So," Mary whispered. "We have a secret. Us versus them, which has gotten a lot of 'us' killed"

"Yes, that's true. How about a talk in the shower, as we may be wired for sound"

"We might be. Good idea." She kissed Kat, took her hand and led her to the shower.

Kat pulled back a bit "Mary, do you want Adam's children? "

Mary paused, started to stiffen, and then relaxed.

"Yes." She whispered "As long as they won't be Squid food. And You?"

"As of today, yes." Kat whispered back. "Children bind most men, even if they won't admit."

"Even Adam?"

"Yes, Mary, when he allows himself to think about it. I need to know when you are ovulating

"Are you thinking what I think you are thinking?"

"Don't be pissed, Mary, but you and I are about to become what certain Mormons called Sister Wives. That is, if you really want kids to survive. Adam must succeed, but we need a plan between the two of us for survival, also. And, in the tradition of many past ruling families, the wives are a power behind the throne. Adams offspring may be allowed to carry on his survival plan if things take longer than he plans. Squids believe in generational family empires, so to speak."

"The...Crèches?"

"Yes, Mary. That's what they are. Super, generational families. Kids are everything."

"So, Kat, we just tried to basically kill each other, and now you want to be pregnant together",

"Yes. If you will have me."

"And If Adam won't agree?"

"He will have no choice. Come on, into the shower. I'll wash your back, and your front if you want."

"One track mind, I see?"

"I worked in porn, remember? I have my PHD in sex."

The Tschaaa surveillance program and sensors that were scanning Mary and Kat had shut down once there appeared to be sexual relations involved. The program was based on an artificial intelligence that did not understand Human Sexuality any more than a live Tschaaa did. As far as it was concerned, humans were a bunch of nasty primates that screwed whenever and whoever they could, gender be damned. Adam had suspicions that he was monitored sometimes, but had no real idea when, where, or the capabilities of Tschaaa technology. If he realized that the proverbial fly on the wall was a reality, it probably wouldn't have done him much good. He knew he lived at the sufferance of his Lord Neptune. He kept many thoughts to himself, but his honesty with the Tschaaa Lord had been a source of humor rather than fear or anger. A master can be very forgiving of a pet he adores, as long as his pet does not bite him badly.

∿

It had been a week since The Fight. Everyone knew about it, (though not the details), but no one broached it in front of the Director or his immediate staff. The work of the Base was completed on a timely basis. Mary and Kat showed up for work, now friendly, almost sisterly.

Kat did a special broadcast on Tschaaa interpersonal relations, including the concept of limited physical conflict between individuals, limited dueling, no Wars, everything for the survival of the Species by complete protection of all the Young. Could humans emulate it?

Adam slept with the Barbie Twins, more for the feel of a warm body than for sex. They seemed to sense this need, foregoing the games they played with each other to cuddling with him. Adam was once again surprised with their depth of understanding and apparent immediate grasp of the situation. He constantly had written them off as possible airheads. He realized how wrong he was. Exactly one week to the day from The Fight, Kathy and Mary respectively requested his presence after work at the suite the women now shared. Adam completed his normal duties, took a shower, put on some casual slacks and shirt. He had two identical bouquets of flowers, as much a peace offering as anything.

He knocked on the suite door. Two voices as one said "come in". He entered to subdued lighting, the smell of incense.

"Come to the bed room, please, Director." instructed Mary. He walked towards the back and into the bedroom. Sitting on the end of the bed were two visions of loveliness and sensuality. Kat and Mary. Both in identical sheer silk robes that revealed the women's breasts were braless. They stood up and he saw they had identical black garter belts and stockings on, with four inch heel sandals. Nothing else. They let the silk robes fall, Adams eyes becoming riveted on their bushy but trimmed sex.

He felt a rush of passion he had not experienced for quite some time. Maybe sex had become too mechanical to him, too much about stress relief. Tonight, it was all passion.

"I want you, Adam." Kat said.

"I want you, Adam." Mary said.

Suddenly, the two women turned towards each other. "I want him. No. I want him." They began a rehearsed, stylized argument.

"Will you fight for him?"

"Yes. Will You?"

"Yes."

They closed, each slowly began a choreographed catfight. They pressed their bodies together, as they pulled each other's hair, letting out small cries of fake pain. They slowly pulled each other's heads back and forth, as if really trying to pull the other woman's hair out. Their nylon stocking legs wrapped around each other, and they fell together back on the bed. Well-choreographed, they rolled back and forth on the bed, legs widened to give Adam an excellent view of all their female sexual parts.

To Adam, they were the most gorgeous and erotic, beings in the world.

The action stopped. Both women stopped pulling hair, stopped rolling and wrestling. They slowly sat up on the bed, facing Adam. Then, they turned towards each other and kissed. The eroticism of Kat and Mary kissing was almost too much to bear. Adam felt like grabbing, squeezing, thrusting. But that would destroy the scene, the moment. He held himself in check.

The women's mouths parted.

"I love you Kat." "I love you Mary."

"Can you share Adam with me?"

"Yes. I love him as I love you."

"And I love him as I love you also."

They both turned to Adam. In unison, they said "Come, Adam. We need you. We need you to make the love work."

Adam went to them, trying to take a condom from his pocket.

Kat grabbed his hand. "No, that is not necessary. We want you, we want your seed. We need your complete love."

Both women stood up and kissed opposite sides of his neck and throat. They unbuckled and unsnapped his pants, each sliding a hand onto his genitals. They seemed to know exactly how to share his stiffened manhood, first one, and then the other.

In unison, they spoke "It is time." and pulled him to the bed.

~~~

He woke after a relatively short sleep between two of the most beautiful women in the world. He had no exact memory of who he had penetrated first, with whom he had first ejaculated. Just as soon as he had one orgasm, then Kat or Mary were using their talents to bring him to 'attention 'for another.

Both women had pressed their bodies against his face, both having the same sensual, musky smell and taste. They climaxed as he did. Kat and Mary had loved each other also, stroking each other as they also loved on Adam. Finally, satiated, exhausted, Kat and Mary kissed each other, kissed him, and wrapped themselves around him from opposite sides. They all three fell immediately asleep.

Adam slowly, gently unwrapped them from him. He managed to get out of bed, and stood up, though he felt almost light headed. He knew from experience certain glands and groin muscles would be sore, but he did not care. He had never felt so good, so loved. As he started to put is pants on, Kat and Mary opened their eyes, smiled at him, and then slid close together, gently hugging. Adam had no idea of the plan behind the smiles. He made it back to his office suite and showered. The nice, long, warm shower, helped to soothe tired parts of his body. He exited, to find the Barbie Twins, Jamey and Jeanie, laying out clean underwear and a clean pair of pants and shirt. In sheer nightgowns, they walked up, kissed him on each cheek, giggled, winked at him with knowing smiles, and then went back to the suite bedroom.

Now he was beginning to wonder. Just who really ran the show?

∽⌒∽

As he was drinking a cup of coffee, his phone rang. It was about 7:30 AM, so it was not that early. But with no Mary, he was his own receptionist. "Hello, Director here."

"Herr Director, Guten Morgan. I hope you had a good night's rest." It was Doctor Fredricks.

He laughed. "You don't know the half of it. What can I do for you Doctor?"

"I was wondering, if I may be so bold to ask, could you meet me at the Sportsplatz, the sports field, please?"

"Uh, couldn't you come here, Doctor?"

"I have something I need to show you here, please."

"Show me there? What..."

"Please, Herr Director. Here at the sports field." There was a sense of urgency, of concern he had not heard before in the Doctors Voice. Something was up.

"Oh, Okay, Doctor. I will be right there."

Ten minutes later, he saw Doctor Fredricks circling on the running track wearing a wide brimmed hat. Adam walked quickly out to meet her.

"Please, Herr Director, please keep walking with me. I need the exercise. And please do not mind that I am looking down. The ground is very interesting."

Adam knew she wanted to shield something she was holding from the Eye in the Sky, and was hoping this area was not wired for sound.

"Here, please, look at this nannite in this small glass tube."

Adam took it, holding it low. "This is one of the newer ones that we just used to fix up the two women, correct?"

"Correct, Herr Director. Now, as I was reviewing the containers of nannites, I found some that had been infused, shall we say, contaminated with this."

Adam looked at the second container. This small almost pill sized object looked more like a chemical pill or capsule than a nannite.

"That, Herr Director, is a highly sophisticated time release capsule with organic, literally living properties. There seems to be a form of virus also. The Tschaaa nannites are like our cruder nannites. Almost little robots designed to repair, to clean, and to make better, with little organic chemical compounds thrown in to speed and help the process. This capsule seems to contain living organisms that eventually wash out of our systems."

"What do they do?" Adam asked.

The Doctor walked a little faster. "As they say, the Devil is in the Details. We Germans had our Devils, the most notorious was Mengele. He experimented with genetics and chemicals to influence the reproduction of the human race, to make a Super Race, a true Aryan. He set back trust in German science at least 25 years. I think it took until the Fall of the Berlin Wall before people began to trust us German scientists again."

"And Doctor, the connection is....?"

Doctor Fredricks stopped short. "That and other capsules directly interferes with our reproductive system and its controlling DNA, genes and hormones. It produces 99% fertility in all females, speeds up the development of the baby in the womb. Seven months will become the standard gestation period instead of nine. Maybe even quicker. Once born, I believe children will develop faster, age faster. A full grown adult at ten years of age, if a women and the child are given a large dose. A smaller dose, everyone gets pregnant, more normal development."

She shivered. "A large dose, massive growth in and out of the womb, Gigantism but without the crippling side effects. Seven feet tall supermen in 12 years of age."

Adam stared at her. "Brain development?"

"There, I am unsure" She chewed her lip. "Over stimulated brain development may cause psychological problems, psychosis. Humans need time to grow and process the worlds around them. Or, we may have geniuses all over the place. Right now, it is a crap shoot."

The Gathering Storm

Adam stood and contemplated. Then, he spoke. "You have found this already in a human, haven't you?"

"Your insight is astounding. This is why you are the Director." The Doctor paused, her brow furrowed with concern. "Six women are pregnant with signs of developing fetuses at a faster rate. After finding these capsules in with the nannites, I did a chemical and physical analysis. I used this as a basis to test the women. They have been infused with the materials in the capsule. Concentrations are hard to judge. "

Adam stood stock still. He stood there for so long the Doctor was beginning to worry that he had slipped into a fugue state. "Director Lloyd?" She finally asked softly.

"Doctor, have you ever felt totally used, lied to?"

"Well, many of my relatives were used totally by the Nazis. By the time they realized that they were being used for the Final Solution, it was either too late or, they decided they did not really care. After all, they were not Jews, were they?"

"Can you keep this quite, Doctor?"

"Of Course. We are here, in the middle of a running track. Is not this secret enough?"

"Thank You." He started to walk away.

"Oh, Director, there is one important side effects in females I believe will show up."

"What is that?"

"They become very aggressive in seeking mates and mating, much more than normal. I believe the substances cause a rise in sexual desire as well as physical aggressiveness towards competitors. That is with even low doses, I believe. I also think in may cause a change in the natural scent of a woman, pheromones, that in men, when they get a whiff, seems to add to the normal randiness, nothing more. After all, women in civilized society limit their sexual availability. Now, their inhibitions have been reduced to a very, very low level. "

Adam stopped. He was squeezing his hands in fists so tight his knuckles were white.

"Thank You, Doctor. You are a treasure for the human species. Please stay healthy".

He strode off.

Doctor Fredricks sighed. mumbled. "My duty is done. Now, I must keep babies and mommas healthy."

Adam went back to his office a bit in a daze. He was still trying to process the ramifications of a modified Human Race along the lines the Doctor had told him. What if people were seven feet tall but so lacking in intelligence that they were easily controlled by the Tschaaa? Would they then be used to wipe out all but the Cattle? What if super intelligence evolved? Would the new over-sized Humans look on normal Humans and even the Tschaaa as inferior beings to be disposed of? Did his Lordship and the other Lordships realize they may have created a Frankenstein Monster that may turn on them? Did they ever really understand the whole Frankenstein concept, the creation of life that back fired on its creator?

He put his face in his hands. What a complete, horrible mess.

Who to tell? The Chief, of course. Then Kat and Mary. Hopefully they would help him figure this out before it became general knowledge. Adam hoped that anything Kat and Mary had in their bodies would not affect their ability to reason this out. He had no idea if nannites, the genetic and the organic material introduced into women's bodies had any mind control properties. But, he had to tell them, as he was sure, based the way they had been acting, they had some dosage of the, what he would call, the Sex Pill. A near perfect combination of libido and fertility. The one bad side effect was the aggression factor. But many men would find women catfighting at the drop of a hat extremely stimulating. Thus, more sex, more babies. Gestation cut down to even seven months would result in a soon to come population explosion. Probably more twins also. He would bet that women would soon becoming pregnant days after birth based on supposed side effects of the Tschaaa capsules. Kat and Mary could be pregnant already.

He shook himself. Can't be frozen into inactivity, thinking about every possible occurrence. Had to start now. He began by calling Kat and Mary....

Kat, Mary and the Chief were all standing on the track at the athletic and parade field. Staring at him after he told them what the good Doctor had discovered. All four humans were wearing wide brimmed hats to help hide their faces from prying eyes form the sky. Adam waited for the information to sink in. Mary began to cry. Kat reached over and put her right arm around her and hugged her close. Kat's own eyes were beginning to tear up. The Chief had a look of stone cold anger.

"Well, friends, now what?" Adam asked.

"In the immortal words of Rickie Ricardo, 'Someone's got some splainin' to do." The Chief finally said.

"Yes, I will be contacting his Lordship soonest. But, you have to remember that, down deep, we are like trained dogs to him. And we screwed with the genealogy of dogs for thousands of years. So, are we morally superior in any way?"

"But they are not sentient beings like us." Kat blurted out.

"From our standpoint, yes. But from the Tschaaa, not necessarily so. At least not at the same level of the Tscahaa. We can get as mad as we like. However, if we bite the hand, or in this case the tentacle, we could be put down."

Mary produced a tissue and dabbed her eyes. "Well, I am pretty sure I am now pregnant. Kat?"

"Ditto, Sister Wife. Don't give me that look, Boss. Yes, we planned on a polygamist relationship with you. And do not tell me you hadn't given it a thought after last night. Sorry to bring this up in front of you, Chief."

"I'm just jealous that I don't have two beautiful wives to take care of me."

Adam harrumphed. "Well, if we are all finished with working over my mind and manipulating me, the question remains. What next?"

Kat answered first. "We get a complete checkup by Frau Doktor, and see if she can determine any side effects. And if there is anything negative, I think I will be going Squid Hunting."

Mary looked hard at Adam. "I will have to second that notion, Director,"

"Chief? Any other suggestions?"

The Chief paused in thought. Then "I am not pregnant with a child that someone is tampering with, whether in a positive or negative fashion. However, if it were my wife, someone might wind up dead. Either me for trying, or the ones who did this by me succeeding."

Adam stood silently. Then he spoke.

"Ladies, although I believe it is early for you to know for sure you are pregnant. Don't argue, please, let me finish. Go ahead and contact Frau Doktor in private. At the least she can determine how much of a dose you Ladies have received."

He paused. Then he continued. "I will have Andrew set up a secure video connection with our Lordship so I can talk to him without being there."

The Chief gave him a worried look. "You want to bring Andrew in on this? Now?"

"Yes, Chief. I am curious as to just how much of his humanity and ability for independent thought and action remains in him."

∿∿

It took Adam a while to get back to his office. He pinged up Andrew.

Thirty seconds later, Andrew called back. "I seemed to remember, Director, a character in a Television Program that used to answer with 'You Rang'?"

Adam smiled. "Lurch, from the 'Addams Family'. I think the actor who played him was taller than you are. He was one big man."

"So, how can I be of service, Director?"

"I need a secure video hookup with His Lordship, if you could, please."

"I will be in your office in ten minutes."

"Thank You, Andrew."

In exactly ten minutes, Andrew walked into his office. "I am here as you requested, Director,"

Andrew removed a communicator from a hidden recess on his body and connected it with Adams computer monitor to give an enhanced image. He made the connection, communicated silently thru his cyber connections, then handed the communicator to Adam

His Lordship known as Neptune appeared on the computer monitor.

"My Director. Andrew says you have some serious matters to discuss. I hope you are not distressed?"

Adam took a breath and exhaled. "Your Lordship, in the name of the continued truthfulness we have always shared, yes, I am distressed."

"How so, Adam?" The Tschaaa moved his tentacles in gestures of concern.

"Lordship, just what modifications have you been doing to our Human Females?" Adam held up the organic object Dr. Hendricks had found mixed in with the medical repair nannites.

The Tschaaa Lord paused. Then he answered. "My Director, I have been providing specially designed organic, genetic, and hormonal substances, including specialized nannites, to improve your species. They have been primarily aimed at your Breeders, your women. These substances were introduced into your populace to help your Species. To make your offspring, your Young, stronger, smarter, larger and more numerous. That is why these actions were taken. Not to harm you. To make your species better."

Adam tried to control his emotions. "Lordship, have you ever heard of the concept of unintended consequences?"

"Yes, of course."

"And, have you heard of the story of Frankenstein?"

His Lordship signed pleasure "Of Course. The Classic with Boris Karloff. His portrayal set the standard as to the image of the Creature. And Lionel Atwell as the Doctor Frankenstein."

"Well, Sir, did you read the book by Mary Shelly it was based on?

"No, Adam. I will have to admit I prefer your Cinema, your Films. They are more enjoyable."

The Gathering Storm

Adam took a breath and let it out, calming himself.

"Lordship, part of the original story emphasized the problem of trying to make human life, and specifically making a Superior Human. The unintended consequence was the Monster."

His Lordship signed calmness, pleasantness. "My Director, trust me. That will not happen. I have studied your human species in depth for some sixty of your years. And, I was able to do this as an independent, outside observer. Not clouded by being part of the grand experiment that is the Human Species. Yes, you are an experiment of what you call Mother Nature, your environment and what you call Darwinian Evolution. "

His Lordship shifted his body on screen. "We Tschaaa developed from much the same environmental pressures. And I do accept the possibility of a 'Higher Power in the Universe' that may have an effect on us, what you call God. But, day to day, year to year, it is the environmental rules that you lump together as 'survival of the fittest', the concept of the Top of the Food Chain that govern our success as a species." The Tschaaa continued. "We Tschaaa have demonstrated our superior position in the food chain. We crossed trillions of your miles of Outer Space, the Galaxy, and Harvested you. Thus, we are the superior species. And, therefore we have a superior ability to see what you humans need to succeed. Adam, I am working to raise you up. To make you as close to equal of the Tschaaa as possible. How is that wrong?"

"Your Lordship, I appreciate all you have done for me, for the humans I have been able bring into your sphere of influence and control. But....why didn't you ask me, tell me, before you decided to try and modify us?"

His Lordship signed concern. "Adam, did you ask your canines, your dogs, before you began to change them through breeding?"

"Of course not. We did not know their language."

"My Director, if you had been able to communicate your desires, would you have told your subjects, asked permission?"

Adam paused. Then, he answered. "I would have liked to say yes. But that would not have applied to all humans. Hell, my previous government performed secret experiments on specific groups and populations without their knowledge. But, two wrongs do not make a right."

"My Director, how is improving your ability to evolve, to survive, wrong?"

Adam realized he had completely misread the Tschaaa Lord in so many ways. He had made the fundamental mistake that because this Tschaaa individual communicated in his language, a human Language, that he processed ideas like a human being. The Tschaaa Lord did not. He had Tschaaa sensibilities, not Human. Time for a different tack.

"May I ask Your Lordship, exactly what else he was trying to do to....improve human stock as a means to help us rise in our standing in the Universe?"

His Lordship gestured pleasure, the equivalent of a smile. "Of Course, My Director. I, with consultation with the best minds in my Crèche, as well as some help from the human scientists on Platform one, were specifically modifying your females, and through them, your Young. First, almost 100 per cent fertility among your females. Then more twins. Next, shortened gestation. Your babies now develop within seven months, thus freeing you mates to either reproduce more, or to free their bodies to the many other tasks that human females do, as opposed to Tschaaa Breeders. Once born, your children will then live longer on average, at least one hundred of your years, possibly longer. Maybe eventually as long as we Tschaaa. That will make you more adaptable to Interstellar Travel."

Adam took all this information in, and began mulling it over. Near 100 percent fertility, and probably a great improvement in the miscarriage rate for all women. More multiple births and stronger offspring to help in species survival.

"Your Lordship, how do you know about the intellectual development? Physical stature is easy to modify and see the results. But Intellect? How do you determine success with that?"

"My Director, nothing is perfect. But with our millennium of developing organic beings as our Grays, our Robocops and other human based beings, you must trust me that the possible problems are few and easily solved. And your human scientists are providing additional insights and suggestions that are greatly speeding up the developmental process."

Adam sighed. What a screwed up mess.

"Please, Director. Do not worry. In a month, we will revisit this subject. I guarantee that I will have solved any problems that may arise."

"Well, Your Lordship, I guess we are definitely in your hands. But, may I ask one more question?"

"Of Course, Adam."

"Did you try any such modifications on any Males?"

Lord Neptune paused. "Just You, My Director. And before you have spasms of worry, all we did was, shall we say, tweak you desirability."

Adam froze. Again, he clamped down his emotions. "And, sir, what does that really entail?"

"You are sexually attractive by human standards already. And power, I believe some of you Humans say, is the Ultimate Aphrodisiac. All we did was a very slight change in your pheromones that you exude, your scent. The already receptive, almost always gravid females of your species are thus given a slight push when they are around you. They become more receptive towards your ideas, your attractiveness, they are prodded a bit to find you sexually desirable at a higher level of frequency. Not enough to make them without free will in the matter, but definitely a push to be receptive to you, to be favorable towards you."

"And the side effect that the females of my species are becoming more aggressive, actually more violent to members of their own gender as they compete for sexual favors and gratification, how do you plan to deal with that?".

His Lordship gave the equivalent of a shrug. "Just a small, how you say, glitch in the development of the process. A slight modification in dosages, strengths of the substances used, slight tweaks to the genetic map, will solve those side effects. To further allay you fears, we have done previous tests in the so-called Cattle Country. That helped us to develop the first base line."

Adam could see that further conversation was a waste of time. The Tschaaa Lordship had decided long ago that he knew what was best for Humankind. Unfortunately, as smart as Lord Neptune believed he was, he really did not understand the possible consequences of genetic or hormonal modifications with a complicated a species as Homo sapiens.

"Well, Sir, I will make the best of it. But, as the information spreads, which it will, people in Tschaaa controlled areas will not be happy."

"My Director, I have complete confidence in your ability to convince your fellow Humans that the course of action I choose for them will be, in the long run, beneficial. Now please excuse me, as I have some other pressing matters. Have a restful day."

Adam handed the communicator back to Andrew, who stowed away on his torso once again. As Andrew disconnected the line to the computer monitor, Adam asked a question. "Andrew, did you know of this modification project of His Lordship?

Andrew stood still for a moment, and then answered. "It is in the voluminous data files to which I have access. But I never really actively review them. I have now through my interfaces."

Adam knew Andrew had almost instantaneous contact with all data bases, both Human and Tschaaa in origin. "Well, Andrew, now that you have reviewed them, what do you think?".

"I think, Director, that the intentions were good, as His Lordship really believes he will improve the human race. But, as the expression goes, the Devil is in the Details. I think that because the human species is so complicated, has evolved in a rather unique fashion on this planet, that no one fully understands the ramifications of such strong modifications in such a short time. My human origins tell me that males and females developed the way they are over hundreds of thousands of years. Trying to change patterns of behavior as well as physical characteristics such as size and period of gestations over a year or two is very… problematical and troubling."

Adam looked at Andrew. He knew now that there was a level of independent thought in him and other Robocop Cyborg type beings that was unrealized.

"That is a very independent opinion, Andrew. Are you not afraid of angering your Tschaaa Masters?"

Andrew paused, then answered. "I and my 249 'brothers' we Cyborg, part human, born here on Earth, part machine, were created since the Strike and Invasion. We have much more independent mental capabilities than those beings produced during the long voyage here. Even though all the Cyborgs are from historical human based genomes. The next dozen or so produced over the coming weeks will be the same as I am. The Tschaaa seem to like this independence because we can operate with a level of autonomy which means we do not bother the Tschaaa with day to day activities. As you have been told, the more Senior Tschaaa have become lazy and stagnate. I function as part of a bureaucracy that keeps things running smoothly with little direction from above. The Tschaaa like it that way."

Adam thought for a few moments, then asked. "If this…tweaking of Humankind produces the literal Frankenstein Monsters of horror film fame, what would you do?"

"I would do what was necessary to preserve life, especially Young Life, both Tschaaa and Human, as it should be."

Adam thought about what he just heard, a*s it should be,* was an interesting phrase. Adam began to think that possibly the Tschaaa had created a creature in Andrew that may be their undoing if he and his brethren decided that the Tschaaa were totally screwing things up. Like Gort, in the original 1950s Movie, "The Day the Earth Stood Still", these supposedly silent and stoic creatures were the hidden power behind the current system. If the system collapses, or seems to collapse, they may take charge….of everything.

"Thank You, Andrew. Your thoughtful analysis helps me greatly."

"I am at your command, Director. Within reason, of course."

As Andrew left his office, Adam knew that the so-called Robocop was much more complicated than anyone realized. The original ones brought for the Invasion were noted for their cool efficiency in destroying anything that disrupted the Harvesting of the Dark Meat to feed the Tschaaa. Initially, they patrolled the population areas, literally taking out anyone who disrupted a quiet street, town, or city. Anything determined a drain on resources was stopped. Public drunks and homeless people were Harvested on the spot. Start a fight when a Robocop was near, you were butchered for eating. Attack or resist a Robocop, same thing. Large scale resistance resulted in large scale destruction, with blood from the slaughtered on the Falcons virtually used to rain down on survivors below. A couple instances of that, no more resistance, no more disruptions in public. Everything nice and orderly when they were watching.

The Tschaaa had the Robocops, with Grey and Lizard help, set up the original electronic fence around what was now Cattle Country. With the help of the remaining Flying Squads, thousands of People of Color not already in Mississippi, Alabama, and Georgia, were herded in like the beef cattle they soon resembled. Adam had added a type of Guard Force and chain link fencing in the last couple of years to help keep the borders of Cattle Country secure. These actions backed up the thousands of miles of the original alien electronic fence. It all acted as an additional reminder that the Director was in charge.

But, who really was in charge?

Adam went to his office wet bar and fixed himself a double Rusty Nail. Too much was happening too fast. He decided he would sleep on it before he gave anybody else the full details of his conversation with His Lordship. The talk with Andrew he would probably only share with the Chief. He took a large swig of his drink and let it burn down to his stomach. Shit. Things were getting more complicated by the hour.

∿∿

"Sometimes in the course of history, a confluence and convergence of independent events occur which somehow connect and form an overriding, forceful event. In the language of weather, this could be called a Perfect Storm. This confluence of forces creates an event of such magnitude that it changes or destroys everything in its path. In the area formerly known as the United States of America, such a Storm of Events began as Free Allied Forces lunched an assault on the seat of alien power in Key West. Florida."

Excerpts from the Literary Works of Princess Akiko,
Free Japan Royal Family

THE PERFECT STORM

While Adam Lloyd was attempting to get a good night's sleep, Colonels Hunter and Bardun were up on Platform One, their third trip to the large

Space Station. After their return from the first trip, Director Lloyd welcomed Cliff Hunter back and offered him a position as a backup Space Plane pilot to Bettie Bardun, soon to be his wife. Within days of their return, the Tschaaa had Grays and Lizards, with human support, replacing the original engines with early models of the pulse engines used in Delta Space Interceptors. THE HOPE became a true space plane, using eject-able rockets to get it off the runway, then kicking in the pulse engines at about 1000 feet altitude. They worked like a charm.

The two pilots were married in a simple ceremony, the Key West Base Chaplain officiating. The Admiral provided a stocked Honeymoon Suite at one of the refurbished shoreline hotels called, understandably, the Republic. The Honeymoon Suite was called the Admiral Suite. Go figure.

Bettie and Cliff spent a glorious three days becoming re-acquainted. Bettie kept pinching herself to insure she was not dreaming. On the final evening they laid in each other's arms, Bettie gently scratching Cliffs somewhat hairy chest.

"You sure know how to treat a girl right." Bettie playfully exclaimed.

"Hell, I thought I was out of practice, being as there weren't exactly a lot of available members of the female gender on the Space Station. I guess it's like riding a bicycle, you never really forget it once you're good at it."

Bettie giggled like a school girl, and gently poked him. "I didn't realize riding me was compared to a bicycle. "

Cliff kissed her forehead. " I wasn't talking about how we... fit together . I mean being able to love someone after six years house arrest in a small room in Space. I'm glad I did not develop some type of psychosis.'

"The strong survive, Cliff. I saw my share of humans who went nuts while trying to survive the Nuclear or Long Winter, whatever title you like. Even when things began to warm up after about 16 months, there were still those who killed themselves, or committed suicide by attacking a Robocop. The rest of us worked to survive, some even had children. The human species has a strong spirit of survival."

"Babe, Bettie, did you ever think about heading North to the Unoccupied States?"

She sighed. "Yes. But I wanted to try and keep the Cape in one piece. I wanted something of my previous life to remain, to exist. I also saw a trip up north as just trading one prison for another one. At least living at the Cape gave me the feeling of some control over my fate, and a purpose for my life."

Bettie rose up on her elbow and looked into Cliffs eyes. "If I had known about your survival, I might have done things different."

"But then you would not have had the chance to fly the Space Plane up and get me. I don't see anyone else trying to go to Space. Things sometime happen for a greater reason."

Bettie kissed Cliff. "I love you. The happiest moment of my life was when I saw you alive on Platform One. The second happiest was when you pulled this ring out of that beat up, bloody, box. Just realize that we are now joined at the hip. Where you go, I go."

Cliff smiled. "I surmised we were joining a little south and to the right of your hip…"

Bettie kissed him again, and nipped his lips. "You can be such an ass**le sometimes. Come here and show me all about being a joiner.…

∿∿

Professor Fassbinder had spent his week on Platform One looking at the proverbial Flying Saucer in the photos the Director had shown him. He and the Olson Twins had spent the first two days clambering around inside a large craft with absolutely no edges or corners. Everything was smooth, almost featureless. Attempts were made to examine its internal workings using X-Rays, MRI like machines, you name it. Everything was blurred. Finally, Joseph walked in the only thing they could get to work, the entrance hatch and stopped.

"Hmmm. Some craft used to have their hatches in the rear. I wonder…" He walked forward to what would be the "front" if the hatch was 180 degrees opposite of the bow of the ship. He suddenly sat down, cross-legged.

And almost jumped out of his skin when the "floor" began to form a seat around his ass.

Somehow, he controlled himself. He was soon in a reclined "pilots" seat. He felt the "armrests" and the area directly in front of him that might have been an instrument console. Parts of the ship formed around his fingertips and palms. When he moved his fingers, a heads up display appeared directly in front of his eyes. Or was it projected into his retina? He saw the wall of the large bay the saucer was in. Sh*t.

"Sandy. Sam. GET IN HERE."

A few hours later, the Twins were able to get the saucers interior to react to them It seemed that the craft, ship, whatever you wanted to call it, took a while to "decide" it wanted to interface with each individual. The craft literally seemed to have a mind of its own. The rest of the week, Joseph spent with the Olson Twins, trying to figure out its system. When he left with thee two Colonels on the Space Plane, the saucer was slowly giving up its secrets to the three scientists. It was as if it was examining and testing them to see they were worthy enough to converse with, to share with. Joseph was glad he did not have to stick around. Not only because he really wanted to get back to his wife, but also he really disliked the Tschaaa Lord in charge of Platform One. Cliff called him the Wizard. Joseph called him Sh*thead. Whenever he was around him, Joseph felt the Tschaaa was sizing him as the main course of a meal. Joseph had visions of himself, on a big table, roasted, with an apple stuck in his mouth.

Joseph felt like kissing the ground when they landed at the Cape. His wife, Sarah, actually brought her school class up to view the landing, getting a complete tour of the Launch Site. Joseph rode back with his wife in an old fashioned Yellow School Bus. It brought back bitter sweet memories. Back at Key West Base, he kissed his wife. "Sarah, I need to check in with the Director."

She smiled at him. "Going to ask him about staying around because I may be….pregnant?"

"Will do, Darling. You'll be the first to know."

He went up to the Director's office, trying not to stare at Mary Lou. Damn, she looked like Bettie Page. Joseph went in with his ducks in line. When he found an opening, he started to explain about his new relationship with his Wife, how they were going to start a family, that….

Adam stopped him short. "Let's cut to the chase, Professor. You think your wife may be pregnant. And you do not want to spend any more time away from her than you have to. Plus you were afraid I would not understand."

Joseph blushed. "Sir, I just…"

"You must think I am the most ignorant, uncaring asshole in the world. Professor, go home. Check in with your Section here. You do not have to go back into Space unless you really want to. The Olson Twins, going by your reports, have things well in hand. Just keep an eye on this project of ours and use your talents with Earthbound Projects. Keep in touch. Talk to you later."

Joseph almost skipped home. He felt that his wife was pregnant. She was happy. Life was good. Little did he realize at that time a couple of catfights and major revelations on modifications of human biology threw everything in doubt.

∽∫∽

Weeks later and the good Colonels were on their Third Trip, Professor Fassbinder staying home. Possibly, had he been along on the second and third trips, things may have been different. They brought up needed scientific supplies, plus some creature comforts that were in short supply, making them the most popular residents (though temporary now) on Platform One. Their expertise on Aeronautical and Space Engineering made them popular help on some of the projects the resident scientists were involved with. Then Doctor Susan Smith and her husband, Robert, found out that Bettie had a Minor in Biology, with a specialized study in Extraterrestrial life.

"Colonel, please. Come to our Lab. We have a special project were have been working on for His Lordship on artificial life. You must see what the Tschaaa growth vats can do, with a bit of tweaking by us humans."

Cliff told her before they set off to the Smiths Laboratory that they were rather 'intense'.

"I haven't been in their section in months. They have a tendency to corner you and go on and on and on. And they also have a tendency to think that the human species are just one big lab rat, ripe for experimentation. I know they were trying to develop new artificial food sources to replace Cattle for the Tschaaa. But they talk and act like they are just making a new kind of sausage."

On the way to the section in which the Smiths Laboratory was located, Bettie and Cliff bumped into Sandy Olson. During the second, previous trip up on THE HOPE, Sandy had been very busy aboard the so-called Saucer and had not had time to even say "Hi". She had even missed meals, spending every waking movement dealing with what the Hell the Saucer was and what did it do.

So, when she saw Bettie and Cliff, she made a beeline towards them in the corridor.

"Colonels. Congratulations on your marriage. How are the Newlyweds?"

"Just Great." Cliff answered.

Bettie felt a bit awkward, after the brief 'affair' she had had with the other woman. She had not had a chance to talk with her, one on one, since Cliff showed up. She turned to her new Husband.

"Cliff, honey, can I have a moment of 'girl talk' with Sandy?"

Having had the situation previously explained to him, he smiled. "No Problem. I think there is a latrine suitable for humans nearby and I need to empty my bladder. See you in a few." He headed towards a small side corridor nearby.

"Uh, Sandy..." Bettie began.

"Bettie, no need to explain anything. You found the love of your life, alive and well. You even told me about him, remember? So, I understand that our, shall we say, fling did not last."

"Sandy, it's just that.... I was NOT trying to use you, to pull the ole f**k em and forget em thing for which men have a reputation. I....we made a connection I did not expect. I will always have good feelings for you and would like you to remain a friend. Is that possible?"

Sandy kissed her on the cheek. "Of course we are friends. I am just glad that you're happy. I wished I could have been at the wedding, but I was stuck in Space. So, one of these days, I'll give you a belated wedding present. Deal?"

Bettie hugged her. "Deal. I just hope you can find someone that will make you as happy as Cliff makes me."

Sandy sighed. "Yes, I wish I could find the 'One'. But to be honest, I'm having some...issues I guess you could say, with a level of randiness and aggression that even my Twin says is worrisome. From some reports I have received from groundside, a lot of women are having similar problems. I mentioned it to the Smiths, who are our primary biologists up here, and they said they would look into it. They mentioned about maybe a mutation or something brought here with the Tschaaa. After all, introducing non-native germs and other species can screw up an environment."

"Well, Cliff and I are headed to their research wing right now. I'll mention it to them."

Sandy looked at Bettie with a thoughtful look on her face. "Just one word of advice. They can get rather intense about what they do, and seem cold as to the effect their research may have on individuals. They have been trying to grow some replacement meat products for the Tschaaa, in order to cut down Harvesting of live subjects. But, I stayed away from their work as, seeing a piece of human looking flesh being tested for Tschaaa consumption gives me the creeps. "

Bettie nodded. "Thanks for the warning. I have definitely seen my share of dead humans over the past six years, so I've probably built up enough thick skin to compensate. But I'll watch myself"

Sandy smiled at her. "Please do that.' Now I have to get back with Sam. We have gazillion things to do over the next few days. Our stay here has been extended for another month. But, it may take a year to really figure the Saucer out. So, keep in touch.'

"Will do, Sandy."

Cliff reappeared and the two Colonels continued their walk to The Smiths' research area.

"Get things worked out, Babe?"

"Yes, Cliff. I just felt guilty, like I used Sandy for some quick sexual gratification. To put it bluntly, I still do not understand how I was so aroused by another woman. I'm beginning to have some suspicions about what has been going on... I feel like maybe my buttons are being pushed."

Cliff frowned. "Well, maybe our visit with the Smiths will shed some light on the whole subject. They are experts in human biology and physiology. Though I have heard rumors some of their stuff can be pretty gruesome, looking more like a morgue scene than a laboratory."

Bettie gave a small smile to her love. "Like I told Sandy, after the last six years, it takes a lot to get to me. Unless it's a lover that is supposed to be dead showing up with a sh*t eating grin and a ring."

Cliff gave her waist a light squeeze.

"I'll never live that down, will I?"

"No, you won't. But I love you to bits anyways."

They arrived at the entrance door to the Smiths Lab area. Cliff found a buzzer when the doors did not slid open automatically a la Star Trek. A couple of minutes later, Doctor Susan Smith opened the access door. Susan was a short, around five foot two, 40ish zaftig woman with large breasts and short, dishwater colored hair. She wore wire rimmed glasses which was surprising, as those with access to Tschaaa medical technologies had used their nannites and organic creature based procedures to fix most of the more mundane human physical deficiencies.

"Colonels Hunter and Bardun. Thanks for coming. I like to have new eyes look at our research once in a while. It helps us to get new ideas. Especially one with a Biology background, Bettie."

A large white haired and full bearded man that looked like Santa Claus' twin, large gut and all, came up. This was Robert Smith, her husband and an expert in all things concerning human Biology. He stuck out his hand and gave both Colonels a robust handshake. "Welcome, my good people. Glad to have visitors of the human variety. I'll let my wife give you the Cooks Tour. I need to go to the supply area and look for a type of widget for an experiment I am doing. Be back in a few minutes, Susan." He kissed his wife on her cheek and strode off.

"Well, if you will follow me, I'll start with something I am proud of."

Doctor Smith took Cliff and Bettie into a large open area that had low illumination lights covering at least two dozen large tubs or vats. There were directional lamps over each of the vats, but only a few were turned on. Susan led them to a six foot long vat nearest the entrance.

"This, Meinen Herr and Frau, is my largest accomplishment. Please take a look." Bettie and Cliff looked in under the lamp and saw an approximate five foot nude adult female form, breasts, nipples and pubic hair included. The head was enclosed in an opaque basketball shaped cover.

Susan grinned. "Say hello to the Other Me."

"What do you mean?" Bettie asked.

Susan grinned broader. "I took my stem cells and, using Tschaaa vat technology, grew "me", a clone to be exact. I have that ball around the head as it is weird, even to me, to look at my face on a body sitting in a vat. But all the organs are functioning."

"How about the brain?" Bettie asked, frowning.

"Just the automatic functions. If you notice the breathing tube. The lungs function at a very low respiration rate, as is the rate for blood flow and heart function. It is basically in a semi-comatose state, much like Tibetan monks claimed to achieve. The body and organs grew and developed quickly, much like the Grays do. But, rather than awakening into a functioning being, like the Grays, I keep it in this state."

"Why?" Bettie asked.

"Well, first, the project was to prove I could produce a full term human body, like the Tschaaa grow Grays. I considered using a similar technique to introduce sentience at an automatic level, programmed to function in certain programmed fashions, like the Grays do. But, it is a human based Clone, not a Gray. I might have to try and educate it to function at least at an idiot level. I really don't have the time nor the facilities to take the experiment to that level. Not to mention the disconcerting idea of an idiot level 'me' wandering around. So I keep it for spare parts and organs.'

Bettie stopped and stared a bit. Cliff's forehead was deeply furrowed "Spare parts, you say?"\

"Yes, Cliff, if I may call you that...yes, thank you. Military Rank seems so formal to me. Anyways, this is the medical wave of the future. Organ Transplants from another "you" to keep you alive and healthy for decades longer. All but the brain, of course. I still have no way to transmit your cognitive abilities to another body. Some brain cells for repair, yes. But right now, if the brain dies, that's it. "

There was something in the back of Bettie's mind that said 'Warning. This is screwed up.'

"But, Susan, how do you decide if this has reached the level of being a ... person? "

"Easy. The same as at an abortion clinic, where I worked at for several years. Until the fetus is "born of woman", pops out, it is not a person. Until we "birth" a clone, wake it up in a sense, it is just spare parts. This experiment was for us humans. The rest of these vats are for experiments and functions for Tschaaa needs. Specifically, Meat sources that are indistinguishable from Cattle currently walking around on Earth. I have achieved that at least in the fresher cuts of Meat,"

"Fresher?" Cliff queried.

"Why yes. First, I took a few eggs and cells from the women up here at the Station, Platform one. By the way, why do they call this a Platform instead of a Space Station? It's confusing. But never mind, I'm getting off subject. Then, cells and eggs were brought up here, first by the Tschaaa, and then you two brought a small quantity up your last trip here."

"Wait a minute." Bettie interjected. "When you say eggs, you refer to human female ovum and gametes, maybe zygotes? ".

"Why yes. Let me show you what we can do with them."

A bit cautiously, Bettie and Cliff followed her to smaller vats a few feet away.

"Here. I can now grow them up to a stage of development where they resemble a fetus and thus provide a vat grown equivalent of veal or lamb for the Tschaaa."

Cliff and Bettie froze. In the smaller vats was each what appeared to be an unborn baby. The one difference was they lacked any part of the head past a rudimentary skull, possibly some jaw development.

"See, these are basically anencephalic fetuses, so called 'brainless' fetuses'. We can easily produce them, thus not having the problem of dealing with true brain development. Once again, the most basic and minimal automatic body functions are evident ...."

All Bettie heard was a nonsensical drone. Near one of the vats were two scalpels and a bone saw.

Cliff, still shocked and staring at the vats, heard this soft keening coming from Bettie's direction.

"Wha...," He started to turn towards Bettie when she slammed a scalpel into Susan's neck.

The Doctor started to scream as Bettie, acting too fast for Cliff to react, slammed the second scalpel through Susan's left glass lens and into her eye. Susan screamed and flailed her arms about. Bettie, with unnatural speed, slashed with the bone saw, opening up the scientist's jugular. Susan Smith spun around, her blood spurting, and collapsed to the floor.

Cliff bear hugged Bettie, "What The ..." and almost had his nose broken as she tried to head butt him. He knew that Bettie was acting on some primal defense level, did not even recognize who he was. He lifted her off her feet and spun her around, his face pressed into the side of Bettie's neck. She tried to bite him, that keening sound coming from her mouth rising in crescendo.

He yelled as loud as he could into her left ear. "BETTIE! It's Me, Cliff! Goddamnitstopit!

She struggled for a couple of more seconds, and then something sank in. She stopped struggling, that animalistic sound from her mouth also stopping.

Cliff set her on her feet, still holding onto her arms. She started to retch. Cliff helped her bend over and she puked all over the feet and shoes of the dying Susan Smith.

Cliff tried to hold her, comfort her. Bettie sputtered, then talked. "My... my... my sister.....gave birth to an anencephalic baby a week before... the first Rock. It lived three days. They named it after ME. Before they realized..." She retched again, and then began to dry heave.

"Bettie, deep breaths Bettie. That's a girl. In goes the good air, out goes the bad."

Bettie finally stood up, and then spat. She looked at the still body at her feet. "I sure screwed this up. But you deserved it, you evil c##t!" Cliff hugged her and stroked her hair.

His mind was racing a mile a minute. Finally, he spoke.

"Babe, we need to leave. In the Space Plane, Otherwise, I don't think the Wizard will understand."

Bettie shook a bit, and then stood up straight, pulling herself together. Her military training and experience took over.

"Your right, let's go." Cliff did not see any cameras in the large laboratory, other than the one at the entrance door. He hit the open button, he and Bettie exited....and almost ran over Robert, "Santa Clause" Smith, carrying a couple of boxes.

"Hey, what's up?" Cliff's right uppercut caught Robert Smith's jaw perfectly, and he went down like a sack of potatoes.

"Those boxing lessons came in handy after all." Cliff stated. They began to run down the corridor towards the docking area where THE HOPE was berthed.

Platform One did have an internal surveillance system on the corridors and main areas. But over the years, the Tschaaa, Grays and Lizards had gotten used to such human activities as running, working out, lots of sexual encounters, etc. The other species believed humankind was a bit "off" and got used to making allowances. The Tschaaa knew that eventually, they could be turned into Meat, end of problem. Thus, no one tried to stop them. Bettie and Cliff made it in record time. There was no security on the spacecraft as why would anyone steal it, and where would they go? The Tschaaa knew they had control of all the good spots on Earth, pretty much ignored the rest. The two Colonels dashed into the berthing area.

The launch bay/berthing area was connected to the outer launch area which would be sealed off by a large airlock/blast door when the craft was getting ready to launch. After being sealed in, the air was pumped out back into the station, and then the outer door was opened. Small maneuver jets and rockets helped nudge and push the craft until it was far enough away to engage the main engines.

The Space Plane was unlocked, there being no one that would steal or molest anything aboard. They grabbed their pressure suits that were hanging up on their special racks, and with practiced ease, had them on in record time. Each checked the other over to insure everything was tight and secured. If they lost air and pressure in THE HOPE, these suits would (hopefully) keep them alive long enough to land somewhere on Earth. Helmets were last, a lot more streamlined than the old Space Shuttle Program ones. Small intercom radios enabled them to talk to each other.

Cliff made a beeline for the left seat pilot's chair. "I know you're senior, Bettie, but I have more experience in actually Space Combat maneuvering. Trust me, we may need it."

Bettie looked at him as she took the right seat. "Dearest, I always have trusted you. But I sure got everything all FUBAR."

"Forget it. It was bound to happen. I'm surprised I didn't pull a Berserker on the assh*le Lordship that runs this place long ago. I think the chance of returning to Earth kept me at least partly in control."

Bettie started to tear up in the helmet, not good as she would have to take her helmet off to wipe her eyes with her fingers, although they had a half-assed bendable little arm controllable from outside the helmet to scratch your nose. "Maybe if you left me…"

"Hey, Dumbass. We're *married*. Remember? For better or worse, in front of God and Country. Can't back out now. Okay, help me preflight this beast, just what we have to do to get it rolling."

"How do we get out the launch door, Cliff?"

"Well, hopefully, no one has raised the alarm yet, so the automatic controls should work. If not, the main pulse engines may be able to knock the doors open.…In Theory, at least."

Cliff hit the release for the magnetic clamps that held THE HOPE in place. He heard the satisfying sound of them releasing. The landing gear the Space Plane was sitting on had electrical motors attached with drive mechanism, allowing a pilot to move the craft around a flat area at about two miles an hour, max. Engaging these motors, and firing a couple maneuver rockets to break the inertia, THE HOPE began to slowly move.

"Remind me to figure out a way to increase the taxi speed on this thing." Cliff said in frustration.

Just then, Cliff noticed his radio phone, attached to a small Velcro pad on the control panel, was flashing. Cliff cursed, managed to untangle and unSEAL his face plate to his helmet so he could hear it. Everyone on the Platform was given a small radio phone that worked in, on and around the station.

"Hunter Here."

"Cliff. It's Sandy. What's going on? I can't raise Bettie. The Tschaaa and their minions are rushing around at the Smith's Laboratory. Was there an accident?"

"Yeah, you could say that. Sandy, I have no time, so listen carefully. I and Bettie are bugging out on THE HOPE. If you can get to the berth and launch area, I would appreciate it. I may need your help. But you may really piss off the Squids if you get caught helping us. Kapish?"

"Tell Bettie I'll be there in five" Sandy replied.

"Thanks." Cliff reattached his radio phone to the control panel.

Under Cliff's control, THE HOPE was now pointed at the airlock door. Cliff hit the automatic door opener and was relieved to see the large airlock door begin to slide open. Slowly, on its motorized Landing gear, THE HOPE crawled to the airlock. It seemed like an eternity, but finally they were in. Cliff paused for just a minute before he signaled the door to close. Now, they would be locked in if the Tschaaa realized what was going on.

"Cliff. It's Sandy. I'm at your launch berth. The doors locked and sealed so I guess you are cycling the airlock to leave."

"You got it. Anybody else there yet?"

"Not yet…..wait. A Soldier's approaching. "

Bettie looked at the closing airlock door.

"We could try blowing the outside blast door. I know there is an emergency exit and launch protocol in case you had to get out of the launch bay with everything jammed up. I think we can do that without the airlock closed and cycling."

Cliff looked at the small rear area view screen. "You had the original in-depth briefings on landing and taking off from this Platform. I just dealt with living on it. I'll leave it up to you. Work your magic."

Bettie quickly brought up the specifics on the launch bay area on her monitor. A quick review and she had the correct emergency procedures in her head. She poised her hands over the controls. She turned her head towards Cliff. "Ready?"

Cliff turned to look at her. "Yes. Blow the Door."

Bettie's hands flew over the control panel keyboard, imputing the correct codes in just the right pattern. A seconds pause, and the outer blast door was blown open, just as the airlock door closed. The air rushed out, and Cliff hit the maneuver rockets, the combination of forces easily lifting and propelling the Space Plane outward. He quickly retracted the landing gear.

"Boy, that's going to piss the Squids off." Cliff said, grinning. Ten seconds later, Cliff hit the Pulse engines. One moment they were slowly moving at maybe 40 knots per hour, the next moment they had a kick in the ass and were traveling at over six hundred knots. He angled the crafts nose downward, towards Earth.

"Man, I will NEVER get used to those sudden accelerations when I hit the pulse engines initially. Zero to six hundred is not exactly fun."

He looked through the cockpit glass straight ahead.

"Bettie, keep an eye on the rear video feed. The Squids have at least one Delta on board the Platform at all times." He activated the various search radars on board, trying to watch everything at once. THE HOPE was in the Earth's Gravity Well, and began to accelerate downward. Its skin and structure was designed to take the heat and stress of reentry at a high angle, using its wing and flaps designs to help control the overall speed. It was easily stressed to take Mach 25, and could take probably a lot more in a pinch due to the "fudge factor".

"Cliff, we have company on our Six."

He glanced at the rear cameras monitor screen and tail radar. A Delta had launched and was trying to acquire them on its sensor systems.

"Bettie, make sure you're strapped in tight and you G-suits cells are inflated. This is going to be a wild ride."

Cliff increased the downward angle of THE HOPE to increase initial speed. He would have to then switch to a high angle of attack to induce drag to slow it down. Based on Space Ship One, it also had shape changeable airfoils that could help to control its descent.

"Let me tell you what I know about the Delta Fighters. They have rudimentary but fairly powerful search radar. This lack of radar capability is because those big eyes of the Squids provide them with outstanding vision, especially for moving objects at long range. The so called Eye in the Sky surveillance system they use is based primarily on lens based optics, not electronic enhanced cameras and radars like our satellites had. "

At that moment the Space Plane was passing fast enough through sufficient atmosphere to cause a sonic boom.

"I hope this bucket is as tough as they say it is. The Delta behind us will pick up our direction of travel and hit their gravity pulse engines to start catching up. In the atmosphere, the ram jets will be used. They can pull more Gs than we can because of the Delta's design and Squid physiology. So, we can't out turn them. I will dive as fast as I can and hope this beast doesn't overheat and come apart. I can jink and release landing flares. Eventually, I'll have to do some s-turns to try and slow us down. That's it. No offensive capabilities."

"You're not headed towards Key West or the Cape, are you?"

"No, Bettie. Luckily, our place in orbit gives us a pretty direct flight towards Montana, U.S.A..

Bettie patted his arm. "I love you. I have a feeling we can do this."

"Babe, I love you to bits. And I hope your confidence in me is not misplaced, or we are going to make one Hell of a fireworks display.

The initial pursuit Delta's pilot was trying to catch up without overheating his craft. The Delta had no specialized force field like protections that the Falcons had, just the tough organically based structure. The Delta was like a chunk of a super barrier reef, reinforced by metal. The Tschaaa Warrior radioed for assistance. From one of the spoke wheel shaped orbiting equivalent of an aircraft carrier, five more Deltas were launched. They were soon plummeting downward in an attempted intercept solution. Bettie, monitoring everything on the rear facing shielded radar systems, picked up new hits on her monitor.

"Cliff, we have new targets, coming in at a bearing of 160 degrees to our rear, about Five 5 O'clock High."

"Shit. Well, they won't catch us before the first one does."

It was a delicate balancing act. Trying to keep speed up to a certain level in order to keep the Delta from catching up, but having to flare out to control the descent and keep from becoming a flaming rock. Cliff knew the tough literally organic grown skin of the Delta, like a super tough carapace of some superior crustacean, could take one hell of a level of abuse and was able to disseminate heat in a superior manner to human made materials. It had been built not as a true space craft, but rather a high atmosphere based attack craft. Swope down from high perch, blow the Hell out of something, use it's gravity pulse engines to boost itself back into low orbit or a high atmosphere perch, then repeat. The Ram Jets gave it control and high speed in the atmosphere, up to about 100,000 feet. One on one comparison, the Space Plane was an also ran even with the Tschaaa technology engines.

"Bettie, I have to start S- curves as the speed is building up way too fast and with it the heat. Start looking for somewhere to hide, if possible."

Bettie felt a sinking feeling in her stomach. Hide? Where? It' was not like there was a foxhole somewhere.

Suddenly, Bettie knew there must be a God.

"Cliff. Two O'clock Low. Thunderhead. A big one too. "

Cliff had been trying to control the overheating and speed so had not noticed the huge cloud formation over the Montana/North Dakota Area. It looked like it came close to reaching 75,000feet. Inside may be large electrical discharges. Lightning. Their craft, built for Earth weather and humans, was grounded and insulated for lightning strikes. Cliff had no idea to what level the Deltas were built to take large amounts of electrical strikes. Well, this seemed like the only game in town.

"Hang On. After this, rollercoaster rides will be boring." He pointed the Space Planes nose down towards the weather formation. The speed picked up, with it heat and vibrations. The forgotten Guard Radio Frequencies, standard still on all Human Aircraft, crackled. "Unidentified Aircraft. We have you on our radar. Turn back or we will fire."

Bettie grabbed the emergency mike and yelled into it. "MAYDAY, MAYDAY ON GUARD. Space Plane THE HOPE with two onboard request emergency with two onboard. Request Asylum. Help us, goddamnit! The Squids are trying to eat us!.

There was a pause as Cliff tried to keep the craft aimed towards the weather formation and in one piece. Something flew by the side windshield.

"Aircraft, you are headed towards Malmstrom Air Base, U.S.A. You will be shot down."

"Go ahead. And shoot the damned Deltas following us!"

THE HOPE hit the top of the huge thunderhead, as Cliff tried to flair the craft out more to slow it down. It began to shake and buck. " Bettie. Escape Capsule Ready Status; Activate."

The Space Plane had been built so that the nose and cockpit area formed an escape capsule. No Shuttle Disaster for future Space trips. The nose area separated from the body, being blown away from the Space Plane body and fuselage. Then, large parachutes hopefully did a controlled descent to the ground. Hopefully.

THE HOPE took a large electrical dstrike. Monitors and gauges flickered; the powered flight controls cut in and out, Cliff cursed and swore.

"I thought this beast was grounded and shielded." He fought to keep the Space Plane under control, fighting the up and down drafts in the interior of the thunderhead. He changed the crafts angle of attack, nose up as best he could to slow it down, and began S-Turns. After a couple of minutes of an extreme rollercoaster ride, THE HOPE popped out of one side of the thunderstorm. Cliff fought to steady the Space Plane. "F#$*! Come on, Baby. Hold together. At least until we get shot down."

Somehow, he began to control the descent. Something large zipped by the left side of cockpit. Cliff glanced over and saw a Delta inverted in a power dive.

"Sh*t. That Squid must have been hit by lightning also. Maybe the water in the cockpit they use as G cushioning help fry him."

"Ah Cliff…I think something is burning." Bettie unlocked and unlatched her faceplate so she could sniff the air. There was the smell of burning electrical wiring and ozone, as well as a little smoke. She could not locate the source.

"Can you bring this thing under control? I can't figure out the source, but something got fried. "

"Just do not turn on any oxygen sources. SEAL you helmet back up, Bettie, so your suit oxygen won't help spread a fire." The suits had a small tank with less than pure oxygen because the cockpit was pressurized. If the cockpit failed and the air escaped, the small quantity in their suit system should last until they landed. They had been breathing it since they left Platform One, due to the threat of attack.

Cliff kept circling THE HOPE at a high angle of attack to slow descent. He had lost sight completely of the Delta that had dived by.

"Bettie, can you get the rear search radar working? I need to know if those other Deltas that were launched are headed this way."

Bettie tried to get the monitor screens up. Nothing. "That burning smell must have been the circuits involved with the screens and monitors."

"Try the Guard Radio."

Luckily, that worked.

"MAYDAY, MAYDAY. Space Plane THE HOPE requests emergency landing instructions. Two souls onboard. Request Asylum."

Someone at Malmstrom Base Control must have figured out something more than a Squid Incursion into their Air Space was happening. A new voice answered.

"HOPE, continue on the exact bearing you are on. Two Aircraft will be intercepting and will try to escort you in. Any sign of Hostile Intent will result in instant destruction. Acknowledge!"

Bettie grinned. "Colonels Hunter and Bardun Acknowledge. "

"I wonder what they are sending up to meet us."

"Well, Good-looking, I hope it's something with some offensive capability. I think the Other Deltas may be catching up."

Cliff kept the heading as ordered, keeping a high angle of attack to slow down the descent of THE HOPE. Years ago he had been at Malmstrom Air Base, after they had reopened the airfield primarily for rotor aircraft. He had a passing thought as to what it looked like now. Finally, he broke through a cloud cover and saw Great Falls. Montana, then located the Base. Everything seemed more sprawling, more recent construction. It looked like a lot of survivors had made their way there, probably because being far up North and far from either Coast, there was less chance of being bothered by The Tschaaa. The Air Force Global Strike Command seemed to have survived the initial attacks. Cliff swung the Space Plane in a wide circle, trying to slow down some more as he lined up on Runway 47 Right. At that moment, he noticed two F-15Es shadowing him as he started to drop below Mach One.

"Damn, Cliff. Those have Japanese Self Defense Forces Markings," Bettie exclaimed. She called them on the Guard frequency. "To the Fighter Aircraft escorting us, do you read me?"

"Yes, HOPE Space Plane. We read you loud and clear. This is Colonel Yakashita. We will escort you until you touch down. Please do not make any rapid course changes. We have orders to launch missiles, fire if you violate instructions".

Bettie believed she heard a slight Japanese accent, especially the "Ls" sounding a bit rounded like "Rs".

"Colonel Yakashita, do you have any other aircraft on your radar?"

"There are some Deltas some thirty miles out and closing. They are being engaged by Ground to Air Defense….Now."

Cliff and Bettie did not see anything being launched, the defense units being in a huge circle around the entire Great Falls Area. Besides, they had their hands full trying to land. They did not want to try and do a go around, not knowing the reactions of the F-15 or even that the pulse engines would work after the lightning strike.

Cliff tried to bring the Space Plane down as best as possible, but landed a little hot as he did not want to try a Go-Around. The landing gear had locked down, one of the few indicator lights that still worked on the instrument panel. They hit hard, and Cliff tried to brake with flaps, speed brakes and wheel brakes. Security and Fire Rescue vehicles went hauling ass down the runway, trying to keep up with the landing aircraft. Cliff used up the total airfield, went onto the overrun area, past that, finally coming to rest with the nose gear in the dirt. THE HOPE had held together. Cliff patted the instrument panel. "Thanks, Honey. You stayed together."

They went through the normal shutdown procedures, and then popped their helmets. Cliff stood up with Bettie. He quickly hugged and kissed her. "We made it so far, Babe. "

Bettie gave him a game smile. "Let's see what our reception is going to be. After all, we are in an Enemy Aircraft."

They went to the airlock and un-toggled it. Not needing to pressurize, they then popped the outer door, and hit the automatic control to lower some stairs. And were facing at least a dozen armed Security Police, weapons all pointed at them.

Cliff quickly raised his arms. "Don't shoot. We are Unarmed." Bettie followed suit.

"Get down on the ground, Squid lovers!" A dark skinned man with NCO stripes yelled at them.

Cliff and Bettie moved to comply. As they started to knell, four uniformed personnel quickly closed on them. The two Colonels were slammed to the ground, arms painfully bent behind them as they were handcuffed. Cliff soon realized that the cuffs were put on so tight that his hands would soon go numb.

"Hey guys. We are not going to do anything. How about loosening these cuffs?"

A foot suddenly forced his face to the ground, embedding rock and soil into the side of his face.

"Shut Up, Squidsh*t. If we want something from you, we'll squeeze it out of you." The black NCO spat at him.

Somebody yelled "TEN HUT. Good Day, General."

A voice he had not heard in years asked. "Cliff Hunter, is that you?"

Cliff, the foot no longer on his face, spit some dirt out. "I think I hear John Reed. Yes, John, it's Cliff. And I'm in the sh*t again."

General Reed chuckled. "That is an understatement. Sergeant, let the Colonels up and take the cuffs off. If they were going to do something, they would have tried it by now."

"General, these Squidlovers helped kill my people." The NCO had a sound of hatred in his voice.

"Excuse me." General Reed began. "Did my Stars fall off my uniform? Let me check...Nope still there. Let them UP! NOW! Take the cuffs off."

The security troops scrambled to comply. No one wanted a pissed off General Reed. He already had two Executions under his belt for personnel who Refused Orders In a Combat Zone.

Cliff got to his feet, and then helped Bettie to hers. "May I present Colonel Bettie Bardun, Astronaut Extraordinaire and my wife."

"Now that is a surprise. It's bad enough everyone believed you dead. Now, someone actually married you? Good Morning, Colonel, and congratulations on your nuptials. "

Bettie tried to salute. "General....." She went white, and her knees buckled. Cliff caught her before she hit the ground.

"EMT. Get up and help the lady" General Reed commanded. The medics seemed hesitant. The General did something he didn't do often. He exploded.

"GOD DAMMIT! Move! If no one likes the fact I'm in charge then shoot me now. Otherwise, Move!"

Then everybody was scrambling.

"Let's get something straight right now. They may have just come from the Tschaaa, but they are still human military officers. You will treat them according to Military Regulations, UCMJ and the Geneva Convention. Clear?"

The Gathering Storm

"Crystal! Yes Sir. Yes General." Suddenly everyone was trying to do everything at once.

General Reed impaled the senior NCO of the EMT personnel with his eyes. "YOU. Senior Sergeant. Take the Colonels to the Hospital. Get them there in good order or you will wish you were never born. And tell the Doctors that I will be there and these Officers had better be receiving the best care possible. Or else. Understand?"

"Yes General."

General Reed wished that Torbin and Ichiro were here. They would go through these Nimrods like butter, kicking ass and taking names. Then he realized. The sun was rising. The Attack on Key West should be in full swing.

The General hot footed it back to his staff car, his driver already had it running and in gear.

"Sergeant Pascal, Hospital, Lights and Siren."

"Yes Sir." He took off like a shot. He was the Generals Driver because he had some Pre Strike experience with NASCAR. He beat everyone to the Hospital by a wide margin. General Reed jumped out of the car, not giving the Sergeant the chance to open his door.

"Once again, Sergeant Pascal, an excellent ride. Keep the motor running."

"Yes Sir, General." When he had gotten the job of Generals Driver, he thought he had Died and Gone to Heaven. General Reed was a Fighting General. Thus, lots of action, fast driving, never a dull moment. He grinned as the General charged into the Hospital. Nut Cuttin' Time.

Five minutes later, as Bettie was being wheeled into the ER, General Reed had almost the entire Hospital Staff 'on notice'. Screw this up, and you'd be up doing ear, nose and throat examines on the remaining Canadians in the Yukon.

"She's going into shock. Get an IV going. Colonel, can you hear me? Good. Hang in there. Focus on me. That's a girl."

Cliff stood by helplessly, watching his love being poked and prodded. He felt heartened when some color came back to her cheeks.

"She'll be okay, Cliff." General Reed had snuck up on him. "Quick and dirty. What happened?"

"General, she saw something that shouldn't be done by fellow humans."

"What was that?" Cliff told him in a few sentences, no frills. He saw General Reed's jaw tighten to the point that Cliff thought his teeth would shatter.

"You were kept incognito on Platform One for six years, no indication what they were up to?"

Cliff took a deep breath, and then let it out. "General, John, to be honest, I think I was trying to be purposefully ignorant. Out of sight, out of mind. I was selfish, trying to survive. Then, we saw those…..babies. And the love of my life may never be the same again." A tear ran down his cheek.

John Reed knew Cliff Hunter as one of the toughest, most competent Fighter Pilots he had ever known. He knew of Cliffs final Kamikaze Mission and, like everyone else, thought he was dead. Just like Captain Bender's brother, William. But he survived. And now his Soul was in Hell.

General Reed then did a very Un-General action. He put his arm around his Old Friend.

"Cliff, it will get better. I promise you. She will live. She's tough. We know all about her history over her last six years. She survived just like you, doing what she had to. "

He took his arm off his friend. "We will work this out. There is a certain Madam President that will want to talk to both of you. And we will need to formally debrief both of you."

Cliff wiped his eyes. "I' m at your service, General. Just, if you need to shoot someone, shoot me. Bettie has suffered enough."

General Reed chuckled. "Colonel, people have done a lot worse than you and were not shot. Just be honest when you talk to Madame President. The She Bear gets pissed when somebody lies to her."

∿∿

About an hour later, Bettie had markedly improved, but still felt like there was a huge weight sitting on her shoulders. A light sedative had helped calm her down so that she wasn't alternating between nausea and hyper ventilating. She had trouble closing her eyes. Images from the Lab kept flashing into her conscious thought. She was in a private room, with two Security Policemen standing guard. From what she had overheard, this had more to do with General Reed demanding she be protected than trying to keep her from fleeing. A small smile formed on her lips. She did not remember meeting John Reed while on active duty. But, since he was friends with Cliff, she knew he was a cut above other men.

There was a light knocking on the hospital room door. An attractive female in European Style Military Fatigues that looked Russian in origin entered. She Saluted.

"Colonel Bardun, Captain Aleksandra Smirnov of the Free Russian Military. Madame President asked me to check on you before she saw you. And, sorry, but she told me to ask you a few questions before she talks to you. Are you well enough?

Bettie nodded yes. "Go ahead and ask away, Captain. But if I suddenly freeze up, I apologize ahead of time."

Aleksandra, with years of interrogation training and experience, could tell something horrific had shaken her to the core. The Colonel had a feral fear and shock look in her eyes of the type Aleksandra had seen when someone had gone through rough interrogation, i.e. torture. But, she had her orders. She had to try and obtain answers.

"Colonel, what made you and Colonel Hunter flee?"

Bettie sat still for a moment. Then "Well, it was like this. I killed a vicious sick C%*t.....I mean, a Human Scientist working for the Tschaaa. She was doing some.....things that made Mengele look like a boy scout." Tears began to run down her face as she stared off into space, her eyes focusing on some un-seeable occurrence. "I stabbed her eye out, cut her throat, and then I puked on her."

"Colonel..."

"I killed her. And I wish I could do it , AGAIN, AND AGAIN AND AGAIN AND......!

Aleksandra saw she was about to go into severe psychological shock. She slapped the Colonels face. Not too hard, just enough to break the psychic loop she was about to go into, reliving something her mind did not want to. In a flash, Bettie's eyes focused on Aleksandra. She began to wail. Not like any type of wail that Aleksandra had ever heard before, but a wail that started deep in the soul of a person who had just seen a level of evil that some ancient peoples would have called the Face of the Devil. Aleksandra stepped out of her role as interrogator and into her existence as a woman. She went to the bed and hugged Bettie to her chest. She lapsed into Ukrainian, her Mothers Language, her father had been Russian. Before she realized it, she was cooing and whispering the same reassurances her Mother had said to her as a little girl. When a Security Officer tried to enter the room to see who was wailing, her Russian Training came to the fore.

"Get out. NOW! I will call you if I need you." She then switched to Bettie. "It is over, dear lady. It is over. You are safe. You are with good men and women again. It is a bad dream, which will fade with time. Trust me. I know."

Finally, Bettie stopped wailing, Still holding on tight to Aleksandra, she quickly blurted out what she had witnessed. Then stopped.

For a few minutes, the two women still clung to each other, finding comfort from the warmth of another human body. Bettie finally let go of Aleks and leaned back. She tried to wipe her eyes with a corner of the bed sheet, but Aleks produced a very feminine lace handkerchief.

"Here. My Yankee Husband gave me a set of these before leaving. Pretty, isn't it?" Bettie wiped her eyes, blew her nose, and then realized she had just messed up a present form Aleks' Man.

"Oh, I'm Sorry, Captain. I'm acting like pig in a slop pit."

"My name is Aleks, Colonel. May I call you Bettie? Thank You. It is now yours. Keep it as a sign of a new beginning. Now, I must fetch Madam President. She wishes to have a few words with you. Are you up to it? Good. Rest here. I will be back shortly."

Aleks patted her leg, smiled, and left the room.

"Men, I will be back shortly with Madam President. Do *not* bother the Colonel unless she asks. And, as my husband Torbin would say, Stay Frosty. Understand?

"Yes, Ma'am." The two Security Policemen answered in perfect unison. Aleks turned and strode down the hallway.

"That's Captain Bender's wife?" One troop asked the other.

"Yes, I guess she is. Man, I bet you he doesn't piss her off. She acts like she would cut your nut sack off in your sleep, and stick it in your mouth for grins."

The both chuckled, then, remembered Captain Smirnov's admonition and went to Parade rest, stern looks on their faces.

Aleks went down the hospital corridor and rounded the corner. She made a beeline to a Ladies Restroom, entered, and went directly to a stall. Aleks went in, noticed she was alone for the moment, bent over and vomited into the toilet bowl. She flushed and wiped her mouth with some toilet paper, spit, flushed, put the lid down and sat. She began to sob quietly. The Russian Spy did that for about a minute. She stopped, pulled a duplicate handkerchief of the one she had just given away, and dabbed at her eyes. Aleks got up, left the stall, went to the mirror for a quick light makeup repair. The statement Bettie had given her had shaken her. Probably because she had been married all of two weeks, her Husband was on a very dangerous mission, and she was sure she was pregnant. The image of the babies, raised without brains, for FOOD. It hit her in her abdomen where her baby would develop.

Aleks pulled herself up straight and looked in the mirror. "You are a Free Russian Officer," she told herself. "You have responsibilities" She took a deep breath, let it out, gave herself a once over, then walked out of the restroom.

She found Madame President with Mr. Williams in the cafeteria.

"Madam President, she is ready."

"Please wait here, George. I need to have some Girl Talk with the good Colonel."

"Yes Ma'am."

Aleks and Madam President walked towards the hospital room. In a few concise sentences in low tones, Aleks told the President why the two Colonels had fled Platform One, what they had seen. Madam President stopped short, staring at Aleks. "She…Said….THAT?"

"Yes, Ma'am. And I have interrogated many a …subject. Her reactions were completely truthful."

Madam President stood stock still. Then, she began to shake with rage.

"Those Mother….. My God, we do things to our own species that the Tschaaa would not dream of doing to their own kind. Maybe they are right. We are a bunch of out of control monkeys who need someone to sit on them."

"Ma'am?" Aleks looked at her with a worried look in her eyes.

She saw Aleks' reaction.

"Don't worry Captain. Just an old She Bear growling a bit, letting off steam. I think we can figure out how to handle our own problems with some ten limbed monstrosities telling us what to do. Let's go see the Colonel."

A couple of minutes later, the two guards were snapping to attention. "At Ease, Gentlemen. Relax. I don't bite." She knocked lightly, and then they entered.

Bettie tried to sit up straight at the sight of the President. "Madam President. Sorry I cannot stand up, but I have these damned tubes….."

She walked straight up to Bettie's bed. "Forget Damned protocol. Girl to Girl, Give me a Hug."

She sat on Bettie's bed and they hugged. Bettie began to cry again.

"It'll be okay, dear. I can say that. I'm the damn President." She hugged and rubbed Bettie's back. President Sandra Paul noticed her waterworks were beginning to flow. She untangled herself from Bettie, reached into the strapped large black purse she always carried and pulled out matching pink handkerchiefs. She handed one to the Colonel, and used the other to dab at her eyes.

"We Womenfolk are huggers, always have been. We have to bond to help each other protect our children from the saber-toothed cats until the Menfolk come home with the mammoth meat. Present day cattiness I think was accentuated by modern society. We left tribal, extended family life behind and looked for the answers in this huge amorphous thing we call Society. "

Bettie wiped her eyes, and then spoke. "Madam President, I am asking for your mercy for me and my husband, Colonel Cliff Hunter. I realize we have been working with the Enemy, the Tschaaa. I ask that we be given a chance……."

"OH, stop that Bettie. I may call you Bettie, can't I? Good."

Madam President continued. "You and your husband have not done anything that hundreds of thousands of others have done to survive this….Infestation. Yes, I think that is a more accurate term than Invasion or Occupations. We have been Infested by some four Alien Species, if you include the artificial Grays. And, they have been manipulating us ever since they landed. Hell, before the Rock Strikes, with their spies that look like us. And besides, your escape has, by some great act of Providence, helped us in our first great counter attack."

Bettie looked at her quizzically. "How so, Ma'am?"

"You took the attention off of our units approaching Key West, distracting one important Falcon and Robocop stationed there, that may have intercepted our units. And, the Eyes in The Sky were distracted also."

"Distracted from what, Ma'am?"

"Well, it's no secret now. Over an hour ago, a tactical Nuke hit the Squids Lord's stronghold off the tip of Key West. Initial reports are of heavy damage. We are hoping so called Lord Neptune is dead and is now irradiated fish food."

Aleks looked at Madam President. "Any word about....my Husband?"

She looked at the Russian Officer, a serious look on her face. "Sadly, no. The last we got from Captain Bender was the signal that the assault on the Director's Quarters had begun. The Nuke did what we hoped it would do...the majority of people at the Base headed towards hardened shelters, the Security Forces helped them according to the plan we had obtained. So, resistance was disorganized. We have intercepted some transmissions from Director's Lloyds Security Control at a listening post we had set up. They are running around like chickens with their heads cut off."

Aleks still looked worried.

"Look it, I ordered that Crazy Marine you married to bring my sainted husband's .44 Mag pistol back. You know he wouldn't dare piss off this old She Bear."

The three women laughed nervously. They all knew the cards were stacked against getting the Director.

The President turned towards Bettie, in low tones she began. "All right. Now, listen carefully. You and Cliff Hunter were part of a super-secret, extra special probation hidden plan to help distract the Tschaaa and the Director from out assault. That is why you left when you did. The death of the cu..., I mean human scientist, was part of the plan. Your extreme reactions were part of this plan. Only the good Captain here; George Williams, my special assistant; Captain Bender, General Reed and myself were privy to your plan. Thus, you will be considered heroes."

Bettie stared at her.

"But, Ma'am, that would be a bald faced lie. We had to escape due to selfish actions on my part." Her bottom lip began to quiver.

The President reached out and grabbed her hand. "Bettie, I believe everything happens for an eventual purpose. You, shall we say, 'saw the light', at just the right time. Who are you and I to defy Divine Providence? I know you want to punish yourself, to beat yourself up for surviving when others did not, for going back to Space on a Tschaaa supported mission. But, it helped you save Colonel Hunter. You got the Space Plane Here. You verified what we believed was going on with those so called scientists on Platform One. So, in the power invested in me as the President of the Unoccupied States, soon to be the United States Again, you and Cliff are Pardoned for any past crimes, know or unknown. Penance is between you and God. "

Bettie sat quietly for a few moments. Then she spoke. "I don't deserve this. But my Husband, Cliff, does. So for his stake, I 'll agree and not ask for a formal Courts Martial for Consorting with the Enemy."

Madam President looked at her intently. "You are extremely hard on yourself. But at least you agreed to my plan. Also, a side benefit to your escape dash is that there are four fewer Squid Pilots and Deltas, and two were damaged. One was taken out by Mother Nature and her lightning. Three went down to six Hawk missiles, two of those because they collided by trying to dodge the Hawks. The two damaged ones were hit by ground fire from a concealed Fifty Caliber Quad Meat Grinder that a military collector donated to us in working order. "

She Chuckled. "Squids have a tendency to break off combat when their Deltas are damaged, usually lacking the drive to risk pressing a kamikaze like attack. So, take my thanks and be done with it. Okay?"

Bettie swallowed a lump in her throat. "All right, Madam President. I will accept your forgiveness, your help. And maybe, someday I can fully forgive myself."

The President looked Bettie in her eyes. "Dear, I would have done the same thing to the so-called Woman Scientist. Only, I would be dead because I would have stomped her into mush and been captured. You and Cliff took the intelligent way out. And in the end, it helped us, the Good Guys. "

Bettie laid back. "Sorry, Madam President, but I am exhausted. I am going to ring my nurse and see if she will give me anything to help me sleep.... without dreaming."

Sandra Paul bent over and kissed her forehead. "Colonel, we are blessed that you and your husband are here. Please believe that. Now, get some rest. I will have Colonel Hunter come over soonest to be with you".

Madam President intercepted the assigned nurse, and had her ring up the Head Nurse and Senior Doctor on shift. Two minutes later, she was giving them their marching orders.

"Colonels' Bardun and Hunter are special heroes that were working directly for me. The details will be released later. You will give them triple A service, especially Colonel Bardun. She had a very horrific experience, and will be suffering from Post Traumatic Shock. Please have the senior psychiatrist on staff contact my Special Assistant, Mr. Williams, to arrange treatment. Any information inadvertently obtained is Classified until I say otherwise. Violate my orders, and I will find some way to send you to the North Shore in Alaska. Clear?"

"Yes, Ma'am." "Yes, Madam President." "Crystal, Madam President."

She left with her assistant George, and Aleks.

"As soon as I have details about Captain Bender and crew, I will call you. Aleks."

"Thank You, Madam President."

She looked at Aleks. "Thank You, my Free Russian Friend. God willing, we women will save this planet. See you soon."

The Perfect Storm had many parts. While Bettie Bardun was stabbing Doctor Smith's eye out, Adam was sitting at his desk. He had not been able to sleep past a few fitful minutes here and there. No one likes to admit they had been made to Play the Fool. Especially not one of the most, if not the most powerful human on Earth. His mind would not stop working. He now knew that the genetic, hormonal, organic manipulation had probably started before the first Rock Strike. How could up to 100,000 Humans actually buy into helping an Alien Species into occupying the Earth without some major manipulation? It made no sense, no matter how racist people were towards each other. Plus, he had been turned into a guinea pig, the ultimate manipulation, as had Kat, Mary, and untold others. This rested on his shoulders. He had helped to rebuild a system, a society controlled by an Alien Species, all in the name of Survival, of Life, the Protocol of Selective Survival. But, as a Human, was it "living" to live at the sufferance of a Species as genetically different from Human Primates as they were from a scorpion? All life in the Universe may start out with the same basic building blocks, but there the connections stopped. Despite the cephalopods native to Earth, the Tschaaa were ALIENS. Illegal Aliens, to be exact.

He sensed another human presence. Actually, there were two. Kat and Mary, soon to be official Sister Wives, softly padded in.

"Adam, are you okay? You aren't sleeping." Asked Mary. Kat walked up and around his desk and began massaging his shoulders.

"Boss, you are way too tight." Kat exclaimed. "Mary, I may need some help here."

Before he knew it, the two women had him lying on the floor on top of sofa cushions, as they worked, kneaded and massaged his entire body. He went with the flow, allowing the two Loves of His Life to do whatever they wished. Waves of relaxation washed over him, and his thoughts finally slowed. He began to lightly snore.

Mary whispered to Kat, so as not to wake him. "This is bad. I have never seen him so tense. Even after he executed that baby raper."

"That talk he had with his Lordship must not have helped at all." Answered Kat. "He won't tell us the details, but it looks like we are Tschaaa lab rats."

The odd tingling vibration that a Falcon produced when flying close nearby woke him. He and his lovers felt, and then heard the Falcon pass by. The Falcon rapidly accelerated, producing a sonic boom a few miles away. He sat up. "That must be Andrew leaving….Fast. Something happened."

Despite Kat and Mary's protests, he hit the Hot Line to Security Control. The phone conversation was short and to the point. The Director hung up the telephone. "There has been a killing on Platform One. And Colonels Hunter and Bardun have fled in the Space Plane. Andrew flew to the Cape in case they try to land there. He has orders to take them into his custody if they show up."

∽∽

The Perfect Storm continued. Because there were Deltas available, with aggressive young Tschaaa Pilots, levels of command lower than His Lordship had decided to launch them instead of sending a bunch of Falcons. After all, the Pilots needed some combat experience. So, they went to intercept, then His Lordship was contacted, being told it was just a matter of a few minutes before Bettie and Cliff were shot down. His Lordship, disturbed from his rest, agreed to the action, then sent Andrew to the Cape, just in case. In addition, since there was a chance they were headed to the Unoccupied Sates, he did not want to risk losing some Falcons. He knew the Humans were building up their Air Defenses. As long as they had no noticeable offensive capabilities to hurt him, he did not care. He had no interest in the cold and dry Midwest.

Another facet of the Perfect Storm appeared. A rebuilt B-25 World War Two Mitchell Bomber, late of a private air museum, was droning its way down Florida. Cutting across the Gulf of Mexico, in connection with the B-25, Ichiro Yamamoto leveled out his captured Delta Fighter, near the deck, at just under the speed of sound. With sudden rough running injectable scram jets, the Japanese Captain alternated cursing the situations with praying to any God which would listen. He needed to keep his speed up until he launched his special payload; a one megaton hypervelocity missile.

The Eye in the Sky saw a Delta, and then ignored it. There was no Squid FAA, no flight plans filed. No real IFF. Tschaaa Warriors followed orders of the local Lordships, so it was their worry if one disappeared. Only Human Craft traveling over three hundred knots an hour perked their interest as a possible threat to someone. This had not materialized. The Tschaaa, never having fought an all-out Air War on their home planet, had never developed a true sense of Detection and Defense. They had been the aggressors during the initial 30 days following the first Rock, had achieved Air Superiority due to all the Rock Strikes and attacks from Space. Earth Forces had made limited offensive responses, so the Tschaaa had seen no need to change their operations.

Now, the chickens were coming home to roost.

Captain Torbin Bender sat on the long jump bench that had been built into the modified B-25. There had been an ongoing discussion during the planning for this attack mission on related subjects. Such as, how big should the assault team be, and what aircraft should be used to transport it? Since the warhead Ichiro had should result in most people hitting the blast shelters, with the Security Forces helping to get the some 6,000 personnel into the shelters, it was decided that a relatively small, hard-hitting assault force was all that was needed. The Marquesas Keys were some 25 Miles away from the tip of Key West, so it would probably not take that long for the Key West Base to determine the level of danger, which was a Nuke had struck.

The rebuilt Director's HQ Building was just over a mile from the main Gate/Pass and ID building located on the Causeway off of Highway 1, the Oversees Highway. Thus, a low level chute drop near the causeway entrance on Highway one, then hot foot it down the causeway and through the Main Gate. It was hoped the Main Gate would be at minimum manning as everyone else hit the shelters. If not, hit fast, fight hard, try to blast through. It was believed that the Director, having the Captain of The Ship idea, would stay above ground in his office until the bitter end. Maybe he never went to any shelter, especially after nothing else hits the Keys.

Thus, twelve troops were selected as the Assault Team, with two more staying with the B-25 as Rear Security. Torbin knew he made 13 with the Assault Team, but was not the superstitious type. The size of the force and its success was based almost entirely on surprise and concentration of force at a weaken spot. Torbin knew the chances of success were low. He had tried to suggest a second small tactical nuke the size of the so called "suitcase device" to hit the Director's Area, but Madame President had refused. She did not want to risk killing women and children, not to mention the Conch Republicans.

The Gathering Storm

Her primary target was the Tschaaa, the attempt at the Director performed in order to capture or kill the Human Head of the Snake. Torbin was a Marine, a Professional Military Man. If he was given a lawful order to "jump" he said "Yes Sir, Ma'am, how high?"

The B-25 WWII era aircraft was chosen for two reasons. First, it was not a current era military aircraft. A C-130 could have been obtained, or maybe two large military helicopters. But that might have raised questions as to who had access to most current military aircraft. The B-25 was like a lot of aircraft that had been found stashed in private collections or on private airfields the last couple of years. Aircraft built to fly Low and Slow were popular, as they drew little if any attention from the Tschaaa and its minions anywhere in Continental America.

The second reason for the B-25 selection was that it was a tough, relatively simple military aircraft that had been easily modified for numerous missions. The current Pappy Gunn's ancestor had become famous in WWII for modifying the B-25 in a variety of ways, which it survived. Thus, the current B-25 was modified with jump benches, additional drop fuel tanks and a larger access/jump door. The two Pratt and Whitney engines were completely rebuilt, unnecessary equipment stripped to make it lighter, with less drag. Crew was just Pilot and Co-pilot. It could hit an honest 300 MPH low down. Now, the B-25 droned along, headed to Key West, Florida. Refueling at an airfield in Kansas, with large drop tanks attached, the B-25 had the Range to reach Key West. The plan was to do a low-level airdrop of some 250 feet near the access causeway to the Base, now defacto capitol of the Occupied States/Tschaaa Controlled areas, just as the nuclear device delivered by Ichiro hit and detonated.

As a connected side note, the 1 megaton bomb was a penetrating "bunker buster". Rebuilt from some former Minuteman ICBM warheads, it would penetrate the coral and tough organic "concrete" that the Tschaaa used as its primary construction material down several dozen feet, then detonate. Aimed at the center of the some 4 mile diameter 90% enclosed complex that had turned the Marquesas Keys into a huge repair, manufacturing, and administrative center, it was hoped the shock waves would cause the complex to collapse. The greater majority of the explosive force would be contained underground and underwater inside the circular Marquesas Keys. There would be a signature mushroom cloud, but the amount of crap thrown into the atmosphere would be reduced. The 25 mile distance from Key West, though over Flat Ocean, would help reduce the negative physical effects on Key West. But not the psychological fear of "Hey, they're Nuking us!" and the resulted flight to the shelters.

Torbin looked at the 14 people seated on the jump benches. The Senior NCO was Gunnery Sergeant Greg Smith. 30 years old white male of generic heritage, he had been a Marine since age 18. Broad shouldered, he still had a lean look about him. He was one of the designated Riflemen with the ubiquitous M-4. He and the other four Riflemen had six 30 round magazines of mixed armor piercing and ball .223/5.56 mm rounds. They also had two hand grenades, one blast, and one shrapnel, in addition to carrying a spare 40MM grenade for the three Grenadiers. Extra stripper clips of ammo were secreted in the spare areas of their combat fatigues for emergency resupply. Slung under his arm was a chopped down M-79 with two CS Gas rounds in a small pouch.

Corporal Manuel Martinez, former Private First Class and Torbin's driver, also fulfilled a Rifleman's slot. He had one additional piece of equipment, which was a WWII era silenced Hi Standard ten round .22 caliber pistol that had been "liberated" from some military museum. Light and proven, it was carried as an anti- sentry weapon. Martinez was a medium complexion and sized Mexican American who was quick and sure about anything he did. He had a Claymore Mine in his small ditty bag.

Privates First Class Moore, Money, and Muller, The Three M's, rounded out the Riflemen. They all had similar builds, medium heights, brown hair, and light complexions, so similar in appearance that they said they were all Brothers from Another Mother. But they were the Best of the Best, or they would not have made it to the Assault Team. In addition to the basic Rifleman load already mentioned, each had a ten round strip of linked ammo for the M-60 stashed in a fatigue pocket. In a flash, a thirty round belt could be put together for use. They also divided between them two LAWS and a Stinger Anti -Aircraft Missile

Corporal Benjamin Black, the Fifty Gunner Who Loved His Job, had turned the Ma Deuce in for a Barrett Fifty with three ten round magazines and a heavy duty scope. In his small back pack he had a thirty round belt of Fifty caliber for additional reloads. Due to the size and additional weight of the weapon and ammunition, he only carried a single hand grenade and a small smoke flare. Rolled up on his butt was a lightweight Ghillie Suit, in case he had to hide to shoot. He sat smiling; his large biceps and huge forearms gave him the nickname of Popeye. Black said his muscle development was due to him lugging around Fifty Caliber Ma Deuces the past years, often by himself with a unique bipod he had designed instead of the heavy standard tripod. He sat on the jump bench with his signature slight "Boy, are we going to have fun" smile. When he jumped, he would have the Barrett broken down into two pieces, barrel and receiver.

Sergeant Joe Hagel, a typical dark haired German of solid build, was equipped with a scoped M21, the semi- automatic sniper version of a Match M-14 7.62 rifle. He had his five-20 round magazines loaded with a Dutch Load of Armor Piercing(AP), Match Ball, and Tungsten Penetrator rounds. In addition to two hand grenades, in one of his fatigue tactical pockets he had a ten round linked strip of tracer for either his or the M-60s use. He had shot some five hundred practice rounds over the last two weeks, using the last twenty-five to sight in a new barrel. Everyone believed him when he said he could hit a gnat at fifty meters.

Sergeant George Washington, very large Black man, was the senior man after Gunny Smith. Sergeant Washington was one of the darkest skinned African Americans surviving in the Unoccupied States. He carried a M-60E1 7.62 Machine Gun with a two hundred round combat pack of AP,, Ball, and Tracer. In his tactical butt pack he had a rolled up 100 round belt. He also carried two grenades and a red smoke flare.

The Three Grenadiers were Private First Classes Joe Trump, a nondescript medium sized man of mixed European Heritage; John Fein, a skinny as a rail, six foot dark haired Irish/English mix; and Mathew Standing Bull, a very large Cheyenne Indian who needed to count some serious permanent "coup" to pay the Squids back for landing a Harvester near Reservation Land in Wyoming. All three men had M16A3 Rifles with attached M320 40MM Grenade Launchers. Each man carried five 40 MM grenades, three high explosive (HE) one newly developed High Explosive Anti-Tank (HEAT) with enhanced anti -armor capability, and one White Phosphorous Smoke Grenade that doubled as an incendiary device. They each also carried one hand grenade and five magazines of .223/5.56 ammo. Standing Bull, due to his size, carried a second Stinger Anti -Aircraft Missile.

The final Assault Team Member was Nick Nelson, a muscular five foot ten native Montanan who carried the M249 .223/5.56 Squad Automatic Weapon(SAW) with a two hundred round assault pack, seventy five round drum, and three thirty round rifle mags that would function in the SAW as well as an M-16. He had a light brown handle bar mustache that he refused to shave off until he had personally killed a Squid. Most of his family had been killed by a large Rock in the early days of the invasion. He carried a smoke grenade as well as a blast grenade.

There were two Rear Security personnel; the Huge Corporal Tatupu and Private First Class Danny O'Brien. Jet black haired "Danny Boy" came from a long line of Irish Cops and carried a sap that had been passed down generation to generation. It had busted many a head. He was the only team member dressed in a semblance of civilian attire, a Glock 26 9 mm with a threaded barrel for a silencer concealed under a Hawaiian Shirt. He was the Front Man, if someone needed to make contact with the Civilian Populace as they beat feet out of the Florida Keys at the end of the mission. Tatupu would cover him with a SEAL Version MP-5 Submachine Gun with the screw on Silencer that looked like a toy in his hands. He had also drug along a friend's .458 Magnum with three rounds of a special hand loaded armor piercing round for Robocop Protection, in addition to three commercial rounds. Tatupu had military camos on as he had to stay in the shadows due to his rather dark skin. His specific emergency skill was as a Special Forces Trained Combat EMT/Medic. He was to bring on board and patch up anyone who needed it as they hauled ass out. And, as added insurance, concealed under a tarp in the former Tail Gunner Position, was a Ma Deuce with a one hundred round belt. The Rear Security Team was to stay with the aircraft, as it flew to land at the Marathon Airfield, some sixty miles or so from the Key West Base.

Because it looked like many a nondescript aircraft that had been put back into service as a "low and slow" transport, after the low altitude insertion during the confusion from the Nuke Strike, the B-25 would land at the Marathon Key Airport. Cover story was that they were operating as a "Gypsy" transport service, one of many that had sprung up over the last year to take items A to point B on consignment, then scrounge a load back. This old style type of transport and capitalism was helping to re-develop an American form of commerce. The Squids couldn't care less, as long as their meat source was not interfered with. Rumors were that some pilots hauled Dark Meat for a price when asked. The two B-25 Pilots, Captains French and Vandenberg, were dressed in non-descript flight jackets and utility slacks. Stashed in the Cockpit, should their cover be blown, were two M-4s.

Tobin carried an M-4 with optics, four magazines of ammo, one smoke grenade, one blast grenade, and a Markarov 9mm pistol with threaded barrel and silencer. Plus he had a Claymore mine in a small butt pack. He also had a special weapon in a shoulder holster with a unique story.

He still remembered the meeting they had in the Hanger at Malmstrom some 48 hours prior. Madame President Sandra Paul had joined General Reed, George Williams and Pappy Gunn for a quick goodbye. As usual, she came in and took charge of everyone.

"Alright, gentlemen, lets form a circle please." The sixteen troops including Ichiro and two pilots quickly complied. Before he knew it, Torbin had his right hand grabbed by her left. "Gentlemen, everyone please grab the hand near you. We are about to have an old fashioned Prayer Circle."

A minute later, Madam President bowed her head a bit, and spoke with her clear, resounding voice. "Lord, we may not be all the same religion here, we may even have an Atheist or Agnostic or two. No matter. We are all Humans! Different colored humans about to make a perilous mission to attack an Evil that has come to Your Earth, home of the first humans. We ask you for your Divine Help, and Blessing on this endeavor. If one of these fine men should fall, please accept them into your Kingdom. For, no matter what flaws they may have, what sins they may have committed, this day they go to Fight and maybe die for all humankind. Please accept my Prayers. And all God's Children say…AMEN."

In that case, Torbin believed the story of there being no Atheists in Foxholes was probably true.

As everyone made last minute equipment checks, Madam President approached Torbin. "Captain, I have one small, unusual request for you."

"Of course, Madam President. "

Sandra Paul pulled a fairly large object from her signature large purse. "Here. This Smith and Wesson .44 Magnum four inch revolver was my Husband's Back-Up Bear Gun. This shoulder holster I believe you can get attached to your gear. You have five rounds of a special armor piercing load for any Robos and one of My Husbands 'bear loads' for a Squid. I have engraved "Property of the President U.S.A." on the back strap so you won't forget where you got it."

She paused then looked him straight in the eye. "I lost my Son, only to gain a Hell of a lot more sons, especially you and Ichiro. I hate sending you all out. But, I must. Please. Do what you can. Come back. I would love to be Godmother of yours and Aleks' child."

Tough, nasty Torbin Bender had a lump in his throat. He swallowed, came to attention, and snapped off a salute. "Yes, Madam President."

She chuckled despite the tears in her eyes. "You can take the Marine out of the Corps, but you can't take the Corps out of the Marine. May Godspeed you on your journey, Captain Bender." She turned and left.

As she walked away with George Williams IV, she reached out and grabbed his arm for support. George worriedly looked at her. "You okay, Sal?"

"Not really, George. This Old Broad suddenly became very, very, weary. Help me back to the Generals office, and maybe I can borrow some of his scotch. Then, I think I need a long sleep."

Torbin snapped his attention back to the present. Sometime in the next ten minutes, Ichiro, piloting the captured Delta, would reach Key West. He would launch the Hyper Velocity Cruise Missile with the one megaton Bunker Buster Bomb. As it sped towards the His Lordships complex, the pilots would get Ground Control on the horn, tell the story that they were a bit lost and would need to follow the Overseas Highway up to Marathon to find the airfield. In his day of limited air travel support, most pilots followed know highways to the desired destination. Ichiro would also try and take out the three ex ship board Phalanx Air Defense Gun systems arrayed in a triangle around the Base. All this activity should distract anyone from noticing the parachute drop.

From some 250 feet, using Russian D6 drogue stabilized chutes that were excellent for tight landing zones from low level drops, 12 team members and Torbin would hit the silk and land a few hundred yards from the causeway entrance that led to the main gate of the base. The Security Checkpoint/Main Gate was about halfway down the almost two hundred meter long causeway that bisected the channel near the entrance of the Former Key West Naval Base/Air Station. Hopefully, though some 25 miles away, there would be some effects from the Nuke that would draw the attention of everyone in the area. Since the attack and air drop were scheduled at dawn twilight, there would be a substantial flash and as well as probably some wind and turbulence, though dissipated by the distance involved. Metrological research pointed to the fact that the prevailing winds would be away from Key West in the impact area, so radiation exposure from any fallout would be reduced.

Torbin scanned his troops one more time. If the job could be done, they were the ones who could do it. He knew there would be casualties, probably death. That came with the territory.

Aleks was pregnant. He knew she was worried sick. Russian Officer or not, she was still a 'mother to be'. Torbin really wanted to be there when she finally gave birth. But, duty and humankind called. They had married two weeks ago, a simple ceremony with the Base Chaplin to give his first child a legitimate name. No Bastards for him. If he did not return, he knew Aleksandra would raise him/her, with help from his military mates at Malmstrom. He shook himself. No more woolgathering. It was time to be focused. Just then, he heard the Pilots Radio Crackle. It was time.

As the B-25 and Delta both approached their destinations, Ichiro cursed and swore in every language he knew. The Deltas Injector Scram Jets were losing power, and when he tried the pulse engine…Nothing. He had substantial momentum from gliding down from a couple of thousand feet as well as the distance where the Scram Jets had worked at full power. So, he would get near the Launch Point. Past that, all bets were off. Ichiro had decided that, if the already armed Hypervelocity Missile failed to launch, and he could not reach the Tschaaa complex, he would dive it into the Key West Base. He knew there would be huge civilian casualties, but he had to at least kill the Director. The Assault Team would die with him. That was unavoidable.

Somehow, Ichiro nursed the Delta along. He knew that the Key West base personnel would not attempt to contact the Delta, as Squid pilots did not carry translators. Ichiro was hoping no Robocop tried an informational interface, as that may be disastrous. Such an attempt would quickly reveal something was wrong, and a Falcon may intercept him. What Ichiro could not know was that two Former USAF Colonels had done something on Platform One that had everyone out of position for any intercept. Then, the Scram Jets sputtered more. Whether he liked it or not, it was time. Ichiro gave a short prayer and then launched the missile. At the same time, he tapped out quick a Morse Code broadcast of the letter "S" twice. A quick three dot reply from the B-25 acknowledged the reception. The Missile launched straight and true, accelerating to some 3600 miles an hour in seconds, turning and headed towards Marqueasas Keys.

Yelling "Banzai", Ichiro fired the plasma energy weapon in the nose of the Delta, taking out the Phalanx System he was lined up on. He skid and jinked the Delta and tried to snap off some reduced power shots at the other two Phalanx sites. He did not see a satisfying explosion as he had seen from the first shot. However, he was pretty sure he had at least fried some of their electronics, limiting their ability to shoot at the missile as it zipped by Key West.

Just then, the Scram Jets quit completely. He was porked. Ichiro made a quick decision. He turned the Delta with the residue energy and tried to aim it at the Headquarters Building. By this time, all Hell had broken loose on the various radio freqs, with the one Phalanx blown up and the other two unable to function, which told Security Control in a flash that something was wrong.

So, Ichiro was rewarded with Fifty Caliber strikes and a Stinger AA missile blowing his right jet pod apart, taking some aircraft control with it. The Key West Base Security Forces were pretty well trained, dammit, to respond this fast. A three inch former ship board gun firing air burst rounds also got a big piece of him. The Delta began to veer to the left, heading towards the entrance causeway. Ichiro tried to bring it back towards the Headquarters Building. No Joy. Seeing he was going down, he managed to regain enough control of the Delta to flair it out, dump air breaks, flaps, and popped the canopy of the modified to human cockpit, anything to slow it and bring it down into the channel water west of the causeway. If he struck the causeway road and bridge, he would damage the route Torbin and his Assault Team had to take to quickly get to the Director's Office area. That must not happen. The Delta flared on the edge of a stall then pancaked into the channel water. It slid on top of the water, then began to dig in. It finally stopped and began to sink, its nose some four yards from the causeway rocky edge near the Main Gate Entry Control Building and Guard Shack.

When Ichiro had sent the quick Morse Code to the B-25, the Pilot, Captain

French, realized he was about thirty seconds early. He had just started talking to Key West Security Control, which also acted as a flight control tower, telling them that they were a bit off course and trying to locate the Overseas Highway to follow to Marathon Airport. Just as the Controller on the radio was telling him to turn to a heading towards Marathon, he suddenly stopped, and yelled.

"Number one Phalanx just blew up! B-25 Aircraft. Leave the area immediately!"

"F@*!." Captain French exclaimed. He hit the jump light to flashing amber. "Captain. Gotta move now. Hang on!"

The Assault Team, seeing the amber light, had already stood up. They had been automatically checking their chutes and gear as they neared the destination, so everything was Go. They all grabbed the solid bars suspended from the top of the fuselage interior, and were lucky they did. The Pilot first banked to the right. Then, he rolled the WWII Bomber into a tight left hand turn, trying to line the aircraft up so as to fly straight up Highway 1. The modern stall warning horn began blaring, and the large airship began to shudder a bit.

"Come on. Baby. You can do it. Did I ever tell you, Joe, my Great Granddad flew B-25s in WWII?" Captain French said to his Co-Pilot, Captain Vandenberg.

Torbin said a quick Prayer. "Lord, send an Angel and give us more lift." He called to his Team. "Visors down." They had visors attached to their goggles that would automatically darken if there was a bright flash, like a Nuke. He knew that the missile Ichiro had launched would take about thirty seconds to reach the target. It should spend a second or two smashing down into the Tschaaa Complex, and then detonate. Despite it burrowing down, there would still be a flash and mushroom cloud. The 25 miles or so the blast would have to cross would take a little time, and the distance would hopefully reduce the physical effects to a little extra heat and a strong gust of wind. The plan had been to be hitting the ground in their chutes just before the wind hit so as not to screw up their tight landing pattern. Now, it was going to be catch as catch can.

Somehow, the B-25 did not stall. Captain French was leveling out when the Captain Vandenberg hit the Green Light and yelled "Jump." As he yelled this, unnoticed by either pilot, Ichiro's Delta hit the channel water. The B-25's wings were just level when Gunny Smith went through the door, with Corporal Black on his ass. The plan was for the Gunny and Black to get to the ground first and provide cover of the landing zone area, Highway One, just North East of the causeway entrance. Like clockwork, everyone was out, tight on the ass of the man in front. The drogues they threw out quickly deployed the chutes, and everyone landed just yards apart, like good Russian Paratroopers would. Torbin was the last out, yelled "Geronimo!" Just because he could.

The Gathering Storm

They had to jump early, so their landing zone was actually closer to the where the causeway connected to Highway One, rather than a ways northeast and up the highway from the causeway. Gunny Smith and Black hit almost at the signal light that controlled the traffic onto and from the Highway to the Causeway. Despite their darkened clothing and dark chutes, the small street light illuminating the traffic signal area made Gunny extremely nervous. The Main Gate Guard Shack was about two hundred feet down the causeway. Early Twilight causes problems with human eyesight, as the eyes are trying to switch from rods to cones. Thus, for a short while, things are a little indistinct, sometimes blurry. This was another reason why the assault was planned for Twilight.

Just after Gunny and Black had hit the silk, there had been a large flash from the Southwest direction of the Base. Ichiro's weapon had detonated. After a couple quick twists and turns, then a final short spiral, the missile had pointed straight at the center of the Complex. A glancing hit from a small plasma weapon, installed after his Lordship saw what the Director did in Key West for air defense, knocked the missile off course. It veered down to its left, and then went straight into the outer southeast quadrant of the circular Marquesas Keys. No longer striking the center of the Complex, the nuke hit the outer structures. It burrowed only some thirty feet down before it detonated. Taking the path of least resistance, a large portion of the blast was directed in a southwesterly direction into the surrounding sea and reefs.

∿∿

Prior to this, Adam had just hung up the telephone with Security Control after an Update on the Space Plane. Then his office windows shook. His radio began to broadcast the yells from the Security Controllers that a Phalanx had just blown up.

He yelled at Mary and Kat. "Shelter. MOVE."

"Adam. "

"Don't argue, Mary, move!."

Jamey and Jeanie came from the sleeping quarters, light robes on.

"Shelter. MOVE." The two Barbies bee lined to the escape elevator. Air Raid sirens began to undulate.

A little over two years ago, Adam had started the construction of a complex of underground shelters capable of holding the population of the Base. It had not been easy, as the Florida Keys sat primarily on coral reef materials, some soil the mangroves grew in, some rock. Using Tschaaa energy weapons, with help from some Grays, Lizards and a few Robocops, he had shelters constructed about two stories down. Soon, local Conch labor came to help, as did some of the new recruits for the New Capitol that came from the rest of North America. The shelters were constructed using a form of Tschaaa organic "cement" to build buried waterproof block houses (waterproof due to the shallow water table) for defense against a nuclear or biological. What Adam did not tell the Tschaaa was that the shelters were built as much for defense against a Tschaaa attack as from any rogue humans.

The elevator dropped down three stories from the second floor, where his office and the living area suites were situated. It dropped and automatically hit the patented Otis Elevator Emergency Braking System that let it slide to a stop on the bottom floor. It opened to an open blast door, which allowed entrance to the large two rooms and a small shower/bathroom room. With substantial emergency supplies, and an escape tunnel modeled after the Minuteman Missile Launch Control Facility tunnel, survivors could last for weeks.

As the women dropped via elevator down to the shelter, Adam grabbed a hotline he had installed a few weeks ago directly to His Lordship. He buzzed the connection. A few moments later, His Lordship picked up.

"Director. It is early and I was still resting. What is happening?"

"Lordship, we are under attack. Get to shelter!"

His Lordship paused, and then hung up. Adam stood up to get his body armor and weapons when there was a flash of light across the lawn areas around the Headquarters Building. Not overly bright, but bright enough to know that a Nuke had detonated off in the distance. Adam heard a distant rumbling, followed by substantial winds blowing across the base. Adam knew a nuke had detonated on top of the Tschaaa complex at the Marquaesas Keys. He punched a direct line buzzer to Security Control that signaled Hit the Shelters. Security Control, if they hadn't already figured out what was happening, immediately began the planned and practiced Shelter Evacuation Plan. A special klaxon went off. Every single Security Soldier, all some 500 of them, were mobilized to get the populace to the shelters. They rushed to put MOPP gear on, as most were to remain above ground to secure the base from further attack. This, if there were a tactical nuke strike follow-up, would be a death sentence. Adam was expecting another nuke in the first minute after the first strike at the Tschaaa Complex. When this did not occur, he knew that they had been spared, for whatever reason. But, depending on prevailing winds, fallout could be the death of them yet.

Chief Hamilton picked that moment to enter his office.

"Well, Adam, I think the balloon just went up."

"I think you are right, old friend. The Ladies are in the shelter. You need to take the ladder down to it."

The Chief snorted, "Yea, Right. You can order me all you want, but I'm staying next to you, watching your back. Just like Old Times."

Adam smiled at his friend. "Willie, no matter what happens, it has been a pleasure." He reached his hand out. Willie took it. "Hell, Director. We're not dead yet. Let's have some fun"

On Highway One, the wind had hit just as the Assault team landed. Only their extensive training enabled them to hit their quick release clasps before the wind began to blow them around. As it was, Torbin was pulled on to his butt before could release his open chute. Luckily, this early in the morning in a limited populated area, there no one moved around or near them. However, they had landed so close to the entrance to the causeway that Torbin was sure someone had seen them and would be sounding the alarm. The Gunny, thinking the same thing, had already told Corporal Black to get his Barrett Fifty Caliber operating and cover the Guard Shack/Entry Control Building. A hundred yard or so shot would be easy for Black. So far, no signs of reaction as the Assault Team formed-up.

What no one knew was that the Sergeant and Security Patrolman who manned the entry point were already scrambling to throw on their MOPP Gear. The explosion of the Phalanx had drawn their attention first, then the Air Raid Sirens. As soon as the warning sounded after the distant flash, even before the accelerated wind hit, they put the MOPP head pieces on, and scrambled to zip up their coveralls. There was no thought of anyone attacking their position on foot. After all, anyone doing so would be hit by radiation. The idea that the detonation was too far away to really irradiate much had not sunk in. They heard a large object strike the channel and send water shock waves up into the causeway, but the explosion of the Phalanx, the Air Raid Sirens followed by the flash and klaxon, had quickly distracted them. They had heard the approaching Delta, but had seen many before this. The idea that a Delta could be behind the attack was not credible to them.

"Hey, hurry up with your gear and see what hit the water." The Sergeant ordered.

Grumbling about possible radiation exposure, the Security Troop finished with his MOPP gear, not bothering to put his weapon and ammo harness back on. He grabbed his M-16 and went outside to look.

Ichiro had survived the impact thanks to tight cockpit straps, though he knew there would be some bruising. He hit the quick release clasps and was out of his unused ejection seat. He had designed and had made a special Quick Release G-Suit. A few Velcro straps and a long zipper and he was out of it. Underneath, he wore a black Ninja suit, traditional head gear and all. Only his eyes showed, though he had a pair of smoked pilot's glasses on to protect him from any residue light from the flash of detonation. He took those off and tossed them into the Delta cockpit.

The Security Troop was hampered by several things when he went to see what had hit the channel. First, the MOPP Gear head piece was not conducive to good sight, it being built primarily for protection with an integral gas mask. Second, his eyes switching from rod cells to come cells due to sunrise twilight, then the weird flash, had made his normal good vision a bit indistinct. Next, the tendency of the human mind to see what it expects to see. When he saw Ichiro clamber into the water and head to the rocks that surrounded the Entry Control Point on the causeway, he surmised it was a Gray or maybe one of those new Soldier Class of artificial being that had been recently introduced. He knew Grays flew Tschaaa craft sometimes, so why not the new Soldiers. Humans did not.

"Hey, if you can understand me, grab my rifle barrel and I will help you up. The safety's on."

The figure grabbed his rifle barrel. Instead of pulling itself up, the figure yanked and jerked the Troop forward and down towards the water. Off balance from standing on the large rocks, he quickly fell into the channel, the rifle twisted from his grip. His cries were muffled inside the MOPP gear, and he soon struggled to stay afloat in the restrictive suit. The Sergeant had heard another large splash and went out to investigate.

"Hey, did you fall in or..." He was face to face with a figure all dressed in black. The Sergeant had a .308 G-3 late from the German Army that he tried to bring into play. A katana parried the barrel up as he fired a single round off into the night.

Ichiro, actions born of a thousand practice sessions, brought his sword down in a half circle and then stabbed two handed upward, low into the Sergeants body to avoid body armor. The Japanese Warriors sharp blade penetrated upward into the lower abdomen, up to knick the right lung and then bumped the spine. Ichiro twisted the blade sideways, hitting the spine with the cutting edge, and then pulled it back out. The move was over in less time than it took to read this passage. The Sergeant collapsed to his knees, his spine partially cut, then fell forward onto his face as he grabbed his abdomen. Ichiro struck the base of his neck with the hard blunt end of his blades grip, and the Sergeant lay still. This was only the second Man he had ever killed. His mission in life was to Kill Squids. But sometimes circumstances dictated your actions. He wiped his katana on the dead Sergeants MOPP uniform, and then ran low down the causeway onto the base, trying to keep to the shadows. As he exited the area he had smashed an overhead light attached to the building with his sword.

When the .308 went off, Cpl. Black was just getting into position with his Barrett. He saw the rifle flash, tried to use his scope to see what was going on. The sun was working its way up over the horizon, to replace the short flash of light from the Nuke. He saw a dark figure move, then disappear past the Entry Point Building as a bright light on the front of the building went out.

"Whadda see?" Gunny Smith asked, crouching down by him.

"I saw the muzzle flash, then a figure running off into the dark, down the causeway. Wait. There is another figure getting out of the channel….And there's something partially submerged in the water. Maybe an aircraft. Want I should take that figure out?"

"No, too much noise, even with the air raid sirens going off. This Fifty has a distinctive bark"

At that moment, in low crouch, the assault team showed up on the entrance to the causeway, Torbin in the lead.

"Cover us, Black." Gunny said. Black just smiled. He loved his work.

Gunny joined the rest of the team across the four lane causeway road, and told Torbin what had just happened.

"Damn it, I bet that was Ichiro and that is his Delta, sure as sh*t. Come on, let's get there before that troop getting out of the water blabs we're here."

They ran crouched down the Causeway, thankful that the Base personnel had been stingy in putting up lights on the Causeway. The one Ichiro had taken out had been a bright flood light, aimed into the eyes of oncoming traffic to slow approaching vehicles and people down. However, the sun was working its way up over the horizon, They had to move fast.

The water logged Security Troop had made it up out of the water and onto the causeway, sans his rifle. He finally deigned to remove his MOPP head piece as he could not see out his soaked integral gasmask eyepieces.

"Soldier, what is going on here?" A stern voice commanded. He looked and saw a Captain he did not recognize, sans MOPP gear, standing in front of him. He heard running figures.

"I don't know Captain. Some Gray threw me in the water...and, OMYGOD. The Sergeants down." As he turned to see to the Sergeant, Torbin hit him at the base of his skull with the butt of his M-4. The man collapsed. Torbin checked his pulse…still alive. No need to kill people unnecessarily. He retrieved the Sergeants rifle. Good, a .308, hopefully with some distinctive tracer rounds in it. Nothing like perceived friendly fire to confuse the issue. He slung his M-4 and held the G-3 at low ready and ran after his troops.

As soon as he saw Torbin take the remaining sentry out, Black jumped up, grabbed his Barrett and began running to catch up on the Causeway. He saw

Hagel waited for him by the guard building. As he closed, he saw the Sniper had a hand held radio in his hand, apparently obtained from the building.

"Come on, Black. I don't want to miss the party." He stepped back into the Guard Shack and ripped the direct land line to Security Control from the wall. Torbin was behind the team, had been delayed by smacking the surviving Security Troop. He glanced back and in the brightening morning, saw Hagel and Black hotfooting to catch up. The front part of the team exited the causeway onto the Base proper at this moment. Off to the right was the Headquarters Building. Gunny Smith used hand signals to spread the team out into a Line Assault Formation. They were approaching the HQ Building from the northwest side, some half mile away. Torbin was catching up when he heard vehicle engines. From his left came three Security Vehicles, a Humvee with a 50 Caliber mounted on Top and two Jeeps. Each had two MOPPed out soldiers in them, so the drivers were trying their hardest not to hit something due to their limited vision.

He turned towards them and began waving at them like he had something to tell them. As the drivers began to slow down, keyed on him, Torbin went into the CQB Groucho Marx Walk, raised the .308 Rifle and fired full auto. He fired at the Humvee driver first, the heavy mixed bag of armor piercing, tracer and ball rounds punched through the front semi armored windshield and hitting the driver. The Humvee skewed off to its right and hit a palm tree lining the HQ Entrance Road, the Gunner on top almost thrown off. The middle jeeps driver was hit by the next burst, which caused him to cut the wheel so sharp the Jeep flipped on its side, and rolled, the passenger being thrown free. The third Jeep Torbin hit with the final rounds in his magazine, the driver slammed on its brakes and try to back up. The radiator was trashed and a round clipped the steering wheel. The driver and his passenger bailed out.

Sergeant Hagel arrived on the scene, heard on his purloined radio screams of "Cease Fire. Blue on Blue. Cease Fire," someone thinking Captain Bender was a Friendly who had opened up by mistake on the vehicles. The Gunner on the Humvee began to fire his Fifty Caliber as Torbin dropped his now empty .308. Luckily, the first rounds went high, and Torbin flattened himself out on the ground, tried to make himself as small a target as possible. The Humvee Gunner started to adjust his fire when his weapons receiver exploded. Sgt. Hagel had hit the Ma Deuce with a .308/7.62 AP and a tungsten penetrator round, detonating the round in the chamber and destroying the receiver. The Gunner fell into the interior of the Humvee. Torbin jumped to his feet and signaled to Black, running up behind Hagel, to take a cover position underneath some bushes in a small depression. His spot would give the Barrett operator the ability to cover the main entrance of the HQ Building as the Assault Team

Members entered.

The two Security Soldiers from the third Jeep fired from some bushes near their disabled vehicle. Once again, the restricted vision from the MOPP Head Gear was not conducive to accurate fire and the first rounds went high. Torbin rolled behind an old U.S. Post Office Mail Box that someone had left in place. He leaned around the right side of the box and fired his M-4 on full auto. Sgt. Hagel fired his M-14 into the bushes also, sent three rounds down range. The firing from the bushes stopped.

A burst of fire from the HQ Building parking lot set rounds ricocheting around the Assault Troops. Before there were any casualties, Sgt. Nelson let loose with his Mini 249. The Security Soldier hidden behind a vehicle was hit and went down. The gunplay stopped. Torbin saw the Gunny, about twenty five yards in front, looking at him. Torbin signaled to continue the Assault to the HQ Building. Torbin started to stand up and leave the cover of the mailbox. Then, all Hell broke loose.

Thirty Caliber auto fire came from the roof of the HQ Building. Chief Willie Hamilton had gotten into the fray with his beloved BAR. Of course, Torbin did not know who it was. The 30.06 AP rounds began striking around the Assault Team Members, as they scrambled for cover behind the few vehicles and light poles in the lot. An AP round went through both of Sgt. Nelson's thighs, taking him to the ground. Rounds hit the mailbox Torbin was behind. He tried to crouch lower. From behind a palm tree lining the parking lot entrance, Sergeant Hagel responded with his scoped rifle. Just as Chief Hamilton shifted the BAR to reload with a fresh magazine, Hagel fired. The AP rounds smashed into the BAR rather than the Chiefs head. He sprawled backwards. Torbin could tell things were heating up, so he yelled at the Gunny.

"Take them into the building!"

As he started to leave the cover of the mailbox, more rounds of a different caliber began to hit it. He ducked back behind it. "This is getting damned ridiculous." He mumbled to himself. Director Lloyd was firing from his second floor office window with a 10mm Ex FBI MP-5. The heavy rounds rang the mailbox like a drum. Torbin snapped a burst out in the general direction before he ducked back behind the mailbox. Just as Adam ducked back into his office, Sgt. Hagel blasted the window area with his M-14. Adam was splattered by pieces of wood molding and he dwent to the floor. Torbin, seeing Hegel's action, was up and ran towards the rest of the Assault Team. Hagel, seeing no motion from the second floor window, began to head forward also.

Torbin yelled at him, "Did you hit anyone?"

"Can't tell, Captain." Although Torbin was supposed to try and capture the Director Alive, that option was rapidly disappearing. He considered blowing the shit out of the office with HE rounds. But then he could not tell for sure if he got him or not. Damn. He had to try at least one assault, as per orders.

As soon as Major Jane Grant had realized that an assault team was on Base, she started to form a fire team sans MOPP gear. She knew that no logical commander would waste a highly trained team if he was planning on Nuking or hitting the Base with a Bacto-bomb. She also knew they were after the Director with the least amount of Collateral Damage. Security Control was only some six blocks from the HQ Building and she began to throw a team together.

∽∽

As this happened, and Adam was on the office floor, a voice crackled over a small radio receiver he had on his desk.

"Director, I will be there in ten seconds." It was Andrew. After getting word of the Nuke Strike, and verifying here was no chance of the Cape being the destination of the Spaceplane, Andrew had elevated his Falcon off the tarmac near the Cape, rotated towards the direction of Key West, then took off like a Bat out Of Hell. Now, he was almost there. Once again, the people on the ground felt the odd vibrating electricity that preceded the arrival of a Falcon. Then it was over the Parking Lot. Torbin swore.

"I need the Grenadiers, Stingers and LAWs up Front. Fire at will!"

Andrew sat the Falcon down between the Assault Team and the front entrance. He had considered just blasting away, but did not want to cause any more collateral damage that he had to. For once in his existence, Andrew had underestimated the capabilities of his former fellow humans and overestimated his Falcon.

Andrew set the Falcon down, and started to scan the area with his sensors. Then the Falcon shuddered with the hits from two HE 40MM and one HEAT round. This was quickly followed by a LAW rocket. A Falcon had a so-called force field or "shield" system. However, it was made to operate in near vacuum conditions, as atmosphere degraded its capabilities. Therefore, the system was rarely operated close to the ground. Only the tough organic barnacle like skin was there for protection. The LAW Rocket, capable of penetrating eight inches of hardened steel, blew a satisfactory hole in the hull, damaging some of its control systems. The 40MM Grenade shells did lesser damage, but some damage none the less. Andrew quickly dropped to the parking lot pavement through an escape hatch. As he dropped, the Falcon began to power up and rise straight up. As it rose, the Stinger missile, with an enhanced warhead, struck the underside of the Falcon, blowing a satisfactory hole. The craft wobbled a bit, and then dashed towards the ocean. Andrew sprinted to the entrance door of the HQ Building at an Olympic Games Plus speed.

Andrews interface system told him that the Falcon had taken some substantial damage, more than he had considered possible. He sent it to a safe distance, saving it from further damage. He may need it to bug out with the Director. Andrew realized he had made a significant error in not taking the chance of collateral damage and should have targeted the parking lot, blasting anything that moved. But he had become so used to people acting in abject fear to the Falcons and the capabilities they reflected, the concept of a substantial attack had become foreign.

The Assault Team let out various whoops of joy and satisfaction at the sight of fleeing Robocop and Falcon. Torbin yelled. "Forget the Falcon. Hit the Building."

There was a loud report from the roof of the Building. A .338 Lapua round smashed through Sergeant Hagel's body Armor and he collapsed. Chief Hamilton, a bit banged up, was still in the fray with a sniper rifle he had as backup. Torbin was close enough to the Gunny that he dashed over and grabbed the loaded Shorty M-79. He spun around and lobbed the CS Shell onto the top of the HQ Building just as the .338 rifle spoke again. The heavy round hit Rifleman Moore's M-4, smashing and jamming the receiver. He yelped and dropped the weapon. Before Willie Hamilton could fire again, the CS Shell hit the roof, began spinning and shooting CS Gas about. With no gas mask, the Chief was soon spitting, sputtering and then retched. He stumbled to the exit hatch in the roof to get away from the gas.

Handing Gunny back the M-79, Torbin went over to Hagel. He was dead, the heavy round overpowering his body armor and hitting his heart. Torbin took his Dog Tags, grabbed the M-14 rifle and a spare magazine. He would grieve later. Three large figures came striding from the far side of the Parking Lot. Torbin immediately recognized them as the new Soldier Class being the Tschaaa had developed. A smaller, Poor Man's Robocop, they were still well over six feet tall and tough. Torbin slung his M-4 and began shooting the M-14 at the figures. He was joined by the Riflemen and Sgt. Washington with his M-60-E1. High velocity bolts of energized metal needle shaped rounds came from the odd looking, large weapons they were carrying. PFC Mooney took a round full in the chest. The round from the Bolt Gun, of the type demonstrated to Adam Lloyd some time ago, blasted through his body armor and through his body. Mooney toppled over, dying. A similar round hit Cpl. Martinez in the chest, and he fell backwards.

Sgt. Washington screamed out a curse and began slamming 7.62 machine gun rounds into one, then another of the Soldiers. Torbin concentrated on one as he yelled "Grenades." Sgt. Washington concentrated his fire on the head of the nearest Soldier, and was rewarded with the head toppling off the beings shoulders. The legs locked and it fell like a tree. Torbin smashed several rounds into the face and neck of one of the remaining Soldiers. Blinded, it started to fire in all directions, a bolt catching Gunny, knocking him over. Then there was a loud report. Black's fifty caliber slammed into the Beings chest, knocking it over. It lay still.

A 40MM Grenade caught the third Soldier full in the chest, blowing it apart. Torbin dashed to Gunny, just as he began cursing and trying to get up. The bolt had hit his body armor at an angle, singeing and bruising his ribs before exiting.

"Going to make it, Gunny?"

"F%*&, yea, Skipper. This is just a scratch." He grimaced as he said that.

Cpl. Martinez stood up, yanking and pulling at his body armor. There was smoke rising from the front of his fatigue top. He threw off his armor, and then pulled a smoldering object from underneath his t- shirt. It looked like a book.

"Santa Maria. My Mom's Bible saved me." Cpl .Martinez exclaimed. The bolt had penetrated his rifles receiver, his front armor plate, coming to rest in the back of a small Bible he was carrying inside his fatigue top. His chest was singed by the fire started in the Bible and his chest was bruised, but that was it.

Tobin gave him his M-4. "Here, use this. Your rifles trashed."

Torbin heard the Gunny curse some more. "Skipper, something hit my rifle. The bolt is fused."

"Go grab Nelsons SAW M249. He can't move with his thighs shot to hell."

Moore went and checked on Mooney. The bolt round had penetrated his body armor and into his chest. He was dead. Moore grabbed his Dog Tags and his rifle. "See you later, Buddy." He would also grieve later, if given the chance.

A thirty caliber tracer zipped by. Everyone grabbed cover behind the few vehicles, light poles and palm trees in and around the parking area. Some three hundred yards away a line of some Non-MOPPED troops were approaching, about seven in number. Torbin yelled for smoke, and two grenadiers each fired a 40MM smoke round in front of the assault line. The WP round set up a thick barrier of white smoke between the attacking Security Forces and Torbin's group.

Gunny Smith crouched next to Torbin behind a staff car that was parked on the edge of the parking area. Torbin said "Excuse me," grabbed the Shorty M-79 from the Gunny again, loading the last CS round. He fired it and the CS round hit near the barrier of smoke.

A couple of Security Troops dashed through the smoke, firing, and then proned out on the ground to provide fire for the others trying to assault through the smoke. They began to cough, choked, then retched as the CS Gas, hidden in the smoke, hit them. With no gas masks, they had no protection. Two more armed human soldiers came through the smoke, and ran into the CS concealed gas. They tried to keep firing, but soon choked, coughed, retched, and their eyes blurred with tears. Two other Security Troops swung wide of the smoke barrier, coming around the North end of the smoke, missed the CS Gas. One fired a grenade, and then was blown apart by Black's Barrett .50 Caliber. His comrade tried to flee back and was hit and downed by rifle fire. The rifle grenade exploded at the feet of Joe Fein, slamming him backwards. It nearly amputated his right leg, and he lay with his life's blood spurting out from a cut femoral artery.

Cpl. Martinez tried to stem the flow of blood, but was unsuccessful as there was more than one puncture. Fein was dead within a minute.

Torbin had to make a quick decision. His small force was being whittled away; the blocking Falcon has delayed the Assault just long enough to allow other forces to arrive.

"Gunny. Base of fire with that SAW. Sgt. Washington. You, Trump, Moore, Muller. Hit the Building. Everyone else, on me, covering fire."

Technically, the twelve man Squad/Assault Force was divided into two Fire Teams, under Sgt. Smith and Washington. Or, it could be reconfigured into three-4 man teams. All twelve men were trained to operate with any others as part of any sized force. So, no matter who was left, they slid into whatever slot was necessary. With the Squad Automatic Weapon as the Base of Fire, Torbin, Standing Bull, and Martinez spread out and began suppressive fire across the parking lot. Sgt .Washington, Trump, Moore and Muller began the mad dash to the entrance door. Nelson lay cursing next to Black's concealed position, his shot up legs preventing him from doing much of anything. He had yelled and had someone throw him Fein's rifle with grenade launcher before they all got busy. He checked it over and it seemed to be still operational. He turned, slid around and faced backwards, cursing from pain. He had refused to take the morphine in his first aid kit, not wanting to dope himself up to the point of ineffectiveness. At least he could be rear security.

The four CS gassed soldiers tried to fire at the figures running at the door, but were too gassed to be effective. Finally, they began to crawl and roll back through the smoke barrier. One was hit and stopped moving. Torbin had the rest hold fire until another threat appeared. The lone gunman, who had fled when his Grenadier Buddy had been hit by Black's Fifty, tried to engage Washington and his men from prone behind a light pole, as Major Jane

Grant tried to help the three gassed survivors to safety behind a nearby small utility building. She received a good dose of residue CS for her trouble. The Major yelled for backup over her radio. The lone gunman, for his bravery, was sieved by the Assault Team. Then they were through the Front door of the Headquarters Building.

The original passenger from the Humvee Torbin had taken out finally made another appearance, MOPP gear and all. He had recovered a rifle and tried to hit the Assault Team in the rear. Sgt. Nelson shot him through his forehead with one round, killing him instantly.

"Get something, Sarge?" Black asked, still providing long cover with his Barrett.

"Yea, some dumbass still in full MOPP gear trying to sneak up on us. You'd have thought he would realize that a full-fledged Nuke or Germ Attack would have taken place by now. Now, he can't realize anything."

"Yea, Sarge. War is Hell. But it sure can be fun." Black smiled, unnoticed under his Ghillie camouflaged poncho.

Through the two sets of double doors in the front of the HQ Building was the foyer, with a large, winding staircase that led to the left up to the second floor. Here were the Director's Offices and the living suites. Andrew had already sped up the stairs, went into the Director's office.

Adam heard something and spun to face it. "Please do not shoot, Director. I just had a new finish put on my body."

Adam smiled. "I still have not figured out how you, being so large and heavy, can move so quietly."

"Superior technique and technology, Director. In that order. And now, I must get you out of here."

"Can't do that, Andrew. I'm the Captain of the Ship. Can't leave with crewmen still aboard."

"Director, Adam. The subject is not up for discussion." Andrew seemed to glide over and picked Adam up effortlessly, holding him under his left arm like a small ankle bitter dog.

"God Dammit. Put Me Down!"

"Sorry, Director, Higher orders." He walked through Mary's office towards the exit to the stairs. He stopped, then set Adam down.

"The enemy is too close to the front door, and too well armed to risk running with you. I will have to dispose of the threat first, and then move you."

"What about the Falcon?"

"Sadly, due to my misjudgment, I underestimated their capabilities to do damage. The Falcon is sitting well off shore. Now, I must engage the attackers and beat them back. Please stay away from the windows, Director, and in the center of the office. I shall return."

Andrew slowly walked towards the winding staircase. He was interfacing with the various cameras, radios, and surveillance equipment in the area to obtain a true picture of the attacking force. He saw the Tschaaa Soldiers had been taken out rather quickly. Then, the Security Forces beaten back. And the attackers were coming straight to the Headquarters Building.

Just then, Chief Hamilton came sputtering, choking down the hallway from the ladder that went to the roof.

"Chief, are you well?"

"As well as one can be, after being gassed and hit with shrapnel. "

"Please, join the Director in the office. I must deal with these attackers directly." The Chief did not have to be told twice. He went in.

Andrew decided he would wait at the top of the stairs, giving him space and distance to use his targeting systems. He had the capability to target any incoming object, including a bullet if given a good distance for response, and hit it with the MP-5K compact weapon he carried on his hip. He had found, as many of his brothers had found also, that their integral interfaced targeting system worked just fantastic with conventional human weapons that threw bullets downrange. One bullet, one hit, at the most vulnerable spot on the target. Using his computer interfaces, he dimmed the lights in the foyer and the upper stairs landing. e stepped back into the shadows and waited. He did not have to wait long.

Washington busted into the building first, and noticed it was darkened. The Sun had begun to rise, so there was some ambient light coming in through the small sun dome that the Director had built above the staircase and foyer. However, all the interior lights were off. He slipped on his night goggles.

"Let me take a look with my night goggles first." He told the other three, as he motioned them to stay put at the entrance. He moved slow but sure into the foyer and looked around. Andrew saw the night goggles and hit them with a pencil beam of light. The goggles safety feature to prevent blindness shut them down, but Sgt. Washington still saw stars and dark dots. He swung his M-60EI up and began firing. The other three Assault Troops hit the doorway and came boiling in.

The small light had told the humans the threat was on the second floor, so they began firing in that general direction. Andrew began to take a few rounds on his armor, so he moved swiftly to the right towards the top of the winding staircase and opened up one handed with his MP-5K. Four targets, four hits on the torsos to start with. The small rounds were stopped by the body armor and had been more of a last minute warning to flee than anything. As he fired, PFC Trump fired his 40MM grenade at Andrew. The Cyborgs fifth shot hit the round halfway to its target, detonating it. Surely the blast would make the troops realize who and what they were dealing with! But Andrew, having dealt with a fairly passive population the last couple of years, dulled by his interface with so many emotionless databases, had again underestimated the enemy's capabilities. And anger.

Large, Black, Sgt. Washington, charged up the stairs, through the back part of the blast, firing his M-60 as he moved two steps at a time. In his hands, the M-60 seemed to be as light as a BB Gun. The AP and Ball rounds smashed into the Robocop, denting the front armor plate. Surprised with the ferocity of the attack, Andrew sped along the top of the stairs back to the shadows where he had been. Sgt. Washington kept firing, some of the rounds hitting Andrew. The Cyborg fired a round into the large man's head, hitting the helmet because the Human happened to duck his head just as he had fired. Washington fired at the muzzle blast, smashing the MP-5 barrel, causing it to jam.

"I got you now, B*TCH!" Sgt. Washington screamed as he reached the top of the staircase. The MP-5, propelled with great force, smashed high into the man's chest, knocking him on his ass. Somehow, the NCO remained cognoscente enough to reach for his hand grenade attached on his left shoulder. He saw a figure approach from his left as he started to pull the loosed pin with the thumb on his right throwing hand. It was the Director, approaching with his sub gun.

In a microsecond, Andrew processed the scene. The Director had not stayed back, was now in danger. He launched himself with inhuman speed, smashed into Sgt. Washington. He ripped the hand grenade from his grasp and tossed it into the foyer. He ripped the M-60 from the assault strap. Andrew held it with his left hand as he turned and threw the African American human by his throat, down at his fellows near the bottom of the stair.

Trump was hit with the flying body just as he tried to bring his 40mm to bear again. His left arm sustained a compound fracture as the heavy human body in body armor smashed the M-16 to his body. The grenade discharged from the launcher, impacting and detonating above the top of the staircase. Andrew was peppered with shrapnel, but did not seem to notice as he threw the M-60 like a spear. The barrel penetrated the skull of Muller between his eyes, completely destroyed his face and head. He did not know what hit him as he died in an instant. Moore emptied the rest of his magazine at the Robocop, then ducked out of the foyer back into the entranceway, just as the spoon popped completely free of the hand grenade that bounced around. Five seconds later it exploded.

With the explosion of the hand grenade, Andrew stopped his descent down the winding staircase. He was on autopilot, in route to turn any surviving attackers into mush. The explosion stopped that line of thinking, his quick assessment was there were no humans in the foyer. The Cyborg turned and hotfooted back to the Director's Office. Moore, outside when the grenade went off, was safe from the shrapnel. He popped a new magazine in and tried to sneak back into the foyer as smoke boiled around. Trump started to scream in pain, drew his attention. Moore heaved the dead from a crushed throat Washington off the wounded man, and helped Trump up. He half carried him from the foyer to out near the entrance. Once under more light, Moore saw the bone sticking out Trumps' left arm. He used a large bandage to secure the arm across Trump's chest. He then helped him out into the increasing sunlight.

Torbin and company had heard the shooting and explosions, then nothing. They stayed in position, waiting to see what happened next.

Finally, two figures appeared, one supporting the other.

"Friendlies. Cover them."

About three minutes later, Moore helped Trump lay down behind the staff car Torbin and Gunny used as cover.

"Did you see him? Did you see the Director?" Torbin asked.

"I don't know, Captain. We blew some sh*t up, but that damned Robocop was in the way. We blew the sh*t out of him and he kept coming."

"F#*&." Tobin had a quick decision to make. He could try with his remaining personnel now, or try a tactical withdrawal. The decision was made for him. He saw at least a couple of dozen Security Personnel approaching from the Northwest. He yelled at his remaining grenadier, Standing Bull.

"Lob a grenade at that office window. Then lob another. Start firing at those troops. Moore. Get Trump back to Black's position. Get Nelson ready to bug out. "

"Everyone with 40MM. Hand it to Standing Bull and me."

Torbin grabbed the Shorty M-79 from Gunny Smith and loaded it with a HE round.

∿∿

Andrew went into the office. "Director, Chief, you must go to your shelter. Go, or I will carry you. I do not know if I can stop another attack. "

Adam looked at him. "Okay. I guess you are right...."

Andrew heard and sensed the 40MM rounds approaching. He grabbed the Chief and Adam like small children under his arms and dashed from the office. The grenades exploded on the window sill, filling the office with shrapnel. He carried them over to the escape ladder that ran parallel to the escape elevator,

"GO, NOW." Andrew ordered. After the last explosions, Adam did not argue.

"Be careful, Andrew."

"Of Course, Director. Caution is my middle name." Andrews's droll humor became more noticeable every day.

The Security Forces began to fire at Torbin's remaining Team. They fought back, hitting many of the soldiers who were crossing open field. But more were coming, trying to encircle them.

"Captain, you need to go."

"Gunny, you stay, I stay."

Gunny Smith stopped firing the SAW long enough to yell at him. "Goddammit. You have a wife and soon a child waiting on you. I lost everything years ago. It's my time to stay. Please, GO."

Torbin paused. Smith continued. "Besides, you need to report to Madam President what happened. Go."

Torbin looked at him. Time to go. "Semper Fi, Gunny. I go with the wounded. Surrender if you get a chance. I was told the Director still has some honor."

Gunny Smith laughed. "See you on the Sands of Iwo Jima." A mortar round landed close. Torbin turned and sprinted back to Black and the wounded.

Gunny kept firing. Standing Bull began to sing and chant a possible Death Song. He let loose with another grenade at the advancing forces.

Martinez and Moore were doing a Fireman's Chair Carry for a protesting Sgt. Nelson.

"God Dammit. I can walk."

"Like Hell you can, Sergeant." Cpl. Martinez scolded him. "That AP round must have tumbled sideways when it was in you right thigh. You're missing a hunk of primary thigh muscles from the exit wound."

Torbin arrived at their position, and heard the nearby Barrett start to fire one round after another. Each round was a kill, and would help break the resolve of the attacking force watching people getting torn apart from long range. A Humvee had made the mistake of exposing itself and now had a ruptured gas tank and a hole in its engine from a SLAP (Sabot Light Armor Piercing) round. However, firing so many rounds would eventually lead to it being located for mortar strikes.

"Corporal Black. Time to leave."

"Alright Sir." Torbin knew he was smiling although he could not see him. The man enjoyed his work. Nelson had a rifle in his hands, being the shooter from the seated carry position for the three troops. Trump, holding his arm in pain, had no weapon. Torbin stepped up, hit him with a morphine shot, and then handed him his Makorav. "Eight rounds, Private. Don't waste them."

Torbin looked back and saw the Gunny had popped his smoke flare, trying to generate some more confusion. He tried to move faster.

∿

Ichiro Yamamoto had actually crossed the causeway first. He had seen the armed guard in the parking lot of the HQ Building and heard the vehicles driving around. He decided that rather than draw possible attention to himself by a frontal assault, he would try and sneak around and find a back way into the HQ Building. The Sun had just started to peak its rays over the horizon when he snuck down the fence line along the causeway, then began to swing wide, stayed in the shadows. He snuck to and from bushes, along small ditches.

He was on the south west area from the HQ Building when the Humvee and two jeeps drove by. Ichiro flattened, willed that they could not see him, and had his katana ready for action. They did not see him. A couple minutes later, all Hell broke loose towards the front of HQ Building. Torbin had arrived. Ichiro jumped up, and ran towards the back of the Building.

Just as he reached a back window, a couple of human soldiers jogged around the corner. They must have come out of a concealed room or basement somewhere. They almost bumped into him before they saw him.

"Hey." One yelled in surprise. Then Ichiro was on top of them.

Five seconds later, they were laid out. He had managed to knock them unconscious, not kill them. After all, they were just ignorant peons, trying to survive. However, judging by the firing, everyone had been alerted to the Assault. Ichiro swore. Just five minutes later, and he would have been inside the building. Five minutes more, the Director would have been captured or dead with a slit throat. He was not an ignorant peon; he was the Leader, a good target for a Ninja.

He sighed. Well, sometimes Fate was just Fate. He started to work his way back to the causeway.

∿

It looked like the survivors would make it onto the causeway before they were blocked. Gunny and Standing Bull were still drawing all the attention, with the Security Forces swinging around close to the HQ Building to encircle them. Torbin and his wounded had made it outside the encircling force. They were about fifty yards from where the causeway intersected with the Base proper. Trump was out front, still holding his badly injured arm close to his body. In a sudden move, what looked like a changing colored mass literally engulfed him. He was gone. Torbin went in the direction the mass seemed to have moved.

"Martinez. Get them to safety." He run towards where Trump had been and took a hard left. It was official Sunrise, things were lightening up. The extra light helped him see that the mass was a Tschaaa. Torbin had not been this close to one, ever. He'd shot at one from a distance during the Invasion, that was it. He saw the characteristic the Tschaaa shared with Earthly Octopi; the ability to change color and camouflage.

He raised his rifle before he realized how close he really was. The long social tentacles wrapped around his ankles and upended him. The rifle went off, he heard an odd hissing noise. The rifle was ripped from his hands by the same tentacles that had upended him.

Torbin rolled to his feet. He grabbed for the .44 Magnum in the shoulder holster. Nothing was there. Somehow, it had been knocked loose from its holster. Out came his K-Bar. A calm hit him. This is like what Ichiro did. Facing a large Alien Beast with a blade.

"Come on, you ugly motherporker. Let's dance."

Dropping the rifle, the Adult Squid lunged at him, its limited cartilage skeleton structure giving it better mobility on land than its Earthly Cousins. The Marine couldn't tell if the rifle shot had winged it or not. It did not matter. He went in under the long grasping social tentacles, slashing and stabbing. The next he knew, the shorter arms where throwing him up and over. He hit hard, some soft grass helping mute the impact. As he got to his feet, the Squid was hissing, clicking, deep belching noises also. One of the tentacles was cut almost all the way through, hanging limp. It clambered towards him. He leapt up, then threw himself onto the main torso and head area. He sunk the K-Bar in as deep as he could, the blue Colored blood spurting a bit around the knife wound. He sailed through the air again, this time sans knife. He did a Judo break fall and managed to get to his feet. The Squid was trying to pull the knife out of its body. Torbin frantically searched for a weapon, any weapon. Stuck in a nearby flower bed was a five foot aluminum pole with a small photocell powered light. Torbin lunged and yanked it out of the soft dirt, just as the Squid charged him with his own knife.

The rest was a little blurry. He remembered colliding full on with the 300 pound Alien, using the pole as a crude lance. Then, he was on his back, looking up into the sky. Combat training and instincts took hold, and he managed to scramble to his feet, almost fell over from vertigo. Then, his sight cleared and he saw the Squid, with its arms wrapped around the pole, which was jammed deep into its mouth. It shuddered, all of its arms twitched. Then it lay still. As his head cleared, he noticed the body of Trump. His neck had been broken.

He saw his K-Bar lying in the flower bed, and he retrieved it. He looked at the M-14 and saw the scope had been ripped off and the magazine was nowhere in sight. He started to look for the .44 Magnum Pistol. There it was, half buried in the flower bed.

"Where the F*&% do you think you're going?" He heard the slightly throaty female voice from behind him and he turned around. A very strong looking 5' 6" female in a set of Combat Fatigues was glaring at him with red, somewhat puffy eyes.

Torbin thought, she looked like she had a dose of the CS Gas. And was now royally pissed off. .'

He had never heard of Heidi Faust, nor she him, but Fate from the Perfect Storm dictated their paths would cross.

"Lady, I just killed this Squid. All I want to do is leave the area. I don't see a gun on you, so I don't think you can stop me. I don't make it a habit to smack women around, Military or otherwise, But…. I don't have time to screw round. So, don't get in my way."

In a flash a rather good sized butterfly Balisong knife appeared in her right hand. She had a throaty, sultry laugh. "I'm in your way. I suggest you surrender so you don't get hurt."

"Shit. Why can't things be easy?" Torbin mumbled

He tried to feint and get around her as he thought he could out run her. She exploded at him.

Her knife was a blur as she performed a type of figure eight Eskrima attack. Somehow, partly due to his body armor taking a couple of nasty strikes and partly due to his ability to move backwards, he managed to keep damage down to a couple minor cuts. He tried to score with his K-Bar in reaction, but was not even close.

Heidi paused in her attack. "Give? Or do I have to kill you?"

Torbin sighed. "Sorry, not in the mood to surrender." He saw the .44 in the flower bed dirt and decided he would make a go for it.

A familiar voice came from his left, Heidi's right.

"Torbin-san. Leave it to you to find an attractive woman in the middle of a battle."

It was Ichiro. Heidi quickly shifted to her left, so that she could see both men at once.

"Please, Gentle Lady. No more fighting. There has been enough death today." Ichiro slowly approached with both palms up, hands empty. Torbin thought he saw his katana handle protruding a bit over his left shoulder. He had removed his ninja headgear so that Heidi could see his face.

"You want a piece of me too? Come on BITCH." Heidi yelled at Ichiro.

Once he appeared in range, Heidi attacked. Heidi was excellent; fast, sure, experienced. But Ichiro was at a whole other level. In a blur, he was inside her attack, knife hand trapped under his left armpit. Before she could react, Ichiro hit her left temple with the heel of his right hand. Her eyes fluttered, and her knees buckled. Ichiro gently lowered her to the ground, removing the knife from her hand as he did.

"She is the fastest woman I have ever met, Torbin-san. You are lucky to be alive."

Torbin quickly strode over and recovered his .44 Magnum. "I sure am glad you have a habit of showing up at just the right time, Ichi." He pulled a plastic tie he carried and secured her wrists behind her back. He checked her dog tags. "Heidi Faust. I think I'll remember that name."

"Let's go, Ichiro."

"One moment, Torbin-san. I have something for you." Ichiro sprinted a few feet and pulled a long arm from a slight depression in the ground. He went and handed it to Torbin.

"Damn. A BAR and a spare magazine. Where did you get this?"

"Let us say, the person has no current use for it. Come, let us move quickly. There is a weak spot in the fence bottom over there that we can bend over and slip through. But we must hurry. We are being encircled."

Torbin followed Ichiro to the spot in the fence. It was a spot that some animal had dug under, probably a dog or raccoon. Torbin pulled a set of wire cutters he carried and clipped the fence wire until he and Ichiro easily bent a section up. Now, they had more than enough room to slide through the fence. Within a minute, they were on the water side of the fence.

He and Ichiro began to head towards the causeway along the channel bank. They moved quick and sure. Some fifty feet from the causeway, Ichiro stopped so sudden, Torbin almost ran into him.

"What..." Ichiro drew and slashed with his katana in one smooth action at something suddenly rising from the water. It was a camouflaged Tschaaa. Two more slashes, then a thrust thru the eye, all in a blur of motion.

"Give me room, Torbin-san." Torbin jumped back and Ichiro became a Whirling Dervish, slashing and cutting at figures trying to exit the water. Torbin raised the BAR, a former Navy version re-chambered and re-barreled in .308/7.62 with two taped together magazines. He fired at something in the water that did not look right and was rewarded by a splashing Squid losing its color blending camouflage. Here he was, after six years without being close to a Tschaaa, and in the last few minutes, had quickly been inundated with them. What was going on?

Ichiro scrambled towards the causeway proper, Torbin followed. From under the causeway as it crossed the channel, figures seemed to be boiling out of the water, some armed with cutting weapons, some not. Torbin swore and began picking his targets.

∿∿

Corporal Martinez had gotten his small four man unit onto the causeway, carrying Sgt. Nelson in a two man Fireman's Chair Carry. PFC Black was watching the rear. They still heard some shots coming from the Gunny's last position, which seemed to have distracted the Security Forces from noticing people were fleeing from the Base across the causeway. They scrambled down the four lane road on the causeway, nearing the Guard Shack at the Entry Control Point. On the way out, Sgt. Nelson had been given a .308 rifle that a defender had no further use for. He carried it as his fellows supported him, scanning in front. He swore and fired up the causeway. "Squids." Everyone looked up and saw Tschaaa crawling up the sides of the causeway road, over the guard rails. Some looked much the worse for wear, appeared as if they had been injured. Some were armed, some not. However, rage was driving all of them. Most were not even trying to use their natural camouflage ability. It was if they wanted to be seen, to strike fear in their opponents.

∿∿

Andrew, after he insured the Director and Chief were climbing down to the Blast Shelter, strode quickly towards the causeway. He knew that a couple of the attackers were pinned down in the HQ Building parking lot. He also knew the others were fleeing across the causeway. Confusion reigned, despite Major Grants attempt to gain control. Security Forces, having now secured everyone else in blast shelters, were flowing to the sound of gunfire. Andrew knew he must go to the causeway and organize what personnel he could as a blocking force. He saw a squad of riflemen come jogging down from a side street towards the causeway. He began a high speed dash to them when Hell broke loose. Tschaaa Adults, Adolescents, some armed Warriors, came scrambling out of the channel water. The riflemen slowed as their supposed allies approached. Without warning, a harpoon skewered one of the Riflemen in his abdomen. Then a Squid literally threw itself on a Human, trying to rip the man apart with its arms and tentacles.

Just at that moment, a stream of data updated his information systems. There had been massive casualties in the Breeding Crèche's from a watery blast wave emanating from the nuclear strike. Because the blast had not been contained in the center of the Marquesas Keys Complex, which would have been the result if the bunker buster had burrowed itself in the center of the Complex, the blast had sent a heated and radioactive tsunami crashing across the ocean. Right into the reef Breeding Areas. It was believed over 1000 Young and Adolescents had been killed, were dying or injured. Dozens of Adults were killed or dying, including 12 breeders. Many others were injured. Still more were insane with rage. They were attacking any humans they found.

Major Jane Grant appeared and emptied her M-9 pistol into the Squid on top of the Security Troop. The creature shivered, then Lay still.

"God Dammit. Don't just stand there. Get it off him!" Major Grant yelled at the surprised and frozen men. Two ran to help their comrade; the rest looked at Major Grant. As this happened, Andrew was broadcasting a Cease and Desist order in the Tschaaa language and frequencies. Some dozen individuals were approaching the rifleman when he broadcast. Half stopped, the other half, enraged, ignored his instructions. Seeing the Tschaaa approaching with murderous intent, Major Grant gave the only order she could. "Fire at the ones approaching."

The riflemen opened up, semi-auto. Most were armed with thirty caliber weapons, so one or two well place rifle rounds seemed to either stop, kill or cause the Tschaaa to flee, wounded. The half dozen attackers were neutralized. Then, one rifleman began to fire full auto on the Tschaaa that had stopped. High velocity rounds ripped into the stationary Squids, ripping alien flesh.

"F@#$king SQUIDS. Kill them all, like we should've done before!"

The Security man screaemed in a rage to match the Tschaaa's. Andrew was then beside him, grabbed the rifle and yanked it from his grasp. Andrews's right hand clamped on the Humans throat, and he lifted him up to look in his face.

"I have stopped those Tschaaa you are shooting. You are wasting bullets, and exasperating the situation. You will stop. Yes?" The man's eyes were bugged out, his breath cut off. Andrew held him for a moment, and then let him fall to the ground. The man laid gasping for air, held his throat.

Andrew looked at Jane. "Major Grant. If you would be so kind as to follow me with these armed soldiers. There are some attackers trying to flee down the causeway.

"Yes, Sir, Andrew. Alright. You heard him. On me." The remaining effectives formed an assault line on Jane, and they began to follow Andrew, who had already begun striding ahead. Other Tschaaa crawled, lunged, slithered, and scrambled from the channel. Andrew tried to stop them with repeated warnings in the Tschaaa language. One refused to stop advancing and, in a blur of motion, Andrew picked up a rock and threw it with blinding speed. It

The Gathering Storm

imbedded between the Squids eyes, stopped it dead. The others began to part away from the approaching Andrew, like the Red Sea to Moses. They hissed, clicked and grunted as the Humans passed. Only Andrews's presence stopped them from mobbing the Security Personnel.

Major Grant called to Andrew. "What the Hell is going on? hy are they attacking us? I thought they said we were their allies."

"They have just experienced a horrible loss in their Young, due to that Nuclear Strike. A loss in such numbers. all at once, is unknown since the Plague hit on their Home World. They are in a murderous rage, a vicious mob similar to others in human history. Almost unknown in Tschaaa history."

Major Grant felt a cold hand grip her spine. If they were not controlled, the Base could be wiped out. Andrew heard shots further on ahead, on the causeway. He began to stride faster.

~~~

Ichiro and Torbin dashed up unto the causeway. Ichiro slashed a rapidly approaching Squid, at least his seventh, taking off two arms and a social tentacle before thrusting home into its brain. Two Warriors came clambering over the causeway railing, edged weapons at the ready. Torbin gave out a war cry and fired the BAR full auto. A half a dozen rounds smashed into the nearest one, a couple penetrating on into the torso of the second Squid. The second Tschaaa slid and twisted, trying to reach Ichiro. The Nippon Warrior parried the long halberd weapon, sliced off the end of the arm holding it, then reversed his katana and thrust its blade through the right eye and into the Alien brain. The creature shuddered and died.

"Quite impressive, Torbin-san." Ichiro said as he flicked Squid blood from his katana's blade.

"And, let me congratulate you on killing that Tschaaa with your K-BAR. Most excellent."

Torbin snorted at him. "I'm going to hurt for days. Let's get moving. My men are ahead, up on the causeway."

Just then, Ichiro looked backwards. "Torbin-san, a Robocop approaches from our rear."

Torbin spun around and looked. "Frack...Ichi, head down the Causeway and catch up with my men. Get them to the pickup point. I'll delay that Robo."

"I cannot leave you, My Brother. We will meet it together."

"Captain Yamamoto, that is not a request, that is an order. Move!"

Ichiro paused for a second, and then saluted with his katana. "Hai. I go. I will sing your praises to My Ancestors. I serve you with Honor, My Brother."

"Just go, and keep my men safe. I'll catch up when I can."

As Ichiro began to run up the Causeway, he yelled back at Torbin. "I killed the excrement Russian Colonel."

"I already figured that out long ago. Now, goddammit move!" Ichiro moved, fast.

Torbin turned and sighted the BAR on the approaching Robocop. The weapon seemed to have a Dutch Load of AP, Ball, and Tracer. He had at least a few rounds left, so hopefully he could do some damage. He fired at Andrew's face at fifty yards. Andrew deflected the round with his arm at blinding speed. Torbin fired a round at the Robocop's chest that ricocheted off. Then Andrew threw a rock with a windmill overhand pitch. It smacked hard into Torbin's helmet, knocking him on his ass and leaving a divot in his helmet. Torbin sat stunned for a few seconds. As he tried to focus his eyes, a large hand grabbed the BAR from his hands. Then, another hand was grabbing his left leg and he was lifted unceremoniously upside down into the air. Andrew dropped the BAR, and yanked Torbin's Dog tags from his neck.

"Hmmm. Captain Bender, Torbin R., U.S.A. Captain, you have caused us many problems and the Tschaaa much pain. I salute the abilities of you and your men, but now I must take you to the Director." Torbin tried to reach the .44 Magnum Pistol, and Andrew yanked it from his grasp.

"The inscription says... Property of the President, USA. That is your Madam President, yes?"

Torbin glared at him upside down. "Yes. Now can you put me down, you big trash can!"

And with that, Andrew dropped him on his head. A moment later, Torbin was hoisted up by the nap of his fatigue top, suspended in the air again. Andrew began to stride towards the HQ Building with his catch.

∽∼∽

Sgt. Nelson soon found out that a thirty caliber bullet between the eyes of a Squid usually put it down. He fired at a fifth Squid, an Adolescent, trying to climb over the guard rail of the causeway. The round hit the guardrail top just below the many armed creature, and it fled back to the channel water. The bolt stayed open on an empty magazine,

"Out of .308. Set me down so I can get the '16 off my back."

Martinez and Moore set him down gingerly, Moore giving him a shoulder to lean on and help him stand with his injured legs. The morphine helped with the pain, but the damage to his thigh muscles made movement difficult. He unslung the M-16 with grenade launcher off his back and adjusted the tactical sling for forward carry.

Cpl. Black, watching the rear with his Barrett Fifty, called out.

"We've got company. A Robocop and some armed soldiers are approaching the causeway…Shit. They just engaged some Squids. Something is definitely weird, the Squids attacking their Lap Dogs."

Moore looked back, and then turned to Sgt. Nelson. "Okay, you go across my back in a shoulder carry. You can watch my rear. Corporal Martinez, can you take point?"

"Gladly. Black, let's get moving."

"Roger." They started to move again, Sgt. Nelson held the M-16 by the pistol grip as he was carried across Moore's shoulder. Wounded extraction had been practiced many times, so all the team members were used to carrying or being carried. PFC Black turned around and looked through his scope again.

"Well I'll Be…The Captains on the causeway, shootin' at the Robo. And Captain Yamamoto is high tailing it to us."

"Keep moving. He can catch up." Martinez said.

Black turned forward again for a few steps, then looked back. An Adult Squid had managed to climb up one of the support pillars and was clambering over the guardrail some ten yards back. Black paused long enough to fire a single Fifty Caliber at it. One second the Squid was there, the next minute it was almost in two pieces, fell back into the channel.

"God Damn you're loud." Sgt. Nelson exclaimed.

"Yea, but when I shoot you, you stay shot."

Ichiro had almost caught up to the fleeing men. He had momentarily thought about disobeying Torbin's direct order, but that would have been a dishonor to him and his friend. He could only hope that Torbin could extricate himself from the enemy. However, he knew that if anyone could, it would be his Blood Brother. As he neared the four survivors, he called out. "I am approaching your rear."

"We saw you, Captain Yamamoto." Cpl. Martinez called back. "Glad you could join us. Now what, Sir?"

Ichiro reached them and matched his speed to theirs. "Captain Bender is delaying the pursuit and ordered I was to insure you escaped to the pickup area at the airport, where the plane is waiting. And, I always follow orders."

"Sir, how do we achieve that?"

"We find transportation for the wounded Sergeant, some type of vehicle or boat. I think a vehicle might be best as the Takos, Squids, seemed to be all over the water. he faster we move on land, the harder it will to get to us. The bomb blast made them very angry, so they are attacking all humans. Thus, the Security Forces may not be able to chase us effectively."

"Well. Sir, lead on, we follow."

Ichiro surged ahead. Then, as they neared where the causeway connected to Highway 1, several Tschaaa rapidly climbed onto the roadway from the nearby channel. Before the men could raise their weapons, Ichiro called out. "Hold back. I will clear them. It is quieter than gunshots."

Cpl. Martinez, PFCs Moore and Black, and Sgt. Nelson were then presented an exhibition of sword play they would never forget. Ichiro strode up to the Tschaaa, Adults with a couple of blade weapon armed Warriors, which seemed to be caught off guard that this lone human was approaching a group of very angry Squids. Then the Samurai was among the leading two. A blur of sword slashes and strikes, and the two Adults were down, eviscerated. He next took on the two Warriors. Parrying and slashing, he sliced off the tentacles of both, and then slashed the forward arms almost in half. He left them writhing on the pavement as the last two Adults tried to encircle him. Cpl. Martinez pulled his silenced .22 caliber pistol and fired two rounds at the one Tschaaa trying to attack Ichiro's back. It turned towards the source of the pain and started towards the four men, rising up on its eight arms. By this time, Ichiro had performed his patented three slashes and a stab through the eye to the brain pan to the others. Seeing the last Squid trying to get to the others, he dashed up behind it and slashed the rear two arms nearly in half, and the Squid plopped to the pavement. He lunged to the left side and stabbed the Squid through its left eye, then leapt back. Writhing in pain, it tried to reach him with its grasping social tentacles. Ichiro danced out of range and signaled the four surviving assault team members to pass to the rear of the Squid. They did not have to be told twice.

Ichiro danced around as the wounded Tschaaa bled out from its wounds. Dodging the badly wounded and still writhing Warriors, he dashed to follow his unit. They were now moving northeastward up Highway 1 towards Marathon Airport. Sgt. Nelson, still laid across PFC Moore's shoulders and back, whistled. "Man, I'll never watch old Kung Fu movies the same way again."

Ichiro snorted. "Japanese sword play is superior to Chinese."

The four enlisted troops chuckled at his comment. Then Ichiro added, "But hear and remember this. Captain Bender killed a Squid with his fighting knife. I saw the end, so take it as true."

Sgt. Nelson, the Montanan, whistled again. "Just like Ol' Daniel Boone or Davy Crockett. We worked with a living legend."

"Yes, Nelson-San. Tell the story, pass on the tale. No matter what happens, his honor must never be forgotten."

TWENTY FOUR HOURS LATER

Torbin Bender had been dozing on and off for most of the time he had been in the cell. He was recovering from the beating he had taken fighting the Tschaaa, not to mention there was not a hell of a lot to do. There was a faucet that provided water in this fairly large cell, so he had drank well. But he had refused the food they had brought; for fear that it was drugged. They had not tried to torture him for information, which was a bit surprising, given the circumstances. But, knowing that the Tschaaa had superior biological techniques, he would not put it past them to introduce some mind control substance.

He began to recollect again the occurrence of events after Andrew, the Cyborg Robocop, had grabbed him up...

Andrew carried him through a gauntlet of Tschaaa at the end of the causeway that had grown to at least a couple of dozen. Some looked as if they had been singed, others battered and bruised. All were almost black with rage. They knew he was involved in the Nuke Strike.

He felt some vibrations emanating from Andrew that told him the Cyborg tried to communicate with the Squids using frequencies out of human hearing. Whatever he had said before or was saying now, the effect was wearing off. The Tschaaa began to crowd ever closer, Torbin feeling their murderous intent.

"Major, please be prepared to open fire again. They are not listening to me." Andrew reached into a hidden compartment in his scratched and battered torso and removed what looked like a flexible length of car antenna. Torbin recognized it as a sheath for a monofilament wire blade, which was capable of slicing almost anything. Major Grant bunched her ten armed men around Andrew and his prisoner. She had her pistol out and ready. Bayonets appeared on the many of the rifles. With our warning, a long grasping social tentacle, five fingers and all, was grabbing at Torbin. A blur of motion from Andrew and the Tschaaa equivalent to a hand was neatly sliced off.

"Please shoot, Major."

"FIRE AT WILL."

Torbin had been involved in Mad Minutes before, but never starting this close, not even the Eater ambush. Hot expended brass was in the air everywhere, some bouncing off of him. A couple of the Major's men were drug from the formation, to be torn apart. Another died from a harpoon bolt through his throat. The humans began to slip and slide on the Tschaaa blue blood as the close range carnage continued. Torbin saw Andrew slice three arms off of one Tschaaa, leaving it flopping on the roadway. Then, it was over. Major Grant tried to recover the dead, but the surviving Tschaaa had scattered, taking with them the human remains.

Jane Grant, shaking with anger and fear, glared at Torbin.

"I hope you are satisfied. You just signed our death warrant."

The cell Torbin was in was devoid of anything except a table and two chairs, one on each side, bolted to the floor; the commode; and the metal sink and faucet. His clothes had been taken and a large chain with a huge clasp had been fitted around his left ankle. The chain and clasp looked like they had last been used in some movie about the French Bastille. Torbin could reach the commode and the sink and walk around a bit. The floor was warm, as was the air. Last night, a mattress, pillow and blanket had been brought in or his use. he jailer had showed him the camera and said if he tried to tear anything up or to harm himself, he would be quickly hogtied. The sleep items had just been removed. He sat cross legged and leaned against the wall. Hopefully, Ichiro got away with the others. There was no way for him to know. He heard the key in the door and stood up, almost hoping it was some good looking woman that he could show his muscled body off to, just for shits and grins. The door opened. In stepped Director Adam Lloyd.

To say Torbin was surprised was the understatement of the year. The Director had a small serving cart that had his clothes and boots on the second shelf and a huge bowl of freshly popped buttered popcorn on the top. Two unopened cans of Miller Light Beer completed the scene. Without a word, Director Lloyd unloaded contents of the cart onto the table, and then pushed it behind him. A very large man took it, wheeled it out and shut the door. Torbin heard the key turn in the lock

Adam tossed his clothes and boots to Torbin. "I see you kept yourself in excellent shape, but staring at a nude man is not my idea of fun. If you had been a nude woman, then, yea maybe.

By the way, Captain Bender. Try to bean me with your boots or any similar action, and you will be castrated. Try it again, you will be blinded. Etcetera, Etcetera. "

Torbin began to dress, Adam sat down. He set the bowl of popcorn in the center of the table, and pushed one of the cans of beer to Torbin's side. The leg chain kept Torbin from reaching the other side of the table.

"The popcorn is fresh, see, I am eating it…mmm, and I am addicted to this stuff. The can of beer is unopened, from a private stash in someone's deep wine cellar. So, it should not be skunky, at least not very much. So, please, join me." He popped his beer can top and sipped it.

Torbin finished putting his clothes on, leaving his boots off as he did not want to screw with the chain on his ankle. Plus, he had no interest in committing suicide by doing a George Bush Iraqi Shoe Attack. So he set the boots on the floor next to the table he sat down and opened his beer. He sipped it.

"Not bad. Tastes a little like can, but not bad." He tried the popcorn. "Now, that is good. Good ole fashioned theater buttered popcorn. Kills you with cholesterol, but Hell, no one gets out of here alive anyways."

Torbin looked directly at Adam. "So, no torture, no drugs? Not even feeding me to the Squids? I have to admit, you have me astounded. Not even a good beating, other than the Robocop named Andrew did drop me on my head."

Adam chuckled. "He and the other recent converts to Cyborg kept their human sense of humor. They are basically enhanced humans rather than machines built on a human frame."

"Well, Lloyd, that still begs the question. What now?' Torbin asked.

Adam sighed. "Well, Captain, to say you and the Unoccupied States have started a sh*t storm would be a monumental understatement. As I have always tried to be truthful, no matter how painful, if I am alive 24 hours from now, I will be surprised."

Torbin stared for a moment before speaking. "I take it from the reactions of the Squids, attacking everything that moved on two feet, there was a lot of Collateral Damage."

Adam snorted. "Your Nuke was hit and damaged. Instead of impacting in the center of the Complex, which was his Lordship location, as you knew, it struck the northeast edge. It burrowed only part way in when it exploded. Thus, a shockwave of heated water and debris was shaped outward. The wave and everything in it slammed into the reefs and shallows in the area, which were being used to raise their Young. Over one thousand Young and Adolescents have died so far. Many are also injured. Twelve Breeders are dead, some with child. Dozens of attending Adults were killed or seriously wounded. And now we have a large area of radiation contamination. All Breeding activities in the area are being moved up to Key Largo and North. "

Torbin knew now that Adam Lloyd was in a serious trick bag. His loyalty and effectiveness as the Director was in serious question.

"So, Director, is his High Lordship alive, or fish food?"

Adam paused, and then answered. "He is alive, though badly injured. I spoke to his Second in Command, one of his offspring we call El Segundo."

Adams memory flashed back to the conversation he had over voice com. The Tschaaa El Segundo had picked a Human Voice that sounded like a broadcaster from a Midwestern Radio Station, no accent.

"He is alive, Director, and asked about your well-being. He is tough, and should heal. But it will be a while. I will be in charge until then." El Segundo paused. "He wants me to assure you of your continued position, but in all honestly, I cannot. There are many Tschaaa who wish that all humans be wiped off of the Earth except a few areas of Cattle. Unnecessary deaths of Young are a psychic blow to all Tschaaa. Some say the Young were targeted. Thus the homicidal rage rather than catatonia amongst the Adults entrusted for their care. That rage is far from over. Since you served my Sire loyally, I suggest you get your affairs in order and be prepared to leave if you wish to survive."

Adam's attention came back to the present conversation.

"And, El Segundo was less than positive about us Humans." Torbin said.

Adam gave a wry smile. "That would be an accurate appraisal. The attack shows us to be Nasty Little Monkeys, to be locked up until eaten."

Torbin shrugged. "With all due respect, Director, by cooperating with the Squids, you perpetuated a system that would always keep us as potential snacks for an entire species, this so-called Protocol of Selective Survival. I and my cohorts were doing what comes naturally to humans; resisting a threat to our survival."

Adam again paused before speaking. "I know you will not believe this, but I have helped save millions by sacrificing one segment of the human genome; so called People of Color. I did this to gain us time. Eventually, I hoped to find a way to replace live meat with types grown in vats, of a type that the Tschaaa could not tell the difference between it and a human born of woman."

"Would there be any… People of Color left by the time this happened?" Torbin responded. "Not to mention the morality of feeding someone our young, our babies. Living under the heel of such an oppressor is not living; it is existing at the expense of some innocent stranger sent to slaughter."

Adam sighed. "Life, and the Universe, are not fair. I did what I could to rebuild the infrastructure to Pre-Strike levels. We have the Internet, food and medical distribution, cross country transportation, operating hospitals. I have not heard of a single case of starvation in the last year. The new Space Program was just an attempt to demonstrate our excellent capabilities and intellect as a species. We would soon be working alongside the Tschaaa as near equals, as are the ones we call Lizards. We would be traveling amongst the Stars within a generation."

Torbin could see a form of almost religious fervor in his eyes. Adam believed that eventually, his way would lead to a better life for most humans. The problem was the word "most". Those not part of the "most" would be the "least", which would mean in this case, food for someone else.

"I have a question, Director. Did the Squids ever eat Lizards?"

Adam stopped. Then frowned. "Not that I know of."

"Then, we are in a little different situation. We would, no matter what we did, always be a hunk of mobile meat on the hoof."

There was silence. Torbin could tell that Adam Lloyd really wanted to help humanity, to be a real Good Guy. He just did not want to admit that, no matter how nice His Lordship treated him, Adam would still be a source of meat when the chips were down.

They dank their beer in silence for a couple of minutes. Torbin could tell Adam was woolgathering, running things over in his mind, both present and past. Finally, Adam spoke, looking off into space.

"You will be transported to the Former State of Utah, now Deseret. I cannot in good conscience hand you over to the enraged Squids, to be ripped apart, and then eaten. ou are an honorable soldier who acted according to Human Rules of Warfare. For your information, you and your people cost us two dozen dead personnel, and an equal number wounded and injured. Not to mention the vehicles you shot up. Plus, a small group escaped to Marathon, and left by plane before we could get organized. The sudden violence perpetrated by the Tschaaa caught us completely by surprise."

Torbin, now hearing his wounded had got away with Ichiro, tried to control his joy. Yes!

"If I may ask, how many people did you lose to the Squids?" Torbin asked.

Adam looked him in the eyes. "They killed at least a half a dozen. As well as an equal number of Conch Republicans. There would have been more but for your people's ability to go through them like a buzz saw, which drew many towards you. Whoever that man with the Samurai Sword is, he is quickly becoming a legend. The fact he went out of his way to incapacitate rather than kill humans helped with this view. He apparently only killed one sentry, at the Main Gate."

Calmly, Torbin spoke. "That is Captain Ichiro Yamamoto, of the Free Japan Defense Force. He's a unique individual, as well as my Blood Brother in Arms."

Adam smiled. "Well, he must have taken out close to a dozen Tschaaa with his sword technique. The lack of projectile weapons helped, but taking on a Tschaaa hand to hand is not something I would want to do."

Then Adam laughed. "But, a certain Coast Guardsman by the name of Heidi

Faust said you took on one with a knife. How did that go?"

Torbin snorted. "I am beginning to feel the aches and pain from that. I was lucky, and I do not want to do that again. "

"Well, you have a legend developing around you also. Especially after the murderous attacks on us, by our so called Friendlies, anyone killing a Squid is beginning to be looked on very favorably. I am working hard not to have an all-out war here. "

Adam looked intently at Torbin, then spoke. "I am about to tell you something I want you to pass on to Madame President. But please believe me that I am not trying to ask for help or mercy, to justify some of my actions. I realize I've made some serious mistakes. But I made my proverbial bed, now I must sleep in it. I will ask that, should my people come under your control at a later date, please show them some mercy. If there is a War Criminal, it is I. They were just trying to survive per my instructions. After I tell you what I know, maybe you will understand better,"

Adam pulled a vial out of his pocket with some small pill like and other round objects. He then began to tell Torbin Bender a story about manipulation and control.

⁓〽⁓

Sometime later, Captain Torbin Bender sat rigid at the table. A rage was building in him that he was having trouble controlling. He sat concentrating, knowing he had to get out of here and back home with the information he just received. He began some of the breathing and mental exercises that Ichiro had taught him as part of some additional martial arts training.

"When things are untenable, when your rage begins to grow to an uncontrollable level, you must breath, control your anger, and become centered. Uncontrolled rage controls you, makes you do stupid things. Control the rage, focus it, and use it, Torbin-san. It gives you additional strength with which to battle your enemies. It can help you survive when all seems loss."

Finally, Torbin had obtained a level of control that he could speak without exploding.

"Those evil mother-----. To manipulate and endanger our Unborn. How dare they?"

Adam waited a moment. before he spoke. "I was told that we did something similar to our dogs to create all of our various breeds. So, His Lordship said he was just trying to improve our 'breed'."

Torbin tried not to glare. "We love our dogs. Most of us do, anyways. And they love us. I have known K-9s to give their lives for their Handlers. I know of Handlers who risked all for their dogs. This mutual love between us, two different species, is strong. I know the Squids do NOT love us, and we sure as Hell don't love them. And I doubt we ever will."

There was a knock on the door. Adam got up and waited for it to be unlocked. Chief Hamilton came part way in, speaking in a low tone. Adam thanked him and shut the door. Torbin heard it being locked

"Pardon me, but did the Chief there have some bandages on his face?"

"Yes, Captain. You got a piece of him when he was on the roof. And, as you can tell, I have a few dings that are not from shaving. It was close. If not for Andrew returning, we would not be speaking."

Torbin nodded. Adam continued. "And, whoever was working the Barrett, he set a new standard for sniping. Six men and a Tschaaa Soldier were felled by him, as well as a Humvee being destroyed. Not to mention he scared the sh*t out of a bunch of people. He needs a promotion."

Torbin gave a small smile. "Corporal Black. He enjoys his work. "

Torbin then asked a question he was dreading. "I had a Gunny and a PFC who were holding you up, letting the others escape. What happened to them?"

"Gunny Smith and PFC Standing Bull, by their recovered dog tags. We had to blast them out with several mortar rounds. Standing Bull was bleeding out when the final assault was made. Someone said he was singing and chanting. I guess he had his own Death Song. They died as soldiers. To many, they would be called heroes. Any remains or bodies I recover will be sent to your commanders with the appropriate honors and decorum"

Torbin was quiet, with a lump in his throat. The Gunny had sacrificed himself for him. So had Standing Bull. He would make sure they were remembered.

Adam cleared his throat. "And now, Captain Bender, it is time for you to leave for Deseret. By the way, the contact person we used knew your name. I guess you get around."

Abigail, he thought. She must have passed on their meeting to the Powers That Be. It would be nice to see her. Maybe, they would use her as a go between. That would be nice.

"I see a small smile on your face. I guess, Captain, you have a friend with the Mormons."

"Yes, I have a friend. And now, Director, I guess I need to put my boots on. Can someone come in and unlock my ankle?"

"Of Course." Adam got up to leave, taking the popcorn bowl with him. He then stopped.

"Captain, in other circumstances, it would have nice to have served with you."

Torbin snapped to attention and saluted the Director. "I will pass on the information and the vial. I am sure Madam President will try and contact you. May God Speed You in your Journey."

"Thank You. Captain. Now, if you will excuse me, I have some things to fix and rebuild."

Two Very Large men came in and removed his chain, watching him closely as he put his boots on. The he heard a familiar voice.

"Well, Captain, you will now get a ride on my Falcon." It was Andrew. "A bit banged up, but we managed to patch it up enough so it is operational. Not pretty, just functional. And I have something I will give you when we arrive in Deseret." He held up a large plastic bag. In it were the .44 Magnum and the six rounds.

"Please give this back to Madam President, with my compliments."

"Thank You, Andrew. I guess I owe you for my life. By the way, why didn't you give me to the Squids? Don't they give you orders?"

"Captain, I am assigned to the Director. My orders from His Lordship were to follow Director Lloyd's orders, as long as they were not suicidal or subversive. I have not received any new orders from His Lordship, so they stand. I was told to collect you, I did."

"And the Squid you killed with a rock I heard the troops talk about? And the one you cut protecting me? What about those actions? "

Andrew paused for a microsecond, and then answered. "I have been given the ability to decide who lives, who dies. I decided you live. So, the others must die. It is simple, really."

Torbin began to wonder, as had others, these Earth Based Cyborgs, just how much humanity did they retain? He would have to watch Andrew during the flight, and see if he could figure it out

They exited the cell, and Andrew told the Two Very Large Men that they did not need to escort him to the Falcon, that he could do it alone. "I do not think Captain Bender will attempt to flee."

Torbin snorted. "What, and get drilled in the back of the head with a one hundred mile an hour plus fast ball? I don't think so."

Torbin thought he saw a ghost of a smile on the exposed mouth of Andrew. The protective visor with a heads up display covered the Robo's eyes, so he could not see a twinkle. But he could swear there was one.

They walked down the hall way to an exit door when he suddenly saw a familiar face. He called out. "Kathy. Kathy Monroe. "

She stopped at the sound of his voice. Kat looked as if she was trying to make the decision to disappear down the hall or greet him.

"You wish to speak to Miss Monroe?" Andrew asked.

"Yes, please."

Andrew put a powerful hand on Torbin's right shoulder and walked with him towards Kat. She tried to beam her signature smile but was having problems. "Hi Torbin."

"Hi, Kathy. Long time no see, at least in person. You look great."

Kat tried to reply, but she was blinking back tears.

"Hey, no need to turn on the water works." Torbin said. "I'm just glad to see you're alright."

Then she was hugging him. She buried her face in his shoulder and began to cry. Torbin immediately stroked her hair and rubbed her back. "Hey, sweetkins, its Torbin. Remember, Mister Smartass? No need to cry. Everything is working out. Andrew is helping me get home, in a roundabout way, but home nonetheless. "

Finally, she stopped crying, and looked him in the face. "Sorry, you just brought back…memories of a much better time. And….I've kind of been on an opposite side for a while."

Torbin kissed her forehead. Then, he reached into his pocket and produced the vial the Director had shown him. "I just had an illuminating talk with the Director. I don't think any of us have been working with a full deck."

She looked at the vial. She hugged Torbin again, and then kissed him. "I missed you. And I still miss your brother. I always will. So, no matter what happens, just remember I loved him with all my heart. He was the best thing in my life."

"Yea, I miss him, too." Torbin had a tear slide down his cheek. He quickly wiped it away, hoping no one saw it. It would ruin his reputation of a Hard Ass Marine.

"Hey, before I go, I'm married, and my wife has a Bun in the Oven." He looked in an interior pocket of his fatigues and found one of the business cards Aleks had hand drawn for him, a little crumpled but still readable. "Take this. Get a hold of me when you can. I will find a place for you if you show up. Okay?"

Kat beamed a smile at him. "Okay. Congrats. Tell your wife to treat you right or she'll have a lot of angry people on her doorstep." She hugged him again and kissed him. Then she turned and walked quickly down the hall.

Torbin took a deep breath.

"Shall we go now, Captain Torbin?"

"Yes, Andrew. Thank You for letting me talk to her. She was like family once."

Andrew stood still for a few moments. "Yes, we all had family, once. For some, like you, family will happen again. The human family is what makes humanity good, no matter what its flaws are. Now, come. We must go. We have some distance to cover."

He and Torbin walked towards the Falcon.

MALMSTROM, MONTANA

As Torbin was saying hi and goodbye to Kathy Monroe, Aleksandra was doing an orientation briefing to a twelve man team of Free Russian SPETSNAZ at Malmstrom Operations, now Armed Forces Base. They had just arrived, having been held at an outpost in Alaska until the word came down that the Nuke Strike had happened. Three days prior, the Russian President had died of a stroke. The Second in Command, the Prime Minister, was a former Female General. Madam President had called her upon hearing of the death. The former Russian President seemed very hesitant to commit much of anything to the Free Alliance, as it was being called now.

A short conversation with new President Alina Federov, Free Russia, and all that changed.

She had said "Madam President, I have lost children, you have lost children. If we are to lose any more, let us lose them together, killing these filthy Aliens."

Finally, the offensive arm of the Free Alliance was coming together. As Aleksandra was explaining the layout of the Base, where their quarters were, where to report in the morning, they suddenly all came to attention and saluted. "Good morning, General." The Senior Lieutenant called out in excellent English.

Aleksandra spun around and came to attention, caught off guard by General Reed sneaking up behind her.

"At Ease, please. I just need to borrow the good Captain for a minute. Aleksandra, please walk with me."

As they turned and walked away, General Reed said. "I have just received word about our Wayward Captain." Aleks held her breath.

"I do not know how that sneaky and crazy Marine did it, but he is being taken to Deseret, formally the State of Utah. We just got a long distance phone call at Security Control that the Squids and specifically the Director, had made arrangements to let him return home via Deseret. Apparently, the Mormons have heard some positive things about Torbin, and are more than happy to get him home. They will provide land transport in the next day or so, and we will meet them on the road. They asked that a young officer be allowed to come to Malmstrom to act as an unofficial liaison. So, The Latter Day Saints are having some thoughts about what the future will look like."

Aleksandra had not really been paying much attention to what the General was saying past the fact that Torbin was alive and coming Home. Tears began to trickle down her cheeks and General Reed provided a clean handkerchief. "Here. Can't let the SPETSNAZ see you blubbering. Blow your nose, dab the tears. The Father of my Godchild is coming home. Now, Carry On."

Aleks blew her nose, stopped her tears. They had heard yesterday that Ichiro and a few others had made it to the Tamiami Trail in the Everglades on the B-25, and were making the rest of their trip by foot, unless the General could arrange some clandestine air travel. But, at least they were alive, and had a chance of sneaking back if they stayed away from the Coasts.

All she had known was that Torbin had been last seen being grabbed by a Robocop. Now, He was ALIVE. And soon to be free.

The rest of the day Aleks felt like she was floating on a cloud. He was coming Home.

ATLANTA, CATTLE COUNTRY

In Atlanta, word quickly spread that a nuclear weapon had been detonated over the Squid Strong Hold. Malcom Carver ordered all further "meat" shipments to Savannah immediately stopped.

"Well what do you know! Those Crackers attacked without us pushing them." Malcom pulled a couple of cigars out of his desk and threw one to Joe. He knew Red did not smoke, so he did not offer her one. But he flashed a big smile at her, which she returned. He had to remind himself that she was not his Bitch, but a needed member of his staff.

"Now, the fun begins. Joe, Red, help our Captains find as much shelter from attack as possible. We are not going to have time for any more construction. We make do with what we have." He lit his cigar and then blew a smoke ring. "Ole Nat Turner. I wished you could see what's about to happen."

PLATFORM ONE

The Olson Twins had been working for over 24 hours straight. The Tschaaa Minor Lord they called the Wizard had flown into a rage over the death of Doctor Smith, the damage to his Station, the theft of the Space Plane. Dark with rage, he almost had Doctor Smiths husband throttled when he began to blubber about his wife. "Shut up, you worthless monkey!" He had screamed over the Translator. "Get back to work and give me Results NOW. I will not be embarrassed again!"

The nuclear strike at His Lordships Complex had thrown everyone into a rage. The humans on the station hid out as the Tschaaa on board raged through the corridors, other than a couple who went catatonic. Then, the humans had been drug out of their quarters and told, again, to get to work. Samuel looked at a tired Sandy.

"Well, here goes, might as well see if we can get this thing to turn on. I don't know how much more time we have." A Soldier stood outside their work area. They clambered into the "Saucer". Samuel took a seat in what passed as the Pilots position. Another one of the form fitting reclined seat positions formed around Sandy's body. Every hour, the craft became more and more attached to them personally. Samuel crossed his fingers, and then manipulated his fingers in the "joystick" that formed around his hand. He thought what he wanted to happen, moved his digits….

Suddenly, they were no longer inside the Station known as Platform One. In fact, they were nowhere near it. "Damn, Sandy. We are in another system."

He thought of the work area they had just left and they were back. He turned to his twin and grinned.

The Perfect Storm had ended. Another kind of storm was brewing.